I0561952

Neither Up
Nor Down

Rob McLaren

Neither Up Nor Down

Rob McLaren

This edition was published in 2023.
Lulu Publishing — www.lulu.com
Copyright © 2023 Dylan Trust

Robert McLaren asserts the moral right
to be identified as the author of this work.

This novel is a work of fiction. The incidents and some of the characters
portrayed in it, while based on real historical events and figures,
are the work of the author's imagination.

All rights reserved. No part of this publication may be reproduced,
stored in a retrieval system, or transmitted in any form or by any means,
electronic, mechanical, photocopying, recording or otherwise, without
the prior written permission of the publishers and copyright holders.

A CiP record for this book is available from the National Library
of Australia and the State Library of Queensland.

Text and illustration copyright © 2023 Rob McLaren
Graphic design, typesetting and map illustrations by Matthew Lin
www.matthewlin.com.au

Paperback   ISBN 978-0-6484-716-2-2
E-book   ISBN 978-0-6484-716-5-3

Typeset in Bembo Semi-bold 12 pt

Neither Up Nor Down
Acknowledgements

I wish to sincerely acknowledge and thank the following people for their contribution to the work:

Peter Cross and Jose de Andrade for access to their extensive Napoleonic libraries.

Gail Cartwright and Lauren Elise Daniels for their rigorous standards and professional guidance as editors.

Sophie Walker, my gorgeous and talented wife, for proofreading.

Matthew Lin for his patience and creative wizardry in the creation of internal illustrations and cover art design.

Matthew Higgins, Graeme Hopgood, Marc Middleton, Mark Robins and Steven M. Smith for their valuable time and insightful feedback as beta-readers.

Victor Eiser for his knowledgeable contributions on regional food and wine.

Neither Up Nor Down
Maps

Neither Up Nor Down
Appendices

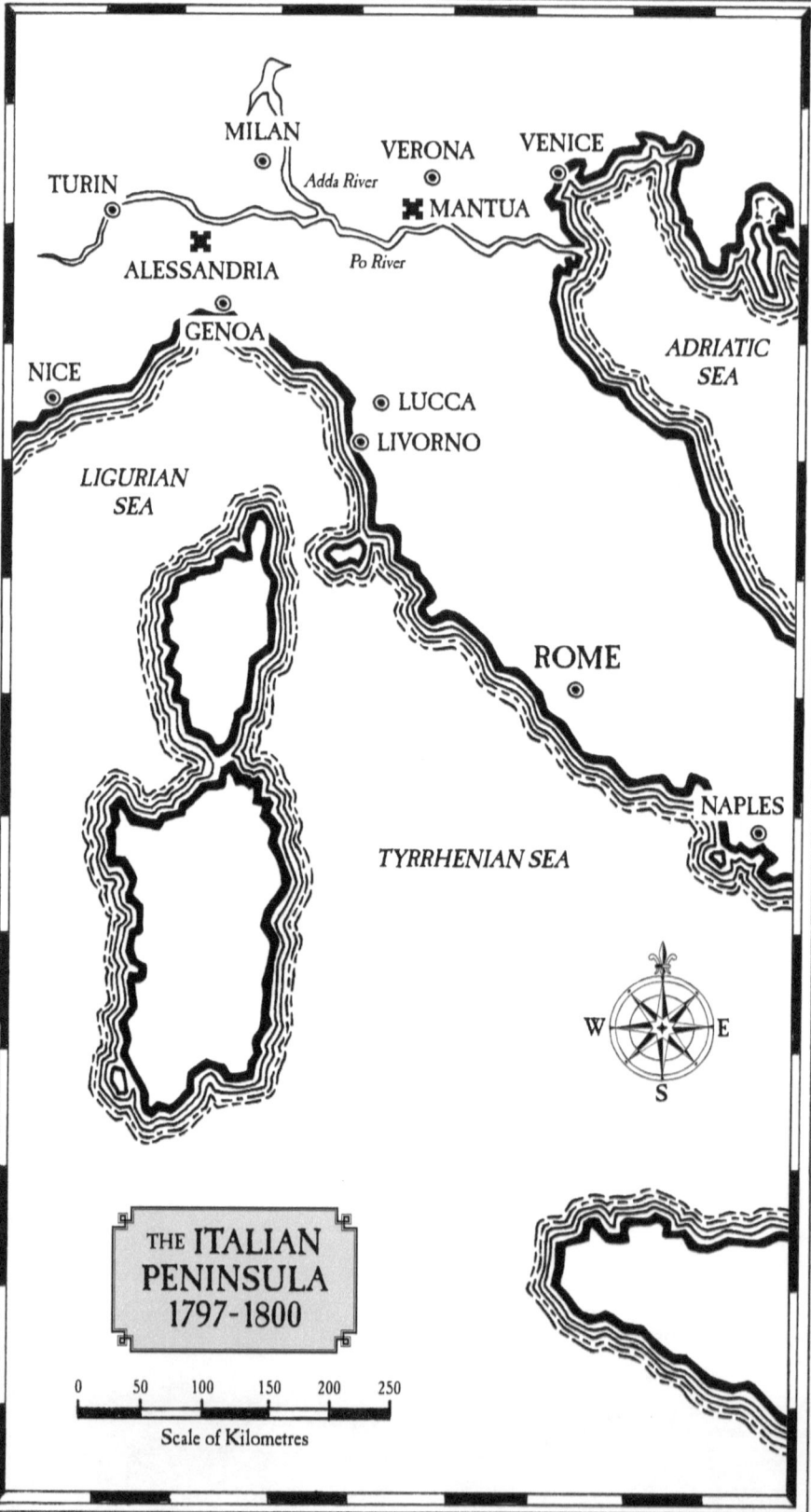

MILAN

TURIN

Adda River

VERONA

VENICE

MANTUA

ALESSANDRIA

Po River

ADRIATIC
SEA

GENOA

NICE

LUCCA

LIVORNO

LIGURIAN
SEA

ROME

NAPLES

TYRRHENIAN SEA

W   E

S

THE ITALIAN
PENINSULA
1797-1800

0   50   100   150   200   250

Scale of Kilometres

Prologue
August 1799, Pasturana, Italy

'Here they come. Eyes shut.'

From the shadows, the glazed eyes of the disobedient dead stared at the corridor beyond the shattered door.

Within the room, amongst the dead on the floor, Lieutenant Colonel André Jobert lay on his back in the ooze from their wounds. The shroud draped across his upper body concealed a cocked pistol. To staunch the pain that wracked his right leg, Jobert crushed the pistol butt with straining knuckles.

The grunts of those who approached echoed along the corridor towards the door, their stealth betrayed as gravel crunched under heavy steps. Their torchlight stabbed through the ribs of the door. The swollen tongues of the fallen licked the glow as it slithered over their faces.

In the shadows of the room, some hidden whimpered in the darkness.

'Shut up,' Jobert hissed.

To ease his distress, Jobert focussed on her memory. He watched her curls tickle her neck. Her lips quivered as her dimples formed. Her slim finger traced the line as she spoke it.

Dost thou love me? I know thou wilt say 'Ay'.

Those who hunted were just outside. One bayonet, then more, impaled the room. Musket muzzles sniffed the stench of sweat, urine and maggots.

A phrase was spat in a foreign tongue. Hungarian? Russian?

A sharp command.

A simpering whine.

A vicious slap.

Through half-opened lids, Jobert watched a ragged scout, silhouetted by the torches in the corridor, creep beyond the broken door.

He snatched at his nose and gagged.

His convulsion alarmed a swarm of engorged flies. He clawed at their darting curtain. He tripped over swollen sausage fingers. He squelched coagulated slime underfoot. He swore at those behind him.

The figure pounced on an infantry backpack just beyond Jobert's feet. He upended the backpack and shook out shit-stained drawers. He exclaimed something emphatic and threw the backpack at the dead slouching along the far wall.

Clenching his jaws against his agony, Jobert's dentures sliced into his gums. *Release me, you bastards,* thought Jobert, *to either to fly to her or free me from this pain.*

Bayonets jerked backwards from their penetration of the doorway. Their boots scurried away.

The corridor choked the retreating light.

Jobert's rigid companions wheezed farts from fermenting bowels.

Jobert's mind reeled with fatigue.

What was her scent?

Chapter One
June 1797, Milan, Italy

Two years earlier ...

A slice of *salame Brianza* taunted Lieutenant Colonel André Jobert from its pewter platter in the midday sun, its melting fats giving the meat a juicy hue.

Captain Chabenac poured straw-coloured *cortese* from an earthenware jug into both their cups. 'You do not care for the salami?'

Jobert's inner cheek rolled against a set of wooden pegs in his aching lower jaw. Glaring at the salami, Jobert peeled a morsel of soft bread from a torn crust, which, soaked in olive oil, melted against his tongue. 'My temporary dentures.' Jobert shrugged as he considered his friend. 'I am tired of chewing on one side of my mouth.'

Chabenac's long legs stretched beyond the shade of the cloisters surrounding Milan's Piazza Duomo. His battered but polished riding boots extended from patched, *chasseur*-green over-breeches. Chabenac's mirliton cap was set atop his sun-browned face and blond queue. Adding a sliver of pear to Jobert's salami, Chabenac popped the combination in his mouth. 'What of your other injuries?'

Does losing Rouge count as a wound? The memory of sawing through his crippled horse's throat at Rivoli still gripped him more uncomfortably than the other physical wounds he received on that day. 'With exercise, my shoulder is now whole again.'

'Come now, sir, your injuries need rest. In the five months since Rivoli, you are still unable to eat chicken. Are you not plagued by headaches?'

Jobert touched the site of his mended skull fracture, conscious of the droop his left eyelid had gained. 'My wounds have healed well enough.'

Jobert's gaze returned to the birds flocking over the morning markets in the Piazza. Doves and crows flapped among the bustling activity. Across the vast cathedral square, their coos and caws blended with the hawkers' cries, the grind of barrows' axles, the snarls of dogs bickering over scraps, lambs bleating for ewes, and the music of competing musicians. Each eager voice of human, animal or tool staked its claim in a multitude of marketplace exchanges.

'Attend the theatre with me.' Chabenac prodded a playbill pinned beneath the platter. 'This play in particular. Have you seen it?'

Jobert twisted his neck to read the woodcut print. '*Romeo and Juliet*? No. Why?'

'The play is a regional favourite, and it might add to your education on matters feminine.' From his extended slouch, Chabenac threw his arms wide. 'Having just marched from the heights above Vienna, exultant in our hard-won victory over Austria, why ever would we not surround ourselves in the fêtes and parades of this new Cisalpine Republic?' Chabenac looked at Jobert. 'All the while we rest and refit our glorious 24th Chasseurs. Are you not pleased with our progress in that regard?'

A sullen smirk twisted a brown scar on Jobert's right cheek. 'To return two hundred survivors to, as Koschak would say, this bountiful sanctuary, I am delighted beyond words.'

'As our administrative commander, do you have authority to return us to full strength? What are your views on attracting local recruits?'

Jobert raised a concerned eyebrow. 'I hesitate to include Italians in our ranks. I shall return a party to Avignon to secure a draft of new men. With the lads now settled in their billets and horses in summer pastures, it is enough to throw off our exhaustion and our rags. I am focussing regimental funds on local tailors and saddlers.'

'Any hint of what will be asked of us next?' Chabenac asked.

'While the armistice continues, I imagine we will return to the Austrian frontier.'

'Then we will be blessed with a spate of regimental weddings. Surely newly promoted Geourdai will pledge his troth?'

'Hah!' Jobert drank deeply from his wine cup. His gaze drifted across the numerous women gathered in the market, young and old, rich and poor, virtuous and fallen, which years of campaigning had hidden from sight. 'I can imagine the odds Moench would offer on that. Short odds on Geourdai taking a knee, and long on Camille's acceptance.'

Chabenac focussed on cutting a wedge of *taleggio* cheese from the platter. 'And your plans in that regard?'

'For whom?' Jobert scowled. 'Tulloc and his maid?'

'Tulloc? Oh, yes, of course.' Chabenac raised a finger to his mouth as he chewed. 'No, I was interested in the progress of such commitments for yourself.'

Marguerite. Jobert clenched his dentures into his swollen gum. 'I am dining with the ladies this evening.'

'Is it still your intent to … approach Marguerite?'

'More than approach her, my friend.' Jobert folded his arms. 'I intend to marry her.'

Chabenac jerked. 'Resolved, indeed.' Chabenac folded his body to lean his elbows forward on his knees. 'As your friend, I feel obliged to tender my views, if I am permitted?'

Jobert huffed as he sloshed more acidic cortese into his cup, before sliding wary eyes towards Chabenac.

'Why not take your time?' Chabenac asked. 'Marguerite and the child are blessed with good health, and she is comfortably situated thanks to her and Fergnes' families, and Raive's ministrations. There is no need to rush.'

'I am aware of your doubts, Chabenac.' Jobert's face tightened at he recalled Fergnes' eyes bulging from a blue, blood-flecked face in the rain of Caldiero. 'I gave him my word.' Jobert drained his cup. 'These last months in Austria I have reflected upon my path. Marguerite is an attractive and pleasant woman, why ever would I not choose her?'

Chabenac opened his palms upwards. 'A proposal of marriage to a woman, for whom you have neither depth of feeling for nor an eye for social advantage, is not the only outcome for your honourable commitment to our dying friend. She demonstrates only a sisterly affection. You have admitted to a lack of intimacy between you both.'

Jobert looked away across the market stalls. His thoughts drifted to Marguerite grinding astride him on his last night of leave in Milan six months ago.

'It has been eight months since we lost Fergnes,' Chabenac said. 'How much time is appropriate? You might care to ask her what she desires most for herself and the boy.'

Jobert inspected his cup. 'I have prepared a letter for her father ...'

'Excellent!' Chabenac refilled Jobert's cup. 'That letter is exactly what Orlande requires to start the morning hearth. Pass it to him this evening.'

Jobert snorted as he swished a gulp of cool, lime-like wine around his throbbing mouth. 'In the spirit of friendship, sir, you press me too hard. I must do what is right by our friend Fergnes.' Jobert shot a sullen glance at Chabenac. 'I will offer my protection to his wife and son.'

With a serene smile, Chabenac bowed his head.

A bell tolled from within the cathedral's spires. A cloud of birds rose above the canvas awnings, causing a momentary pause in the market's tumult.

Jobert stood and flicked crumbs from his faded tailcoat. 'I must away.'

Chabenac glanced at Milan's towering medieval spires. 'Communion or confession?'

'Worse.' Jobert raised his gaze to the swirling birds. 'A tailor's fitting and the receipt of new dentures.'

Jobert strolled through the busy streets. Civilian commerce pulsed in every doorway, on every corner, down every lane. Soon he reached Fergnes' apartments. The dusty air cooled as he crossed the tiled floor.

'Good morning, sir,' Orlande said, Jobert's valet and cook. 'Would you care for refreshment?'

'No, thank you, Orlande. Are the ladies at home?'

'The ladies are attending a recital at Madame Bonaparte's.' Orlande swept back his fringe of red hair, where it promptly flopped back across his forehead. 'Before the tailor arrives, are you available to review domestic matters?'

Jobert grimaced then nodded.

Descending the worn stone stairs, Jobert and Orlande entered the large, whitewashed kitchen to find Jobert's chasseur groom, Tulloc, and his teenage wife, Maria. The hearth-warmed air smelt of baked bread and split timber. Steam rose from soaking laundry in frothy coppers to mist across pots and pans hanging from the walls.

The tall young man drew back his broad shoulders, to extend a hand from beneath a shawl-swaddled bundle. 'Sir, may I introduce my fiancée, Maria.'

'*Buongiorno,* Maria,' Jobert greeted her in Italian. 'How have you found Madame Fergnes' household?'

A slim girl, in a grey apron, bobbed in curtsy, her eyes on the stone floor. 'Very good, thank you, sir.'

'Speak up, Maria,' Orlande said. 'Colonel Jobert cannot abide mumblers.'

Maria cringed.

'Ah, sir, may I introduce my son, Andrea?' Tulloc said, staring down at the bundle in his arms. 'We named him after you, sir, but in Italian ... umm, since you were so kind and—'

'You honour me, Tulloc.' Jobert clasped his hands behind his back before he bent over the sleeping infant. *Good grief, another mouth to budget for.* 'Welcome, little man. Well done, Tulloc. How old is he now?'

'Nine weeks, sir.' Maria curtsied and glanced up from beneath the peak of her cloth cap.

'A fine boy, Maria.' Jobert's eyes narrowed as he turned to Tulloc. 'What of the horses?' Jobert had chargers to maintain, Bleu and Jaune, and packhorse Grenzer, as well as Tulloc's regimental remount. 'Despite your paternal duties, Tulloc, I require your full attention in returning our horses to condition.'

'Yes, sir, of course, sir,' Tulloc said. 'They are comfortably settled in the stables and are gorging themselves on grain and hay.'

'I require you to take them out for green pick each day, Tulloc,' Jobert said.

Tulloc blinked and his mouth hung open as he looked to the baby for a solution.

'Perhaps, sir,' Orlande said, 'with one in the shafts and three tied on behind, the horses might graze while we picnic beyond the city walls?'

'There we have it,' Jobert said. 'Tulloc, Maria, I shall not keep you from your duties.'

Both Tulloc and Maria bobbed their heads. She performed multiple curtsies as they departed the kitchen.

Jobert gave Orlande an anguished look. 'Have you allocated sufficient duties to the girl to justify her cost?'

'I have tasked her with as much as a seventeen-year-old nursing a babe can manage, sir,' Orlande said. 'It is all in hand.'

'And their wedding?' asked Jobert.

'This Sunday in a chapel on the Pavia road.' Orlande looked pointedly at Jobert. 'And at a very reasonable cost for the gentleman giving away the bride.'

Jobert shook his head. 'Oh, good grief.'

'Of course, sir—' A muted knock sounded from the back door. 'Ah, here is your tailor now.'

Jobert rolled his eyes. *More expense.*

Jobert turned to find Madame Quandalle, 2nd Squadron's *cantinière*, and her teenage son entering. 'Good afternoon, madame.'

Madame nodded but kept Jobert's eye. 'Good afternoon, sir. May I beg a moment of your time?'

'It is always a pleasure, madame.'

Madame tugged her worn apron straight and took a deep breath. 'With the regiment now returned to Milan ...' Madame Quandalle dropped her face. 'I have chosen to return home to my family, sir. These last years on campaign have been ... too ...'

Jobert reached out and gently squeezed her elbow. 'Madame, I understand your decision. I have often remarked upon your resilience. As the regiment endured prolonged hardships, your resourcefulness as our cantinière contributed significantly to our fortitude.'

Madame's shoulders slumped. 'Thank you, sir. I have been ever so grateful for your sponsorship of me. Could I call upon our association to ask one last favour?'

Jobert's eyes slid to the boy. 'You can ask, madame.'

'You have known my lad for four years, sir. He has always been a good boy, and strong. He is well regarded by your Orlande. He is fourteen now and has always respected your kindness to us.'

'What is your request, madame?' *Another mouth.*

Her lips trembled. 'Sir, would you include him in your personal retinue?'

Jobert looked hard at the boy. *An apprentice to Tulloc? A kitchen hand for Orlande?*

Young Quandalle held Jobert's gaze and straightened his bony frame.

'He is strong and honest,' Madame Quandalle said, 'and willing—'

'Madame,' Jobert raised a finger, 'I acknowledge your boy's attributes. Allow me to discuss the situation with Orlande?'

Tears filled Madame Quandalle's eyes.

Jobert watched Marguerite's blown kiss dissolve her two-year-old son's smile to sadness.

'Goodnight, darling boy.' A flutter of Marguerite's fingers dismissed the maid. 'That will be all, Anissa.'

'But mama—' The child wriggled to keep his mother in view as he was taken from the dining room.

An inner pressure squeezed Jobert's heart. A silhouette of his own mother's back stared into an anxious twilight. Jobert reached for his *lambrusco*.

'Jobert, did you see Vienna,' Camille asked across the table.

'Ah ... our vedettes were one hundred kilometres from the city.' Jobert evaluated Camille's stillness. 'Some say they saw sunrise glint from the city's spires.'

'And what of the peace, darling?' Marguerite asked.

Camille sliced her pork. 'Leoben brought us only an armistice, cousin.'

'Indeed, we still await the peace,' Jobert said. 'General Bonaparte's negotiations continue with the emperor's plenipotentiaries in Udine. Do you ladies still attend Madame Bonaparte's salon?'

Camille snorted. 'That lady has enough protectors, thank you, Jobert.'

'Will the regiment contribute to the occupation of Venice?' Marguerite asked. 'If so, I would dearly love—'

'I am afraid not, madame,' Jobert said, 'the regiment is too weakened to participate without much replenishment.'

The candlelight rocked in the summer breeze. A small tinkle sounded as Jobert's soup spoon trembled against his bowl.

'You seem so solemn, darling.' Marguerite looked at his broth. 'Are you not restored?'

Camille's gaze pierced him. 'Did you not receive your new dentures today?'

Jobert placed down his disloyal spoon and anchored himself on the stem of his red wine glass. His mind groped for an opening move. 'Might I take his sabre from storage? I wish to have—'

Marguerite's cutlery clacked on her plate. 'It is an ugly thing. I do not want it in my home. I should have thrown it on—'

Jobert's placating hand wavered. 'It is an item that will have meaning for your son.'

'I do not want my son to know that of his father.' Marguerite's flushed face turned to Jobert, daring his disobedience. 'Take the wretched object. Do not return it.'

A weak thrust smartly beaten. Jobert bowed his head.

Camille's fork slid into her meat. 'I suspect dear Jobert seeks to petition you, cousin.'

'A petition?'

Jobert's eyes locked on his fingers turning the stem of his glass. 'I am keen to write to your father, Marguerite. May I ask for his address?'

A half-smile curled Camille's full lips. 'Whatever for?'

'To let him know of the regiment's return and inform him of your good health.'

Camille raised an eyebrow. Marguerite blinked.

Jobert swallowed against a dry throat to look at Marguerite. 'When Fergnes passed in my arms, dear lady, I swore to protect you and your son.'

Marguerite covered his left hand with her right. 'I am blessed with the love of our families, and also the love of our friends. But Colonel Raive has already spoken to Papa.'

Raive? thought Jobert.

'Having escorted poor Colonel Spiccard home to recover,' Marguerite continued, 'dear Raive took the opportunity to call upon my father.'

'How might you offer what you have sworn to give?' Camille's eyes pierced him. 'An uncle for master Fergnes? Possibly a little soon, Jobert?'

Heat pricked at Jobert's chest.

Marguerite stroked the back of his hand. 'Raive returns tomorrow morning, darling. Why not chat further when he delivers his news?'

Later that night, Jobert sat naked on the edge of his bed. 'Marguerite, please ...'

Standing before him, she placed his hands on her bare hips. 'Surely, you are not concerned for my reputation?' Marguerite laughed. 'Society allows abandoned wives and young widows their amusements. Observe the licence extended to Madame Bonaparte. Do you not want me, darling?'

Jobert's hands vacillated at the heat of her perfumed skin. *Stop her? Take her?*

He lowered his face towards the divested robe puddled around her ankles. 'Yes, of course, but—'

'Then silence, my gorgeous man.' Marguerite took his fingertips and lifted him to stand. 'Then let us not waste ...' her eyes reflected the candle's flame as they lowered to his waist, '... the moment. Come, I want you this way tonight.'

She turned him then she knelt on the bed.

Sometime after, Marguerite whimpered in half-sleep. The wafting bed-curtains rippled moonlight along her naked back and thighs.

Jobert disentangled himself from the knotted sheets and rose from the bed.

What in hell am I doing?

Chapter Two

The next morning, Jobert's finger twirled his breakfast coffee cup. High on the sunlit balcony, he sought answers across Milan's undulating mash of rooves. Darting pigeons matched the rapidity of his thoughts. Last night, desperate to be soothed, he had buried himself within the softness of Marguerite. Now, as smoke from numerous kitchen chimneys eddied, his confusion returned.

A staccato of capped heels drummed across the tiled entrance behind him. 'Is anyone within? I am returned.'

Feminine delight squealed from an inner chamber. 'Dearest Raive, you are back. Quickly, he is here,' cried Marguerite.

Jobert returned through the languid curtains to the breakfast parlour. 'Good morning, sir.'

Colonel Raive's eyes glinted as he espied Jobert. 'Jobert! Excellent! I have news. Much news. Where do I begin?'

Marguerite descended the stairs in a flutter of morning robes, her curls hastily piled with combs. Her maid raced to wrap madame's shoulders with a shawl.

Raive knelt at the bottom of the stairs. 'My dearest Marguerite, would you make me the happiest man on earth by consenting to be my wife?'

Ice skewered Jobert's heart.

Marguerite's trembling hand grasped at the banister. 'Darling, what of Papa?'

Raive withdrew an envelope from an inner pocket. 'I have a letter from your father blessing the proposed union. Further, to secure the harmony of the household, I have assumed the lease of these apartments.'

Marguerite cupped Raive's hands in hers. 'Oh, I accept, dear Raive. Yes, of course, I do.' She kissed him on his cheek.

Jobert's eyes flickered to Orlande standing by the breakfast buffet. Orlande's lips convulsed to suppress his bemusement.

'To confirm the arrangement,' Raive asked, 'would you permit me to present a token of my eternal affection?' From a velvet box, Raive revealed a two-part, interlocking gimmal ring, set with a large ruby nested within diamonds.

Marguerite's eyes and lips widened. 'Oh, darling, you always know how to please me.'

Jobert turned back toward the balcony. *Not on a colonel's salary.* He gripped the railing to steady himself.

Raive swaggered onto the balcony. 'The moment calls for something a little stronger than coffee, eh, Jobert?'

'At the very least, sir.' Jobert sought Orlande. 'Orlande, might you fetch *amoretto* to … celebrate. My warmest congratulations, sir.'

'Thank you, dear boy.'

Jobert gulped the liqueur Orlande delivered and poured himself another. 'You lease a fellow's apartments and gain his widow, child and household into the bargain. Some might baulk at the arrangement.' Pressed by the uhlans' lances, Fergnes was fast disappearing into the mud of Caldiero.

'More fool them, I say.' Raive smoothed his moustache with the back of his finger. 'Sweet Marguerite, I could not suffer her a widow too long. And that beautiful little boy needs a father. It is only right. Do you not agree?'

'You certainly have my blessing, sir.' Jobert raised his glass. 'The happiness of three such deserving persons could not be more complete.'

Raive sipped. 'I have so much news, Jobert. Are you aware I have been posted to Bonaparte's staff? I am to be the Inspector of Cavalry here in the Cisalpine Republic.'

'Again, my sincere congratulations, sir.'

Raive clamped Jobert's shoulder. 'You too, Jobert, have been blessed by the bounty of this golden Milanese summer. You will accompany me to the Army of Italy's staff.'

Jobert choked. He jerked away from Raive's grip, his cough of amoretto spraying his dolman's sleeve.

Raive searched Jobert's expression. 'Surely, not an unexpected arrangement?'

Jobert frowned. 'These last seventeen years, I have only known service beneath the regimental standard.'

Raive's eyes narrowed. 'You will never command a regiment without experience on the staff.'

Jobert wiped his lips. 'What of the regiment, sir?'

'The 24th Chasseurs are to return to Avignon to be brought back to full strength. They will depart Milan at the end of the month.'

'But the horses—'

'But nothing, Jobert.' Raive toasted the blue Alps beyond Milan's walls. 'The regiment will graze the largesse of the Po on the march to Avignon. As a new chief of squadron, Geourdai is more than capable of rebuilding their strength. Spiccard will shake his Italian contagion and resume command. The 24th Chasseurs are no longer your concern.'

'But ...'

Raive returned his firm grip to Jobert's shoulder. 'You need to return to your brother, Jobert. You have not been home in nearly four years. Your leave has been approved. Take rooms here in Milan. Sort your arrangements. Attend our wedding in Avignon in September. Then rest at the farm in high autumn, returning to Milan next spring. Perfect.' Raive's beaming smile caused him to bounce on his toes. 'But first, galas and fêtes. Is your number-one tailcoat brushed? We shall attend today's parade of the newly formed Cisalpine Legion.'

Jobert looked down to straighten his patched dolman. The amoretto stains had soaked in like blood. He had never noticed before how his jacket's capucine cuffs had faded to grey.

Jobert let the excitement wash across him as the Milanese thong pulsed to view their own Lombardian Legion. Summer gusts whipped green, white and red flags and bunting. Coats, dresses and parasols were a jostle of colour. Wafts of pies, sweat and dust enriched the air. As commands were bellowed, bands tootled and ale hawkers cried.

Looking about him, Jobert searched for Marguerite and Camille. 'The ladies?'

'Shopping?' Raive shrugged. 'Races, games and double rations. This is our reward for our service.'

In the crowd, Jobert saw familiar ghosts. He greeted his phantoms with a grim smile. Chattering young men, their bodies emaciated, their chasseur uniforms torn, years of privation ended, risen from their mud graves to strut for the attention of maidens and gorge on pastries.

'Are your thoughts still with the 24th Chasseurs?' Raive asked.

'Four years of service and suffering, over twenty engagements, over six hundred brothers lost. Why would my thoughts be anywhere else?'

'What of you, Jobert? Those years ago, did you not desire to extend your abilities? Did you not depart the 5th Chasseurs for the 24th Chasseurs? Come now, allow your injuries of the past year to heal, attend my wedding, take leave at home, and then return refreshed to new possibilities. Why not?'

Jobert frowned. 'Perhaps.'

'I shall report your overwhelming gratitude to Bonaparte. He will be delighted that his posting order was so appreciated.'

'Bonaparte?' Jobert sighed. 'Am I to be his coffee-boy?'

'No, Bonaparte is attended by his favoured aides. The peace negotiations are slow, but I expect he will prevail. He always does. France shall have this Cisalpine Republic recognised and the Papal States secured as allies. The Austrians will absorb Venice and maintain their allegiance with Naples. With Austria's demise, Britain now becomes our foremost enemy. We must defeat Britain before Austria can rebuild.'

'Perhaps now is the time to transfer to the Army of the North?'

Raive's face jerked with alarm. 'Would you really swap the Adriatic coast for the channel?' Raive shivered. 'If action is your desire, Austria will recover soon enough, and you will have action aplenty.'

Jobert winced. 'I hear Austrian troops will occupy Verona and line the Adige River. We will be pressed hard to defend Milan and the Po Valley.'

'It is in our interest that this new republic endures as a buffer between ourselves and Austria. We now have the great fortress of Mantua, and thirty-five thousand French troops are to remain. But Milan requires an army. Today, we have the first of its many battalions. Ah! I see friends.'

Raive raised his hand in greeting at two approaching civilians. 'Jobert, have you met Signore Bernasconi, the Prefetto of the Mantua Council.'

Bernasconi, a solid man in black velvet, reciprocated Jobert's bow with weary eyes. 'I have had the honour of Lieutenant Colonel Jobert's acquaintance.'

'Are the 24th Chasseur's debts to the communities around Verona settled to your satisfaction, sir? Jobert asked.

'They are, sir,' said Bernasconi. 'In these times of upheaval, it is a rare treat to do business with a man of his word.'

Raive extended his hand towards Bernasconi's companion. 'Jobert, may I also introduce Signore Rizzoli of Milan?'

Jobert bowed toward a tall man in an emerald wool suit, whose benign smile lifted his thick moustache. 'The pleasure is mine, sir.'

Raive clapped Rizzoli on the upper arm. 'I understand you have been confirmed as the commanding officer designate of the new Cisalpine *Chasseurs à Cheval.*'

'I have, sir,' said Rizzoli, 'and my thanks to your support in that regard.'

Jobert interrupted with a polite cough. 'Excuse me, gentlemen, the colours approach.' The four men turned towards the troops marching along the packed boulevard. A green, white and red standard fluttered above the heads of the cheering throng. Jobert and Raive saluted.

Jobert turned to Bernasconi. 'Does the parade bring you to Milan, sir?'

'I am here with family,' Bernasconi said. 'My son, Silvio, hopes to engage regimental tailors and procure pistols, much against his mother's wishes.'

'I can recommend a Brescian armourer here in Milan, sir.' Jobert swallowed a bitter memory. 'I have just purchased a new brace of cavalry pistols. Superb workmanship.'

'Ooh, I see her parasol!' Bernasconi pointed over Jobert's shoulder. 'My daughter, Gianna. She is so elusive. I must not lose her.' Bernasconi's body shuffled in the direction his finger pointed. 'Whenever you are in Mantua, Jobert, you have an open invitation to call upon my home and we might dine together. I beg your forgiveness, Raive, would you excuse us?'

After hurried bows, Bernasconi and Rizzoli became obscured by the crowd in the pursuit of a bobbing umbrella.

'New men, Jobert,' said Raive. 'The revolution created a France teeming with new men. You and I rose from sergeants to colonels. Now, this Cisalpine Republic is a new country, with Bernasconi and Rizzoli, her new men, indebted to us for their opportunity. Would not our lost brothers urge us ... nay, demand we grasp the flame their cold hands kindled?'

'Perhaps if I am to serve on the staff, I too will require assistance.'

Raive's moustache shivered. 'Do I detect commitment?'

'A lieutenant at most.'

'Hah, my funding does not extend that far. Which of your scoundrels? Bredieux? Peugeot?'

Sergeant Major Koschak folded his thick arms and squinted as he considered Jobert. 'You, sir? An aide on army headquarters?'

The shutters of Jobert's office, a farmhouse kitchen occupied by the regiment, were open. Wrens twittered in the lush foliage.

Couriers' horses slurped at a trough.

Jobert leaned back from his document-cluttered desk. 'As I said, Sergeant Major, I will be working for Raive. Probably fetching coffee for generals.'

'And you need an aide? A lieutenant?'

'Someone has to carry the *biscotti*.' Jobert smirked at Koschak's grimace. 'To separate from the regiment will be unbearable. Why should you not suffer beside me?'

Koschak scowled. 'Me? An officer?'

'The alternative is to return to Avignon with the regiment.' Jobert held up his palms. 'You may have said "no" to entering the officers' mess in the past but expect to be offered company command as the regiment rebuilds. This is the dividend of peace. The window of opportunity is closing.'

Koschak squirmed. 'So, train a company of recruits in Avignon or fluff around here in Lombardy? What, running errands? Counting blankets?'

'More or less.' Jobert mouth tightened to a solemn smile, thinking Koschak will never accept this.

Koschak scowled. 'It will sting to leave the regiment.'

'It will. So, is that a "yes"?'

Koschak folded his arms across his chest. He squinted as his jaws ground an internal conversation. 'Why not? It might prove interesting.'

Jobert grinned with surprise. 'There we have it.'

A rap on the door frame. Koschak turned to find Trumpeter Moench saluting.

'Good morning, sir.' Moench's handsome moustache curled in a smile. 'May I be one of the first to congratulate you on your posting.'

Koschak harumphed. 'Stand to arms, sir, you have a petitioner.'

Jobert folded his arms. 'Thank you, Moench, you crafty prick. Was I in your book? How much did you make?'

Moench beamed. 'Enough for a new bow and a full set of strings, sir.'

Jobert raised an eyebrow. 'What do you want?'

'Oh, no, sir, it is not what I want. It is what I can do for you, sir.' Moench's eyes narrowed. 'A senior aide on the Army of Italy's headquarters will need someone to attend to horses, act as messenger, arrange billets, scrounge food on the road.'

Very well, let us haggle. Jobert shook his head. 'Piss off, Moench.'

Moench spread his palms wide. 'A senior officer, renowned for his tough standards, would only accept a hardened veteran. A seasoned sergeant well known to him, ready to anticipate his every need. Only his loyal trumpeter, who has covered his sabre arm these long years, could be considered for this position of trust.'

Jobert frowned at Koschak. 'Is it your impression that Moench will miss me?'

Moench winked at Koschak. 'More so Orlande's cooking, sir.'

Jobert set his hands down on his desk. 'No, Moench, there is not enough money for a sergeant. I doubt Colonel Raive will stretch his purse for a corporal.'

'Corporal, sir?' Moench's appeared offended. 'I am sure to make sergeant as the regiment's senior trumpeter.'

'Ah!' Jobert raised his hands in revelation. 'There lies the better path. Return home to Avignon, where your mother will appreciate your sergeant's pay.'

'I cannot, sir.' Moench slumped, hooking his thumbs in his sword belt. 'Too many Avignon husbands with short cocks and long memories.'

'Corporal Moench.' Jobert winked at Koschak. 'A fine title for a hardened veteran.'

Koschak threw Moench a malicious grin. 'A fine title for a hardened veteran who can handle two horses. One for Lieutenant Colonel Jobert, here, and one for his aide, Lieutenant Koschak.'

Moench's jaw dropped. 'Both of you are leaving?'

Koschak's eyes widened in mock surprise. 'Am I not worth wagering upon?'

Moench squinted. 'Two horses definitely need a sergeant.'

'Corporal's lace only, Moench.' Jobert leaned back with his palms raised. 'Or return to the cuckolds of Avignon.'

In the last week of June, the two hundred sabres of the 24th Chasseurs paraded past Jobert.

Jobert's heart pounded in his chest as he saluted the regimental standard. He dammed his welling emotion by grinding his dentures into his raw gums.

The chasseurs, keen to march home, puffed with pride as they passed him. Each grim face gave Jobert a nod of acknowledgement. Their calves squeezed a lift of energy from their remounts. The horses' strides surged, necks arching towards lowered faces.

Leading their columns of soldiers, his friends passed him with their sabres lowered in salute. Their lips twisted in grimaces of parting. He had hugged each of them prior to mounting parade – Chabenac, Geourdai, Neilage, Voreille, Bredieux, Yinot, Peugeot – brothers together through four years of hard service.

'We will be together soon enough, sir,' Chabenac had said before the parade, as they gripped each other in a hard squeeze. 'Raive's wedding is only weeks away. I can only imagine the regiment returning to Lombardy next spring.'

Madame Quandalle's was the last wagon of the trains to rumble past.

Jobert leaned on Bleu's neck as the screech of axles and the clip of iron-shod hooves faded. Straight green backs, white cross belts and nodding capucine plumes diminished until the street refilled with local traffic.

Jobert squeezed the base of Bleu's hogged mane. 'We knew them all, brother, did we not?' Jobert wiped the corner of an eye with a gloved fist.

Bleu's ears flicked towards Jobert.

'Are we ready for what lies ahead, my beautiful lad?'

Bleu pawed the ground.

'Impatient bastard.'

Chapter Three
September-December 1797,
Auvergne, France

Three months later, on the heights of France's Massif Central, three colts stiffened in alarm. In unison, their heads pivoted towards the deep shadows of the surrounding forest.

Jobert and the other two riders searched the dark branches towards which the young horses' ears were pricked. Jobert scented the pine-laden air.

'Lynx, Uncle?' Didier, Jobert's elder brother, whispered.

'Probably mouflon,' Yann said.

A sharp crack split the forest's brooding. A heavy branch fell with a swoosh.

A solid shadow darted. Wild hooves clattered on unseen boulders.

The colts spun in fear on the tight mountain path. Rider's knees collided as they all shortened their reins.

'Shit!' Yann cried as his spooked horse leapt. Falling, Yann grabbed at his pommel and thrust his other arm out to break his impact. The spinning momentum of his horse flung his body headfirst. Yann's movement ceased with a loud thwack as his skull struck a rock. Yann's horse bounded down the steep path, reins trailing.

Jobert swung down from the saddle. 'Didier, take my horse.'

As Jobert rolled his uncle over, Yann groaned. Jobert's fingers searched Yann's scalp for lacerations. 'No blood.'

Didier worked to settle Jobert's agitated colt, upset at the rapid departure of its paddock mate. 'Solid Chauvel bone, I am sure,' he said.

'Can you sit, Uncle?' Jobert asked.

'No, let me—' Yann twisted onto an elbow and vomited.

'André, here. Water.' Didier fumbled to disentangle the battered Prussian canteen's straps from the nervous horses' reins.

'I am fine.' Yann swished a limp hand. 'Allow me a minute.'

'André, remove this idiot's bridle and release him,' Didier said, thrusting his chin at Jobert's prancing colt. 'Two empty saddles will raise the alarm in the pastures below. I will descend and send a cart up the gully road to the upper glade. Yes?'

'Release him?' Jobert grunted as he struggled to lift Yann to sit. 'You cannot lead him?'

'The paths are too tight to lead ... without my foot.' Didier hung his head with despair. 'I no longer have any feel for my stirrup.'

After tucking his stirrup leathers through their irons, Jobert undid the bridle's throat latch and slid the bit from his colt's mouth. The liberated youngster squealed as it bounded down the mountain path. Didier's gelding shuffled in agitation.

'Can you ...' Jobert glanced at Didier's right boot, 'manage the descent?'

Didier glanced at his right stirrup. 'I will have to, will I not?' Didier pressed his skittering horse over the lip of the trail and disappeared.

Yann slumped against a rock, panting hard.

'Where does it hurt?' Jobert asked. 'Broken bones?'

'Nothing. I am dizzy. I need to piss. Unbutton me and I will take care of the rest.'

Once settled, Yann closed his eyes and breathed deeply. 'I have been meaning to find a quiet time with you. There is a flask in my waistcoat. Chartreuse. Its weight is a burden.'

Jobert ruffled Yann's inner pockets for the hipflask. 'You have selected a pleasant spot for a picnic.'

'Piss off.' Yann coughed as he sipped. 'We need you here at home, André. Times are bad. The Directory is in anarchy. Those bastards could not organise a fuck in a brothel with a fist full of gold louis.' The old sergeant shook his head. 'The declaration of bankrupting two-thirds of the nation's debt has caused this recent Jacobin coup. Negotiations with Austria struggle to manifest a peace. People are desperate, lad. The roads are choked with unprecedented banditry, the towns fevered with royalist uprisings.'

Jobert rolled the liqueur in his mouth and stared into the haze of the Allier Valley below. 'And how does me being here on the farm change that?'

Yann gripped Jobert's sleeve. 'You bloody well know why, boy. Our family has raised horses on these slopes for over fifty years. Our herd of three hundred and fifty horses supports near two-hundred villagers and amputee veterans. The current chaos drives up costs. Loan repayments are becoming harder to meet. We cannot lose what we have gained, André.'

Jobert hung his head. 'What do you expect of me?'

'I am now sixty,' Yann said. 'I am getting old and getting hurt. I am juggling the production of forty colts per annum for the artillery and the scheduling of twenty wagons to and from Paris for your Raive. You are respected by the men here. Your place is with us now.'

'Has Didier proved himself unworthy?'

'The farm does not suit him.' Yann sucked deeply at the

hipflask. 'The slopes do not suit a man without a foot. His balance in the saddle is unreliable. His heart is not in the Auvergne. He yearns for Paris.'

Jobert sighed. 'Can we not make a proposal to Duque?'

'Duque does not graduate for another eighteen months. I know full well the army has an expectation of service following four years of veterinary training.'

'What of Michelle? Our uniform contracts?'

Yann shrugged. 'With Aunt Sophie nearly eighty, Michelle manages the workhouses well enough, but I despair. An unwed mother, attending Parisian parties semi-naked. These de Colbert brothers lurking, with one of the bastards proposing to her but claiming he is too poor to marry. If this Édouard does marry her, how will that impact on the percentage ownership of our company?' Yann wriggled against the rocks beneath him. 'In the meantime, we are threatened by our own generosity.'

'How?'

'How? We harbour these de Chabenac women while Parisian gangs hunt *émigrés*. Our military contracts are imperilled should these bloody noble women be discovered under our beds. We must fight for what our family has struggled to earn.'

Jobert rubbed his eyes with the heels of his hands. 'But, Uncle, I cannot resign so easily. I have been a soldier all my life. I have only ever known the regiment. Now, as regiments are being rebuilt after the war, I could be promoted to command.'

'Oh, bullshit, lad.' Yann kicked at the rocks near his feet. 'You have been cast adrift from your regiment. The life of a general's dandy is not for you. If you seek the responsibility of regimental command, the management of the farm is the equivalent to brigade command. What is more, you are thirty-two, André, and not yet married. Have you met any eligible brides?'

Jobert slumped. 'How is that relevant?' Visions of Marguerite's recent wedding to Raive, blurred with her wedding to Fergnes nearly three years before.

'Just answer. Have you?'

'No, Uncle.' Jobert coughed to clear his throat. 'I have been at war for four years.'

Shuffling clouds covered the sun. A sharp wind hissed though the pines' shadows.

'How is your head?' Jobert asked.

Yann winced as he stretched his neck. 'Tougher than that bastard mouflon's skull.'

'Come,' Jobert said, 'shall we descend to Didier's cart?'

'Avoid the subject if you want,' Yann scowled at Jobert, 'but you need to know our family's wellbeing is dependent upon you.'

In a storeroom within the rambling Chauvel-Jobert farmhouse, warmth from the kitchen hearths below rose through the floorboards. The rich flavours of herbed roast goose seeped through the door. Laughter from those preparing the evening meal leapt up the chimney and rebounded in the storeroom's unlit fireplace.

Seated on one of many dusty crates and chests, Jobert angled Fergnes' sabre towards the dull winter light filtering through the storeroom's small window.

Dried blood pitted corrosion along the length of the blade.

The first essential skill of the cavalryman, he thought. Jobert had never cleaned the steel of Fergnes' last moments in battle. He never would. Jobert dabbed a fingertip against the dried blood.

Black pockmarks stared like his friend's calculating dark eyes. Jobert's last memory of Fergnes were his half-lidded gaze set in a blue-grey face as the clods of a mass grave were packed upon him.

Jobert enfolded the sabre and its scabbard in a worn blanket before settling it in a long, wicker linen basket.

Sitting across from Jobert, Didier inspected the scrollwork around the etched relief of a boar's head within the silver inlay on a long-barrelled cavalry pistol. 'Do you have other pistols?'

As the long-held tradition in the Chauvel farmhouse required, the brothers conversed in German.

'Yes. I purchased a brace in Milan. Made in Brescia. They are very good. Why?'

'These bastards took my right foot. I want to know why.'

Jobert rummaged in another chest in the storeroom.

He unwrapped a feathered helmet plume, chasseur-green with a yellow tip. It was a regimental plume of Jobert's mother regiment, the 5th Chasseurs à Cheval. Before transferring out, it had also been Didier's original regiment. Jobert stared blankly as he ran the plume through his loose grip. Yann had served his entire military life with the 5th Chasseurs, rising to the rank of sergeant-veterinarian. Jobert and Didier's father had become its regimental sergeant major. Jobert frowned when a few feathers floated free.

'At the end of '92,' Jobert said, 'the 5th Chasseurs were brigaded with the 3rd Chasseurs at Jemappes. In the rain, we stumbled across the Austrian artillery park beyond the town. It was protected by Dutch hussars. We charged and counter-charged in the mud, our horses exhausted, our musketoons drenched. One of the 3rd Chasseurs' squadrons was to be taken in the flank—'

'Raive's squadron?' Didier asked. 'With Koschak?'

'Yes.' Jobert looked beyond the plumes. Beyond the floorboards. 'My company advanced in reserve. With no higher authority present, I chose to take the kaiserliks in their flank. We saved Raive's lads with a slog in the mire. Duque was struck down by a hussar officer—'

'One of these bastard von Maefelds?'

'Yes, this particular von Maefeld dropped my Blanc with his pistol. With me on foot covering Duque, two other brothers joined the fray. We cut at each other in the mud. I ran two of them through.' Jobert hung his head. 'Having dispatched Blanc with a captured pistol, I bludgeoned the third brother to death with it.' He snorted. 'Or so I thought.' Jobert shrugged. 'I saved Duque. I took the pistols as a prize to remember Blanc.'

Didier's stare lifted from the plumes to his brother's face. 'How does this Belgian affair link with Italy?'

'Perhaps with Austria's loss of her Belgian and Dutch provinces, the surviving von Maefeld – Victor, the one I pistol-whipped – rejoined an Austrian regiment assigned to Lombardy.' Jobert wrapped the regimental plume and replaced it within its chest. 'After Castiglione last year, Victor attempted to settle a duel with an officer of the 24th Chasseurs—'

'Yes, I remember, Voreille—'

'Quite so.' Jobert's hand brushed at Didier's interruption. 'During that affair, Victor and his nephew, Wolff – the son of the man whose pistols I took – identified my pistols. More importantly, Wolff identified me as the man who slew his father.'

Didier's eyebrows arched. 'You gave him your name?'

Jobert's focus returned with a jerk. 'The turd stole one of my pistols. I demanded he attend me to return it. He gave me his word he would.'

Didier nodded slowly at his own memories. 'And north of Trento, my hussars crossed blades with Wolff's hussars. He must have heard my name called aloud in our melee. In his rage, bellowing about debts of honour and demanding satisfaction, the bastard drove my horse into the ground, his mount crushing my ankle.'

Jobert dropped his eyes to the wooden prosthetic strapped to Didier's lower leg. 'Does knowing relieve the ache?'

Didier shrugged.

Jobert reached out for the pistol. His voice growled low, 'I will avenge your loss.'

Didier hefted its weight before handing the pistol across butt-first. 'Perhaps.' Didier groomed his moustache with the back of his finger. 'Another souvenir for your chests?'

'No.' Jobert wrapped the pistol in an oiled rag. 'It will return with me to Lombardy. I will have it with me when I reclaim the other.'

'The old plume brought back memories. How are you finding separation from your regiment?'

'The 24th Chasseurs?' Jobert shrugged. 'I have memories and scars a plenty.'

'And your wounds from Rivoli?'

Jobert's face creased in a slow smirk. 'Well, enough.'

Didier leaned back and folded his arms. 'What next for you, André?'

'I do not know. Someone will tell me when I return. Everyone is heading for this intervention in Switzerland. With the treaty with Austria signed, the Army of Italy is likely to be committed.'

'Then it is lucky Bleu and Jaune are mountain bred. Do you need more horses as an *aide de camp*?'

'You are quick to hand out the farm's hard work.' Jobert took a deep breath as he considered his brother. 'After his fall on the mountain, Yann spoke of the difficulties arranging herds and hands as well as coordinating Raive's cartage with the senior colts. Why does Yann ask for me to stay? Are our enterprises in need? You are well respected by both the village herdsmen and the veterans who drive the cartage teams. Your horsemanship and your keen financial eye make you a good manager. Does the family farm not suit a colonel of hussars?'

'Does he doubt me? I feel mildly insulted. I have been here a year. I play my part.'

'Yann says he feels his age.'

Didier held up his palms. 'What rubbish! Look at what Aunt Sophie undertakes at seventy-nine.'

Jobert evaluated his brother as Didier wriggled on his crate before fussing with the iron latch of a chest behind him. 'How are Sophie and Michelle with their contracts?'

Didier continued to wrestle with his composure on the wooden lid. 'Michelle is as ebullient as ever.'

'I hear the Paris mob hunts émigrés. Are the de Chabenac women in danger?'

'No, the de Colbert brothers take good care of them.'

'And de Colbert's child?'

Didier sat still and frowned at Jobert. 'Are you referring to our nephew, Jacques de Colbert-Chauvel? His father, Édouard, has been dealt a rubbish hand.'

'Yann thinks ...' Jobert began. Didier tilted his head in enquiry. Jobert shook his head and smiled. 'Speaking of the de Chabenacs, at Raive's wedding, Chabenac told me he has been promoted and also posted to the Army of Italy.'

'Raive is poaching his favourites. It can only bode well for you.' Didier smiled at a whiff of scandal. 'What do you make of Raive's unseemly haste to marry Marguerite. He proposes to the woman eight months after she is widowed, then marries her three months later. I cannot imagine Raive siring such a beauty.'

Jobert twitched. A waft of dread slid around his belly.

A knock on the doorframe. The brothers swivelled to peer

through the dust motes floating on the last rays of the day.

'Excuse me, gentlemen,' Orlande said, raising a sealed document, 'a military courier from the Army of Italy for Lieutenant Colonel Jobert. Otherwise, dinner is ready.'

'Thank you, Orlande.' Jobert considered Raive's wax seal before unfolding the parchment. He read it and then passed the order to Didier. 'As Orlande says, my goose is cooked. I am recalled to duty.'

'It is the recent unrest in Switzerland, no doubt.' Didier flicked the paper with his fingers. 'The establishment of another republic, perhaps?'

Jobert shrugged. 'Well, Milan initially. I do not know after that.'

Didier looked over his shoulder to confirm Orlande's departure. 'I envy you. An aide is an opportunity to be in the thick of the action under the eye of your commander. Oh, forget the farm, brother. Think of the glory.' Didier's face tightened in calculation. 'Does Bonaparte still command the Army of Italy?'

'He did when I left in September. With the treaty signed, who knows? Possibly Masséna or Berthier?'

'Excellent! All men who know your mettle.' Didier reached out and gripped Jobert's knee. 'André, now is your time to ascend.'

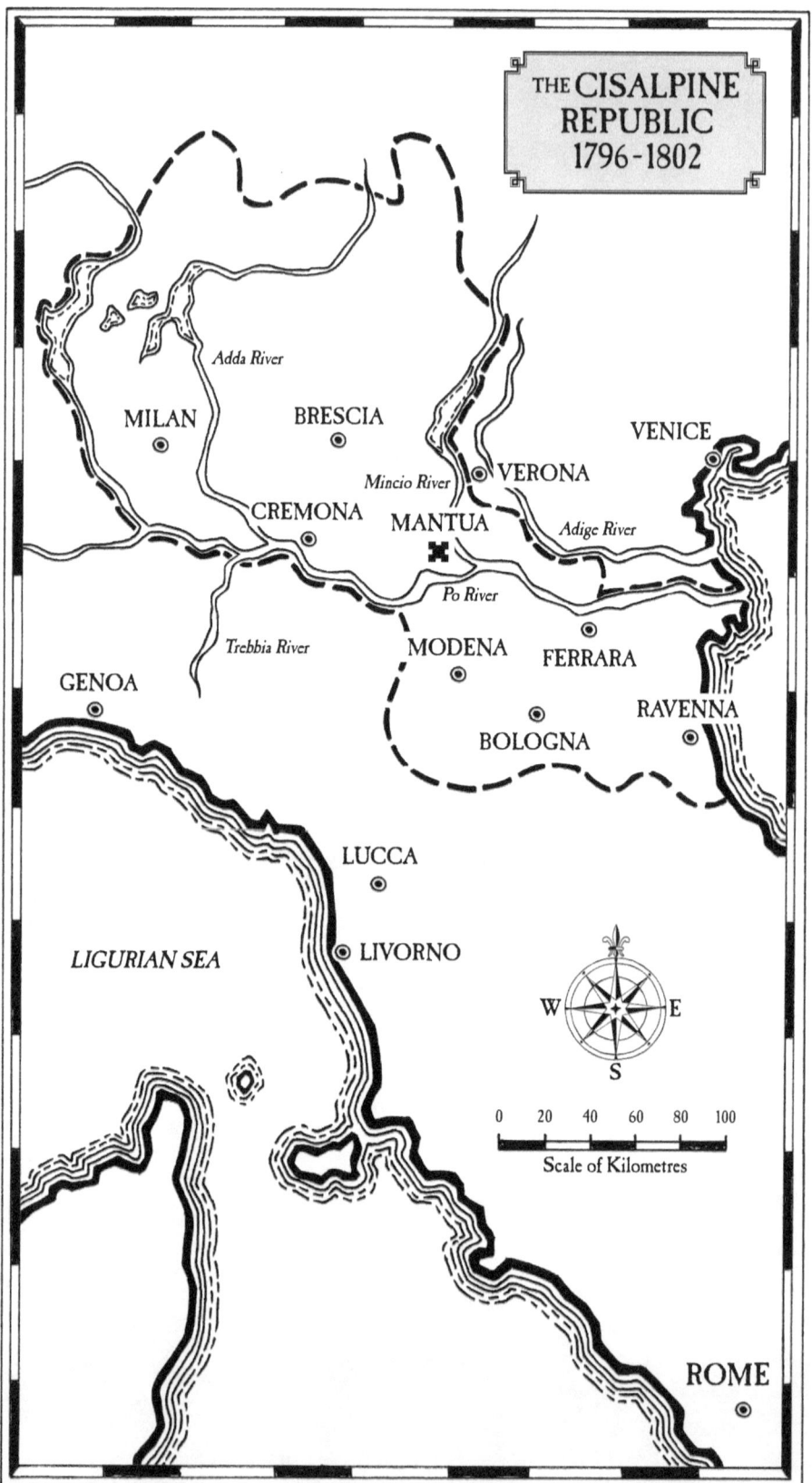

THE CISALPINE
REPUBLIC
1796-1802

Adda River

MILAN

BRESCIA

VENICE

Mincio River   VERONA

CREMONA   MANTUA

Adige River

Po River

Trebbia River

MODENA   FERRARA

GENOA

RAVENNA

BOLOGNA

LUCCA

LIGURIAN SEA   LIVORNO

W   E

S

0   20   40   60   80   100

Scale of Kilometres

ROME

Chapter Four
February 1798, Milan, Italy

'We have created what?' Jobert reeled with confusion. 'An Army of England? Were our expeditions to Ireland and Wales not defeated around this time last year? Why does the Directory persist with these pinpricks against Britain?'

Raive wobbled his head as he sought wisdom within the flames of his hearth. 'Perhaps that is why Bonaparte has departed Italy to command this Army of England. Perhaps the Directory hope for him to deliver great victories across the channel. Who knows?' Raive rocked back in his chair and gave his thighs a slap. 'Of greater relevance to you and me, your fellow Virginian, General Berthier, now commands the Army of Italy.'

Jobert rolled his eyes. 'I regret reminding Berthier of our time together there. Nevertheless, the musical chairs of command resume. What of Switzerland, sir? Are we being swept up in the invasion?'

'No, Rome.'

Jobert's face went blank at the unexpected destination. 'Rome?'

'There has been an uprising in Naples. The Holy Father attempts to raise an army. Berthier has directed our good friend Masséna to occupy Rome.'

'Have I been assigned to Masséna's staff?'

'No,' Raive said. 'You have been assigned as an *attaché* to the Cisalpine Chasseurs à Cheval.'

'An attaché! To whom?'

'The Cisalpine Chasseurs à Cheval. Both you and Major de Chabenac—'

Jobert's face creased with concern. 'De Chabenac, sir?'

'I am sure I told you at the wedding de Chabenac was posted to the staff. Are you surprised at his promotion?'

'It is neither his posting nor his promotion, sir, but his name. DE ... Chabenac? Has he resumed his nobility?'

Raive spread his hands in conciliation. 'A small allowance has been made. These new Italians relish associating with aristocratic stock.'

Jobert gave the burning logs a stern look. 'He resumes the mantle of petty nobility to further France's influence, while his mother and sister are hunted by the Parisian mob for the same name.'

'Ah, quite so. Shall we resume the details of your assignment with the Cisalpine Chasseurs?'

Jobert's dentures stabbed his mouth as he drew a notebook and pencil from an inner pocket.

'You have met Prefetto Bernasconi,' Raive said. 'He has been appointed by the Cisalpine Republic's legislative assembly to raise military forces. Do you remember meeting his friend at the parades last summer? Colonel Rizzoli now commands the regiment.'

'This regiment was raised before winter?'

Raive winced. 'Nearly. On paper, companies exist in Milan, Cremona, Mantua, Brescia, Bologna, Modena, Ferrara and

Ravenna.'

Suspicion jabbed at Jobert's guts. 'What experience does Rizzoli have?'

'None.'

'Then why was he ... ah.'

'Indeed,' Raive said, 'he and Bernasconi both have invested heavily.'

'Then who does have regimental experience?'

'Quite a number of the junior officers and non-commissioned officers are Lombardians who served previously in the Austrian Army. They have been spread throughout the regiment.'

Jobert raised his eyebrows. 'Kaiserliks? Is that so? Then what is required of me?'

'Provide advice ...' Raive pursed his lips, 'if asked.'

'Is that the extent of my involvement?' Jobert slumped. 'To make suggestions?'

'Suggest ... delicately.'

Jobert breathed deeply. 'Do you require me to report on their ... progress.'

'Monthly will suffice.'

'Shall I report to Rizzoli in the morning?'

'That is not necessary,' Raive said, 'as de Chabenac attends Rizzoli here in Milan. The regiment has orders to march for Rome. I recommend you ride for Mantua, ingratiate yourself with Bernasconi and move with the Mantua Company.'

'Yes, sir.' Jobert stood, saluted and turned to depart.

'And Jobert,' Raive looked up from the documents on his desk, 'once in Rome, you may be sought out ... by an old friend.'

A swinging red flare popped in Jobert's memory. *Bloody Inoubli!* His throat convulsed as if he had swallowed chain-shot.

A nervous look flittered across Raive's face.

Jobert's sour look deepened. 'Anything else, sir?'

Raive fidgeted with a sharp letter opener. 'Speaking of the wedding, Jobert, you may not be aware. Marguerite and I have received a great blessing.' A grin curled Raive's moustache. 'Marguerite is with child.'

A week later, in Prefetto Bernasconi's mansion, just around the corner from the Piazza Sordello in the heart of Mantua, Jobert and three guests joined the Bernasconi family for dinner.

Prefetto Bernasconi sat at the head of the table on Jobert's right. 'Our family home in Verona is now occupied by imperial troops. Here in Mantua, I hope to err towards some modesty. With prevailing sentiment for the new republic, a Veronese lording himself amongst the Mantuans is viewed dimly. Regional rivalry is fraught.'

'Your home is very handsome, sir,' Jobert said. 'The Mantuan architecture states your authority, where your Veronese furnishings describe a modest family. I believe you have achieved the balance you seek.'

Across the table on Bernasconi's right sat Colonel Rizzoli, the new commander of the Cisalpine Chasseurs Cheval. His gentle, debonair look akin to a theatre's leading man, his half-smile stretched beneath a lustrous moustache.

'Major de Chabenac,' Rizzoli said, 'surely your ancient family has a military past?'

Seated on Rizzoli's right, de Chabenac bowed his blond head. 'Our ancestral home has sufficient suits of plate and halberds bolted to the wall to raise a regiment should they be so called upon.'

'I can only imagine your attachment to my staff,' Rizzoli said, 'is a brief honour, as I am sure calls for regimental command will soon take a gentleman of your breeding from us.'

De Chabenac presented a warm smile and bow of his head.

'What of you, Jobert?' Rizzoli asked. 'Did you attend the theatre this evening? *The Marriage of Figaro*. Marvellous!'

'Ah ... unfortunately not, sir.' Jobert twisted the stem of his crystal glass. 'Do you have plans for the regiment, sir?'

Beside Rizzoli, de Chabenac's smile broadened. *Is he warning me?*

'My plans?' Rizzoli's eyebrows arched. 'I have raised a regiment of four squadrons and now march on Rome. Is that not sufficient?' Rizzoli returned his smile to de Chabenac. 'I am guided by the wisdom of Prince Eugene. Have you read de Saxe, sir?'

'As a boy, I was a student of the classics, sir,' de Chabenac said, 'but Colonel Jobert is our scholar of contemporary tactical thought. Within his library I have found much to reflect on with de Maillebois, de Guibert and Bourcet.'

'My goodness, comparing de Guibert to Eugene of Savoy. Now that will not do. And *Principes de la Guerre des Montagnes* will be of little value in the Po Valley.'

'If only to chock a wagon's wheel, sir,' said Jobert. The gentlemen around him chuckled softly. 'And it certainly did that as we drove Piedmont out of the Maritime Alps in two weeks and chased the Austrians over Carinthian Alps to the gates of Vienna.'

Rizzoli's moustache flickered with indignation, and he directed his handsome smile towards Bernasconi.

Jobert leaned back in his chair. 'On our march to Rome, Colonel Rizzoli, will you be taking the opportunity to further the regiment's training while in the field?'

'Whatever for?' said Major Zenari, a young man with a drooping moustache and tight brown curls, seated on Jobert's left. 'We were up to the task at Arcole. I cannot think why we cannot be now.' Like his regimental colonel – and his uncle, Jobert was informed – Zenari wore a dolman of verdant green, the bright scarlet facings highlighted with white trim. Mirroring de Chabenac seated opposite him, Zenari wore the crisp new lace of a chief of squadron.

Jobert's head pivoted to Zenari, making an effort to close his mouth from the surprise revelation. 'You served at Arcole? With whom did you serve?'

With hooded eyes Zenari shot a smirk towards Rizzoli. 'With the Cisalpine Chasseurs, of course.'

'You have me at your advantage, sir, I thought the regiment was raised—'

'Yes,' Bernasconi said, 'the regiment was authorised to be raised last June. Although a company of chasseurs was raised a year earlier, mid-'96, when General Bonaparte initially established the republic. And yes, that company did contribute at Arcole later that year.'

Signora Bernasconi coughed. All eyes flickered towards the lady of the house at the foot of the table, seated between her son and daughter. Signoras's slim shoulders hunched over her setting, her trembling left hand gripped her daughter's fingers, her grey face twitched towards her son on her right.

'I hesitate to bore the ladies with such menial details, Jobert,' Rizzoli said, 'but it is not my intent to degrade the condition of the horses with schemes and distractions.' Rizzoli exchanged a nod with Bernasconi.

'I want to participate in a charge,' said Bernasconi's teenage son, seated beyond Zenari from Jobert.

'Silvio!' Signora Bernasconi's eyes burned bright as she flinched her arm away from her daughter's soothing.

Squirming under his mother's gaze, Silvio shot pleading

glances at Rizzoli.

Diagonally across from Jobert, beyond the small moths fluttering about the table's candelabra, sat Signorina Gianna Bernasconi. Seated between de Chabenac and her mother, Bernasconi's daughter contemplated the dinner's guests with cautious glances.

Turning toward her, de Chabenac asked, 'Were you aware, Signorina, that Colonel Jobert's family have been breeders of fine horses from their estates in the Auvergne for generations.'

'I was not, sir.' Gianna smiled nervously at Jobert, as if apologising.

Gianna was full-figured in a modestly cut gown of a rich yellow silk.

Certainly, the only person of interest, Jobert thought. *Mid-twenties, perhaps?*

Her brown hair was bound up with black ribbons. Her green eyes, or perhaps hazel, had only engaged Jobert the once. It was her mouth that held Jobert's attention. As she spared small courtesies to de Chabenac, her lips and dimples quivered with a playful tenderness.

'Jobert?' Rizzoli asked.

Jobert's thoughts jerked back from their distraction beyond the candelabra. 'Forgive me, sir. Thoughts of home.'

'Estates, Jobert?' Rizzoli smile returned from across the table. 'I understand your family has enterprises around Paris. With peace now declared, are you not eager to return to your estates?'

'I am a professional soldier, sir. My immediate task is to contribute to the security of your new republic.'

'Is that so?' Rizzoli's face shuddered with disappointment. 'Oh, well then ... ever our thanks to our French friends.'

'My family is of humble origin, sir.' Jobert's chest swelled. 'For over three generations, we have striven to establish ourselves as horse-breeders and manufacturers of uniforms.'

Rizzoli beamed at Bernasconi. 'My goodness, how fascinating.'

'A burgeoning industry in France, I am sure.' Zenari shot a smirk towards Gianna, before turning to run an eye over Jobert's tailcoat.

Jobert could imagine a comment beginning to form on Zenari's lips. 'From which your new republic benefits. Is that not so, Zenari?'

Zenari's face soured before he spun to signal the wine waiter.

Jobert caught the flash of Gianna's dimpled smile.

A plate smashed onto the table. Cutlery clattered on the tiles.

'I cannot do this.' Signora Bernasconi's knuckles were white as she gripped both halves of her shattered plate. 'I cannot sit here with them. I will no longer listen to their tongue at my table.' Signora thrust a jewelled-laden finger at Jobert. 'They upset the tranquillity bestowed by the Holy Roman Emperor. They took my son's life and ruined my daughter's future. Now they move to abuse the Holy Father and rob me of my baby.'

She struggled to stand from her heavy chair. Footmen surged from the shadows to assist her. The gentlemen grabbed at their napkins to stand.

'I must pray.' Signora Bernasconi lurched away from the table.

Gianna caught her mother's elbow and guided her from the dining hall.

'Gentlemen, please sit.' Bernasconi's jaw trembled with embarrassment as he flicked a finger towards the attendant staff. Dishes, half consumed or broken, were removed as the gentlemen resumed their seats. 'I beg your forgiveness. My wife has found adjusting to these tumultuous days difficult.'

Silvio's eyes darted to de Chabenac. 'Mama cannot abide the French.'

'Did France take your son, sir?' de Chabenac asked. 'The lady cannot be denied her grief.'

Bernasconi levelled his gaze at Silvio. 'My eldest son chose to be a soldier. He reaped a soldier's harvest.'

Silvio dropped his face to his glass.

Rizzoli's fingertips tapped Bernasconi's forearm. 'A terrible price to pay for the blessing we now receive.'

'Hardly blessings, Uncle.' Zenari rolled his eyes. 'We have long deserved these days. Despite the price, all of us here now benefit. We would do well not to imperil any future gains.'

Bernasconi's face soured.

'Sir, gentlemen, would you excuse us?' Jobert glanced to de Chabenac. Jobert stood and de Chabenac followed. 'Prefetto Bernasconi, sir, would you accept my sincere condolences on the loss of your son. I cannot imagine Signora Bernasconi's pain at having us join your table. We have disturbed the happiness of your household, and for that I apologise. With your permission, we shall take our leave.'

Bernasconi stood and offered his hand. 'You have done nothing to apologise for, Jobert. May the Lord bless your travels to Rome. Upon your safe return to Mantua, I must insist you dine with me.'

Chapter Five

February 1798, Modena, Italy

On the road to Rome, Rizzoli held his evening open table at a Modena salon, the haunt of the officers of the regiment's Modena Company.

Jobert found the dainty glass he held too small for his needs this evening. Any reasonable sip of the delicious *ramazzotti* would empty it. To distract himself from the irritation, Jobert approached Rizzoli.

Rizzoli beamed as he surveyed the buzz of excited young officers around the salon.

'I have taken steps to acquire de Saxe, sir,' Jobert said. 'Did Eugene compose his own memoir?'

Rizzoli's merriment faded to his sad-eyed smile, as if he regarded Jobert with pity. 'No, Jobert, he did not. I am surprised you have joined our jaunt to Rome.'

Jobert winced. 'As a liaison officer from the Army of Italy attached to the regiment, is that not assumed, sir?'

'You do not have to if you do not wish to.' Rizzoli shifted his view to the movement of others over Jobert's shoulder.

My wishes?

'My duty demands I attend your regiment, sir.' Jobert dabbed his upper lip with wine from his ridiculous glass. 'Sir, your views on our progress to Rome?'

'No need to rush. Cavalry can do little in Rome.'

'You do not wish the regiment to participate?'

'Why not arrive with distinction? As a parade, a triumphal procession amidst the Romans?'

'Indeed, sir.' Jobert suppressed a frown by inspecting the crystal thimble between his fingers.

Rizzoli swung his view towards the officers around the room.

My company inadequate?

Jobert smiled at the opportunity to give a touch of spur. 'The regiment is authorised to raise eight companies, until now only eight troops are on the rolls seven months later. May I ask, sir, have you faced difficulties with recruitment or the provision of horses?'

Rizzoli swung back to face Jobert. 'I have no difficulties, whatsoever, Jobert. I am justifiably proud of the regiment's achievements. Why? Have you observed anything untoward?'

'I am aware that flints have not been ordered for your musketoons.'

'A minor obstacle. Beneath my station. Indeed, is that not what we have you French for? Perhaps I might call upon your assistance in that regard. You may have greater influence amongst the lower—'

'Uncle, you must attend us.' Zenari had stepped between Jobert and Rizzoli, the back of his shoulder to Jobert. 'Differing views on Eugene's passage by Cremona are on the verge of blows. A matter only you can resolve.'

Rizzoli seemed to increase in height at the challenge. 'Lead on, sir.' Rizzoli spun and strode towards the group of chattering young officers.

With such a snub by Rizzoli and such blatant rudeness from Zenari, Jobert fought the urge to throw the petite goblet at the back of Zenari's head. Jobert scowled as he investigated the room.

They look like officers, but they are not. Where am I?

'Excuse me, sir.' Jobert turned to the voice behind him.

'Would you forgive me for introducing myself. I am Captain D'Onofrio, commanding our Mantua Company.' D'Onofrio held himself in an erect, soldierly pose, his thick black hair pulled back from his thick eyebrows into a long, tight queue. So dark was D'Onofrio's beard beneath the skin, his clean-shaven jawline was blue. D'Onofrio's eyes flickered with unease across Jobert's face. 'I feel we may have met previously. Under adverse conditions.'

'How so, sir?'

'Am I correct, sir, you served in Italy with the 24th Chasseurs since 1794?'

'I ... did.'

'In '94 and '95 I served across the field with His Imperial Majesty's Chevau-léger de Kerzy. My regiment had the honour of crossing blades with the 24th Chasseurs on numerous occasions.'

Jobert's cheek creased in a half-smile as he recalled his days as a company commander in the Maritime Alps above the Ligurian coast.

A hint of smugness twitched the edges of D'Onofrio's mouth. 'If I am not mistaken, you and I met on the heights above Finale Ligure in July of '95 following our capture of Savona. Your company led us a merry chase through the mountains to Rocca Barbena.'

A brown scar on Jobert's right cheek twisted as his harsh grin spread. 'Yes, I remember our encounters, D'Onofrio. From the heights above Dego in September of '94 all the way to our recapture of Savona in November of '95, I recall.'

D'Onofrio stiffened.

'And yes,' Jobert continued. 'I remember you from Finale Ligure.'

D'Onofrio gave a stiff bow.

'How have you found the transition to serving in the Army of ... the Cisalpine Republic?' Jobert asked.

D'Onofrio shuffled. 'In imperial service, there was clear structure which both drove you and supported you. Here there is ... more latitude.' He forced a smile. 'Greater freedom for initiative.'

'Eugene himself would be delighted. How would you describe the state of your company?'

D'Onofrio took a series of short breaths as he contemplated the scene around him. 'Satisfactory, sir.'

'I am aware that only a troop has been raised in each company and even then only a platoon complies with orders to march on Rome. As one experienced campaigner to another, do you find that curious?'

D'Onofrio's eyes darted to Jobert as he thrust out his chin. 'Headquarters felt that was all that was needed.'

'Is that so? Deploy on operations with half your available force?' Jobert considered D'Onofrio with care. 'May I request your permission to observe your men in their duties, sir?'

D'Onofrio stiffened further.

'I only seek any small measure,' Jobert said, 'where I might support their performance. Perhaps in the provision of flints for their musketoons. I have contacts at the highest level that will respond in the regiment's favour.'

D'Onofrio wilted briefly. 'That would be appreciated, sir. You are welcome to review them.'

Jobert glimpsed Koschak moving across the room with a silver jug of something and three long-stemmed silver cups.

'Then allow me to thank you, Captain D'Onofrio, for reminiscing of our time together, and the hope that our shared adventures will contribute to a fine body of horse under your command. Would you excuse me?'

Jobert caught Koschak by the elbow and looked at the silver chevrons of a commissioned officer above Koschak's cuffs. 'Give me two cups of whatever you have.'

Koschak regarded Jobert suspiciously as he poured. 'Is something amiss, sir?'

'I am confused. This regiment has only raised half of its establishment in seven months. The colonel believes he can build a regiment by reading the strategic designs of a grand master. Rizzoli then complies with higher orders with only half his available force because he deems it sufficient. The situation is inconceivable.' Jobert thrust out his cup for another serve. 'I am unsure of my place.'

Koschak laughed at Jobert's disquiet. 'These ninnies are beneath us, sir. They are not real soldiers. This is a carnival, a dividend of the new peace. They have challenged me to a round of cards to which I shall relieve them of their purses. A source of income denied me if I had forsaken a commission.'

Jobert studied Koschak's relaxed grin. 'I feel uneasy. It is only a matter of time before ...'

'Whatever could go wrong, sir?'

Jobert watched de Chabenac across the room laughing with Rizzoli. 'De Chabenac told me of the reaction to this twenty-day march to Rome. Rizzoli did not send out his own regimental orders for two days and we have stayed two days in each company barracks we have traipsed through. We are already one week behind Masséna's corps.'

'Oh, sir, we should allow ourselves a little licence.'

'Did we not recently endure a brutal military endeavour? It is only a matter of time before Austria strikes. These people are making no effort to prepare, but they are receiving pay to make such effort. Are you not dismayed?'

Koschak eyes softened to pity. 'I am attending a travelling card evening with teenage dandies. The sons of the bourgeoisies speak only of opportunities to parade their uniforms.'

'I see. I am in a nightmare where I have returned to the old royal army as an officer of fortune up from the ranks? I now understand how it was for Didier. Look there! Bernasconi's son is sporting a hussar's pelisse of his own design.'

Koschak coughed a gruff laugh. 'What is more, he wears a dress epée instead of a sabre.

'What are we doing here, Koschak?'

'Adapting to peace, sir.'

'Really? I despair.'

In Bologna three days later, Jobert and Koschak stepped into the stables housing the horses of the twenty-five-man platoon from D'Onofrio's Mantua Company.

The dark interior reeked of urine. Thirsty horses neighed and thrust their noses against their confining halters. The horses snickered and stomped, their tails flicking and eyes rolling with irritation.

Between the empty water buckets, six chasseurs wearing their soft *bonnets de police*, whistled a tune in unison as they raked the piles of manure under the horses' rear hooves.

Jobert's head swivelled down the line of hooves. 'Nine days into a twenty-day march and their feet are in this state.'

'A nine-day march we have taken fifteen days to complete.'

Koschak lifted stirrups on saddles to find the harness dry for want of oil. 'Another rest, I am told, before we cross the Apennines.'

'Which is your horse, chasseur?' Jobert asked a teenage chasseur in Italian.

The boy ceased whistling and braced his rake to attention.

Jobert smiled. 'Your horse, lad?'

The soldier pointed to a nearby horse.

'Follow me and look here.' Jobert picked up a rear hoof with overgrown toes and wiggled the loose shoe. 'Tell your company farrier—' The chasseur frowned. 'Do you have your company farrier with this detachment?'

'No, sir, but there is a farrier with Brescia Company.'

'What is your horse's name, lad?'

'San Marco, sir.'

'San Marco must not be harmed with a nail from a loose shoe piercing his foot. Tell the farrier.'

Outside down the street, a trumpet sounded for morning stables.

Koschak closed his pocket watch. 'Seven o'clock! Will the princesses take a turn around the park after morning tea? Fuck me!'

'Tsk! Language, lieutenant,' Jobert chided. 'You sound like a sergeant.'

'Huh!' Koschak turned to an older soldier carrying an armful of hay, and asked in Italian, 'Chasseur, where are your sergeants?'

The soldier dropped the bundle of fodder, braced to attention and frowned.

'Where are your sergeants?' Jobert asked in German.

'Sergeant Fazio normally arrives after breakfast, sir.'

The clack of a pistol's hammer being drawn back caused Jobert and Koschak to spin.

'What are you doing here?' A wiry sergeant rocked the barrel of a pistol between them both.

'Sergeant Fazio?' Jobert asked as he and Koschak stepped swiftly apart.

'That made it easy.' Fazio spoke out the side of his mouth from beneath his thick black moustache. 'As I shall shoot the bastard with the most lace.' The reek of alcohol reached Jobert as Fazio exhaled and swung the barrel.

Koschak's right hand brushed against his left cuff, drawing a dagger.

'Sergeant, stop!' Jobert said, raising his palms. 'I am Lieutenant Colonel Jobert, assigned to Colonel Rizzoli's staff. Captain D'Onofrio—'

'French dog! You ought to eat my ball.' Fazio aimed at Jobert's belly.

Koschak threw his dagger.

Fazio recoiled from the dagger's handle striking his face. The pistol fired.

Jobert dropped to one knee. The ball zipped past.

A horse screamed and kicked out.

Koschak twisted the pistol from Fazio's grasp, then kicked Fazio hard in the crotch. Fazio collapsed with a strangled scream.

'Good throw to strike with the handle,' said Jobert, brushing green manure from his over-breeches with a handful of straw.

'That was not my intent.' A sour look twisted Koschak's face. 'On your feet, Sergeant!'

Fazio rolled onto his knees and vomited. Grappa was the dominant odour in the thick bile.

'What is going on—' D'Onofrio searched the gloom of the stables.

'Is this man Sergeant Fazio, Captain D'Onofrio?' Jobert asked.

D'Onofrio stiffened. 'Yes, sir.'

Koschak's boot toppled Fazio into his pungent puddle. 'Stand up, Fazio!'

'This man threatened me with a pistol,' Jobert said, 'then fired it at me when I declared who I was. He has wounded a remount. Captain, march this man to the cells and have him charged with assaulting a superior officer and inflicting injury on regimental property.'

D'Onofrio spun towards the line of rigid troopers. 'Corporal Cieno, form an escort for the prisoner. March him to the city's gendarmes. Fetch the sergeant-veterinarian for the horse.'

'Stand fast, Cieno.' Zenari swaggered into the barn. 'That will not be necessary.'

'Captain, I gave you an order,' Jobert said. 'Execute that order. Now!'

Zenari stood with his hands on his hips. 'That is not how we conduct business in this regiment.'

'That is exactly how business is done in the French Army,' Jobert said, 'of which this regiment is a part. Captain D'Onofrio, carry on. Major Zenari, outside with me. Now!'

The sky threatened a storm as they walked out of the stables. Jobert hooked a finger. 'Come here, Major Zenari.'

'I am not your dog to be called to heel,' said Zenari. 'I shall report this outrage to my … to Colonel Rizzoli.' Zenari strode up the lane towards the tavern which housed Rizzoli's headquarters.

Koschak and D'Onofrio exchanged dumbstruck stares at Zenari's disobedience.

'D'Onofrio, what was Fazio's previous service?' Jobert asked. 'Your regiment of chevau-léger?'

'No, he was not, sir. Fazio was a corporal in the horse artillery.'

'Is that so.' Jobert ground his teeth. 'When in doubt, attack!'

Jobert followed Zenari at a steady pace. Koschak fell into

step beside him.

'Do you know Zenari's previous service?' Jobert asked.

'A second lieutenant in the original Cisalpine Chasseur Company.'

'Hence his claim to honour on the field at Arcole.'

Koschak spat. 'They patrolled the routes from the divisional trains back to Verona. They never crossed the Adige.'

Jobert pumped his fist in which he carried his scabbard. His sabre rattled its desire for action. 'But sufficient for this prick to know everything about soldiering. Since Rizzoli has never served before, this ought to be interesting.'

Jobert entered the tavern. Rizzoli sat at a breakfast table in his shirtsleeves. Zenari helped himself to a jug on a side bench.

Rizzoli blinked at the pistol in Koschak's hand. 'I believe you have caused a ruckus, Jobert.'

Jobert bristled. 'I am a lieutenant colonel in the French Army. I do not cause ruckuses, sir. I was observing the conduct of morning stables when I was fired upon by one of your drunken sergeants.'

'Why did you need to attend morning stables?'

Jobert's face crimped with incredulity. 'Why was I shot at, sir?' He pointed at Zenari. 'And why was this officer deliberately insubordinate to me in the presence of junior ranks?'

Zenari puffed up. 'Me? Insubordinate?'

'Gentlemen,' Rizzoli said, 'this is unseemly. I request everyone withdraw to allow me to reflect upon the matter. I shall give my verdict at dinner this evening.'

'Dinner where?' Jobert asked. 'You have not received my report on the matter.'

'Why, dinner here, of course. And I have heard enough, I assure you.'

Zenari banged the jug on the bench top. 'What of our Fazio being held in the cells, Uncle?'

'Oh, we cannot have that. What an impost upon the town. Zenari, be so kind as to arrange his release, and beg the forgiveness of the Chief Constable.'

'Colonel Rizzoli, you must reconsider.' Jobert's voice was low and measured. 'I have ordered Fazio be detained in custody prior to being charged with a serious military offence. Under Austrian regulations, he would be hanged. Under French military law, he will serve in chains on the road gangs.'

Zenari coughed with surprise. 'French regulations?'

'Gentlemen, please.' Rizzoli held up his hands. 'I have considered, Jobert. There has been a misunderstanding. Upon my order, Jobert, Fazio will be released forthwith. And Jobert, can I trust you to act in the best interest of the regiment?'

Jobert rocked back as if struck. 'Sir, never in my eighteen years of service, under either king or republic, has my loyalty ever been questioned.'

Rizzoli's handsome smile curled his moustache. 'You are assigned to my regiment, Jobert. I sit here now certainly unsure of your loyalty to me.'

Jobert clamped his jaw. His dentures pierced his gums. 'Sir, I am loyal to the commander of the Army of Italy, of which this unit is a part, and General Masséna, upon whose orders we march to Rome. I shall comply with my orders, sir, with the alacrity they demand. I will depart within the hour and report to General Masséna on the delays to your progress.'

'Go ahead if you must. You add nothing of any value here. I will require de Chabenac to remain with my retinue. There is a gentleman with whom I can converse.'

Zenari waggled his wine cup. 'Perhaps you might arrange suitable accommodation in Rome.'

Jobert stepped towards Zenari, stabbing towards him with a rigid, flat palm. 'I am not your quartermaster, Zenari.'

Zenari stumbled backwards into the bench. The jug and cup

clattered to the tiles.

Jobert hissed through bared teeth. 'I am a lieutenant colonel, and I am entitled to be addressed as "sir" by anyone of inferior rank. And you, Zenari, are most certainly my inferior.'

Chapter Six
February 1798, Rome Italy

Ten days later, Jobert entered the murmur of the dingy, crowded salon.

Over a dozen amused French officers and Roman courtesans glanced at Jobert as he entered. The sharp flames of the room's many candles were blunted by the grey cloud of tobacco smoke. In the dim light, the colours of the many officers' uniforms and prostitutes' gowns were muted. While the crowd hummed, the string quartet was silent, their violins resting on knees, their faces locked on the central spectacle.

An Italian chasseur officer flung his slim arms in mad gestures and babbled incoherently. The central spectacle was young Silvio Bernasconi.

'Sir!' Koschak raced to Jobert's side. 'Young Bernasconi has challenged a dragoon captain to a duel. The boy is drunk. I have tried to placate the dragoons, and the captain has stayed his hand so far, but that bastard Zenari is stirring the shit-pot with his tongue. Zenari is a disgrace. The bullshit of being an officer does not allow me to sink my fist into his throat.'

Jobert took measured strides across the centre of the gathering. He spun the boy by the shoulder to face him.

Bernasconi wobbled and drooled. 'Who dares—'

Jobert slapped Bernasconi with the back of his hand. 'Shut up, idiot!'

Bernasconi tottered backwards, more from surprise than sting, and dropped onto a chair to gulp air.

Jobert approached the captain in question. The dragoon stood squared and balanced, his fingers hooked in his sword belt. His surrounding associates muttered close by.

'Captain,' Jobert said, 'my name is Jobert.' With a glance at the lace of rank on Jobert's cuffs and thighs, the captain stiffened as a slight sign of respect. 'I am ashamed to declare I am connected to this buffoon. What can I do to repair your evening? Would you be satisfied if I removed him from the venue? Is your table owed a debt?'

'There is no need for your intervention, sir. I have a second lieutenant from my squadron able to give the fellow satisfaction on my behalf.'

'With our recent imprisonment of the Pope and on the eve of Masséna declaring the Roman Republic, could we not jeopardise the mood further with the slaying of a Cisalpine officer?'

'Perhaps a firm kick down the stairs may save the pup's hide.' The captain jabbed a finger at Zenari as he seethed. 'But that Italian ... gentleman needs a slapping too. Who gave him the rank of a chief of squadron? He will get men killed with his crap.'

Jobert gave a grim wink. 'Submit a report of this disgrace to your commanding officer. I confirm they are both Cisalpine Chasseurs à Cheval.' Jobert turned to Bernasconi. 'Lieutenant Koschak, escort Lieutenant Bernasconi outside.' Jobert pointed at Zenari. 'You! Outside now.'

Koschak gripped Bernasconi by the elbow.

With a cry of pain, Bernasconi scrabbled at the grip of his dress epée.

The crowd hooted at the development.

As Bernasconi stumbled, his scabbard snagged under a card table. Attempting to free his blade with his left hand below the hilt, Bernasconi sliced open his palm. He squealed as blood pulsed onto his tailcoat.

The gathering roared with glee.

Bernasconi began to sob as he swiped at the blood stain with his bleeding hand, spreading the dark ooze further. Koschak reapplied his grip and thrust him towards the stairs.

Zenari stepped alongside Jobert. 'Call off your dog, Jobert.'

'Or what?' Jobert descended the stairs at speed. 'Would you care to call me out?'

Zenari gripped the rail to steady himself. 'Since we are not of the same rank, propriety forbids me.'

'That did not stop you forcing an affair between this second lieutenant and that captain.'

Outside, Jobert and Zenari followed Koschak and Bernasconi into a side lane. A punch of stale urine burnt their nostrils. Without torchlight from the street, the light of a full moon illuminated Bernasconi kneeling against the wall in a puddle of mud, hugging his stomach and choking on vomit.

Zenari stepped to Bernasconi's side. 'This is an outrage, Jobert. This is the son of the regiment's patron.'

Koschak spun, feet wide, fists curled into thick bone hammers. 'Is it the same son of the regiment's patron that you attempted to murder in a duel? We averted a tragedy of your making.'

'Address me as "sir", you impudent dog. As a commissioned veteran of Arcole, I deserve it.'

'Why should I?' Koschak tipped his head forward, teasing Zenari to act. 'You fail to address Colonel Jobert with respect. He and I too fought at Arcole. Tell me of your drawn sabre on the field?'

Jobert raised placating palms. 'Major Zenari may not have drawn a sabre as he may not have received an order to do so.' Jobert turned from Koschak to Zenari. 'But you were there at Arcole, Zenari. You appreciate the gravity of being there. How does that experience allow the licence for this ludicrous situation?'

Zenari, realising what mire he was standing in, stepped away from Bernasconi. 'Regimental honour was at stake. It would have been good for the boy to be blooded.'

Koschak spat. 'Blooded? The dragoon would have run him through.'

'I would have insisted on pistols.'

'You idiot, Zenari,' Jobert said. 'Bernasconi claimed the affront, did he not? The other man chooses the terms. Your lack of judgement is appalling. As for your vaunted regiment, those dragoons regard it as a laughing stock. What gall to stage a triumphal entry with your gaggle of platoons into a city two weeks after it has been occupied.'

Zenari stepped forward with menace. 'How dare you impugn my regiment.'

'Enough, Zenari!' Jobert held up a flat hand. 'Bernasconi has impugned the regimental name with your contrived display. Now step back. You are in a back alley in Rome, Zenari. If it were not for our protection,' Jobert drew his dagger from his left cuff, 'your throat might be opened.'

Zenari stumbled backwards, tripping over Bernasconi's prostrate form, and splattering in the gutter of urine. Zenari bellowed in indignation and thrashed at the slime.

'Koschak, assist Major Zenari, please?' Jobert asked.

'It would be my pleasure, sir.' Koschak stepped onto the tail of Zenari's jacket, pinning him in the filth. Capped boot heels crunched on metal watchcase and polished dress scabbard.

'Here let me help you, sir.'

'Get off me, you ... ah! My fingers!'

'Allow me to retrieve your bicorne, sir.' Koschak dragged the hat and its plumage through the mire. Koschak offered the hat to the struggling Zenari, the saturated feathers dripping stale piss across Zenari's eyes and mouth.

Zenari moaned and spat. 'Get off me!'

'Stand up, Zenari,' Jobert said. 'A soiled jacket is the least of your worries. The officers of the 16th Dragoons want to gut you like a rabbit. I would hasten to your bed with a wary eye for any brass helmets.'

Zenari stood hunched, fingers spread, dreading the touch of his sodden clothes on his skin. 'Come, Bernasconi, we have better company to keep.'

'No. Bernasconi is in my custody. His wound needs attention.'

'You cannot detain an officer of my regiment. You failed to hold Fazio, you shall certainly—'

'Prick!' Jobert lashed out with a stiff arm to pin Zenari's throat to the wall, his dagger tip pressing into Zenari's lower left eyelid. 'You just do not know when to shut up.'

Zenari's eyeball bulged as he wheezed and wriggled before becoming still and meeting Jobert's menacing eyes.

'Your arrogance makes you oblivious to the danger around you.' Jobert released his hold.

Zenari spun and slid on unseen filth, only to fall again. As he scraped the stone wall, the pommel of his epée struck up under his ribs. On his hands and knees in the sewer, he panted.

Jobert stood over him. 'You are a disgrace, Zenari. You are no soldier.'

Zenari stood and limped to the street. At the corner, the lanterns lit a blaze across his face. 'And you are no gentleman, Jobert.'

Koschak lifted Bernasconi to his feet.

'Hmm, Arcole.' Jobert slid his dagger back into his cuff. 'I have an idea that will impose a penance on our boy for his lack of judgement. Furthermore, Lieutenant Koschak, did I see you lift Major Zenari's purse?'

Koschak threw and caught the heavy bag of coins in his fist. 'No, sir, you are mistaken.'

A shaft of moonlight caught Jobert's cruel smile. 'Then accept my apologies.'

Jobert saluted Rizzoli. 'I am aware of the regiment's orders for this evening. Shall I report to you here at ten o'clock?'

'No, Jobert, I am not participating in this midnight convoy escort.' Rizzoli's nostrils widened with apparent distaste. 'It is a minor matter when I am engaged in weightier duties. This evening I will be meeting with Roman dignitaries. As I represent the Cisalpine Republic, I will be confirming our reputation. I shall have Zenari command this. He can stretch his wings with an independent command.'

'Command the regiment's first assignment, sir? How is Major Zenari?'

Rizzoli appeared confused. 'He is fine. Why?'

Jobert suppressed a smirk knowing that Zenari had kept his drubbing to himself. 'I am so pleased to hear that, sir.'

Rizzoli waved the papers. 'Must you attend? There is no need to lower yourself unnecessarily into areas that are beneath you.'

'My copy of the same order, signed by General Masséna, clearly states that I am to accompany the convoy. Should I not comply with a direct order, sir?'

The smallest of the three bells of San Pietro's Basilica struck midnight. At the Porta Settimiana, Jobert, Koschak and Moench joined ten empty carts lining the street. The warmly rugged drivers moved under lantern light to check the harnesses of their teams.

'Your family's teams tonight, sir?' Koschak asked. 'Perhaps some veterans from the 24th Chasseurs. Then this should roll smoothly.'

A teamster waved to Jobert. 'Well met there, Colonel Jobert.'

The wooden crutch of the one-legged man clattered across the cobblestones to Jobert.

'Allow me to introduce one old sergeant to another,' Jobert said. 'Koschak this is Lamy, recently of my brother's hussar regiment, our convoy commander tonight.'

'Evening, sir,' Lamy said. 'I am unsure which of us has the greater inconvenience. My crutches or your officer's lace?'

'How many wagons tonight, Lamy?' Jobert asked. 'How many teamsters?'

'Ten wagons, forty lads, but do not assume eighty arms and eighty legs, sir.'

'And our guide?'

Lamy nodded towards a Franciscan monk who, having uttered a benediction to a line of kneeling drivers, moved towards Jobert. His cowl covered his face. His voice a whisper. 'With our Lord's blessing, sir, are we ready to depart?'

Jobert stared at the shadows within the cowl. *Raive's spy, Inoubli!*

The stone walls of the street echoed the clatter of iron-shod hooves, as D'Onofrio arrived with his chasseur escort.

'Captain D'Onofrio,' Jobert said, 'you have only a troop. Our orders from headquarters specify a company. Where is Major Zenari?'

'Ah, sir ...' D'Onofrio said, 'he is indisposed this evening and, ah ... sends his apologies. He stated to me that a troop was sufficient.'

Koschak snorted a laugh.

Jobert stomped with anger. 'Then Zenari has placed us in a position where we are disobeying a direct command. Very well, which chasseurs do you have?'

'Those from my squadron, sir. Mantua and Brescia.'

'Have you trained your men in convoy escort?'

D'Onofrio shifted with discomfort. 'I have discussed the topic with the officers of the Mantua Company.'

Jobert looked to Koschak. Koschak shook his head. 'Post Mantua forward and Brescia rear. Koschak, will you accompany the guide?'

Inoubli lifted a lantern on a pole. 'Douse the lights. I will lead.'

The convoy and its escort snaked east through the twisting lanes towards the Tiber's wharves. The river fog pressed the stench of sewers and rotting garbage upon their nostrils. Rats and dogs gnawed on shadowy scraps beneath shuttered windows and gantries protruding from warehouse doors.

Jobert noticed the soldiers and the veteran drivers humming a tune in unison as they rode. Jobert turned around in the saddle to a softly whistling Moench. 'What is the tune?'

'The overture to *The Marriage of Figaro*, sir.'

In a lane behind the quayside warehouses, Inoubli stopped at a set of iron-hinged double doors.

'D'Onofrio,' Jobert said, 'set a section at both ends of the street and have the other platoon stand to horse as a reserve. Let us see what this load is about."

Inoubli creaked the gates inwards to a dark portcullis grill beyond. Inoubli unlocked a side door and descended steps. 'Follow.' In a dim basement, Inoubli placed his lantern on a barrel and stepped back.

Jobert, D'Onofrio, Koschak, Moench and Lamy saw the musky warehouse was full of hessian wool bales, double sewn at their folded throats. Jobert rocked the closest bales. Within the bale, paper swished and crunched. 'Documents of some form. I count thirty bales at two hundred kilograms each, at least. Can your veterans handle this?'

With a snort, Lamy shook his head.

Jobert turned to D'Onofrio. 'Each bale is a six-man lift. Have your reserve platoon form four teams to load. How long will it take?'

Lamy shrugged. 'At three bales per wagon, not more than two hours to load and lash.'

'Surely, my men cannot be expected to load, sir?' D'Onofrio said.

'You cannot expect amputees to load this lot.' Lamy said.

Jobert held up his hand. 'D'Onofrio, your chief of squadron chose to countermand orders and send only half the force allocated to the task. Your men will bear the burden of his decision. Post Bernasconi to lead the southern section. Koschak, stand post with the northern section. Questions? No? Then to your duties.'

Once D'Onofrio, Koschak and Lamy had exited the basement to brief their men, Moench asked. 'May I enquire what … crime we commit?'

'Shall we see? Pick a bale.' Jobert drew his dagger from his left cuff.

Jobert cut a wrist-sized slice at the neck of a bale indicated by Moench.

Moench slid in a hand and withdrew a scroll. He leaned

towards Inoubli's lamp to read it. 'Title deeds. Six tonnes of title deeds. Why title deeds?'

'The monk said for safekeeping.' Jobert looked about the shadows for Inoubli. Inoubli was no longer in the room. 'Extortion, I imagine. The owners will a pay ransom to France to re-own their properties.'

'But that is ... not right. Is it, sir?'

'You want France to buy bread and grappa from Italian peasants to fill your belly? Then Roman noblemen must pay the bill.'

Two hours later, the last of the bales were manhandled out of the warehouse.

Koschak's spurs and scabbard clattered on the steps. 'Sir. A disturbance at the southern post.'

Jobert and Moench hurried outside and remounted before trotting to the southern post on the quayside. Bernasconi had Fazio and twelve chasseurs mounted in two ranks, with musketoons resting on thighs.

'Not a move, you fucking slugs.' Fazio swayed in his saddle as he slurred at his chasseurs.

Beyond the chasseur line a crowd of citizens gathered. 'What are you stealing now?' The mob began to shout as the Franciscan outline of Inoubli moved among them. 'They are ransacking the papal warehouses. Their rapacity has no bounds.'

'Fuck these Roman shits,' Fazio said. 'What have the Romans ever done for us?'

Jobert twisted in the saddle. 'D'Onofrio, silence in the ranks!'

A cobblestone hurtled through the night sky to strike a horse. A second stone struck a chasseur.

The two ranks of chasseurs bellowed curses at the crowd. Some turned their horses up the street toward the convoy.

'Are your men at the load, D'Onofrio?' Jobert asked.

D'Onofrio looked at his reins. 'Ah, no, sir.'

'What? Why not?' Jobert dismounted, handed his reins to Moench and drew his sabre. 'D'Onofrio, on me!' Jobert pushed through the ranks of horses to stand in front of the chasseurs. 'Mantua, dismount! Form one rank on Sergeant Fazio, ready! Horses to the rear.'

Fazio and eight chasseurs dismounted with a rattle of slung equipment on stirrups and formed behind Jobert with musketoons at the ready. Three horse holders walked their dozen remounts further up the street.

'Mantua, load!' The chasseurs cursed as they scrabbled at their cartridge boxes in the dark.

Fazio spat the residual gunpowder from his mouth. 'Shut up, you piss-poor bastards.'

The crowd murmured. Cobblestones were grabbed.

'Mantua, aim high.' Muzzles were raised. 'Fire!'

An explosion reverberated off the walls and echoed across the river. The street filled with smoke and floating cartridge papers. Balls cracked off the surrounding stone walls. Ricochets pinged off iron work.

The crowd screamed and shrank backward.

'Sabres!' Jobert cried. 'Mantua will advance in line five paces forward. Quick, march!'

Those at the front of the crowd lurched back onto those behind.

'D'Onofrio, call out what I say,' Jobert said.

'We are Cisalpine Chasseurs, men of Mantua.' A few in the crowd spat. 'We safeguard the Holy Father's decrees. We need to take them to safety within San Pietro's vaults.' D'Onofrio added, 'before the French find them. Withdraw to your beds, citizens.'

Horses clattered up behind the chasseur line.

'The loading is complete,' Koschak said. 'Convoy ready to march, sir,'

Jobert sheathed his sabre. 'Well done, Mantua, on completing the regiment's first assignment. I noted your steady bearing under pressure.'

Fazio shook his head and spat on the ground.

'You proved yourselves worthy of the regiment,' Jobert continued and the eight soldiers swelled with pride. 'Sergeant Fazio, remount and re-join the convoy. Carry on.'

With one eye on the retreating crowd, Jobert spun to D'Onofrio. 'We have faced each other across the field. Despite our preparations, we never doubted the readiness of the other. Do you agree?'

D'Onofrio shuffled backwards, glancing at the receding chasseurs.

Jobert followed jabbing his flat hand at D'Onofrio. 'When have you ever experienced such a sham as this regiment? Rizzoli has the honour and the resources to raise eight hundred sabres but chooses to only enlist four hundred. Despite his orders, he chooses to deploy with only two hundred sabres, without flints in their musketoons, arriving two weeks behind the main column.'

D'Onofrio put up his hands. 'My loyalty is to Colonel Rizzoli, sir, I will not—'

'Oh, loyalty to the colonel as demonstrated by his nephew, Zenari. Ordered to command one hundred chasseurs on a delicate mission, he chooses to dispatch only fifty then absents himself from the duty.'

D'Onofrio slumped.

'What regiments allow sergeants, such as Fazio, to be constantly drunk, negligent in their duties, abusive of their soldiers and be pardoned when firing their weapon upon a superior officer?'

'With respect, sir, Sergeant Fazio is not negligent in—'

'Bullshit, D'Onofrio. His horses' feet were not prepared for the march to Rome. His men's saddlery was not in inspection order. The call to stables was at seven o'clock. His soldiers – your soldiers – are incapable of loading their weapons whilst dismounted in the dark. Am I wrong?'

'He is the most experienced sergeant we have, sir,' D'Onofrio said.

'What of the abuse he levels at his soldiers?' Jobert asked. 'These chasseurs are volunteers. They should be inspired by Fazio and have confidence in his leadership in battle, not dis- illusioned by his drunkenness. Imperial training methods will not work with patriotic volunteers, D'Onofrio. Your chasseurs will desert at the first shot.'

Jobert peered at furtive figures sloping down the street away from the site of confrontation. 'Are you seeing what I am seeing, D'Onofrio?'

D'Onofrio opened his mouth then closed it.

Jobert regarded Moench holding Jaune in the shadow of the stone warehouse. 'I remember the exploits of my old regiment, and I despair at my current situation. I am trapped in a nightmare. Where is D'Onofrio, my respected foe who tested me in combat?' Jobert poked D'Onofrio in the chest. 'Where is he?'

Chapter Seven
March 1798, Rome, Italy

'Frankly, I am disappointed, Jobert.' Rizzoli spread his hands wide upon his polished desk.

'Did you say, sir, that I disappoint you?' Jobert's fists clenched behind his back.

Rizzoli's shoulders slumped as his eyes softened with pity. 'What ought to have been a simple loading of wagons becomes a massacre of civilians narrowly averted. I expected better of you.'

'One volley was fired high. No one was struck. The information you have received is incorrect.'

'How else might you be employed, Jobert? Is de Chabenac not sufficient? You seem ill at ease with us. You meddle unnecessarily.'

'Meddling! My reasonable enquiries have unearthed irregularities in regimental finances—'

Rizzoli raised a hand. 'Do not speak of regimental irregularities, Jobert, when your French troops mutiny here in Rome.

'The soldiers demand their rightful food and pay. They have marched, fought and bled for Italy. It is their entitlement.'

'Hah! The conduct of your army is woeful. The Holy Father snatched prisoner and escorted to France. A fine use of French cavalry. Masséna is a disgrace.'

Jobert took a step towards Rizzoli's desk, his rigid finger raised as if he held a pistol. 'Our commanding general—'

'Now, Jobert,' Rizzoli raised a warning finger, 'I have no wish to report you to General Berthier.'

Jobert lowered his hand. 'Report as you see fit, sir. Berthier and I have an acquaintance of eighteen years since serving together at Yorktown.'

Rizzoli blinked. 'Where?'

'The battle of Yorktown, in the colony of Virginia.'

'Oh ... how pleasant for you both.' Rizzoli shook his head. 'Jobert, do you intend to threaten the regiment's good name?'

'A regiment only earns its reputation in battle, not on parade.'

'How can we make this arrangement satisfy us both? Raive supports our logistics. Perhaps you might take on the role of fencing master or riding master?'

Jobert stepped back and slowed his breathing. 'Sir, you and I read the broadsheets from Paris and Vienna. The French Government's ... meddling in Switzerland and Rome will not be tolerated by the regents of Europe. War is inevitable. If not this spring, then next, Austria will launch from across the Adige to tear the Cisalpine Republic to shreds. Your personal desires and mine will be crushed by that onslaught.'

Rizzoli braced his hands upon his desk.

Jobert brought his fingertips together in supplication. 'Will you not accept what I have to offer? Has my experience nothing to provide the regiment?'

'How?' Rizzoli asked.

'A comprehensive approach. I am well able to design field exercises.'

'Such as?'

Jobert softened his pose. 'Staff rides to investigate battlefield problems, sir. Investigate the battles that were fought last year? Company exercises.'

'That sounds a pleasant outing.' Rizzoli's handsome face smiled. 'Might you prepare a list of possible opportunities?' Rizzoli looked to the documents on the desk indicating their meeting was at an end.

'I request permission to travel between each of the eight companies of the regiment,' Jobert said. 'I ought to be able to spend a few days with each company every two months.'

Rizzoli's shoulders sagged. 'May I request you focus on the southern companies – Mantua, Brescia, Modena, Bologna, Ferrara and Ravenna. Major de Chabenac is all we require for Milan and Cremona. Your experience is best elsewhere.'

'I am aware that the regiment has received orders to depart Rome for home barracks. With your permission, I will return ahead of the regimental column. Prefetto Bernasconi is keen to know how his son's wound heals.'

'Do what you feel best.' Rizzoli waved a sealed envelope. 'If you ride north, would you take this letter to headquarters in Milan.'

Two weeks later, Jobert approached Gianna Bernasconi in the Bernasconis' drawing room.

'Permission to join you before lunch is served, Signorina?' As Jobert sat he was enfolded in her perfume of lavender and orange.

Gianna smiled. 'Thank you for the safe return of my brother, Colonel Jobert.'

'Is your mother well?' Jobert asked. 'I want to know what I can do to make some amends. My condolences on the loss of your brother. A soldier? Do you know the circumstances of his passing?'

Her smile faded. 'He was an artillery officer. He died during the French ... your invasion in April 1794. I believe it is referred to as the battle of Saorgio.'

Ponte de Nava. A memory of an artillery officer firing a pistol. The brown scar on Jobert's right cheek blazed with heat. 'Your mother spoke of a future ruined. Were you betrothed?'

Gianna twisted a ring on her finger on her right hand. 'Yes.' It was an interlocking gimmal engagement ring.

'Was he also taken in battle?'

'Yes.'

'I am sorry for your loss.'

Gianna fingertips caressed the ring. 'He served with my brother. We lost him in late '95 on the coast west of Genoa.'

The battle of Loano. Jobert's mind swirled with images of dragoons in the snow and the grunts of pain under his spinning blade.

'Now I am twenty-three, and too old for ...'

'For what?' Jobert asked. 'Marriage?'

She looked up.

'I am unaware of the ideal ages of women to wed,' Jobert said, 'but I assure you, Signorina, any man would be blessed beyond measure to have you ...' He frowned at his clumsiness.

She looked at him in surprise. 'Our family has not had the honour of hosting cavalry officers.'

'Since our revolution, our cavalry officers are no longer noblemen, as the Austrian regiments might be. I am a man of humble origins.'

'I overheard you describe your family the last time we dined. Your parents are well, I trust?'

'My mother and father have passed. My uncle manages a horse-breeding business in the mountains of the Massif Central.'

'The Auvergne, no?'

'Quite so, Signorina. My cousin produces military headdress in Paris.'

'He must be busy.'

'She is, that is. My cousin, Michelle, is busy.'

'Oh my, your revolution has allowed the most extraordinary developments.' Gianna leaned closer. 'My family too is of humble origins. To become a Verona magistrate under the Austrian administration, my father had to break from our family's origins in tanneries. Were it not for the creation of this new republic and my father's rise ...'

'Yes, your world and mine have been turned upside down.'

Gianna placed two fingers on the back of Jobert's hand. 'My mother would be scandalised should she learn I have told you.'

Jobert's heart leapt at her soft touch. 'I shall not betray your confidence, Signorina. I understand your mother's distress. The loss of her son and her daughter's fiancé conflicts with the rise of her husband. How have you adapted?'

'I remain at my station and focus on my duty.'

'An answer befitting a soldier, Signorina. Your brother would approve.'

'Speaking of brothers ...' Gianna sipped at her *brachetto*. 'I am aware of the assignment you tasked Silvio with. Was it meant as a punishment?'

Jobert remembered binding Bernasconi's cut hand in Rome. *Write a report on the actions of light cavalry in France's recent Italian campaign.*

'No, not at all,' Jobert lied. 'He requested to learn more.'

'He has certainly taken to the task with relish. He sprouts

all manner of tales from the recent campaign ... when mother is absent.'

Signora Bernasconi sat on the other side of the drawing room, glowering at a bible on her lap.

'What constitutes your library, colonel?' Gianna asked.

'My leisure only allows the study of military texts.'

'My friends and I are reading the play *Romeo and Juliet*. It is a local favourite due to its setting in Verona and Mantua.'

'I attended it last summer with Major de Chabenac, but my knowledge of Italian that evening failed me.'

Gianna considered him. 'I have a copy of it in both French and Italian. We could read it together. Perhaps I could assist you in expanding your Italian.'

Jobert studied her. 'That is a most generous offer, Signorina. One that I would be honoured to accept, but I hesitate to do so.'

Gianna looked miffed.

He continued. 'Will it not interrupt your duties to your friends and add distress to your dear mother?'

Gianna's smile caused her dimples to twitch. 'Would you like to improve your Italian through the study of this play?'

'If you were my tutor, yes. I would like that very much.'

A bell rang for lunch.

Jobert followed Prefetto Bernasconi, Gianna and Silvio to their places in the dining room. Signora Bernasconi swept from the drawing room to her prayers.

Bernasconi leaned upon the table and his stare grilled Jobert. 'Tell us, Jobert, of the action in which my son was wounded. He is evasive in the retelling.'

'A wound of honour received on a midnight mission,' said Jobert.

Silvio cringed. Gianna covered her open mouth with her fingertips.

Jobert continued. 'We were ambushed. An assailant's blade

was drawn in the dark. There is always risk of harm. Silvio deflected the thrust and was awarded his wound, before overcoming his foe. His fencing lessons are reaping their reward.'

Gianna's eyes widened as she regarded her brother.

Prefetto Bernasconi raised his glass. 'A toast to give thanks for Silvio's safe return.'

Silvio shot Jobert a glimpse to acknowledge the save. 'My wound heals swiftly, thanks to the attention of Colonel Jobert.'

'Our Jobert not only administers healing,' Bernasconi said, 'but administers essays in the art of war. Silvio, is your essay on the use of cavalry in the recent campaign complete?'

'Yes, Father. It has been most enlightening.' Silvio glanced at Jobert and blushed. 'Thank you, Colonel Jobert.'

Bernasconi coughed a laugh. 'As the son of a tanner, I now purchase fencing and dance lessons for my son as befits his station.' Bernasconi nodded toward Silvio. 'Might I ask you, sir, to test his blade? Frequently.'

Jobert bowed his head.

'With the loss of his elder brother,' Bernasconi said, 'I invest heavily in the boy. Might I prevail upon you to safeguard my investment?'

'Sir, I am at your service.'

Bernasconi squeezed Jobert's forearm. 'Silvio is not the only investment I seek to protect. Again, I seek your support.'

Jobert investigated Bernasconi's firm eyes, the look of a seasoned magistrate seeking leverage.

Bernasconi's face softened with a smile, but his eyes remained calculating. 'Frances' occupation of Switzerland and the plunder of Berne's treasury, and now Rome's, has led the great houses of Europe back onto the path to war. And so, your oversight is valued. Indeed, it is vital.'

'Within the regiment that is not a widely held opinion.'

'The regiment needs to be ready for war, Jobert.'

Jobert placed down his cutlery and dabbed his mouth with his serviette. 'I have experienced both combat and the preparation needed for success in the field. But my views are treated with disdain by the regiment. The regiment is not ready for war, sir, and it shall remain thoroughly unprepared while regimental leadership has neither experience of battle nor an understanding of the exhaustive preparation required.'

'I implore you to persist, Jobert,' Bernasconi said. 'I will speak to Rizzoli.' Bernasconi leaned forward to bind Jobert in his confidence. 'The politics of the Cisalpine Republic are precarious. You know the factions. I am appalled at the news of how Paris conducts ... I was distressed at the conduct of both Masséna and the Directory's Deputies of the People in Rome and am shocked at their reported conduct in Switzerland. Do not underestimate my depth of sentiment on the matter, Jobert. It is more to me than my current investment in sons and treasure. What is the regiment's greatest need?'

Jobert met Bernasconi's eyes with a grim look, thinking, *Men capable of leading it.*

'The regiment must expand from eight troops to eight companies,' Jobert responded. 'That cannot be accomplished without sound leadership and over four hundred horses.'

Ten days later Jobert arrived at Raive's office within the headquarters of the Army of Italy in Milan.

'What have you done now, Jobert?' Raive waved Rizzoli's letter in his hand. 'Rizzoli requests you be employed elsewhere.'

'Then support his request, sir.' Jobert threw up his hands. 'Rizzoli has no desire to address his regiment's incompetence. He has no respect for my experience. I want to be employed elsewhere. Is there no other more pressing assignment on the staff? Why me? Why this?'

'When presented with a list of officers, Bonaparte picked you.' Raive raised a warning finger. 'He could not have seen the outcome, but if he placed a trustworthy man at the heart of it ...' Raive shrugged. 'I do not understand, Jobert. You are well paid. You want for nothing. Enjoy what you have suffered to earn.'

Jobert folded his arms. 'I have not suffered to earn disdain. My home is the regiment. These Cisalpines reject me. They are not my brothers. You have done me a great disservice, sir, removing me from the 24th Chasseurs. What of this scheme to Egypt? If Bonaparte considers well of me—'

'Egypt is out of the question. If given the opportunity, what would you offer Rizzoli?'

'I have a program here.' Jobert scrabbled at the contents of his sabretache. He passed a document to Raive. 'A program of company activities across a period of a week. Eight weeks in the field. I know the terrain across which the Austrians will assault. I can work with a squadron of dragoons and a battalion of infantry as our training enemy. The regiment's ammunition stocks have not been touched and flints have now been issued.'

Raive skimmed Jobert's training plan.

'Can you not influence Rizzoli to agree, sir?' Jobert asked.

On the Corso Lodi, towards Milan's outer ramparts, Jobert and Bleu entered the tavern gate. The weak March sun filled the tavern yard with soft light. With the stone walls anchored against a chill northern breeze by lounging tavern dogs, the members of Jobert's retinue busied themselves.

Stripped to their shirtsleeves, de Chabenac and Koschak thrust and parried with their fencing. Tulloc supervised fifteen-year-old Quandalle with the tacking of a shoe on Grenzer, the pack horse. The five other war horses, tethered to the tall wheels of Jobert's trap, snoozed under the sun's meagre warmth.

A musical riot spilled from the kitchen door. Moench played a fife. Orlande sang whilst juggling a jug of cider and a tower of cups in one hand and Tulloc's toddler with the other. Maria hummed as she bore a tray of cherry tarts towards the fencers.

As Jobert dismounted and unbuckled Bleu's girth, de Chabenac and Koschak broke from their ripostes and flopped on camp stools set out at the rear of the cart. 'Ah, well timed. Join us for cider.'

'Since I paid for it, I just might.' Jobert slid his saddle over Bleu's rump. 'What is the opera of the day?'

'*The Marriage of Figaro*,' de Chabenac said.

'Bach?'

'Tsk, Mozart. Did you see Raive? Are we off to Switzerland? The new Helvetic Republic?'

Koschak wiped his mouth of dribbled cider. 'Better still, Egypt! Will Berthier command in Egypt?'

Jobert ran a currycomb over Bleu's loins. 'I have heard Bonaparte will return to take Egypt. Berthier will join his staff. Brune now becomes the new commander of the Army of Italy.'

De Chabenac held out a cup of cider towards Jobert. 'And our friend, Suchet, becomes Brune's chief of staff.'

'More friends in high places,' Koschak said. 'Oh, shit—'

Koschak leapt to his feet.

Jobert turned toward where Koschak was trotting. A potential situation was developing. Tulloc's one-year-old son was tugging at a crust in a puppy's mouth just behind the rear hooves of Bleu and Jaune. Tavern dogs were beginning to circle the two infants and their tug-o-war food. Bleu stomped a warning with a hind foot.

Koschak scooped up the infant who screamed at being separated from his snack. Koschak picked up the puppy by the scruff of the neck. As Koschak entered the kitchen with his squirming bundles, little Andrea snatched the crust from the puppy's mouth and placed it his own.

'You met with Raive,' de Chabenac said, 'and your dilemma remains unresolved.'

Jobert slouched his elbows on his knees. 'What of you, de Chabenac? Where does your font of motivation lie within this assignment?'

De Chabenac stiffened as he raised his cup to sip. 'Italy accepts the circumstances of my birth. With every prayer I give thanks to your family's care of my mother and sister, yet France rejects my family.' De Chabenac stared into the depths of his cider. 'My growing connection to Bernasconi and Rizzoli increases the possibility of me providing a safe home for my mother here in Italy.'

Crows hopped across the tavern yard, nipping and tossing strands of straw.

'Why?' De Chabenac asked. 'What is the essence of your frustration?'

'War is possibly months away,' Jobert said. 'I am lost without the regiment. My eighteen years' experience is wasted here. I appear unable to adapt, unable to deliver. How did I go from a place where I was respected to being held in such disdain?'

'Is there nothing that brings you pleasure?'

'Perhaps ... Gianna Bernasconi. Where does my commitment lie?'

A sad smile creased the tanned skin around de Chabenac's mouth and eyes. 'So much for your esteemed *coup d'oeil* in combat, Jobert. Here you are, as you say, in the midst of turmoil and you fail to observe around you.' A sweep of the tavern yard. 'Here is your family. Happiness is staring you in the face.'

Chapter Eight
April 1798, Mantua, Italy

A year ago, Jobert spent his thirty-second birthday in a freezing valley above Vienna. Today, with the air infused with her lavender and orange scent, he stole glances at the curls on Gianna's neck. His birthday could not be sweeter.

Jobert and Gianna sat at a wrought iron table on the tiled patio of an inner courtyard opening onto a small garden. Bees hummed as they flitted between the flowers. Within the open doors of the drawing room, Jobert hoped just out of earshot, Signora Bernasconi attended to her needlework.

'Father is expecting Colonel Rizzoli from Milan,' Gianna said.

'Ah, the good colonel comes to pay me birthday compliments. Then, *Signorina Professoressa*, shall our studies extend until his arrival, so that I might pay my compliments to the colonel?'

Gianna guided Jobert through the Italian version of *Romeo and Juliet*, comparing it to her French book of the play. They laughed as each assumed a comical voice for each character. Jobert enjoyed the swordplay with teaspoons, he as Benvolio and her as Tybalt. When she gripped his gloved hand to smite his knuckles a deadly thrust, Jobert baulked as his chest tightened.

In the second scene, Gianna faltered in her lines. '… let two more summers wither in their pride, ere we may think her ripe to be a bride.' Her nostrils flared as she breathed.

Jobert frowned. 'These lines upset you, Signorina. Memories of your fiancé, perhaps. We can stop.'

Gianna raised her chin to look at Jobert. 'I was engaged at eighteen, and a spinster at twenty.'

Jobert blinked to calculate the ten years between them. 'Signorina, with peace returned, be certain you will attract more suitors.'

'There have been others already, sir,' said Gianna, 'but war has swept them away.'

Jobert winced.

Gianna whispered as she lowered her eyes. 'Just as Lord Capulet bemoans his daughter's youth, so my mother bemoans my increasing age.'

Jobert closed the book he was holding. 'Perhaps we should pause our studies. This student—'

'No,' said Gianna, 'let us continue.' Her eyes were earnest. 'Please. This foolish melancholy will pass. I was enjoying your … studious efforts.'

They resumed their lines. Emboldened, Jobert attempted a nasal voice for Nurse in the exchanges with Gianna's Lady Capulet and Juliet. Laughter soon followed.

Jobert noticed how, with each humorous passage, their heads hung closer over the shared pages. He found himself examining her freckles and her eyebrows. 'Where am I up to?'

'Here!' she said. 'You are the most exasperating student, sir. Just read. It is about to become interesting.'

'Which is which?' asked Jobert. 'Saints and pilgrims?

'Romeo is the pilgrim hoping to receive the blessed kiss from Saint Juliet.'

Jobert scanned the page to find his line. 'Have not saint's lips, and holy palmers too?'

'Ay, pilgrim,' Gianna read, 'lips that they must use in prayer.'

Jobert studied the curl of her lips, the wrinkles in her cheeks. He slid his eyes to the page between them. 'O, then, dear saint, let lips do what hands do: they pray, grant thou, lest faith turn to despair.'

'Saints do not move, though grant for prayer's sake.'

'Then move not—' Jobert coughed to remove the husk in his throat. 'Excuse me ...' He continued, 'then move not while my prayer's effect I take. Thus from my lips, by thine, my sin is purged.'

A sound of mischievous pleasure purred from Gianna's throat. 'This is where he kisses her, and Juliet says ...' Gianna glanced at Jobert. 'What are you looking at me like that for?' Her cheek rippled in a half-smile. 'Stop it, sir.' Gianna placed a finger on the page. 'Then have my lips the sin that they have took.'

Heat scorched Jobert's chest. *I want her.*

'It is your line.' Gianna's voice trembled.

'Where?' His finger searched the page.

'Here.' She slid his finger with hers. 'Where he kisses her again.'

'Sin from my lips? O, trespass sweetly urged!'

This is unbearable.

'Give me my sin again.'

Gianna turned her face to his. 'See there, written in the margin ... they kiss again.' Her breath was warm upon his cheek. 'Juliet then responds to his kiss by saying "You kiss by the book". Now, does her comment infer she enjoyed the kiss?'

Jobert turned his face. Their lips were a handspan apart.

He searched her eyes and sensed they sparkled. He leaned his mouth towards hers.

Gianna's eyes widened before she jerked upright. 'Stop, sir! You have gone too far.'

Jobert sat rigid. 'Signorina, I …'

'Gianna, are you well?' Signora Bernasconi asked. Then to a footman within the drawing room, she called, 'Fetch Senor Bernasconi.'

Tears welled in Gianna's eyes as she clutched a handkerchief to her mouth. 'You know my loss in this regard.'

'Forgive me, Signorina.' Jobert stood.

'You have not listened to me at all, sir.' Gianna's eyes pleaded. 'These violent delights have violent ends.' She closed the books. 'Perhaps I have done wrong by sharing the play.' She stood. 'Perhaps it might be best if we took a little time in reflection. Good day to you, sir.'

Jobert entered his rooms with the Mantuan tavern. At the table, Moench played sheet music propped up by a jug and held firm by an apple. Orlande sat with his feet up by the fire, little Andrea giggling on his knee.

'Ah, sir, A glass of birthday *recioto*?' Orlande rose to place the baby on his seat.

'Please.' Jobert nodded towards Moench as he removed his number-one tailcoat. 'Figaro?'

Orlande poured the smooth brown liquor into a Venetian glass. 'Indeed, sir.'

'Then at least I got that right.'

'Was your Italian tuition not ...'

Jobert pressed his lips into an unhappy smile as he took his glass from Orlande.

Orlande frowned. 'No matter.' He took an envelope from the mantelpiece. 'Perhaps some birthday cheer from your family.'

Jobert opened the envelope.

Chauvel Farm, Auvergne
13th March 1798

André,

A brief note to inform you that Yann has fallen and broken an elbow. He has had his right arm amputated.

Jobert sagged 'Shit!'

Orlande pressed his glasses onto his nose. 'Are your family well, sir?'

Thankfully, he recuperates slowly. His fevers are mild and intermittent. For some reason, he accuses you of his misfortune. I must admit I am shaken. I have sent for Michelle. Not only will Yann benefit from her ministrations, but I expect I will lean on her experience.

Although home eighteen months, I had been blithely unaware of Yann's efforts in maintaining the farm's routine and finances. As I now assume the reins of the farm, I confess to being somewhat overwhelmed. I am sure I will cope.

Can you return at your earliest opportunity? I need your assistance.
Ever yours,
Didier

Jobert's hand holding the letter dropped loosely to his side.

Orlande pushed his spectacles onto the bridge of his nose. 'What news, sir?'

Feet pounded on the steps outside. The door burst open with Quandalle and Maria entering breathlessly. Maria scooped up her infant.

Quandalle's eyes searched his open hand. 'Sir, from Lieutenant Koschak.' He struggled to breathe as he counted on his fingers. 'A local child has been killed by a regimental wagon. Two chasseurs have been killed by the mob. Fazio is leading his platoon in a rampage. Lieutenant Koschak requests you come quickly. Tulloc is with him.' Quandalle checked his fingers again before searching Jobert's face.

Jobert clapped Quandalle on the shoulder. 'Well done, lad. We will make a chasseur of you yet. Come with me in case of further messages.' Jobert handed his letter to Orlande before shrugging on his tailcoat. 'Orlande, I will return to the Bernasconi residence to inform Colonel Rizzoli who is arriving from Milan. Moench, go to Koschak and inform him of my visit to Rizzoli.'

Jobert strode with purpose the winding streets to the Bernasconi residence. Quandalle trotted to keep up.

Leaving Quandalle in the courtyard, Bernasconi's chamberlain had Jobert wait outside in the anteroom. Women's voices came from beyond the salon door. An inner door closed. The chamberlain appeared before the open salon door. 'Sir.'

Jobert entered the salon to find Rizzoli seated on a plush divan with a full glass in hand.

Jobert saluted. 'Good evening, sir. I hope your travel was uneventful?'

'Most satisfactory, Jobert. Thank you for attending me. Unfortunately, your appearance has disturbed the ladies. It appears the prefetto remains in council within the palazzo. I await his return. Would you care for recioto?'

'Thank you, sir, but no. Are you aware there has been an incident here in the Mantua this evening? The Mantua Company is involved. There is a possibility that the situation—'

'I am aware, thank you, Jobert. D'Onofrio has briefed me.'

'Should you care to attend, sir, I would accompany—'

'Why would I do that? Forego my courtesies to the prefetto? No, I have given sufficient instruction to D'Onofrio. As for you, Jobert, do not reel off a report to Milan. General Brune does not need to be distracted by an occasion of no consequence.'

Of no consequence?

A sickle swung towards his abdomen as he tore through the barricades. At the end of his pistol blast, a woman whipped back into the roiling smoke of burning homes. Memories howled at Jobert of when he accompanied Bonaparte at Binasco and Lannes at Pavia during civilian uprisings.

'Each of these small injustices spur the release of deeper resentment leading to wider suffering,' Jobert said. 'Does the current unrest in Naples not sound a note of alarm, sir? I strongly suggest your presence with your chasseurs—'

'Mantua is not Naples, Jobert. Allow us a moment of calm and consider what would Eugene advise.'

Jobert lowered his face. *Eugene would not have allowed such a situation to develop.* 'I am at a loss to say, sir.'

'Then I recommend further study. Speaking of which ...' Rizzoli emptied his glass. 'I have been reflecting on your offer of instruction.' Rizzoli poured himself another recioto. He slicked back his thick moustache with the back of his finger before sipping. 'What did you have in mind?'

Jobert blinked with the change of tack. 'Ah, sir ... to take individual companies on a week-long campaign against a training enemy.'

'A week! Is that really necessary? As much as a company?

How much will the enemy cost?'

'At the very least to refine the requirements of camp.'

'You really will be impacting on the chiefs of squadron's training.'

'And what training is that exactly, sir?' Jobert asked.

'Last week we charged. It was a marvellous day out.'

'And I was not invited to observe?'

'We had de Chabenac.'

'What did you charge, sir? An infantry square? A battery of guns? An escorted train?'

'What does it matter?' Rizzoli expanded his arms. 'The length of a field. We charged. Glorious!'

Jobert examined the exotic carpet beneath his boots. A clock on the mantlepiece chimed once. 'What if smaller initial steps were taken, sir? Perhaps a troop for three days?'

'I can imagine stretching to a platoon.'

'A sergeant and twenty odd men? How would the officers be involved?'

Rizzoli recoiled. 'Do they need to be? They are rather busy. What if it rains? Taverns can be expensive.'

'Why would we not be under canvas?'

'Why ever would we be?'

'What occupies captains and lieutenants more than them preparing their men for impending battle?' Jobert asked. 'Having served in a chasseur regiment, not for one year, but seventeen years, I assure you I know exactly how busy company officers can be. Do we not agree our hopes are threatened by a renewed war with Austria?'

'Perhaps. The greater threat may well be the egregious meddling of your Directory.'

'Does imminent war not concern you, sir? I know the Austrian army, encamped two-days-march east, concerns Prefetto Bernasconi.'

'Undoubtedly,' Rizzoli said, 'but there is only so much an individual can do in such circumstances.'

'An individual who commands a regiment of eight hundred sabres?'

'My regiment stands ready.'

'I beg to differ, sir. My near five years' experience of constant campaigning—'

Rizzoli raised his palm. 'Lieutenant colonel, I will not be spoken to in this way. Perhaps our conversation is at an end.'

The clock ticked.

Jobert took a step backwards. 'Is there nothing I can offer the regiment, sir?'

'Have we not agreed to you taking each of the platoons out for a day or two?'

'That is the responsibility of their company captains, sir.'

A log in the hearth crumbled into coals.

'Is the task beneath you, Jobert? Are we an inconvenience to your martial desires? I sense your attachment to us does not align with your active spirit.'

A slash of flames gripped the exposed timber.

I have failed.

'Perhaps I should seek another post, sir.'

'If you feel it the best application of your talents, then should you request, I would do my utmost to support your advancement elsewhere.'

Raive slammed his desk with his palm. 'I will not have you posted out, Jobert.'

Wringing his hands behind his back, Jobert seethed. 'How many times must I report their persistent incompetence? What else can I provide but the same report? For how many months must I endure this indignity? Is this the worth I represent to France?'

Raive shook his fist at Jobert. 'With the Directory's ill-advised invasion of Switzerland, only now sending in troops to crush the Swiss uprising, the treaty of Campo Formio that Bonaparte negotiated, is void. War is upon us, Jobert. The Army of Italy needs every experienced man.'

Jobert held out his hands in placation. 'Is there no other posting? Does no other chasseur regiment require a commander or a second-in-command? There must be vacancies in the dragoon regiments.'

Raive slumped in his chair. 'If such regiments exist, then they have marched from the Rhine. As you are unknown on the Rhine, any general would be unwilling to accept your nomination.'

'Is there no other task on the staff that requires attention or liaison? In Switzerland? In Rome or Genoa?'

Raive's head gave a regretful shake.

'Rizzoli is right,' Jobert said. 'Bonaparte is wrong. Is there no other commander who respects my previous service?'

'There are so few who know you. Masséna is in disgrace after the plunder of Rome. Victor is returning from the Army of England.'

'What of infantry regiments in need of a second-in-command?'

'Your desperation is unbecoming, Jobert.'

'Horse artillery?'

'Stop it. You are not a gunner.'

'But I can be quite capable of administrating a regiment comprised of men, horses, wagons and ammunition.'

Raive rubbed his chin. 'Perhaps I could investigate a position in the commissariat.'

Jobert blanched. 'You know my family's circumstances, sir. Both my uncle and my brother are now amputees. Your own enterprises, on behalf of France, are endangered should Yann's and Didier's restricted abilities imperil the movement of wagons. I must return to the farm. I request three months leave.'

'Request denied, Jobert.' Raive leaned back with his eyes pressed shut. 'The commander has rejected the leave applications of others for more strenuous reasons. You cannot expect your leave to be approved during a summer in which the armies of Austria grow stronger. Have you heard of the riots in Vienna against our diplomatic mission there?'

'Why should I be concerned with Austria's growing strength? Colonel Rizzoli is not. Which general is driving him to that imperative?' Jobert's eyes scoured the beams above Raive's head. 'Now there is an option for me.'

Raive scowled. 'What option, Jobert?'

'I could join an Austrian regiment.'

'Have you been accessing your hashish oil?'

'Their light horse may not accept my lack of noble blood, but their uhlans would be grateful for my service.'

'Ah, Fergnes rolls in his grave. Is it really that bad?'

Jobert leaned forward and wrung his hands. 'It is intolerable. My experience is wasted. My life is being wasted. I have not endured the loss of so many brothers to suffer this indignity. I want to return to the 24th Chasseurs.'

'You cannot. That ship has sailed.'

'Sailed? What of Egypt?'

Raive shrugged. 'There is no need of cavalry officers.'

'What of Bessières and Murat? What of our old friends Clemusat and Huin?'

'There is no other task on this staff that has greater need than your attachment to the Cisalpine Chasseurs.'

Jobert became still as he considered Raive. 'No posting to

any other staff?' Raive shook his head at each suggestion. 'No posting to any other regiment? No posting to any other corps? No willingness to be granted extended leave?'

'Not while an avalanche of enemy divisions is poised to drive across the Adige.'

'No chance to leave the army on half pay?'

Raive's face creased with a humourless grin. 'You can always apply but it will be immediately refused.'

Jobert remained still. The letter in his tailcoat pocket grew heavy. 'I have failed to deliver, sir. I am irrelevant here. I am not valued anywhere. I am beyond my level of competence. Sir, my service to France is at an end.'

Raive scowled. 'Do not be ridiculous, Jobert.'

'Am I valued, sir? I have been idle for a year and can expect the same for the foreseeable future. And what if war comes? What then will be my value? Rizzoli will dither at his luncheon table. Zenari, D'Onofrio and Fazio will emerge drunken from their whores' beds, barely capable of forming battleline before they are ridden down. The survivors will desert. How then will I be of value to Bonaparte, or Berthier, or Brune this week, or perhaps Masséna next week or—'

Raive raised both palms. 'Enough, Jobert, enough. Return to your post.'

Jobert drew himself upright. 'My family needs me within our business, sir. There is nothing that keeps me in Italy. If I am unable to be posted somewhere my experience will be appreciated, then ... I shall—'

Raive poked a rigid finger at Jobert. 'Do not say it, Jobert. Do not!'

Jobert straightened himself to attention. 'Sir, I hereby resign my commission.'

Alarm flashed across Raive's face. 'A rash declaration that smacks of poor judgement, Jobert. Enough! Return to your quarters and reflect upon your situation.'

'I agree sir.' Jobert posture slackened. 'Enough. Before I return to my post, sir, I have one last request.' Jobert drew a sealed envelope from an inner pocket. 'Would you pass my letter of resignation to General Brune?'

Raive shook his head slowly. 'Do not do this, Jobert.'

Jobert pushed the envelope towards Raive's desk. 'I do not belong here.' Jobert's voice wavered. His fingers found it difficult to release the envelope.

His fingers opened.

The envelope slithered onto Raive's desk.

Raive pointed to the envelope. 'Pick that up, Jobert. Remove it.'

'Good evening, sir.' Jobert saluted. 'Would you excuse me.' He departed the room.

That evening, Jobert took the small square of paper from Orlande. He broke the wax seal of the Commander of the Army of Italy and opened the folds.

Milan
25 April 1798

Lieutenant Colonel Jobert,

General Brune requests you attend him promptly at ten o'clock tomorrow.

Brigadier L-G Suchet
Chief of Staff, Army of Italy

Pressure gripped Jobert's heart. His stare burrowed through the floorboards beyond Suchet's note. He swallowed before he spoke.

'Orlande, would you prepare my full-dress uniform for tomorrow morning.'

Chapter Nine
April–August 1798, Milan, Italy

The next morning, the tiled corridor within the headquarters of the Army of Italy echoed with the traffic of capped boot heels. Jobert adjusted his weight to his other hip where he hoped to both maintain his bearing and cultivate his composure in front of the general.

The door opened across the corridor from where Jobert waited. Out bustled two clerks each hugging an armful of files and scrolls. Behind them, a sombre-faced major swept his hand towards the chamber beyond. 'Lieutenant Colonel Jobert, sir?'

Jobert straightened his shoulders, tugged on the lapels of his tailcoat and took up his scabbard. The wood-panelled room he entered smelt of ink, cigar smoke and coffee. The staff major shut the door behind him.

'Ah, Jobert,' said Brigadier Suchet to Jobert's salute. 'Are you here to see the commander?'

Jobert stiffened further. 'General Brune has summoned me at this hour, sir.'

'You have missed him. The commander is out dispatching the

Army of the Orient.'

Jobert's eyes widened with surprise. 'They have sailed for Egypt?'

'Yes, today was the first contingent. Let us chat. Please sit down.'

A table by Suchet's hearth was set with a blue and gilt-edged coffee service. An envelope lay unopened beside the tray.

My envelope.

Jobert sat on the edge of his chair. 'Congratulations on your promotion, sir.'

'You congratulate me on my promotion to brigadier general, but let me regale you, my old friend, of my misfortune.' Suchet smiled as he poured coffee. 'Being promoted to become the chief of staff of the Army of Italy now fills my days and nights with reading. Not just reports and returns from units, but the contradictory intrigues from Paris.'

Jobert broke his rigid posture to accept the offered cup.

Suchet's eyes drifted across Jobert's uniform. 'As regimental officers in the salons we would bemoan the mystifying intrigues of government. Did we not? Now I am buffeted and bounced by daily contradictions. Many of our friends elevated to general – Victor, Masséna, Joubert, Bonaparte – are trapped in this vicious whirlpool. Deputies of the government work tirelessly to plunder the lands we occupy, draining anything of value to Paris, denying our hard-pressed troops their rightful pay. I am buffeted not just by ill winds from Paris, but also by the unseemly gusts of local politics. We have regional politicians conniving to gain leverage, attempting to renege on the fair and legal payments due to our troops.' Suchet's face soured. 'We won these lands. We occupy them for the defence and glory of France. Still the Directory insists on these local puppet regimes. Why? I do not know. We should annex the country and be done with it.'

Suchet's eyes narrowed as he looked across his porcelain cup. 'This is where you come in, Jobert.'

'Indeed, sir? How am I of any value attached to an Italian gentlemen's riding club?'

'But you are of value, Jobert. You are trusted. You know this country. You speak the tongue. You fought the kaiserliks here. You lost men here. You move at ease amongst the Italian officers and their soldiers. Your reports are read closely. We need your understanding ... your connection to Italy.'

Jobert fiddled with his cup on its saucer. 'These people are charlatans charading as soldiers.'

'That may well be, but their incompetence does not distract from the vital nature of our work.'

Jobert's stared hard at Suchet, his voice emitted a deep growl. 'I am wasted in this role, sir.'

'That is not true, my friend.' Suchet leaned forward, his elbows on his knees. 'You have friends, such as I, who can only deal with the political duplicity in the face of the Austrian threat, because we are strengthened in the knowledge that utterly trustworthy men like you watch and wait in readiness.'

What bullshit!

Jobert clenched his jaw. 'Is that the extent of your requirements, sir? For me to just sit on my hands.'

'And watch.' Suchet sipped his coffee. 'And report what you observe. Is that not the role of the chasseur?'

Jobert ground his dentures as he searched in the hearth beside him. In the fireplace beside him, a black skin hardened on the untended coals. Their orange hearts pulsed dully as they cooled.

'Is this not your envelope?' Suchet raised his cup. 'Pick it up.'

Jobert scanned Suchet's face. Suchet had found something of interest within his coffee grounds.

Jobert turned towards the yellow parchment and its anger-smeared seal before extending his gloved hand. Jobert reread the brief contents in his mind. The envelope seemed to writhe as Jobert picked it up between the tips of three fingers.

'Either pass it to me, Jobert,' Suchet bobbed his head to sip his coffee, 'or place it on the fire.'

Jobert's heartbeat pounded. His arm cramped with hesitation. *Where can I go?*

On a warm day in late May, the plaster walls of Mantua reflected the heat down upon Jobert as he rode Jaune along the busy road. He guided Jaune into the direct sunlight allowing passers-by to weave within the limited shade.

At a street corner ahead, two women emerged from a side street, their backs to him, their faces hidden under a shared parasol.

Gianna!

The women continued up the street in advance of Jobert and Jaune.

'Excuse me, ladies?' With no breeze within the city's walls, the humidity seeped from Mantua's surrounding lakes. Jobert shrugged at the weight of his woollen tailcoat and waistcoat. 'Signorina Bernasconi?'

Gianna turned. 'Colonel Jobert.' As she drew herself up, a wry smile dimpled her cheek.

Jobert dismounted Jaune and respectfully touched the brim of his mirliton cap. 'Forgive my intrusion, ladies. I was hoping to speak briefly with Signorina Bernasconi.'

Gianna's friend whispered into Gianna's blue bonnet.

'Perhaps you might escort me, Colonel Jobert,' Gianna said. 'That will be a relief to my friend who can then return home.'

Jobert bowed to Gianna's friend. 'Might I be permitted to escort the lady home?'

'That is unnecessary. Her residence is close by.'

The woman failed to suppress a conspiratorial grin as she embraced Gianna. With a curtsy to Jobert, she departed.

Jobert took a deep breath. 'Signorina, can you find it in your heart to forgive my unseemly impropriety last—'

Gianna raised a finger for Jobert's silence then pointed to his horse. 'Who is this?'

Jobert blinked. 'Ah … Jaune.'

Gianna beamed as she rubbed Jaune's brown nose. '*Enchanté*, Jaune.'

Jaune lowered his head with a sigh.

'You have the spell of inducing pleasure in all those you greet.'

'Why, thank you, sir.'

'Are you on your way home, Signorina?' Jobert asked.

'I am, sir.'

'May I take your basket?'

'Thank you, sir.' Gianna removed her arm from under the woven cane handle but kept the basket by her waist. Jobert took a step towards her to lift the basket from her grip. Gianna said quietly, 'I am so pleased your inspections return you to Mantua.'

Jobert maintained his proximity to her. 'Mantua has only one attraction that compels my return.'

Gianna twirled away from Jobert, along the lane. 'Is it your intent to pay me court?'

He thought her tone playful. With Jaune in tow, Jobert strode out to walk beside her. 'It would be my desire, but I feel confident your mother will not allow it.'

'Then it is a shame you are unable. I like the way you look at me.'

'How do I look at you?'

'As an equal.' Gianna smiled revealing her teeth. 'You take your French values very seriously.'

What must I do to receive that smile from you every day?

'How do other men look at you?'

'Some look at me to appraise my father's value in their own ascent. Some appraise how I might appear should I be promenading in Vienna or on my first occasion in front of their mothers. Others, feeling I am above their station, appear sullen or ogle me like a pastry to be devoured.'

'Surely you have undone many a love-struck young fool?'

Gianna wobbled her head. Loose curls caressed her neck. 'Yes, one or two. It has been a rare and sincerely appreciated compliment to be in the company of a love-struck young fool.'

'Two? I have an adversary for your attentions?'

Gianna peeked from beneath her bonnet. 'Are you doubting my virtue?'

'I am surprised there have not been more.'

A handcart of fish rumbled towards them. Jobert extended his basket arm to guide her towards the wall, as he lifted the reins to yield Jaune sideways.

Gianna inspected the fish as they passed. 'So far, I have only noticed two.'

'Your fiancé and ...'

'His brother.'

A frown twitched Jobert's eyebrows. 'Is this gentleman quite well?'

Ginna's lips twisted. 'He was wounded at Rivoli and returned to Salzburg.' She placed her hand on his forearm. 'You both have scars. It is the nature of your trade.'

Jobert hesitated in his stride. 'But I represent the instrument that has wrought great loss in your life.'

Gianna turned back to him. Her eyes were sad, but her lips curled into an encouraging grin. 'And now you bring me pleasure.'

She stepped back into the stream of people entering the Piazza Sordello. Jobert and Jaune quickened their pace to return to her side.

'We were speaking of love-struck fools,' Gianna said. 'You are aware of another?'

Jobert contemplated the duomo on the far side of the piazza. The morning's sunshine had crawled halfway down the cathedral's columns. 'What factors do you consider when you appraise such men?'

'Do I admire them?' Gianna glanced at Jobert. 'Do I respect them? Do I trust them? If I were with him would the connection in any fashion create a scandal causing suffering and humiliation for myself and my family. Should we ever marry would he be able to provide a home?'

'Then if it is scandal you seek to avoid, you had best stay clear of Frenchmen.'

'Scandal undoubtedly and the loss of my heart and ... the loss of my soul. Have you ... your government not thrown the church out of society?'

'Be assured, Signorina, now the Terror has passed, every soul in France is safe. It is the power of the church over French purses that has been broken.'

'What of you, sir?' Gianna asked. 'I sense a hunter in pursuit of his prey.'

'Have I ever acted in a predatory ...' Jobert blushed as he remembered the attempted kiss.

She considered him with a tilted head with the tip of her tongue on her lips. 'No.'

'So, why would you sense—'

'Here is my door. I shall take my basket, thank you.' She stepped close to slide her bare arm under the handle beside his. 'May I prevail upon you, sir, to keep my secret?'

Jobert frowned. *What secret?*

'The price of my silence is considerable.'

Gianna looked up. 'How so?'

Jobert's gaze roamed her face. Green eyes.

'The resumption of my Italian tuition.'

Gianna's cheeks dimpled with happiness; her eyes softened as she arched an eyebrow. 'Ah, so you seek the return of the love-struck fool.'

The warm July breeze leaned against the gauze curtains in Raive's Milanese salon. Jobert slouched against a cool column. He avoided the energy of the baptismal breakfast, by raising his face to inspect the ornate fixtures of the room,

A string quartet competed with the babble. Suchet spoke to Rizzoli, a discreet finger waving near his waist in time with his speech. Rizzoli nodded towards Suchet's finger while he shifted his stance from foot to foot. Marguerite laughed with Madame Bonaparte. De Chabenac, his hands clasped behind his back and head inclined, listened to Prefetto Bernasconi.

Raive promenaded around his guests. 'So much for British superiority at sea,' Raive said. 'An entire embarked army has outwitted their squadrons of frigates.'

Camille, the bemused godmother, followed Raive holding the swaddled infant. The baby bawled incessantly as it had done throughout the ceremony in the cathedral. Behind Camille, trailed the three-year old son of Fergnes gripping the apron of his wet-nurse.

Jobert appraised master Fergnes. The child's soft hair curled on his embroidered smock. A pudgy hand clutched a wooden horse on wheels to his chest. Jobert recognised the calculating eyes of the boy's father.

Jobert smiled as de Chabenac approached.

'Ah, the lurking godfather, spent from his duties,' de Chabenac said.

Jobert shuddered. 'To think this could have been me.'

'It may still come to pass.' De Chabenac gave a tight-lipped grin. 'What is it about babies you are not comfortable with? I think the newborn has a striking resemblance to his father.'

Jobert grimaced. 'How can you tell when the child's face is beet red from crying. Thankfully the child is being removed.' Jobert shook his head. 'Give me the cannons' roar any day. Does the constant wailing disturb no one else?'

De Chabenac gave a shrug of nonchalance. 'You live with Tulloc's child by your soup kettle.'

'Enough of babies, sir. Is Senor Bernasconi quite well?'

'He is disturbed by the recent Jacobin coup in Paris, and that General Brune has exacerbated the situation, in his opinion, by installing a Jacobin Directory here in the Cisalpine Republic.'

'Bernasconi feels comfortable confiding his politics to you?'

'Perhaps he assumes a fellow named de Chabenac would be anti-Jacobin. Bernasconi fears for the Cisalpine experiment. He has hopes for further duchies to unify within the republic. Whilst you accompany him back to Mantua, I am sure your opinion will be sought.'

Jobert shrugged. 'It is just over twelve months since our return from the heights above Vienna. Bernasconi's vision may play out yet.'

At Jobert's elbow, Orlande made a polite cough. 'Excuse me, sir.'

Jobert took the note Orlande extended towards him. He frowned as he read it. 'Would you excuse me, de Chabenac?' Jobert followed Orlande into the apartment's vestibule. 'I do not understand the secrecy, Orlande.'

'All will be revealed, sir.' Orlande scanned the room before ushering Jobert through the servant's entrance and up the worn timber stairs. Orlande opened a door to reveal the nursery. The small room had been whitewashed and its floorboards covered in oriental carpets. Two single beds sat neatly made either side of a white cot.

A young wet-nurse, the same maid who had accompanied Raive downstairs, leapt to her feet in surprise.

The three-year old pumped a rocking horse to the point of toppling over. 'Look! Me running, Uncle Jobbie.'

With a flourish of his hand, Orlande indicated the baby. Propped up by cushions in the centre of a thick carpet, the child gnawed on a wooden block.

'I am pleased the howling has ceased.' Jobert gave a pained look. 'Otherwise, I do not understand, Orlande.'

'The child is sitting, sir.'

'So?'

'Downstairs, the swaddled infant was declared to be one month old, sir.' Orlande pushed his spectacles onto the bridge of his nose. 'This baby is not one month old, sir. He sits. He must be four months old, at least.'

'I am too tired to calculate conception and be titillated by scandal.'

Orlande frowned at Jobert. 'Then let me assist, sir. If the babe was conceived after the September wedding, then a birth one month ago is a blessing. But the child was not born in June. It was born at the end of March.' Orlande raised an eyebrow. 'It was conceived last June.'

'Last June?' Jobert blinked as his memory stirred. 'We had returned from Vienna last June.' A glimmer of realisation lit Jobert's eyes. 'Raive proposed last June.' He smirked. 'We are both aware of Marguerite's midnight passions. Perhaps Raive received a hearty welcome—'

'Yes, sir, we are both aware of madame's proclivities.' Orlande said with exasperation. 'Who does the child look like, sir? Does the baby look like Colonel Raive?'

Jobert glanced at the gurgling infant. 'You know I am not good with—'

'Look closely, sir.' Orlande bent towards Jobert, then whispered, 'Perhaps the child looks like your Uncle Yann?'

In that moment Jobert recognised the distinct Chauvel face. Jobert's expression of realisation swiftly transformed to a frozen mask of alarm.

'It is my lady, O, it is my love!' Jobert's voice rasped as he read aloud from Gianna's book spread upon the iron-lattice table. 'O, that she knew she were!'

Jobert paused to savour the August air beneath the apple tree that dominated the Bernasconi's inner courtyard. Overripe fruit under the marble birdbath absorbed the attention of pecking wrens. The perfume of lilies and violets attracted darting bees. Gianna's perfume of lavender and orange was all that Jobert cared for.

Gianna smiled encouragement. 'Read on ... André.'

Jobert's throat tightened with each line that Romeo revealed his love. He felt Gianna staring at him, though he remained focussed on the page.

Gianna's voice betrayed how affected she was by Juliet's heartfelt declarations. 'In truth, fair Montague, I am too fond, and therefore thou mayst think my behaviour light.' Earlier in the scene, while they had jested as Benvolio and Mercutio, Gianna's tone had been whimsical. Nervousness now edged her whispered lines. 'But trust me, gentleman, I'll prove more true.'

Jobert felt light-headed. His vision clung to her fingertip tracing the lines on the page.

'O, wilst thou leave me so unsatisfied?' Jobert read.

We incant a spell. The more we utter, the greater the demon we awake.

'What satisfaction canst thou have tonight?' Gianna responded.

'Th' exchange of thy love's faithful vow for mine.'

'I gave thee mine before thou didst request it: And yet I would it were to give again.'

Jobert was aware of his breathing. 'Wouldst thou withdraw it? For what purpose, love?'

'But to be frank and give it thee again. And yet I wish but for the thing I have. My bounty is as boundless as the sea. My love as deep: the more I give to thee, the more—'

A tap of heels sounded from the tiles. Signora Bernasconi swept across the grass towards Jobert and Gianna, followed by a maid bearing a tray. 'You appear in need of cold water, Colonel.'

Signora Bernasconi took from the maid the tray heavy with a jug and glasses. She placed the tray on the table with such determination that Gianna fumbled to remove the books in time. Gianna and her mother locked eyes. Their faces, carved in stone, strained to conceal the emotion cracking through.

'Ah ... that would be delightful, Signora.' Jobert leaned back as lemon water was poured.

Signora threw Jobert a look of disdain. 'I would expect you to be more attentive to your regimental duties, Colonel.'

'I have inspected the Mantua Company, Signora,' Jobert said with a smile. 'I assure you, I shall depart Mantua at the end of the week on my tour of the companies.'

'Then I would recommend the remainder of your visit to Mantua on your knees in the duomo repenting your sins, sir.' Signora swept away from the table.

'No chaperone today?' Jobert asked as Signora Bernasconi returned indoors.

'She watches.' Gianna raised a defiant chin to look at Jobert. 'Forgive her, André, she is lost without her Veronese friends. She is disoriented here in Mantua.'

Jobert considered Signora's retreating bustle. 'I know her concern.'

'Shall we resume?'

They bent their heads to the page. Jobert's senses filled with Gianna's scent. Dissatisfaction had swelled in his chest. 'Such a short distance separates the lovers. Romeo overcame the orchard wall. Why can he not ascend to her balcony?'

Gianna tilted her face to his. 'Only he knows what stays his final effort.'

'How delightful a world that is manufactured by the play-wright's quill.'

'Can true love not find a way despite the obstacles?'

Jobert's gaze drifted across the wrens chirping around the fallen apples.

Gianna withdrew her finger from the script. 'Your answer, sir?'

His mind yawed without the anchor of her finger upon the page. 'I know the answer I want to give, Gianna.'

'Then give it to me. To yourself.'

Jobert lifted his stare from the page. He regarded her cautiously then lowered his gaze to contemplate her mouth.

The tip of Gianna's tongue moistened her lips.

Jobert swallowed against a granite-dry throat. He leaned forward.

Gianna did not move.

His fingertip touched her chin.

Her palm cupped his jaw. She watched her thumb brush across a scar under his right eye.

They kissed.

Chapter Ten
October–November 1798, Mantua, Italy

A scraping against the door caused Jobert to glance up from his cousin Michelle's letter. Juggling the door latch with his elbow, young Quandalle entered their Mantua apartment with an armful of split logs for the night's hearth.

Jobert tipped Michelle's pages back towards the candlelight.

The poor darling is distressed at his restrictions, the ongoing discomfort in his stump and the shifting arrangements between he and Didier. Like wounded old bulls, they grumble and lean on each other, but never lock horns. My reminders to Papa of his own clashes with Grandpa were not well received.

I am not sure why Papa blames you for his accident. He grumbles that you are not overseeing training standards and herd management. As far as I can see, the annual rhythms of the herd are unchanging, and the overseers and hands know their duties. I am more concerned with the accounts and loan repayments, but I am swiftly and gruffly assured all is in hand. Perhaps your presence here would settle affairs. If you can return home, it would be of benefit to us all.

Jobert bowed his head as remembered his commitment to Suchet. As Quandalle's fire flared with a new log, so Jobert saw his letter of resignation cringing in flame.

Jobert's musings were interrupted by the others in the dim room. Orlande was bent over the stockings he was darning. Maria washed the dinner platters in a frothy tub as her eighteen-month-old son bashed at a sponge with a ladle.

At the table, whilst cleaning his pistols, Koschak leaned sideways into the candlelight to glance at a Parisian newssheet at his elbow. 'I see we have invaded Ireland again. How many times is that now?'

'Twice, I think.' Orlande poked at his memory with his needle. 'The winter before last. Or was one of them Wales?'

Koschak returned his attention to his pistol's jaw screw. 'Paris is bruised by the mauling the British gave our fleet off Alexandria. They say Bonaparte is now trapped in Egypt.'

'Which de Colbert brother went to Egypt to make his fortune, sir?' Orlande asked Jobert. 'This will delay his return to your cousin and their child.'

Jobert flapped the letter in his hand. 'Michelle writes that both Édouard and Auguste are—'

Shouting sounded from the street below.

Jobert opened the shutters and peered down at the crowd surging into the dark streets. The flow of people, mostly men, rippled with shouts and agitation. The stream of torchlights tumbled around the corner and onwards to the centre of Mantua.

Jobert's eyes narrowed. 'Something has happened. People are massing—'

A sharp rap on the door preceded the screech of the iron latch. All heads turned.

Moench entered. 'There is a gathering in the piazza, sir. Local Jacobins, or so the tavernkeeper called them.'

Jobert exchanged a concerned look with Koschak. 'Jacobins! Orlande, prepare to break camp. Moench, saddle our horses and harness Grenzer. Koschak, we ought to have loaded pistols to hand.'

Orlande looked over the rims of his glasses. 'Are we in danger, sir?'

Maria scooped her toddler towards her.

'A Jacobin sentiment in Mantua may possibly turn anti-French,' Jobert said as he loaded his pistols.

Moench lingered at the door. 'Why, sir?'

Koschak glared at Moench. 'Saddle the horses, Corporal.'

Moench shot Jobert a look of appeal.

Jobert paused his ramming. 'In brief, Moench, there is a tussle over who receives the wealth of Lombardy. In August, General Brune established a government of his liking in Milan to increase the flow of local taxes. Last month, our minister to this republic dismissed Brune's government. Last week, the Directory replaced that minister and re-established the Cisalpine government. Perhaps the agitation outside is dissent against Paris' latest levies.'

The door latch screeched, and the door swung to shove Moench in the back.

Koschak cocked and levelled his pistol at the face that peered around the latch.

'Is Colonel Jobert—' Silvio Bernasconi froze at the sight of Koschak's barrel. Koschak raised the muzzle.

'Forgive my intrusion, sir,' Bernasconi said. 'My father has been arrested. Colonel Rizzoli advises caution, but I cannot stand idle.' Bernasconi dropped his face to the floor. 'I do not know who else to trust.'

Jobert frowned. 'And Gia—' Jobert bit down on his impropriety. 'Your mother and sister are well?'

'They were quite safe with Colonel Rizzoli when I departed,

sir,' Bernasconi said.

Why would Jacobins not sweep Rizzoli into their bag?

'Why would the Jacobins be motivated against your father?' Jobert asked.

'I do not know.'

'Does the French garrison still control Fort San Giorgio and the city gates?'

'I believe so, I am not sure.' Bernasconi jerked with agitation. 'Why, sir?'

'You spoke of Rizzoli. Where is he?'

'Here in Mantua,' Bernasconi said. Jobert flinched in surprise. 'I have just left him and Major de Chabenac at our residence.'

'Koschak, we must attend Rizzoli. Orlande and Moench, continue our preparations for departure.'

Caped to conceal the pistols in their sashes, Jobert and Koschak jostled their way through the chattering groups milling in the streets towards Prefetto Bernasconi's residence. Young Bernasconi jogged to keep up through the milling crowd. They were received by nervous members of Bernasconi's staff at the outer gate, before being shown into an upstairs drawing room.

'Good evening, sir.' Jobert saluted Rizzoli before giving de Chabenac a curt nod. 'With the disturbance throughout the city and having received the news of Prefetto Bernasconi's arrest I came immediately. Is the household safe?'

'Indeed, it is, Jobert. The ladies have retired.' Rizzoli threw Bernasconi a look of irritation. 'There was no need to create a fuss, Lieutenant.'

'Do you have news from Milan, sir?' Jobert asked.

'I do. General Brune has conducted a *coup d'état* in Milan.' Rizzoli brushed his moustache with the back of his gloved finger. 'Three weeks ago, your Minister of the Cisalpine dismissed our government. A week ago, Paris replaced him with a Jacobin who re-established our assembly. This, at the same time as Paris establishes a new republic in Piedmont. This would appear not to Brune's liking and he now has assumed the authority of the republic.'

Jobert glanced at de Chabenac. *Your careful smile conceals what?*

Jobert asked Rizzoli, 'Then why has Prefetto Bernasconi been arrested?'

'Bernasconi has the authority to call out the legion.'

'Against whom, sir?'

Rizzoli straightened his bearing. 'The fellows who took him appeared to be Jacobin opportunists, in favour of a republic not under Brune's dominion. Perhaps they hope to avert any disruption of their momentum.'

'You were here when Bernasconi was taken, sir?'

'Yes. Why?'

Jobert's jaw clenched. 'You allowed him to be taken, sir. Why? As a senior commander of the Lombardy Legion, why were you not arrested?' Jobert swung his scowl towards his lounging friend. 'Or you, de Chabenac, as a senior French officer? You, who know full well what an enraged mob can do.'

De Chabenac tensed at the reprimand and straightened in his armchair.

Rizzoli raised a finger. 'It was—'

Jobert turned to depart. 'You must have arrived with an escort, sir. May I take temporary command of your escort that might support our immediate release of Senor Bernasconi?'

'Our escort has returned to barracks.' Rizzoli raised his palms. 'I would advise caution, Jobert. I will not have my chasseurs ignite such a volatile situation.'

'Come, de Chabenac.' Jobert gave Koschak a nod toward the door. 'When the situation is confusing is when swift action triumphs.'

Within the hour, Jobert marched at the rear of a formation of six chasseurs moving across Mantua's Piazza Sordello. Led by Koschak with sabre drawn, Jobert, de Chabenac, Bernasconi, Moench and Tulloc followed. Only their implacable faces could be seen above their capes and beneath the oilskin covers over their mirlitons. Each man had a pistol in his sash. Each man carried a his cocked musketoon at the ready across his chest.

Once under the high porticos that marked the inner walls of the Ducal Palazzo, at a nod from Jobert, Moench and Tulloc peeled away from their formation to seep into the shadows of the palazzo's gatehouse.

Within the gardens of the palazzo's courtyards small knots of men flapped and argued. They reduced their political conversations to nudges and whispers as the column of chasseurs crunched along the gravel paths, their scabbards slapping against their legs in forbidding rhythm. Underneath their capes, the links of iron chains clinked. Having recoiled from the chasseurs' passing, the citizens followed, their mutterings alert to the possibility and implications of further arrests.

Koschak halted his armed party in front of a collection of well-dressed city elders. Jobert, de Chabenac and Bernasconi, their faces known by some of the elders, turned away toward the crowd to secure the conversation.

'Gentlemen, I am Major Zenari of the Cisalpine Chasseurs,' Koschak said. 'Colonel Rizzoli commends your foresight in securing the councillors to safeguard the republic. I have orders to escort the councillors to Milan. They are to be moved before the French garrison can deny justice. Who here is able to authorise their release?'

'Colonel Rizzoli is here in Mantua?' asked one member of the group. 'He supports our gathering?'

'Of course, citizens!' Koschak said. 'The Cisalpine Chasseurs are of the people and for the people.'

'Why are the councillors not secure where they are?' asked some of the other men. 'How are they more secure in Milan? They will be surrounded by even greater numbers of French.'

'But the French will be unaware of their presence in Milan,' Koschak said. 'Their location will remain secret until your negotiations deem it necessary for them to be revealed.'

Moench and Tulloc arrived behind Koschak. 'Sir, the French infantry are beginning to move out of Fort San Giorgio. French patrols are confirming the security of their guards at the city gates.'

Koschak gave a nod to this whispered intelligence. 'Gentlemen, there is no time to lose, and you have more immediate priorities. What is your consensus? Should the councillors be taken into our custody, the chasseurs will be able to evade the French net. Gentlemen, the fate of our republic is at stake.'

One heavy set man in rich robes stepped forward. 'Come with me. I shall inform the gaoler of the transfer.'

As Koschak and his chasseur escort followed the city elder, Moench marched close to Jobert. 'I saw Fazio in the crowd.'

'Did he step forward?' Jobert asked.

'No. He took pains to remain obscure.'

'Then we need to move fast.'

Once within the palazzo's dungeons, Koschak nodded towards the imprisoned councillors. 'Open the gates and remove their chains.'

Prefetto Bernasconi stepped forward. 'I protest—'

From within the prisoner escort Silvio gave a nod silencing Prefetto Bernasconi.

Koschak's broad chest swelled in front of the elder and the gaoler. 'Sir, I have the authority to detain you in my custody.'

'Whose authority?' asked another of the detained councillors.

With a nudge, Bernasconi silenced his colleague's protest.

'You are obliged to comply with my directions,' Koschak said. He waved his hand between the chasseur escort and the prisoners. 'Manacle them.'

Jobert, de Chabenac and Silvio stepped forward to wrap capes around the shoulders of Bernasconi and two other councillors. Under the capes each man was given lengths of trace chains to hold. They all accepted their bondage with a nod.

Once out among the palazzo's raised garden beds, Bernasconi whispered to Jobert, 'How are my wife and daughter?'

'Colonel Rizzoli is safeguarding them, sir.'

'Did Rizzoli authorise this release?'

Jobert looked to de Chabenac. 'Ah … he supported it, sir. Where is the safest location for you?'

'Milan. With my sister-in-law.'

'Then I urge you to depart the city immediately. The situation is volatile.'

Bernasconi grimaced in agreement. 'But I sense the situation will stabilise within a few weeks.'

'Until then, may I offer my protection?' Jobert gave a nod to Koschak, Moench and Tulloc. 'My men will escort the prefetto to Milan.'

'Horses?' Koschak asked.

'Silvio,' his father said, 'return home. Bring three saddle horses to Jobert's stable. Keep my whereabouts secret from your mother. In the coming days, they cannot know. Do you understand, Silvio?'

Silvio's head bobbed in acquiescence.

'They must remain here. If they are seen to flee, they will become complicit. We must avoid scandal.'

Chapter Eleven

The following morning, Maria entered the tavern's rooms, her baby clutched to her chest, her eyes seeking Jobert. 'Soldiers are coming, sir.'

Jobert stepped to the window and looked down through the shutters. A few chasseurs of the Cisalpine Regiment dismounted in the tavern yard. Horses jostled as reins were passed to others designated as horse holders. The soldiers' shouts leapt up the wooden stairwells. Their scabbards clattered on door frames and balustrades as their boots crunched on the stairs.

'Orlande, quickly!' Jobert said. 'Take Maria and Andrea and step outside these rooms. There is no time for explanations. Send for de Chabenac.' Jobert slipped on his coat and sword belt. He tipped a few coins into his hand before passing his purse to Orlande. 'Orlande ... look for me in the dungeons of the palazzo.'

As Orlande closed an inner door behind himself and Maria, Fazio burst through the door, pistol in hand. Fazio's face was twisted with sinister glee. Two chasseurs entered behind Fazio, one with manacles.

Zenari entered with sword drawn, bloated with authority. 'Jobert, I have a warrant for your arrest, issued by the Council of Mantua. I demand your parole.'

'On what charge?' Jobert asked.

'Upon the suspicion of you participating in the abduction, and possible murder, of Prefetto Bernasconi. Your parole?'

'You have my parole.'

'Remove your sword belt,' Zenari said.

'Take my sword, Zenari. It will not burden you long. You will return it to me upon my imminent release.'

Zenari's lip curled. 'And remove the dagger in your cuff. I have not forgotten the back lanes of Rome.'

Fazio snatched the dagger from Jobert.

Jobert fists clenched. 'Leave it on the table for my valet, Fazio.'

Fazio rubbed the dagger's grip between his fingers, his look daring Jobert to strike.

'Steal it from me at your peril, Fazio,' Jobert said. 'Upon my release yours will be the first throat I open with it.'

Zenari scoffed. 'If you are released.'

'With a battalion of French infantry secure with the city's Fort San Giorgio, I have no doubt the garrison commander will act swiftly to right this abuse.' Jobert pointed. 'Table, Sergeant. Now!'

Fazio spun the blade in the air. The dagger fell point first to dig into the table and quiver. 'The manacles, sir?'

Jobert gave a laugh of contempt. 'You would manacle a paroled officer upon unproven charges? Do not push your theatrics to the point of self-destruction, Zenari.'

A biting northerly had brown leaves dart and pounce as Jobert was marched through the streets to Mantua's prison. Zenari led the mounted escort that surrounded Jobert.

Fazio rode on Jobert's left, his drawn sabre poised above

Jobert's shoulder. 'God's teeth, this chilly day reminds me of Bologna this time last year. Nothing like being marched to the cells to stir the soul.'

As Jobert passed through the gate of the barred cell, Jobert passed a few coins to the gaoler. 'Thank you, sir. Would you accept this for my accommodation? My valet will soon arrive with food. He will pay for your generosity in allowing him access.'

Two hours later, the gaoler opened Jobert's cell. He passed Jobert a small loaf and a half-wheel of *mascarpone* cheese. Jobert noticed the man's black-grimed fingerprints squeezed into the cheese. 'Where is my valet?'

A black-gowned man with a soft black cap approached the bars of the cell. 'You have been forbidden visitors until I have spoken with you.' De Chabenac stood behind him. 'As a warranted magistrate representing the Mantua Council, I am authorised to interrogate you. Where is Prefetto Bernasconi?'

'I do not know.' Jobert recognised the magistrate from the group of city elders.

If he has not recognised de Chabenac, then perhaps ...

The magistrate scanned Jobert from head to toe. 'Prefetto Bernasconi and two other councillors have been abducted. The council is concerned for their welfare. A delegation from the city escorted them to the palazzo. They came willingly to join the assembly of concerned citizens.'

Jobert pressed his lips together to avoid his face betraying him. 'What does the politics of your city have to do with me?'

'A party charading as Cisalpine Chasseurs presented falsified documents to have the councillors released and detained under their escort. You, Colonel Jobert, have access to Cisalpine uniforms. You have loyal soldiers on your staff. It is reasonably expected that an officer of your rank would be capable of drafting potentially convincing documents.'

Behind the magistrate, De Chabenac's gentle smile spread wider.

His mask against worry.

'I will accept your word for it, sir,' Jobert said, 'as I was not at the exchange.'

The magistrate waved a rolled scroll bound with a black ribbon. 'I have a written deposition from Colonel Rizzoli stating that no order was ever given or received for the republic's chasseurs to act as described.'

Jobert's eyes slid to de Chabenac. 'Does Colonel Rizzoli swear to my involvement?'

'He does not,' the magistrate said. 'But we do have a witness who describes you as a member of the party.'

Fazio!

Jobert willed himself not to be drawn into any revelations. 'This person bears false witness. I was not present.'

'If you claim you were not party to the abduction,' the magistrate said, 'can you, Colonel Jobert, account for your whereabouts yesterday evening?'

Jobert drew back his shoulders. 'I was at my rooms in the tavern. I remained there during the evening as the crowds gathered in the streets. I learnt the crowds were unfavourable to towards the French, so I felt it wise to remain indoors. I was unaware of Prefetto Bernasconi's location throughout the evening.'

The magistrate's gaze drifted around Jobert's cell. 'Can anyone vouchsafe your location?'

'My valet and my groom.'

The magistrate's eyes leapt back to Jobert. 'Anyone who is not a member of your household? An independent witness?'

'Perhaps the tavern staff.'

The magistrate smiled warmly. 'Come now, Jobert, where is Prefetto Bernasconi?'

Before dawn the next morning, the duomo's bells woke Jobert. The dungeon was dark. Beyond the bars, no guards patrolled with lamps. Chains rattled, throats coughed and moaned, as those manacled stirred in neighbouring cells. The wracked breathing shifted to a hum of desperate whispers. Buckets full of human waste splashed and gurgled as inmates emptied their bladders and their bowels. The disturbed faeces in the buckets pulsed a stench of stale urine through the odours of rancid wounds and ripe bodies.

Jobert's shoulders ached from using his arm as a pillow. He sat up against the stone wall slimy with mould and body grease. As he converted his tailcoat from blanket back to coat, he heard small, clawed feet scrabble across the straw. He reached down his legs to find midnight teeth had gouged his boots.

He knew would exact a revenge on Zenari and Fazio for their shabby performance. *But was Rizzoli involved?*

Jobert stood over his piss bucket. His movements alerted him to fresh irritations on his skin. A volley of tiny bites was initiated along his ribs and hair line.

To endure such indignity was beyond his commitment to Suchet. *I have given much to France, but my acceptance of this, France does not deserve.*

In the half-light, Jobert knelt over a water bucket encrusted with black mould. He scooped a handful of water and sniffed.

In his mind he saw the bleak road home, across ice-locked streams and snow-choked rocks.

My infatuation with Gianna is part of my punishment.

Keys scraped in his lock. The gaoler swung open the door. 'You are released, Lieutenant Colonel Jobert.'

D'Onofrio stood in the corridor between the grids of bars.

Jobert flicked away the handful of water. 'On what terms, D'Onofrio?'

D'Onofrio passed Jobert his sabre. 'No terms, sir. The council has ordered your release.'

Jobert strapped the sword belt around his waist. 'Where is Colonel Rizzoli and Major Zenari?'

D'Onofrio surveyed the stone at his feet. 'They have returned to Milan.'

Jobert snorted.

'Major Zenari asked me to pass a message.'

Jobert clenched his teeth as a wave of lice bites nipped into his skin.

'He hopes you were not too inconvenienced.'

'Inconvenienced? I have been abused, D'Onofrio. Those responsible will account for this injustice.'

D'Onofrio gaze swept the straw in Jobert's cage. 'You have no headdress, sir?'

'No, D'Onofrio, Zenari denied me such respect.'

D'Onofrio swept off his mirliton. 'Then would you take mine, sir? And please take my horse to convey you to your rooms.'

Jobert gripped D'Onofrio's upper arm. 'Thank you, D'Onofrio, but no. I will not allow the shame Zenari has flung at me to stick.'

Jobert paused as he moved past the gaoler and pressed his remaining coins into the man's hand. 'Thank you for your kindness, sir.'

Jobert walked alone through the bitter streets. As he entered the tavern rooms, he received a downcast welcome by de Chabenac and Orlande.

'How was my release arranged?' Jobert asked.

'The garrison commander,' de Chabenac said. His wan face

was focused in discomfort on Jobert's stained tailcoat. 'But I am at fault, sir. I beg your forgiveness. I was not swift enough to prevent a further calamity.'

'What has happened?'

De Chabenac raised his chin. 'An alibi for your whereabouts presented themselves to the Council.'

Jobert blinked. 'An alibi! Who?'

'Signorina Bernasconi.'

'Gianna!' Jobert recoiled. 'What perjury has Gianna committed? I would have been released from Zenari's abuse by the garrison commander. Or a week at most awaiting a response from headquarters in Milan. What did she say? Can anything be salvaged?'

'Gianna stated she was with you in these apartments,' de Chabenac said.

Jobert reeled as if punched. 'No!'

'The discretion of her movement was ensured by your valet escorting her. The arrangement had been in place for some time.'

Jobert slid his gaze to Orlande. 'Orlande, did you concoct this with her?'

Orlande attempted to conceal his trembling lips by pressing his spectacles up his nose. 'No, sir, she—'

'Did you corroborate her statement?'

'Yes, sir.' Orlande straightened. 'As did Tulloc, Maria and Quandalle. If it meant securing your release, then yes.'

'She has sacrificed her honour for me.' Jobert sought stability by gripping the back of a wooden kitchen chair. 'Her reputation in society is ruined. I must go to her. Orlande, fetch a bucket of water, a fresh shirt and my number-one tailcoat.' Orlande stepped smartly to fetch the wash basin and soap. 'De Chabenac, what was Rizzoli's role in the scandal? Did Rizzoli engineer Bernasconi's arrest? And mine?'

'I was with him throughout. He knows it was you … I mean, us, from the exchange in Bernasconi's salon. Rizzoli was incensed that the reputation of the regiment was impugned. He upbraided me severely for it. Your arrest, I am convinced, was of Zenari's manufacture. Some small revenge, perhaps?'

Jobert towelled his face and armpits of lather. 'As I thought.'

Once cleaned and dressed, Jobert marched swiftly to the Bernasconi's residence.

Upon his announcement there, he was invited into the drawing room before Signora Bernasconi, Gianna and Silvio.

Signora wrung a handkerchief between her white knuckled fists. 'Where is my husband? He will return to a family embroiled in scandal.'

Silvio stepped forward and placed a hand on her forearm. 'Perhaps mother we might thank Colonel Jobert for securing father's release from the dungeon's chains.'

Signora jerked her arm free. 'That he is not held by the mob does not infer his safety.'

Jobert took his eyes from Gianna. 'He is quite safe, Signora. At his request, the best of my men have escorted him to your family in Milan.'

'Milan?' Signora clenched her handkerchief to her lips. 'Is that not where the brute Brune —'

Silvio stepped forward again with a hesitant placating hand. 'I hear Brune has departed Milan.'

Gianna smiled as she rocked on her toes. 'With a significant amount of cash.'

'Signora,' Jobert said, 'the excitement in the city will soon subside and your husband shall return soon enough.'

Signora spun away. 'I will retire to pray. Gianna, attend me.'

Gianna slipped her hands behind her back. 'No, Mother, I will remain.'

Senora Bernasconi's eyes bulged.

'Attend to your prayers, Mother,' Silvio said. 'Gianna and I shall attend to our guest and give thanks and care to the man who was imprisoned to save, if not your husband, then our father.'

With lips clenched and tears brimming, Signora departed the drawing room.

Jobert evaluated Gianna. 'Does your mother not know of your ...'

Gianna raised her chin. 'Not yet.' She stepped toward him, her fingertips intertwining. 'Not until I had seen you walk free.'

He tentatively opened his hands towards her. 'I warn you, Gianna. I have come direct from the cells.'

She ran to be engulfed within his embrace.

Silvio mumbled and exited.

Jobert's hands cupped her shoulder blades as he looked down at her. 'I am astounded at your sacrifice for my freedom.'

Gianna rubbed his lapels. 'Some are sacrificing more than their good name. I exchanged that to repay the debt of my father's release.' Gianna held up a finger. 'That does not infer any obligation on your part, André.'

'On the contrary, Gianna. I am forever in debt. Your reputation is of great value.'

Gianna fought back tears. 'You risked yourself for my father. In his absence I value you. Our family is safer with you on the outside of a dungeon.' She sniffed. As he smudged a tear on her cheek with his thumb, she asked, 'How else might we resume our study of Italian? Are you not interested in what the third act has in store?'

A laugh of surprise spasmed in Jobert's throat. 'You have compromised your honour for me, beautiful Gianna. I will do more to restore your good name, than excel at my lessons.'

Gianna beamed. Her dimples squeezed his heart. 'How might you do that, Jobert?'

One of his hands slid to the small of her back. A finger of the other hand traced her jawline and brushed her lower lip.

'By you becoming my wife.'

Chapter Twelve
December 1798, Piedmont, Italy

After Brune's failed coup in November, the new commander of the Army of Italy occupied Lombardy's neighbouring state, Piedmont. The Cisalpine Chasseurs accompanied the French column to capture the Piedmontese capital of Turin.

In a Piedmontese village south-east of Turin, on the road to Alessandria and Milan, D'Onofrio's squadron of the Mantua and Brescia Companies sought stabling for horses and billets for the men. Across the square from a tavern and its stables, between the buttresses of a church, Jobert's retinue made their camp beside Jobert's two-wheeled cart.

Jobert busied himself brushing his horses' tails. At least Bleu, Jaune and Grenzer enjoyed his company and appreciated his attentions, such as an itch relieved under the bridle's cheek straps.

'Gentlemen, I seek your views,' Koschak said.

Jobert looked up from the knots in Bleu's black tail towards Koschak and de Chabenac.

'With Cisalpine's government resettled and our occupation of Piedmont complete,' Koschak asked, 'do you feel we will march on Naples?'

De Chabenac raised his eyebrows to anticipate Jobert's answer, and when none was forthcoming, he said, 'With Brune summoned to Paris, General Joubert has sufficient to occupy the army with this occupation of Piedmont. Does Joubert still call you "cousin"?'

Jobert harrumphed and shook his head. 'With Piedmont's king having fled, Koschak, and General Grouchy installed as the governor, the occupation is to remind the Piedmontese they answer to France and secure our flanks against the Alps for the coming campaign.'

'In my view,' de Chabenac said, 'Paris' actions create contradictory results. The Directory create these liberated republics allied to France and then drains them of their wealth. Who is surprised when these self-governing republics take umbrage at being heavily taxed? Such resistance compels successive commanders of the Army of Italy, with their agenda of receiving sufficient funds to pay their regiments—'

'And line their pockets.' Jobert sneered. 'Masséna in Rome, Brune in Milan.' *And Raive.*

De Chabenac gave a small bow to the interruption. '—our generals assume control of the republics to ensure the flow of gold and food to the troops and to Paris.'

'And that brings our latest commander, Joubert, to Piedmont,' Jobert said.

Koschak squinted. 'So, we will not march to Naples?'

'No,' Jobert said, 'that task falls to our new Army of Naples. They have brushed aside the Austrians and Neapolitans north of Rome. Rome will be resecured soon enough.'

'And with the destruction of our Mediterranean fleet in Egypt, what will be done with the British re-establishing themselves at the port of Livorno?' asked Koschak.

De Chabenac raised a finger. 'Now that affair the Army of Italy will be called upon to resolve.'

Koschak leaned forward on his mount's withers. 'From what I read, as many as six hundred thousand Austrian, Russian and British troops are being mobilised for the coming spring.'

'In four months, when the snows melt in the alpine passes,' Jobert slapped his brush at the church's brickwork as much in irritation as to remove the dust from the bristles, 'war will come to Lombardy.'

A shout from the Brescian chasseurs bustling around their stables caused Jobert to look across the cobbled street. Beyond their small camp, the weary chasseurs of the Ravenna Company entered the square.

'Have you noticed there are no babies in the streets?' Jobert said.

'Babies, sir?' asked de Chabenac.

'We see them in every Lombardian street we ride through. Little girls supporting a baby's first steps. Pudgy toddlers sitting in puddles eating goat shit. Small children throwing mud and sticks at dogs. But not here in Piedmont.'

De Chabenac looked between Jobert and Koschak. 'Where are they then?'

'Their mothers have taken them off the streets,' Koschak said. 'The children we do see are old enough to run fast, deliver messages. Something is afoot. We are being watched.'

'By whom?' de Chabenac asked.

'Partisans,' Jobert said.

'Are the villages dangerous?'

'We compromise our security when we disperse men and horses by billeting throughout the village. Whenever did the 24th Chasseurs billet our troops in Ligurian villages?'

De Chabenac scowled as he tried to remember.

'Do you feel this threat warrants us shifting camp?' Koschak asked.

Orlande, Moench and Tulloc paused in their tasks around the cart and turned toward Jobert. Not one attentive face revealed any apprehension of the effort required to pack and move.

'We are fine where we are.' Jobert saw their disciplined masks melt with relief. 'Though tonight will be the last night we bed down in the towns. Now that Rizzoli has recruited full companies and deploys with all of his force available, our numbers are too much to halt together in one town. Each evening, Rizzoli establishes his headquarters in the mayor's house, then disperses his squadrons to far flung farms. Isolated targets are easy to attack.'

'Have you informed Colonel Rizzoli of the disadvantages of his dispositions?' de Chabenac asked.

'He will not listen to me. Have you no influence with—'

A chorus of anger flared across the street. A dozen chasseurs were flailing their arms into each other.

'Where did that come from?' de Chabenac asked.

Koschak laughed. 'Looks like Ravenna and Brescia are keeping each other warm. One company feeling the other had taken more than their fair share of stabling.'

Men from Ravenna dismounted to join the fight as more chasseurs from Brescia and Mantua emptied from the stable.

'The companies' regional identities are proving their downfall,' Jobert said. 'Rizzoli has made no effort to bind them together.'

Officers and sergeant majors roared at the brawlers to cease their stupidity to no avail.

At the corner of the village piazza the clatter of hooves, sharp in the freezing air, bounced off stone walls. A squadron column of green-jacketed French dragoons marching for Turin came into view. The column of silent horsemen approached the brawl.

The chasseurs began to step apart from each other as the dragoons marched past.

The French dragoons looked down at the chasseurs, their black horsetail manes swinging from the backs of their brass helmets.

The embarrassed pugilists returned to their horses or their stable duties, whipped by their sergeants' curses.

The dragoon column continued out of the village.

With hands on his hips and head low, D'Onofrio ambled out of the stable. He glanced at Jobert, straightened his shoulders and began walking in the opposite direction.

'Captain D'Onofrio!' Jobert called.

D'Onofrio turned with a blank expression on his face.

Jobert beamed. 'Is it too late to re-join your previous regiment?'

D'Onofrio squirmed.

Jobert's grin widened as he said, 'When you go, take me with you.'

Outside Piedmont's capital, Turin, mounted on Bleu to the flank of the three-hundred metre line of chasseurs, Jobert stared at the snow-churned field and contemplated Rizzoli and Zenari. His face soured as he shrugged his shoulders within his jacket at imagined lice.

I will observe and report. Nothing more. Nothing.

Since his overnight incarceration in Mantua, Jobert had avoided Rizzoli, but had maintained an implacable stare towards Zenari. If Zenari even thought of smirking, Jobert was ready to open his belly. Whether by luck or good sense, Zenari maintained his arrogant posture but never acknowledged Jobert's presence.

Under Rizzoli's anxious eye, Zenari prepared the regiment for an inspection by a commanding general. Zenari drilled the regiment in marching at the walk, then wheeling in column of platoons. Two thousand hooves swirled snow and mud and levelled the furrows beneath. Now, as Rizzoli conversed with his officers, sergeant majors prowled the ranks and troopers dismounted to make final adjustments.

Leather creaked as de Chabenac mounted beside Jobert shifted in his saddle. 'Why is General Victor inspecting the regiment today? Have you set Rizzoli a trap?'

'I have done no such thing.' Jobert stared along the line of chasseurs. 'Suchet may have warned Victor when the regiment was placed under his command. Victor, disappointed that we are being wasted as diplomatic cannon fodder, sought my views on ... areas of concern.'

Disappointment creased de Chabenac's face. 'Will the soldiers be asked to perform a task they are unprepared for? It is one thing to embarrass Rizzoli. It is another to shame the men in the ranks.'

'It is better the regiment fails a simple task in front of Victor now,' Jobert said, 'than in front of the enemy in a few months' time. Look! Here comes Victor. I had best accompany Rizzoli.'

Jobert cantered Bleu to approach Victor's party behind Rizzoli.

Rizzoli saluted. 'The Cisalpine Chasseurs on parade and ready for your inspection, sir.'

'Thank you, Colonel.' From his vantage point, Victor scanned the ranks. The chasseurs' drawn sabres quivered revealing the cold seeping into their erect, but inactive, bodies. 'Colonel, I wish to see a demonstration of your regiment firing their musketoons whilst mounted.'

Rizzoli's brow creased as he smiled. 'Certainly, sir.'

Victor's smile effused confidence. 'Nothing unduly complex, Colonel. May I request your regiment fires two volleys to your front.'

Rizzoli blinked with confusion as he stared down the empty field. 'Certainly, sir.'

'Do you have any questions, Colonel?'

'No, sir.'

Victor drew his watch from his pocket. 'Then carry on.'

Rizzoli and Jobert rode back to the centre of the chasseur line. Rizzoli faced the ranks and looked up and down the length of the battleline.

Jobert fought the impulse to offer suggestions.

Rizzoli took a deep breath before calling, 'Major Zenari, attend me.'

Zenari trotted over and saluted.

'General Victor requires the regiment to fire two volleys,' Rizzoli said.

Zenari slid a suspicious scowl towards Jobert. 'Mounted, sir?'

'I believe so. Are you familiar with the orders to fire?'

'Yes, sir,' Zenari said. 'It is as simple as Ready! and Fire!'

Jobert smiled. *A little more than that in a fire order.*

'Oh, yes,' Rizzoli said, 'I am quite aware of the orders, Zenari. I wished to confirm that you are. Very well, carry on.'

Zenari screwed up his face as he looked the length of the line. 'So, do we fire both volleys as a regiment? Not as companies?'

Rizzoli looked towards Victor. 'I am unsure.'

Zenari's eyes flicked in annoyance towards Jobert.

Jobert softened his face to indicate he was receptive to joining the conversation. *You idiots are completely lost in the simple act of discharging your firearms.*

Zenari looked away, blinking, calculating. 'Might I discuss the options with Captain D'Onofrio, Uncle?'

Rizzoli glanced at Victor's party. 'Do hurry.'

Upon being hailed by Zenari, D'Onofrio trotted to join the cluster.

'D'Onofrio,' Zenari said, 'if a regiment was to fire two volleys, how might it be executed?'

D'Onofrio darted a frown towards Jobert. 'In battleline or skirmish order, sir?'

Zenari turned to Rizzoli.

Rizzoli licked his lips. 'Ah, I ... ah.'

'Did General Victor specify skirmish line, sir?' Zenari asked.

'No.'

'Then as we are in battleline, D'Onofrio, fire the volleys in battleline.'

'Very good, sir. Will you execute rolling fire by half-companies?'

Zenari slumped as he turned his face to Rizzoli.

'Yes,' Rizzoli said, 'that sounds quite smart. Do that.'

Zenari's clenched fists shook his reins. 'The men have never executed that order, sir.'

'What?' Rizzoli jerked. His horse took a nervous step. 'Never! Oh, good grief. What have you been doing all this time? Let us fire our musketoons and be done with it. What are the commands? Ready and fire?' Rizzoli stood in his stirrups. 'Cisalpine Chasseurs, ready!'

The chasseurs, with sabres drawn, looked left and right at their sergeants. Some attempted to sheath their sabres. Others let their sabres swing on their sword knots around their wrists as they took up their musketoons.

Jobert sighed. 'Perhaps sir, we might retire the officers behind the second rank prior to firing?'

Rizzoli shifted in his saddle. 'Shall we retire, gentlemen .'

As he squeezed Bleu through the muttering ranks, Jobert glanced at Victor's party watching the fiasco from the slope.

'Sir,' Fazio hissed at Zenari as the officers pressed through the agitated horsemen, 'the regiment is at the unload.'

Zenari rolled his eyes. 'Sir, might you give the command Load! to the regiment.'

'Why were they not ... oh, very well. Regiment, load!'

Jobert had only observed a few of the companies practice this fundamental chasseur skill. He felt embarrassed for the soldiers as they fumbled with their reins and cartridge boxes. Some dropped their cartridges. Some dropped their ramrods. When a few troopers dismounted to collect their dropped ram-rods from beneath the hooves, sergeants roared for their men to remount.

'Are we ready?' Rizzoli gave a slight cough. 'Is there not a trumpet call for this?'

'I do not believe so, sir,' Zenari said.

'Oh, very well. Regiment, ready!'

Nearly six hundred and fifty hammers were cocked.

Jobert gritted his teeth. 'We are firing by ranks, are we not, sir?' A growl edged his voice. 'Otherwise, the second rank will shoot the front rank in the back.'

'Yes, thank you, Jobert, I am quite aware of the procedure ... front rank, fire!'

A cackle of explosions expanded from the centre of the line. Horses in both ranks snorted, reared and bucked. Sergeants screamed for dressing of the line and to reload.

D'Onofrio gave a nervous glance to Jobert before addressing his commanding officer. 'Shall we advance the second rank before they fire, sir?'

Rizzoli spluttered to breathe in the swirling gun smoke. 'Advance them, D'Onofrio.'

D'Onofrio's company trumpeter gave two short barps.

Silence fell along the ranks. 'Second rank, advance through!'

As the second rank of three hundred horsemen surged through the front rank, the front rank unleashed a rumble of dissent as comrades passing them disturbed the reloading process, causing a clatter of ramrods to fall on the sods beneath. The whole manoeuvre was punctuated by the fire of five or six prematurely discharged weapons.

In the spluttering discharge of powder, horses grunted and surged in distress. Sergeants screamed 'Not us!' at those chasseurs of the initial front rank, now standing behind, attempting to aim between their second rank comrades, now standing in front.

'Regiment, second rank, fire!' Rizzoli called.

'No!' Jobert screamed. 'Front rank—'

Musketoons exploded. Men screamed. Two men were punched to the ground. Three others lolled in their saddles as they were gripped by comrades shouting for wound dressings.

Jobert eyes widened with alarm. 'Sir, cease the exercise as we have wounded.'

One of Victor's aides reined in beside Rizzoli's party. 'General Victor orders the regiment to cease fire, sir, and for you to attend him at your earliest convenience.'

Rizzoli's face was white as he watched a moaning chasseur lowered from the saddle. 'Very well. Zenari, have the regiment cease fire.'

Rizzoli and Jobert cantered to Victor's position just beyond the edge of the regimental line.

Victor closed his watch cover and slipped his watch into his fob pocket. 'Rizzoli, had such military incompetence been described to me, I would not have believed it had I not observed it with my own eyes.'

Rizzoli's head wobbled as he assumed a weak smile.

Victor's eyes drilled Rizzoli. 'That display was appalling. I am saddened I was unable to transmit the order to cease fire before soldiers and horses were wounded or killed. When was the regiment raised? Last June? Eighteen months ago?'

'Indeed, sir.' Rizzoli panted through his nose. 'Prince Eugene of Savoy once remarked—'

'Jobert,' Victor said, acknowledging Jobert for the first time that day, 'did you not raise a regiment of chasseurs from scratch in '93. How long was the period from initial recruit arrival to their first combat?'

'Three months, sir.'

'What would you say was the longest period your squadrons engaged with the enemy?'

'Three years, sir.' Jobert sat straight in the saddle. 'My regiment was in continuous contact from April '94 to April '97.'

'I find it extraordinary, Rizzoli,' Victor said, 'when asked for your regiment to discharge your weapons twice, I witness such a debacle.' Victor swept his hand towards Jobert. 'Yet you have immediate access to such an experienced officer attached to your staff for that exact purpose.'

Rizzoli shuddered. 'My sincere—'

'Today was a disgrace, Rizzoli. I shall be making an enquiry of General Joubert as to why you ought not be stripped of your command.'

'Indeed, sir.' Rizzoli's jaw spasmed to form his words. 'Is ... is there any other aspect of the regiment you wish to review?'

Victor rocked back in his saddle. 'Why ever would I, man? Have I not seen sufficient of your regiment's ability to perform in battle? Austria, Britain and Naples attack us in the south. Russia marches to join Austria in the north. War will be upon us in weeks. Your regiment has much to do in a very short time, Rizzoli. You will march from Piedmont this very day for your home garrison. Upon your return to barracks, you are to correct this alarming deficiency. Good day to you, sir.'

Rizzoli saluted. As he turned his horse towards his chasseurs, Rizzoli pierced Jobert with a bitter glare.

Chapter Thirteen

'Good afternoon, sir,' de Chabenac said to someone approaching over Jobert's shoulder.

Jobert turned to see Rizzoli striding through the icy slush in the village square.

'Jobert,' Rizzoli asked, 'am I correct in understanding you are a close acquaintance of General Victor?'

'We met during the siege of Toulon, sir,' Jobert said. 'We fought together at Dego in '96 and at Rivoli nearly two years ago.'

'It is reasonable to assume you informed him as to how best to disgrace the regiment.'

'On the contrary, sir, I was adamant that General Victor request the simplest of tasks for such untrained troops.'

Rizzoli raised a rigid finger towards Jobert's face. 'My chasseurs are not untrained.'

'In the time it takes for every man to fire one round, your soldiers have shot five of themselves. You have not trained your men for the tasks required of them.'

'That is not my role, that is the job of captains. You are the architect of the trap which led to the deaths of my men.'

'You ordered your chasseurs to fire,' Jobert said, 'not I. What steps had you taken to ensure—'

'Enough!' Rizzoli held up a firm palm. 'Your insolence is unbearable. Your long, sour face. Always picking fault.'

'You are so determined to despise me, sir, we are incapable of conversing on any matter. What I observe is fine chasseurs being led to their destruction by officers too idle to educate themselves.'

Rizzoli turned away and then back again. 'For all your supposed experience, you are a great disappointment.'

'Sir, may I warn you—'

Rizzoli leaned toward Jobert. 'Do you now threaten me, sir?'

'—warn you of a threat to the regiment on our march to home barracks.'

Rizzoli turned away.

Jobert lowered his voice. 'Please, sir.'

Rizzoli kept his back to Jobert. 'What threat?'

Jobert glanced at the locked shutters on the stone buildings surrounding the square. 'I have a strong sense we are being tracked by Piedmontese partisans.'

Rizzoli spun on his heel to face Jobert. 'Who? Partisans! Bandits at best. Why would peasants track us?'

'To kill. To plunder.'

'Do you share this opinion, de Chabenac?'

De Chabenac glanced sideways at Jobert. 'I feel these suspicions warrant attention.'

'And if we humour ourselves with these suspicions,' Rizzoli nodded to de Chabenac, 'Jobert, what attention might you warrant?'

'Enhance security, sir. Move the troops out of the villages and dispersed farms. Concentrate in a regimental camp.'

'A camp? Where?'

Jobert swept his arm wide toward the bare-limbed orchards. 'In any open field surrounding the village.'

'That is your experienced solution? To bivouac in the mud of an alpine December.'

'It is the first step of—'

'Enough!' Rizzoli turned and walked away.

Jobert exhaled a long breath of steam.

De Chabenac shuffled beside Jobert. 'You are aware, sir, that the regiment blames you for ...'

Jobert gripped his hands behind his back. 'Perhaps the vilification of me will finally unite the squadrons above their petty regional differences.'

De Chabenac checked who was in hearing distance. 'The regiment is ashamed of their performance in front of Victor.'

'That performance may well generate shame,' Jobert said. 'For in front of the kaiserliks, that performance will generate their destruction.'

As Jobert turned and walked away, D'Onofrio emerged from the door of Rizzoli's evening headquarters. Glimpsing Jobert, D'Onofrio turned and increased his stride.

'Captain D'Onofrio,' Jobert asked, 'may I have a moment of your time?'

D'Onofrio's shoulders slumped before he turned to face Jobert. 'Sir?'

'Were any of the men wounded from your company?'

D'Onofrio's face soured. 'Thankfully, none, sir.'

'Are you one of those who believe I deliberately designed the injury of those chasseurs?'

D'Onofrio clenched his jaw as he looked towards the stables.

'Can your Mantuans fire two volleys mounted?' Jobert asked.

D'Onofrio's fierce eyes returned to Jobert. 'Yes, sir.'

'And what of the Brescia Company when it joins your

squadron?'

D'Onofrio shook his head at the ground.

'Why is that? Your previous regiment were highly skilled with their musketoons. I experienced that mastery at Finale Ligure. What malaise grips this regiment?'

D'Onofrio shuffled in the mud. 'I do not know, sir.'

Jobert leaned close. 'Bullshit!'

D'Onofrio winced as he sought solace on the rooves over Jobert's shoulder.

'How are those men who were wounded?'

'Their injuries have not soured, sir. A greater contagion – our corrupted morale – crawls through our ranks.'

Jobert sneered. 'Perhaps attach a section of dragoons to the regiment to shame the men into soldierly discipline?'

'Will that be all, sir?' D'Onofrio asked.

'Fractures within the regiment, D'Onofrio. Not the best condition to receive a strike from the enemy, would you agree?'

D'Onofrio squinted at Jobert. 'An enemy strike, sir. Who? The Piedmontese Legion?'

'Piedmontese partisans, more likely,' Jobert said. 'Where is your company tonight?'

'We have been billeted in the town.'

Jobert leaned toward D'Onofrio and lowered his voice. 'Have you established a guard force capable of assembling and mounting swiftly? If you are attacked here, are you aware of any other company ready to come to your aid? Do you have orders to be prepared to march to the aid of another company under attack?'

D'Onofrio looked worried.

Jobert assumed a look of nonchalance. 'Would my questions have been out of place in your previous regiment?'

'No, sir.'

Fazio marched up, cracked to a halt and gave a brisk salute

to D'Onofrio. 'Excuse me, sir. Sentries posted.'

'May I ask tonight's password, Sergeant?' Jobert asked.

Fazio shot a look of enquiry to D'Onofrio. D'Onofrio nodded. 'The challenge is "horse". The response is "shoe".'

'The same as last night? Is that wise?'

Fazio gritted his teeth.

Jobert evaluated Fazio. 'Sergeant, here in this Piedmontese village, have you noticed a lack of men between the ages of fifteen and fifty?'

Fazio's eyes flashed to Jobert.

Jobert smiled. 'As have I. What does your gut tell you?'

Fazio glanced sourly at D'Onofrio. 'We are walking into an ambush.'

By the next afternoon, following a day's march by the regiment, Jobert entered the next town's mayoral house where Rizzoli had established his headquarters.

Zenari smothered a laugh as he walked past Jobert. 'At least I will not be cowering in the mud afraid of Piedmontese peasants.'

Jobert turned on his heel and watched Zenari's departure.

De Chabenac coughed at his elbow. 'I did not see you during the march today, sir. Where did your investigations lead you?'

'Koschak and I rode at the rear of the column,' Jobert said. 'Along the length of the march, I counted six pairs of boys, with bundles of kindling, sitting by the side of the road as our column passed.'

'Obliged to collect firewood in December, surely?'

'I saw clear enough that four of the six pairs either kept neat bundles of twigs between their feet or they whittled branches, each stick with cut notches along their lengths.'

De Chabenac frowned.

'They are counting us, de Chabenac.'

De Chabenac slid his hands behind his back. 'Perhaps tonight we can unburden ourselves of our concerns. We have been received by a company of Piedmontese fusiliers.'

Jobert frowned with alarm. 'Received?'

De Chabenac raised his eyebrows in surprise. 'The Piedmontese are not our enemies. These fellows march to Turin. They have promised a reception this evening for our regiment's officers.'

Jobert looked about him. 'Does that not sound suspicious? Remember Masséna had us host the Neapolitan dragoons in Villafranca in mid-'96. We poured wine down their throats while we milked them for information. With their guts full of grappa tonight, how will our officers react to any midnight attack. Where is the reception to be held?'

'The fusiliers have foregone their billets in the village and have invited us to a farm along the north-western Turin road.'

Jobert scowled. 'Within the confines of their encampment?'

'No, they are billeted in farms on the north-eastern road.'

An inner door opened. Rizzoli and two blue-coated infantry officers emerged. The officers took their leave, placing on their embroidered mitre caps, before saluting Rizzoli and departing.

Rizzoli noted Jobert's presence and moved swiftly to re-enter his inner office and close the door.

'Grenadiers!' Jobert said. 'They are not fusiliers, de Chabenac, but grenadiers. The fiercest men in their battalion. Utterly delighted, I am sure, that their homeland has been overrun by the French, their king fled into exile, and now loathsome Lombardians waddle along their roads gorging themselves on the spoils.'

De Chabenac attempted to mask his concerns with his urbane smile. 'Sir, I have never doubted your soldierly wisdom. But is it possible the isolation you feel here in the regiment is souring your disposition?'

Jobert's head swivelled towards his friend. 'Are you accusing me of imagining phantom threats?'

De Chabenac held up both hands. 'Do you feel you are observing our march home with undue concern?'

'Do I anguish at our situation?' Jobert threw up his hands. 'Tell me, de Chabenac, how will Rizzoli and Zenari act should an enemy strike? The regiment is moments away from its first enemy engagement. The men are enraged with their recent embarrassing volleys and vent their frustrations by brawling with each other in the streets, to which Rizzoli disperses the companies in case they attack each other.'

De Chabenac maintained his gaze of concern.

Jobert gripped de Chabenac's shoulder. 'I shall not attend the grenadiers' reception. I am sure Rizzoli would not extend an invitation to me. I strongly suggest, brother, you also submit your apologies for this evening. Again, my camp tonight will be in a field as suits my imagined threats. As ever, you are welcome to join me.'

Later that evening, an explosion of musketry woke Jobert like a kick in the guts.

He rolled out of his blankets, leaned groggily against his trap's wheel, checked his musketoon was cocked and stared into the darkness. The shuffling and snickering of disturbed horses obscured his ability to listen to the night.

Clouds covered a waning moon. Tendrils of river fog crept across the surrounding stubble and slid blades of ice into Jobert's abdomen. The musket fire continued but at some distance to the south.

Satisfied his camp was not under immediate assault, Jobert buttoned up his cape. 'Piquet, report.'

'I have not detected any movement near us,' said Koschak from the darkness. 'We are not the target. I am not sure which farm is being attacked as I cannot see muzzle flashes. I believe it to be the Bologna and Modena Companies' farm beyond the village south from us.'

'Koschak and Tulloc,' Jobert said, 'we will patrol towards the firing. No sabres, one pistol in your waist sashes. Tulloc, sling your rifle. Moench, Orlande, and Quandalle, secure the camp. No fire, no smoking. Maintain a double-staggered piquet that changes on the hour.'

Jobert led his patrol, Koschak and Tulloc on his flanks behind him, out into the mud and the fog. 'We will set a route that keeps clear of the farms,' he whispered.

A long whistle blast pierced the night.

Musketoons cocked and with fingers on their triggers, Jobert, Koschak and Tulloc knelt on the ice-hard earth and listened.

The firing stopped.

'They are waiting to see how the chasseurs react,' Jobert said, slipping his finger out of his trigger guard. 'Whether a patrol emerges from the farm or reserves arrive from elsewhere.'

They continued their patrol until, in the mist ahead, loomed the outline of trees.

'The Turin-Milan road,' Koschak said.

They sank to their knees and listened. Within the dark tree line, slung equipment clanked, gravel crunched beneath booted feet and instructions were hissed.

'Infantry on the road,' Koschak said. 'They are setting ambushes for chasseur patrols.'

Jobert growled in agreement. 'Let us report to the mayor's house in the village. If his throat has not been slit, Rizzoli ought to have returned from his grenadier's dinner.'

Creeping parallel to the tree line, well away from the road, the patrol moved towards the village.

A firearm cocked in the darkness ahead. 'Halt. Who goes?'

'The Cisalpine Republic,' Jobert replied. 'A foot patrol to report to Colonel Rizzoli. May I advance?'

'No, Stay there.'

'Sergeant Fazio sets tonight's password. What is the word you must challenge me with?'

'I do not ... just shut up and wait.'

Voices mumbled in the gloom.

'Horse.' It was Fazio.

'Shit,' Koschak whispered. 'D'Onofrio needs to change his password.'

'Shoe,' Jobert responded to Fazio. 'Sergeant Fazio, it is Lieutenant Colonel Jobert reporting to Colonel Rizzoli.'

A firearm cocked.

A storm of musketry unleashed on one farm. The lightning flashes lit up the bank of fog.

'You pissing idiot, Fazio,' Koschak's anger rattled his musketoon in the dark. 'The Bologna and Modena Companies are being struck again. There is no time to waste.'

'Fazio, listen to me,' Jobert said. 'The enemy is firing on our squadrons. Now is not the time for your bullshit.'

'Advance one and be recognised,' Fazio said.

Jobert remained still. 'Make safe your weapon, Fazio.'

'Why would I do that, Jobert? You are my enemy.'

'Really? You shot at me in Bologna. You marched me to the cells in Mantua. Are your grievances not sufficiently satisfied that we cannot see off this immediate attack?'

A hammer was released forward with a dull clack.

Jobert approached the dark outlines of Fazio and his sentry. Jobert found Fazio easily enough due to the alcohol on his breath. 'Be patient, Fazio, there will come a time to settle our differences. I promise you.'

Jobert and his flanking shadows moved along the road, into the town and arrived at the headquarters.

At headquarters, Jobert found D'Onofrio and the captain of the Brescia Company standing motionless as Zenari struggled to pull on his boots.

'D'Onofrio, have the Mantua and Brescia stand to arms.' Zenari fumbled with the clasp of his sword belt. 'We shall counterattack.'

'A mounted charge, sir?' D'Onofrio glanced at Jobert. 'On a night like this? We will be shot out of the saddle.'

Zenari drank deeply from a wooden mug. 'Do not challenge my orders. We must do something.'

'D'Onofrio, where is Colonel Rizzoli?' Jobert asked.

'He has not returned from the Piedmontese dinner, sir.'

Jobert sighed as he turned to Zenari. 'May I suggest, Major Zenari—'

Zenari clacked the empty mug on the table and attempted to stand. 'Thank you ... sir, but that will not be necessary.'

Jobert stepped towards Zenari. 'Shut up and listen, man.'

Zenari plopped back into his seat.

'Tonight is your regiment's first engagement with an enemy. An enemy cloaked in fog on a moonless night. An enemy that holds the roads between the farms. Indeed, your first affair under fire, Zenari. At least, listen to my suggestion.'

Zenari shrugged. 'How do you know these peasants control the roads?'

'Because I have already conducted a silent dismounted patrol as soon as the firing began.'

D'Onofrio's eyes widened as he regarded Jobert.

Jobert turned to D'Onofrio and the captain commanding the Brescia Company. 'Send Brescia to disrupt the attack on the farms and to confirm our communication with them. Best patrol dismounted. Best without sabres. Stay off the roads as Piedmontese ambushes await. D'Onofrio, hold your Mantuans as a fresh reserve.'

D'Onofrio nodded his agreement to the captain of the Brescia Company.

'There may be wounded in the farms,' Jobert continued. 'Take the regimental surgeon.'

D'Onofrio's face creased with frustration. 'The surgeon is another senior officer not returned—'

A roll of drumming sounded outside.

'Go now, D'Onofrio, swiftly,' Jobert said.

The officers jostled to exit the room. Outside, Koschak strained to identify a location of the noise reverberating off the stone walls of the village. 'The drums approach along the north-east road.'

'The grenadiers,' Jobert said. 'Are they attacking?'

Winding between the stone houses marched half a company of grenadiers, bearing lit torches. They halted in the small piazza. Their commander, a lieutenant, approached and saluted Jobert. 'We heard firing, sir. We marched immediately. Shall I set my troops in a defensive perimeter around the town?'

'Where is the rest of your company, lieutenant?' Jobert asked. 'Where is your captain?'

'The other half-company is encamped further way. They are an hour behind us. Our officers were at the reception.'

The sound of distant musketry increased.

'A second farm,' Koschak said. 'That containing the Ravenna and Ferrara Companies, is now under attack.'

'Shall we secure the north-east road we marched in on?' asked the grenadier lieutenant.

'Yes, do that.' Jobert spun towards Zenari, who wobbled with inebriation. 'Zenari?'

'Yes?'

'Tie-in the grenadier's defence with D'Onofrio's chasseurs. Can you do that?'

Zenari smiled. 'Anything else … sir?'

'The attacks are against two of the three billet-farms. I shall take my patrol on the western road to the third farm containing the Milan and Cremona Companies. I shall report back.'

'Do not let me … detain you.' Zenari re-entered the headquarters and slammed the door.

Jobert stiffened as the sound of a dungeon door's lock clanked in his memory.

Next morning, the grating caws of ravens acknowledged the dawn twilight.

Jobert and his staff, their cart and horses, passed through the outer sentries and wound their way through the village lanes. As the team set up a breakfast camp between the buttresses of the church, Jobert and Koschak reported to Rizzoli's headquarters.

Jobert entered the mayor's house to find a press of tired and muddy officers. Jobert squeezed through them to de Chabenac. 'Casualties?'

De Chabenac grimaced. 'Three dead and eight wounded.'

'Any Piedmontese found on the field?'

De Chabenac shook his head.

Rizzoli and Zenari emerged from an inner room.

'Not today, Jobert,' Rizzoli said on seeing Jobert in the crowd. 'I will not accept your criticisms today.'

'Ah, Lieutenant Colonel Jobert,' Zenari said, 'once the smoke clears and the bodies collected, he emerges for—'

Jobert stepped forward, his finger pointed at Zenari's face. 'I will not—'

Zenari fumbled with his cuff to draw a dagger.

With an open hand, Jobert slapped down on the dagger, sending it spinning across the floor. Jobert then reversed his swing and unleashed a sharp backhand to Zenari's jowl.

Zenari's head whipped back, and he stumbled to his knees.

'Jobert!' gasped Rizzoli.

Jobert looked down at Zenari wiping blood from his mouth. 'On your feet, Zenari, battle fatigues us all. Do not allow weariness to undo your soldierly discipline.'

The room was silent. Some faces expressed shock. Some faces expressed delight. No one assisted Zenari to his feet.

Zenari wiped the drool from his lips. 'Jobert weakened the defences of the town by—'

D'Onofrio stepped forward. 'The timely patrol by the Brescia Company broke the attacks on both southern farms.'

'D'Onofrio,' Jobert asked, 'how many of the Brescians were lost?

'Two wounded, sir.'

Koschak grinned. 'A dismounted company patrol by night fared better than a mounted regimental volley by day.'

'Shut up, Koschak!' Rizzoli swept the air with curled fingers. 'I will not accept ...' Rizzoli slumped and ran his long fingers across his thick, queued hair. His voice wavered as he rubbed his forehead and groaned. 'Enough.'

Surely not a hangover, sir, thought Jobert.

'Permission to speak, Gentlemen.' The regimental wagonmaster stomped to attention. His erect posture and unwavering stare at a point on the opposite wall identified him to Jobert as ex-Austrian army.

Rizzoli ignored him.

'Yes, Captain,' Jobert said.

'Were any wagons relocated during the night to reinforce the defence of the town, sir?'

'Zenari?' Jobert asked.

Zenari spat blood on the floor towards Jobert's boots. 'I have no idea.'

'Why, Captain?' Jobert asked.

The wagonmaster stiffened even further. 'I am unable to locate nine wagons.'

Jobert spun towards the man. 'Are you missing drivers and teams, or just wagons?'

'Just the vehicles, sir.'

'What were their loads?'

The wagonmaster thrust his chin out further. 'Five regimental drays holding ammunition, brandy and horseshoes, a regimental forge-caisson and three company carts of tentage.'

Jobert bared his teeth. 'Where were the wagons last seen?'

'Drivers and teams were billeted around two taverns on the north-east road. I had—'

'The north-east road!' Jobert clenched his fists. 'The road along which the grenadiers were billeted.'

'D'Onofrio,' de Chabenac asked, 'do the grenadiers still occupy their defensive positions within the town?'

D'Onofrio frowned. 'What grenadiers, sir?'

Jobert spun towards Zenari. 'The grenadiers that Major Zenari ...' Jobert hung his head and rubbed his eyes. 'The grenadiers and the partisans worked together. The theft of our wagons was the target of their attacks.'

'What target, Jobert?' Rizzoli said. 'I do not understand.'

Chapter Fourteen
January 1799, Lucca, Italy

Under the clawed branches of winter-stripped trees, the frigid air pressed wafts of smoke from the blacksmith's forge. In the whirl of smoke, Jobert caught the sharp smell of roasting chestnuts. Across the frozen river in a snow-bound wagon park, oxen could be heard lowing.

As he adjusted his woollen scarf within his cape, Jobert reflected on what had brought him to this winter scene. Upon return from Piedmont, the Army of Italy was tasked with ejecting the British fleet from the port of Livorno. In the Apennine ranges above Livorno nestled the city of Lucca. The French troops were subsequently ordered to strip the vulnerable city of its wealth.

The Cisalpine Chasseurs and Jobert were now employed around a crossroad junction four kilometres east of Lucca, on the road north to Modena. That crossroad lay beside the River Serchio where one road emanated from the junction, crossed a timber bridge and ran to the village of Il Colle. Between the village and the bridge, on a rutted field churned to icy slop, a wagon park had been established. On the hills east of the crossroad, the road twisted to ascend to the Villa Reale di Marlia, where pillaged goods were recorded, bundled and stored before shipment.

The Mantua Company stood guard at four vedettes around the crossroads. Two posts north and south on the Lucca-Modena road, one west of the Serchio bridge and one beside a wayside shrine as the road climbed to the villa.

In a corner of the crossroads, with its back to the frozen river and the wagon park, a blacksmith's forge was tucked snug beside the bridge. Jobert ducked his head and reentered the heat of the low-roofed shelter. Within the warm smithy, Moench tootled his continuous fife practice.

Bloody Figaro!

'What, sir?' Moench's grin responded to Jobert's scowl. 'Everybody loves Figaro. The lads. The villagers.'

Tucked in tight beside the forge, Koschak reclined on a folding camp chair with a Parisian broadsheet angled to a stub of candle. Koschak poured a cup of *tuaca* wine and handed it to Jobert. 'A liar, a thief, a rogue. What is not to love?'

'You describe the aspiration of every Italian chasseur.' Jobert savoured the citrus wine. 'Anything of interest?'

Koschak squinted as he adjusted his vision up from the paper. 'This new Army of Naples has occupied Naples. The declaration of a Neapolitan republic has caused a local uprising.'

Beside the glowing forge, D'Onofrio peeled the charcoal shell of a chestnut with his gloved fingers, before popping the doughy-tasting dumpling in his mouth. 'New year's greetings, sir.' D'Onofrio puffed around the scalding heat of the chestnut to form his words.

'And my best wishes for the new year to you, D'Onofrio. Are your guard posts set?'

'They are, sir. Do you know if we have been successful at

chasing the British fleet out of Livorno?'

'I believe so,' Jobert said.

'And your views of General Sérurier's current orders, sir?'

'To strip Lucca of her wealth?'

D'Onofrio's face soured as he gulped the remains of his snack.

'If you want to be paid for your services,' Jobert said, 'and feed your men and horses, then a necessary requirement.'

'Here, sir.' Koschak poured a cup of tuaca and passed it to D'Onofrio. 'It will help you swallow it all the better.'

'What? The chestnut or the task?'

Koschak gave a wicked grin.

Jobert plucked a chestnut from the forge's coals and began to peel the shell with gloved fingers. 'How many of your company deserted on our return from Piedmont?'

'I lost over twenty men. A platoon's worth.'

'A quarter of your company.' Jobert hissed through his teeth.

'Not as bad as other companies, sir,' D'Onofrio said. 'What broke their spirit was the order on Christmas Day to join General Sérurier's column immediately. I marched with a troop, with the remainder in barracks regathering those who have absconded. It has been a bitter tonic for those designated to march far from home's hearth.'

'Every company searches for its lost men,' said Jobert through gulps of air around his burning morsel. 'Only a troop from each has deployed. That tonic is spooned liberally throughout the regiment. Do your lads who remain with the standard still grieve their losses at the hands of the Piedmontese partisans?'

D'Onofrio searched the bottom of his cup. 'That still galls. But now a fresh barb pricks them. There is a bitter mood throughout the regiment. News of our shame with the volley exercise outside Turin has reached other units within this column to Livorno. Their taunts are a shower of sparks on powder.'

Koschak stood from the anvil stump and turned his backside to the forge. 'That would explain Colonel Rizzoli's orders for capes, no plumes and oilskin covers over mirlitons to hide our facings.'

'To hide our shame,' D'Onofrio said. 'To deny us our pride. He would have us bury our *tri-couleur* under a mound of horse ...' D'Onofrio hung his head. 'Forgive me, sir. Would you excuse me?' D'Onofrio shuffled around the anvil blocks to move outside.

This morning, across the road from the smithy, the village priest stood by a wayside shrine blessing those who passed. A column of six empty wagons with a mounted escort from the Modena troop had descended from the villa and halted by the shrine. Steam swirled from the rumps and nostrils of horses and bullocks. The men dismounted their vehicles and mounts to receive a blessing. Should a congregation of passing troops gather, the blacksmith's son would hawk a basket of roasted chestnuts. Some knelt receiving their benediction, some rifled through their pockets to find coins for the scalding tidbit.

A shout alerted Jobert to another column of wagons approaching D'Onofrio's southern guard post from Lucca. The carts were laden with appropriated stocks of leather, fabric, felt and shoes to be sorted and baled in the villa's temporary warehouse.

The escort were chasseurs from the Ferrara troop. Led by their sergeant, a group of Ferrarese chasseurs strode towards the Modena men at the shrine.

Shouting erupted. 'Unblock the lane to the villa, you dumb Modenese bastards!' Ferrarese complaints were based upon the weariness of their wagon teams, the pervasive cold, and the unloading task ahead.

'Trouble.' Jobert drained his cup. 'Koschak, fetch D'Onofrio.' The surly Ferrarese troopers formed a phalanx behind their sergeant. The Modenese men stepped forward, arms loose, fists clenched.

'Fuck you, you Ferrarese turd,' called the sergeant of the Modena escort, 'or we will shoot you properly!' Jobert winced at the reference to a Ferrarese casualty during the volley exercise.

'Is that fucking right?' A right cross was thrown. The Modenese sergeant reeled backwards.

Unable to see D'Onofrio, Jobert bellowed, 'Sergeant Fazio, stand the guard to.'

Around the shrine, a melee of over a dozen men erupted. Swinging fists. A flurry of capes. Civilian drivers shoved to protect the priest and themselves from the barrage of blows. Chestnuts and mirlitons flew. Men grunted and fell. A flash of a booted stomp.

'Guard, by the left, double march.' Fazio and a dozen Mantuan sentries trotted for the brawl, as more Modena and Ferrara men abandoned their convoys at the sprint to join the fray.

'Now stop this bullshit,' Fazio cried. 'Stop, you fucking idiots!'

'Stop this, you Mantuan prick!' A punch from the crowd struck Fazio. He flew back and tripped on his scabbard. His Mantuan chasseurs bellowed as they drove their musketoon stocks into faces and ribs.

A scream.

'Shit! The bastard has pulled a knife.'

The near thirty combatants froze. Some caped figures knelt around a fallen whimpering comrade.

Jobert strode towards the melee. 'Koschak, D'Onofrio, on me! Cisalpine, stand fast!'

'You miserable prick!'

A pistol shot.

A hiss of pain.

The men pointed at the firer and howled abuse at each other.

Jobert drew his sabre. 'Stand fast! Silence! Sergeants, back away and call your men to you. Now!'

A circle of bruised faces smeared with blood and spasming with hatred surrounded Jobert, Koschak and D'Onofrio.

'Well, look here. Chestnuts in the fire.' One soldier looked to Fazio. 'Let us finish the French shits.'

Fazio hesitated to contemplate.

'Stand fast!' With his hilt in front of his face, Jobert stared down the length of his curved blade. 'I will run through any man who draws a blade or lifts his pistol.'

Koschak's and D'Onofrio's blades carved a wide circle around the two sobbing wounded.

Jobert's blade tip aimed at Fazio's chest. 'The wounded to the smithy now, Sergeant Fazio. Corporal Cieno, fetch the surgeon.'

A half-smile creased Fazio's swollen cheek. 'The fun is over, boys. Fall in!'

That evening, in the village church, Jobert and de Chabenac stood further along the side wall than the near sixty regimental officers and sergeants. Zenari, standing at the right of the line, called the assembly to attention.

Rizzoli swept through the entrance doors and marched down the nave. He appeared thinner, his face lined, his tailcoat looser. Rizzoli genuflected towards the altar before turning to his commanders standing rigid against the wall.

'Gentlemen,' Rizzoli said, 'chasseurs wounded from regional feuding has only brought more shame upon the regiment's good name,' Rizzoli said. 'From an auspicious beginning, our regiment was bound for glory. However, we are now beset by misfortune. I am reminded of Prince Eugene of Savoy when ...'

Jobert stared beyond Rizzoli. *A unit reflects its commander. How would I fix this mess?*

Rizzoli continued his address. 'I demand you restore discipline and good order in your companies. We have failed to identify the chasseur who drew his pistol and wounded his comrade.' Zenari glared at the audience from his position at the end of the line. 'We are blessed that both ball and blade did not rip deep. In the future, I will commit each miscreant guilty of shaming the regiment's honour to the road gangs. Furthermore, the man's sergeants and sergeant majors will be discharged forthwith.'

Jobert looked along the back ranks of sergeants and sergeant majors. These older men's faces seethed with offence and injustice, with Fazio's face sourer than most.

'I am severely disappointed. That is all.' Rizzoli moved towards the church's vestibule. 'Carry on.'

'Officers,' Zenari called, 'to your duties. Regimental Sergeant Major, carry on.'

D'Onofrio raised a hand. 'Excuse me, sir.'

'No, D'Onofrio,' Zenari said, 'the colonel's orders will not be questioned. That is all.'

Jobert's face twisted with disappointment. He reached forward and touched D'Onofrio's arm. 'War will be upon your squadron in one hundred days, D'Onofrio. Focus on your squadron. Do everything you can to prepare. If you need to speak, I will listen.'

As they left the church, Jobert nudged de Chabenac. 'We desire them men of Verona, but they insist on remaining Montagues and Capulets.'

De Chabenac swung his head slowly towards Jobert, his mouth agape.

'What?' Jobert appeared offended. 'Have you never heard me utter a literary reference before.'

'Ah, no, no,' de Chabenac said. 'I am impressed … as to how profoundly apt it is and how I must commend your tutoress when next we meet.'

Chapter Fifteen

A few days later, Jobert rode with the Mantua troop escorting empty wagons up to the warehouses at the villa. In a fog of exhaled breath, horses stepped short on the iced ruts. Ahead of Jobert on the bridge, the Milanese sentries stomped their frozen feet and shrugged deeper into capes. Many had their blankets crusted with ice around their shoulders.

Moving out of the wagon park, the Mantuan column had pulled over to the verge to allow a column of Ferrara troop, on their way to conduct a guard relief at the post up at the villa, to pass the slower vehicles. As the Ferrara troop walked their remounts onto the bridge, derisive laughter was heard from the dozen bridge guards.

'Piss on that, you Milanese turds!' The Ferrarese chasseurs leapt from their saddles and assaulted the mocking guards.

'Stand to arms, Milan!' The guards from their posts around the crossroads ran to their comrades' aid.

'Stand fast, Mantua!' called Jobert. He swivelled in his saddle and thrust an accusatory gloved finger at Fazio. 'Not a move.'

Jobert jerked at the sound of trotting hooves and the clacking of scabbards on spurs. One of General Sérurier's aides, with an escort of two dragoons, clattered into the crossroads.

Some of the chasseurs slowed their grappling and wild swings to appraise the mounted party. The young officer, aghast at the scene of brawling troops, spun his horse and, with smirking dragoons following, cantered back south towards Lucca.

Jobert lifted Jaune and entered the fight at the trot. Jobert aimed Jaune's shoulders at scuffling chasseurs. Men were knocked to the ground. They scrambled and scattered at Jaune's momentum. 'Stand fast, all ranks. Moench, sound Figaro.'

A gloved hand flashed from under a cape at Jaune's reins.

Jobert kicked the hand away. 'Moench, Figaro! The first bars of the overture.' By dropping his hip and twisting his toe outwards, Jaune spun his rump and bowled the chasseur over. 'You play it often enough. Sound it now.'

Moench closed his eyes, nodded the tune in his head, then blew into his trumpet. The fighters jerked at the loud, familiar tune. Moench played it again with gusto. The chasseurs stepped apart bemused.

'Listen to me, you stupid bastards!' Jobert called. 'The general's dragoons will be upon us. Either shut up and obey me now or roll up your trouser leg and make ready to receive your chains.'

Sullen men spread their attention between Jobert above them and their rivals beside them. 'Listen in, Sergeants. Regiment, on parade! Form a single troop rank either side of the road. Mantua to the east. Ferrara to the west. Mount! Milan guard, form a single rank dismounted in front of the horses, half guard east, half guard west.' Along the road to the south a trumpet sounded Trot March. 'The dragoons and the commanding general are coming. Move!'

With grumbled curses and hands brushing mud from knees,

men ran for their horses. Sergeants shouted to set markers.

'Stow capes and oilskins. Let us reveal our pride.' Jobert thrust a pointed finger at the lead driver of the wagon convoy. 'Not a word.' The driver bowed his head, raised his hands in submission and leaned back in his seat.

'Bernasconi, take post as parade commander, front and centre.' Jobert took post to the right rear of Bernasconi. 'Draw sabres and shoulder arms.'

Bernasconi gave the commands as a troop of forty dragoons came along the road, their dragoon muskets on their thighs, hammers cocked. The dragoons halted before entering the defile of ramrod straight chasseurs.

'Pass through, Captain.' Jobert barked at the suspicious dragoon commander. 'Make way for the general to receive our salute.'

The dragoons moved through the Cisalpine formation at the walk.

General Sérurier and his staff approached at the walk. Jobert glanced to confirm Rizzoli was in the party. 'Bernasconi, general salute.' Jobert whispered.

'Cisalpine Chasseurs, general salute. Salute!' cried Bernasconi.

'Thank you, Lieutenant.' General Sérurier halted and accepted the salute. He acknowledged Jobert with a nod. 'I heard that assistance might be required at your post, but I must have been misinformed.'

'Bernasconi, invite the general to inspect the troops,' Jobert said.

'Would you care to inspect the troops, sir?'

General Sérurier spoke with sufficient volume for the assembled soldiers to hear. 'Your invitation honours me but my duties at the villa preclude me from inspecting your men more closely. The fine reputation of the Cisalpine Chasseurs is well known throughout the Army of Italy. From here I observe the fine dress and bearing for which your regiment is renowned. Men of Cisalpine, I commend your steadfastness. Thank you for the honour you pay me. I bid you a new year bountiful of glory. As storm clouds gather, I am heartened we stand together.' Sérurier bowed his head.

'Bernasconi, general salute.'

'Regiment, general salute. Salute!'

Sérurier's party followed the dragoons east up the villa road.

'Regiment, attention!' As Rizzoli approached, the dismounted guard shouldered arms and the mounted chasseurs completed the movement of the salute so that their sabre pommels rested on their right thighs.

'Bernasconi, salute and invite the colonel to inspect the troops.'

'Silence, Bernasconi!' Rizzoli hissed. 'Piss on your inspection. The general's aide reported a brawl to the general. This is unforgiveable. I want names. I want names now.'

'Ah ...' Bernasconi's chest rose and fell. 'Ah—'

'The aide was wrong, sir.' Jobert narrowed his eyes at Rizzoli. 'I am at a loss to explain his report. Your chasseurs have been performing their duties in an exemplary manner all morning. I have seen nothing to fault. The Milan troop man the crossroad vedettes. The Ferrara troop are proceeding to the villa for a guard handover. The Mantua troop are escorting empty wagons into Lucca, sir.'

Rizzoli's eyes swept across the ranks on either side of the road, stopping on those soldiers who attempted to snort dribbling blood back into their bruised noses. Rizzoli's moustache betrayed his demeanour. Beads of sweat oozed from the brow of his mirliton. He swallowed hard. 'Is this the truth, Bernasconi?'

Bernasconi pressed back his shoulders. 'Yes, sir.'

Rizzoli shortened his reins and squeezed his mount into a

trot to follow Sérurier.

'Regiment, regimental salute. Salute!' Jobert and Bernasconi swept up their blades in unison as the chasseurs' sabres followed their movements and musketoons rattled to present arms.

Across the road, Fazio thrust out his stubbled chin and gave Jobert a wicked sneer.

The light was dimming rapidly under the leaden clouds when Jobert, Koschak and Moench, inside the blacksmith's hut, heard shouts of alarm.

Guards from the Bologna troop sprinted towards the bridge.

A chasseur ducked his head into the smithy. 'Where is the captain? A mob from the village is approaching the bridge.'

'Gentlemen, to horse,' Jobert said to Koschak and Moench.

As they rode across the bridge, bellows of rage and high-pitched wails were heard from the far end. A crowd of villagers had gathered.

A ragged explosion of shots was spat from within the throng.

Ahead of Jobert, two sentries fell. Spent balls zipped past.

'Partisans!' The Bologna troop assembled its guard and prepared to fire.

The mass of people retired into the gloom towards the village.

Coming abreast of the Bolognese captain, Jobert lifted his reins and sank his hips. Jaune halted within a stride. 'Bologna, remain at your post.' Jobert twisted in his saddle. 'Koschak, ride to the wagon park and ensure the Milan and Cremona Companies remain at their posts. Moench, ride to the villa.

Inform the commander there that the Modena Company must remain at its post. I will ride for Rizzoli's headquarters.'

As Jobert entered the village, smoke lay heavily on the evening air. Silhouetted by firelight, shapes of armed men, wearing bonnets de police and tailcoats, smashed through cottage doors. Weapons fired. Screams and the crackle of flames rebounded off stone walls. The church bell began to toll.

Jobert arrived in the central piazza. Men dashed with buckets from the pump. Wounded villagers were carried into the church. Women laden with baskets dragged crying children and bleating goats.

'Colonel Rizzoli is meeting with the priest in the church, sir,' said a headquarters sentry as Jobert passed him Jaune's reins.

De Chabenac hailed Jobert from the steps of the church. 'From what we understand, some soldiers from the reserve companies, Mantua and Brescia, have broken into a store of grappa. They have attacked some youths and threatened young women. The village men gathered and ran them out of town.'

Jobert peered about the chaos in the piazza. 'I have come from the bridge. A mob confronted the crossroads guard. They fired upon each other.'

De Chabenac nodded. 'Hence the cry of "Partisans!" through the town.'

'What is Rizzoli's plan?'

'The priest is urging the citizens to take refuge in the church. Rizzoli ...' de Chabenac shook his head. 'Rizzoli has taken to his prayers. There is no plan.'

'Zenari? D'Onofrio?' Jobert asked.

De Chabenac shrugged. 'Somewhere in the streets. The village we are defending is under attack from our own soldiers.'

'De Chabenac, can you arrange the regimental trumpeters to sound Assembly?' Jobert said. 'And send the regimental surgeons and the sergeant-veterinarians to the church.'

With a grim smile, de Chabenac hitched his scabbard to stride down the steps towards the headquarters.

Jobert moved to assist villagers seeking sanctuary. As they limped with burnt skin, bleeding faces and broken arms towards the shelter of the church, the villagers screamed, 'Take your filthy hands off him.' 'He has been killed protecting his children!' 'Shame!' 'Your soldiers are raping our daughters and burning our homes!'

As the trumpets, in their call for Assembly, pierced the shouts and the imploding rooves, de Chabenac rejoined Jobert.

With a clatter of iron-shod hooves on cobblestones, Koschak reported at the base of the steps. 'Milan and Cremona remain on guard at the wagon park. They are fearful of a partisan attack.'

Jobert peered at a few stragglers crossing the village square. 'Koschak, return to the wagon park. Tell the Milan troop that Rizzoli orders them to parade in the piazza.'

Gripping hammers, pitchforks and knives, able bodied men from the village gathered at the door to the church. A small group of officers and sergeant majors formed a line at the base of the stone steps.

D'Onofrio and Bernasconi appeared through the smoke, guiding terrified villagers, bent with sacks of belongings. A few local men snatched the people D'Onofrio and Bernasconi supported and swept them and their chattels into the church.

D'Onofrio dusted and straightened his tailcoat. 'Our disgrace has found a new low. A few drunks have interrupted the roasting of chestnuts. They beat the young men and forced themselves on the young women.'

'I smell Fazio,' Jobert said. 'I have sent for the Milan Company. And look who we have now.'

From the lanes and the shadows of the village, around forty drunken chasseurs formed a threatening crescent around the front of the church. Jobert saw Fazio in the centre of the mob.

Backing away from the pack, Zenari held his sabre and pistol. His spurs snagged on the cobblestones as he shuffled rearwards. He glanced over his shoulder and spun when he saw the village men on the top steps. Zenari brandished his pistol in a wild arc towards those securing the church's entry. 'Those partisans have stolen musketoons.'

The rioters and the defenders all jerked at the rattle of shod hooves in the lanes. Jobert grinned. 'Here is Koschak with the Milan Company.'

'Sergeant Major,' Zenari shouted to the Milanese sergeant major, 'there are the source of our shame.' Zenari swept his sabre at the soldiers. 'Shoot them.'

The miscreant soldiers, grubby from their pillaging, edged towards their shadows.

Jobert stepped forward and clapped his hand down hard on Zenari's shoulder. 'Silence, man. They are your soldiers. They are not the enemy.'

'Then who is the enemy?'

'No one here, you idiot.' Jobert looked to the line of mounted chasseurs. 'Sergeant major, assemble your men in the piazza. Have half dismount and protect the church.'

The sergeant major drew back his shoulders. 'May our Lord forgive us, sir. My men will not participate.'

'Why?' Jobert asked.

The sergeant major shook his head.

'Then march them back to the wagon park.'

'Is that your suggestion, Jobert?' Zenari rushed forward.

A thrown cobblestone arced out of the dark to strike Zenari on the chest. With a screech, he collapsed to the ground.

The hissing chasseurs in the piazza advanced. 'The arrogant prick deserves it.'

Fazio held out his arms. 'No, boys, no.'

With blade raised, Jobert stepped in front of Zenari's writhing body. 'D'Onofrio, recover him.'

D'Onofrio did not move.

'Get off me, you French bastard.' Zenari slapped at Jobert's legs.

Bernasconi dashed forward.

At the head of the church stairs, the defensive villagers parted as Rizzoli emerged from the church doors.

'I will punish these mutinous dogs.' Zenari flapped to recover his sabre as Bernasconi assisted him to stand.

Jobert turned and stomped on Zenari's blade. 'There are no bad soldiers, Zenari. Just bad officers.'

Jobert sheathed his sabre in a fluid movement then strode toward the gaggle of chasseurs. He raised the back of his hand and threatened to slap any chasseur brandishing a weapon or fist. Jobert grabbed Fazio by the lapels and dragged him out from the crowd.

Fazio exhaled grappa fumes at Jobert. 'Let me fucking go.' Fazio whipped a knife from his sash and jabbed it into Jobert's waistcoat.

'Gut me or not, Fazio, your choice. But listen!' Jobert shook Fazio like a limp sack. 'You are condemning your company to years in chains. All ringleaders will be shot by the next battalion to march through here. Is that what you want?'

The mobs' shoulders slumped. Their heads swivelled to gauge the shifting mood. Their fists and weapons fell to their sides.

'Tomorrow's sunrise will be your last, Fazio.' Jobert released Fazio's lapels with a flick of his fingers. 'I cannot imagine your imperial horse battery descending to such depravity.' Jobert leaned forward to Fazio, jabbed Fazio's chest with two rigid fingers. 'Where did that fine soldier go?'

Fazio searched the cobblestones.

'Milan and Brescia!' Jobert called to the subdued rioters. 'Form four ranks on Sergeant Fazio. Move!'

The chasseurs shuffled into formation.

Jobert turned towards the church, his eyes brimming with contempt for the dejected Rizzoli. 'Captain D'Onofrio, march your squadron back to their lines.

Chapter Sixteen
February 1799, Milan, Italy

Two weeks later, in a tavern in Milan, Jobert stood over the hearth in his rooms. He placed one of the envelopes Orlande had handed him on the mantlepiece and opened the other.

'Are Colonel Raive and his family quite well, sir?' Orlande asked.

With its contents digested, the letter wilted between Jobert's fingers. 'Raive writes of nothing to the contrary.'

'Unwelcome news then, sir?'

'Raive is offering me a colonelcy ...'

'And that is upsetting?'

'In the commissariat.'

Orlande straightened. 'Oh ... where would that base us, sir?'

Jobert reviewed the letter. 'Either Nice or Genoa.'

'Where does your concern lie, sir? The rank, the service or the location?'

Jobert peered at the swirling flames at his shins. 'Signorina Bernasconi.'

'You felt compelled towards Madame Marguerite based on

honour.' Orlande pushed his spectacles onto the bridge of his nose. 'With Signorina Gianna providing your alibi during the coup, are you now obligated by a sense of honour to her?'

'I can undo Gianna's shame through marriage, but my admiration for her is profound.'

'Unlike Madame Marguerite, the depth of your feelings for the signorina is most evident. I am delighted that you declare them aloud.'

Jobert inclined his head toward Orlande. 'Should I be considering establishing a household for her in Nice or Genoa?'

'Perhaps ... perhaps seek out how she views the situation between you both. If her response is favourable, ask her father's permission to marry and his views on where you might settle. If Nice or Genoa find approval with him, propose to the lady and respond to Colonel Raive.'

Jobert gripped Orlande's shoulder. 'Thank you.'

'May I be so impertinent to ask, sir ...'

Jobert folded Raive's letter and placed it in his inner coat pocket. 'Anything.'

'Have you reflected on Madame Marguerite's second child?'

'Neither Marguerite nor Raive had made any comment, nor has their attitude towards me changed. Both parents appear most happy with ... their child.'

'And you, sir?'

'If, Orlande ... if the child is mine, his situation is best where he is. As godfather and uncle, I shall keep my eye on the growth of both of Marguerite's sons.'

Jobert picked up the second letter to be received that day. It was addressed to Colonel Jobert, Army of Italy, Milan. Jobert flipped the envelope over.

Within the letter's red wax seal, a boar's head emerged, jaws agape and tusks prominent. Just this morning, Jobert had polished the same boar's face on his silver engraved pistol. He cracked the seal, opened the envelope, and sought the signature on the bottom of the short note.

Wolff von Maefeld!

I am coming, Jobert. Attend me. Have my father's pistol ready.

Jobert turned his back to Orlande and folded the note for his inner pocket.

One foe at a time.

Jobert picked up a book from his trunk. 'Orlande, is the household ready to depart for Mantua once my appointment with Colonel Rizzoli is complete?'

'We shall begin loading and saddling once you and Major de Chabenac depart.'

Jobert stepped out into the Milanese lane and espied de Chabenac tucked in the fragrant steam of a coffee house across the way. Jobert waved to his friend, who joined soon after. De Chabenac twisted his head to read the book's title tucked under Jobert's arm. 'You will proceed to Mantua once you have spoken to Rizzoli?'

Jobert nodded.

'How is everything between you and Gianna?' de Chabenac asked.

'I have not seen her since the coup affair in November. I presume ... I hope her affections remain.'

'And your primary motivation towards her continues to be love?'

Jobert stopped in the street, turned to de Chabenac and frowned.

De Chabenac raised his hands. 'You advanced towards marriage with Marguerite motivated by honour. I was just ...'

Jobert exhaled a long breath of steam. 'My feelings for Gianna are ... very strong.' He viewed the cart traffic, both foot and horse, in the street about him. 'What is the aftermath of Lucca?'

'Nine ringleaders will be sent in chains to the road gangs.'

'Fazio?'

'No.' De Chabenac tilted his head in concern. 'Why?'

'In the month that we returned from Piedmont and marched for Lucca,' Jobert said, 'the regiment has imploded.' Jobert shrugged as he began to walk. 'I have no control. I have no influence. This descent into madness is sickening. In my mind rages an endless debate. What potential exists for a fine body of men, brothers under the standard, bonded with pride in their glory? And the blame is laid at my feet. I am French. I suggested the volley firing exercise. I was aware of the Piedmontese partisans—'

De Chabenac raised a pointed finger. 'More than that, you brewed the grappa and tipped it down their throats that caused them to loot, rape and murder. All your fault, undoubtedly.' De Chabenac gave Jobert a stern glance. 'Rizzoli has been deflated as a result. Is this an opportunity to work with Rizzoli to rebuild the regiment? How will you re-establish yourself with Rizzoli?'

Jobert tapped his book. 'Perhaps Prince Eugene has the answer.'

They navigated around a dray loaded with firewood to cross the street.

'Are you aware of the reason for General Joubert's departure?' de Chabenac asked.

'Yet another general,' Jobert said. 'The shift of political alliances is always the reason.'

'Thoughts as to his replacement?'

'With Masséna embedded in Switzerland, I have heard Moreau might depart his command on the Rhine.'

'Have you heard that the Russians are now in the northern reaches of the Austrian Empire?' de Chabenac asked. 'What of their General Suvorov? He has a fearsome reputation.'

'I remember our struggles against the Austrians in '96 and '97. I cannot imagine when that onslaught includes the Russian hordes. Here we are.' Jobert looked at the entrance of Rizzoli's Milanese headquarters. 'If I cannot win this next engagement, then the Russians matter not.'

Jobert entered Rizzoli's office. 'Excuse me, sir, forgive my intrusion.'

Rizzoli slumped at Jobert's entry. 'What is it now?' Rizzoli had lost weight. Black bags sagged under his eyes.

'May I ask a question, sir?' Jobert asked. 'Of Prince Eugene.' Rizzoli's eyebrows raised warily. 'Maurice de Saxe writes when Prince Eugene was defeated at Staffarda, he found strength from unexpected quarters. What is your opinion of how he recovered his reputation by Ryswick?'

A look of suspicion on Rizzoli's face lifted to a smile. 'I imagine he found himself undermined from where he expected support, and then an ally emerged to support his flank. Are you reading de Saxe?'

'Anything I can find on Eugene, sir. Our books provide such sweet distraction. You had said you had not had time to review Bourcet. Have you had the opportunity? Might I offer my copy?' Jobert held out his leather-bound book.

'With a war in mere weeks on the plains of the Po, I am not sure a review of mountain warfare would be the best priority for my attention.'

'Pursuit is the role of light cavalry, sir. Soon the Austrians will break and flee to their Tyrolean Alps as they have done before. A commander whose troops operate effectively in such terrain would be highly valued.'

Rizzoli smiled. 'If you can bear such esteemed knowledge to depart your library for a short period, I would be honoured to accept your offer.'

With the book held in both hands, Jobert extended his arms to Rizzoli.

Rizzoli opened the cover and examined the title page. 'Jobert, what are ...' Rizzoli's fingers turned the pages with a light touch. 'What are your views of the Russians who march to join the Austrians?'

Jobert took a deep breath before he lied. 'The Russians will be exhausted by their march to foreign lands, sir, and their numbers will be less than the Austrians they support. Our Army of Italy has much experience defeating successive Austrian armies in Lombardy. The coming campaign will be hard-fought, but I feel confident in our superior determination.'

The creases in Rizzoli's forehead diminished. 'Will the Army of Naples march north to join us?'

'Yes, sir. With Rome and Naples secured, and republican governments established, it would be wise to concentrate our forces in the north.'

Rizzoli wagged his finger in warning. 'Despite the defeat of the Neapolitan forces, this latest republic has caused a violent uprising amongst the Neapolitan citizens against the French. That might tie down French forces.'

'You make a good point, sir, indeed it might.' Jobert suppressed a twitch of delight. 'I shall not distract you further. Thank you for your time, sir. Would you excuse me?'

'Might you stay, Jobert?' Rizzoli inspected a map within the chapters. 'I have had the good fortune to enjoy an audience with General Joubert.' Rizzoli smiled. 'Whatever shall we do now he departs for Paris?'

'I hear our General Moreau is being transferred from the Rhine to command us. A general renowned for his luck in battle.'

'Moreau, indeed! Then we will be in good hands' Rizzoli appeared to concentrate on the text. 'General Joubert and I discussed the best utilisation of the regiment in the coming conflict. We agreed that escort and screen duties suited the regiment best.'

Jobert's eyes narrowed as he nodded slowly.

'With some weeks before our commitment to the field, I felt an opportunity existed to enhance the regiments skills in this regard. May I prevail upon your support, Jobert?'

Jobert straightened. 'I am at your service, sir.'

Rizzoli's moustache lifted over his sad smile. 'Do you still maintain your rotation of visits to each company barracks?'

'I do.'

'Would you feel comfortable delivering to each company a short address on the subject of escorts and screens? Perhaps accompanied by a simple field exercise? I would provide a letter of authorisation ordering the company commanders to comply with any request you might have to facilitate the instruction.'

Jobert hesitated. *This moment has taken a year and a dozen deaths.*

'You honour me, sir,' Jobert said, 'with such a generous invitation to make such a contribution to the regiment. But I would seek your guidance in one respect.'

Rizzoli raised his eyebrow.

'It takes me two months to rotate around all the companies in the regiment. With your deeper insight due to your conversing with General Joubert, do you feel sufficient time is available?' Rizzoli opened his mouth to answer, but Jobert continued. 'What would your opinion be of assembling all captains, second lieutenants, sergeants in Milan for a centralised presentation overseen by yourself? Companies can remain in home locations under the supervision of company second-in-commands and sergeant majors.' Rizzoli nodded. 'Couriers sent today would have all assembled within ten days.'

And I can dash to Mantua in the meantime.

Rizzoli smiled. 'Why am I not surprised with your alacrity, Jobert. I feel confident you have a program of instruction tucked into your sabretache.'

Four days later, Jobert entered the drawing room of Prefetto Bernasconi's Mantuan residence.

Bernasconi strode across the room to grip Jobert's hand. 'My thanks, Jobert, for intervening in that coup business.' Bernasconi's face was tight. 'I am saddened that you were incarcerated as a result and that your release had wider impacts.'

'I have given my word to your daughter, sir,' Jobert said, 'that I will remedy that grievous situation.'

Bernasconi smiled. 'I look forward to discussing your ongoing engagement in that regard. Do you feel that conversation will be soon?'

Jobert considered Bernasconi. 'It is my ardent intent, sir. With your permission, I hope my discussion with Signorina Bernasconi this morning will direct my next steps towards your door.'

'Good.' Bernasconi smiled briefly before turning to the fire. 'Have you heard? Your Bonaparte has invaded Syria.'

Jobert stepped to stand beside Bernasconi at the hearth. 'France is on a war footing everywhere, sir. In weeks, there will be war here in the republic.'

'And what are your views on the state of the regiment? Rizzoli informs me it has acquitted itself well recently. Defeating ambushes by partisans in both Piedmont and Lucca. More distressing, Rizzoli took swift action to stomp out a few bad apples in Lucca. Nine men sentenced to serve in chains on the road gangs, I hear.'

'I defer to Colonel Rizzoli's detailed reports on the matter, sir. But I can report on the disciplined performance of your son in the erudite conduct of his duties.'

'I am pleased. I am wearied by the preparation for war in weeks. That my boy is swept up in its violent tide inflames my anxiety. The dread with which people speak of the approaching Russians. Dear Lord, forgive me! I nearly forgot. I have a gift for you, Jobert.'

Bernasconi peered around the tables and mantels of the salon before espying a book on the sideboard. 'I have procured a copy of Suvorov's book in German, *The Art of Victory*. What is your view of these fellows?'

'I remember the immense challenge the Austrians presented in '96 and '97. I cannot imagine a renewed onslaught strengthened by the Russian hordes under the hand of Field Marshal Suvorov. Yes, in weeks there will be war here, but feel confident your son will acquit himself bravely.'

'Yes ... yes.' Bernasconi's eyes took on a sharp glint. 'I foresee Rizzoli becoming the commander of the Cisalpine Legion in due course. Would you consider the rank of colonel in the Cisalpine Legion? Rizzoli would be well served with you as his chief of staff. You both appear to work well together. Why change the recipe and spoil the soup, eh?'

'As attractive as that proposition is—'

A knock at the door. Gianna entered with her books clasped to her chest.

Bernasconi gave a quick bow of his head. 'I should leave you to your instructress.'

Gianna sat at the table with her books unopened. 'Please sit, sir.'

Jobert sat beside her and breathed her lavender and orange

scent. 'No chaperone today?'

'Spoiled produce has no value and does not merit protection.' Gianna raised her chin as she looked at Jobert. 'My mother has not forgiven my admission last November.'

Jobert placed his fingertips on the back of Gianna's hand. 'I owe you a debt of honour.'

Gianna overlapped his fingers with hers. 'Nothing more?'

'Gianna, I am neither poet nor playwright. I do not have the words to express the intensity of my feelings for you. You know you have my heart. When I saw you three months ago, I spoke of you becoming my wife. Have you reflected on such a situation?'

Gianna's smile was mischievous. 'Are you proposing to me, André, or telling me?'

'Before I can ask, I must seek your father's permission. Before I approach him, I need to understand how you feel.'

'Have we not sealed our declaration to each other with a kiss?'

'May I confirm that commitment?'

Gianna looked around the room for any witnesses. Her hands gripped his upper arms as he squeezed her waist. They leaned toward each other, noses touching.

Their lips brushed, before Gianna kissed him ardently.

They pulled apart, their breathing ragged.

Jobert coughed to regain his voice. 'An opportunity has arisen for us in Genoa or Nice. Does such a distance from your family cause distress?'

'Father has expressed the chance of an Italian commission on offer. Perhaps we could be—'

'I cannot wait.' Jobert stood. 'I shall ask your father's permission now.'

'No, no, André, sit. Forgive my timidity, as I have arrived at this ... delicious moment before.' Gianna reached out for his hands. 'Allow us to weather the coming storm. Then return to me once it has passed. When you ask father, I know he will be delighted.' She tapped the cover of *Romeo and Juliet*. 'Today's lesson, the third act, may be enlightening in that regard.'

Jobert knelt in front of her. He cupped her hands holding the book with his. 'Gianna, I belong in your arms.'

'You do, my gorgeous man. As I belong in yours. Therein lies my anguish.'

'How so?'

'Your arms are occupied wielding rein and sabre. There is no space for me within them. Do your duty, André. Then once done, return to me. To where you belong.'

Emotion squeezed Jobert's throat as he slid his hands to her waist and lifted her to stand. He cupped her ribs in his palms and drew her body into his. She clung to him. With his nose in her perfumed curls, Jobert looked down her back at his hands.

For this forever, simply release rein and sabre.

During the reading of the play's third act, both Jobert and Gianna had difficulty giving voice to the deaths of Mercutio and Tybalt.

'Outside the streets speak of the coming onslaught,' Gianna said. 'Is it that easy to kill?'

'The playwright's pen makes sport of the act and the suffering that comes of it.'

'You never speak of your experiences.'

Jobert's eyes were solemn. 'You have never asked.'

Gianna trembled.

Jobert touched her cheek. 'Once we are together once more, we will have time for me to answer any question you have. In the meantime, as Romeo is banished, I must undertake my punishment far from your side.' Jobert frowned. 'As we read of Juliet's impending marriage to Paris, may I enquire of another man.' Gianna crinkled her nose in confusion. 'You spoke once of your fiancé's brother, who returned to Austria wounded.'

'What of him?' Gianna's eyes searched his face. 'Dominic sought comfort after the loss of his brother. We became close. He lost an arm at Rivoli. He can no longer serve his emperor as a soldier. He has seen the end of war.'

Jobert was unable to mask his doubts.

'You are the man I desire, sweet André.' Gianna's hand crept out to tug at his sleeve. 'Not him.' As she withdrew her hand, Gianna's fingernails scraped along Jobert's thigh. 'We still have two acts in the play to go. When should we attempt Act Four? Ought I present you with the book as a keepsake?'

'No, my sweetheart, I will return. Reading is nothing without you.'

'Is this our farewell?'

'No.' Jobert's lips throbbed as he attempted a smile. 'What is the line I just read … I will omit no opportunity that may convey my greeting, love, to thee.'

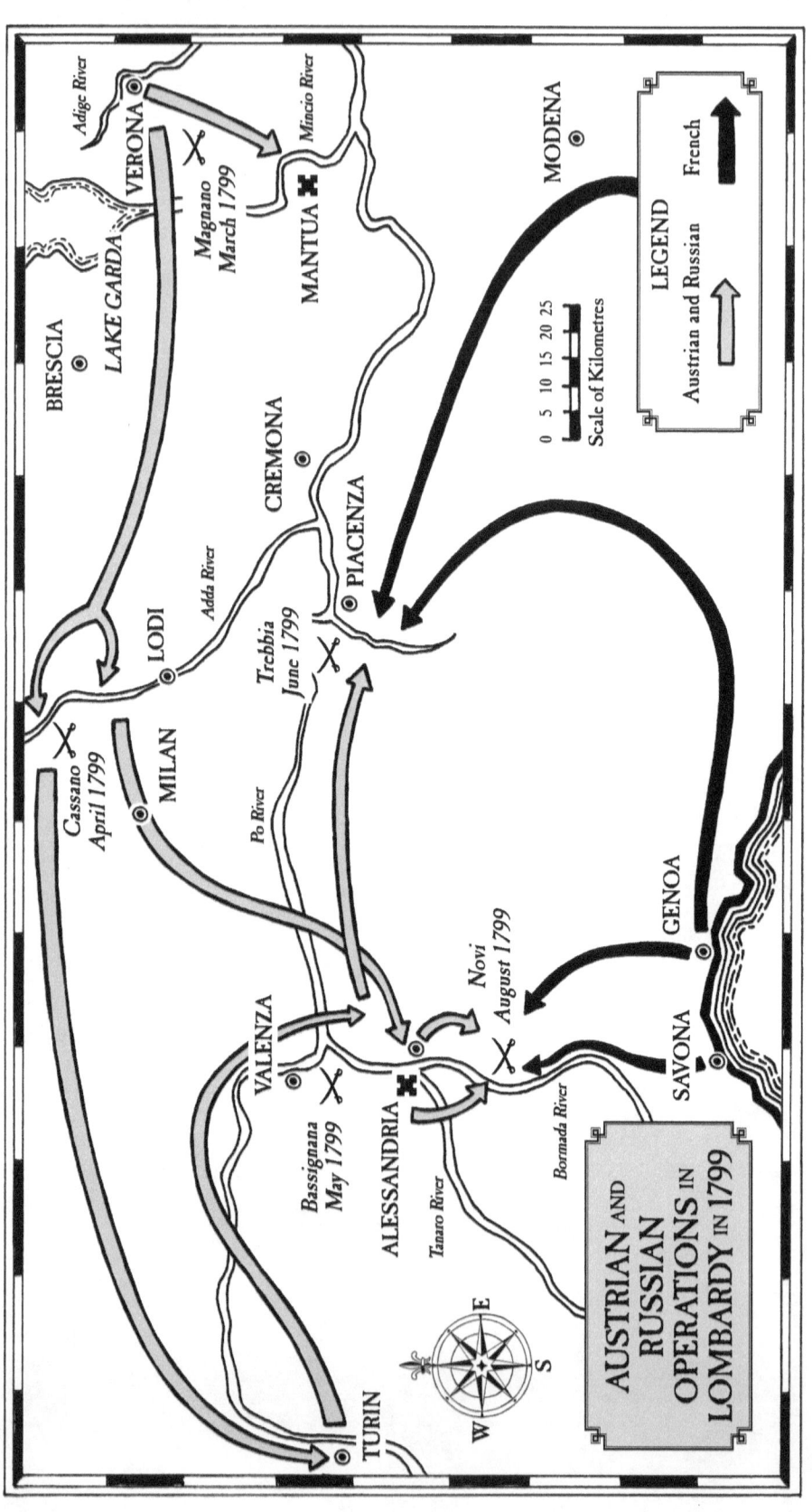

Map labels:

Adige River

VERONA

LAKE GARDA

Mincio River

Magnano
March 1799

MANTUA

MODENA

BRESCIA

LEGEND

French

Austrian and Russian

0 5 10 15 20 25

Scale of Kilometres

CREMONA

PIACENZA

Adda River

LODI

Trebbia
June 1799

Cassano
April 1799

MILAN

Po River

GENOA

Novi
August 1799

VALENZA

SAVONA

Bassignana
May 1799

ALESSANDRIA

Bormada River

Tanaro River

N
W E
S

TURIN

AUSTRIAN AND RUSSIAN OPERATIONS IN LOMBARDY IN 1799

Chapter Seventeen
March 1799, Milan, Italy

'As we are to be attached to General Victor's division, sir,' Jobert said, 'I have an idea that you might consider.'

Rizzoli's face tightened with caution. 'An idea, Jobert?'

'More of a surprise after we receive Victor's—'

Musket fire cracked from the front of the convoy.

Jobert shortened Bleu's reins as D'Onofrio cantered forward to the shouting advance guard. 'Colonel Rizzoli, sir, would you care to ride forward and view D'Onofrio's response, sir?'

'Indeed, Jobert, let us see what that dastardly Koschak has in store for us.'

Koschak's attack on the training convoy with a troop from the Milan Company was the culmination of Jobert's program of screens and convoy escorts. Today, D'Onofrio led the ad hoc training company of the regiment's captains, second lieutenants and sergeants.

'Pin the front, then attack the flanks,' de Chabenac said pointing across a field. 'Here Koschak comes now.'

At three hundred metres across the field, two ranks of chasseurs emerged from their shadows into the light.

A trumpet sounded from the front of the column.

'What was the call?' De Chabenac twisted in his saddle to Moench. 'Was that the opening bars to Figaro?'

Moench's moustache curled over his wide grin. 'Yes, sir. The companies have taken it as their signature tune.'

In response to the call, Bernasconi led the escort reserve out to meet Koschak's marauders. Koschak's attack was advancing towards the convoy at the trot, sabres drawn. In front of his single rank, Bernasconi held his arms wide before touching his fingertips above his mirliton. 'Troop, extended converging fire, ready!'

Rizzoli reined in beside Jobert. 'What evolution is this, Jobert?'

'A simple drill, sir. With musketoons held at forty-five degrees we achieve a dispersed strike at a range of one-hundred-and-fifty metres. With a troop of forty aiming at the centre of the enemy line, we can expect to bring down a dozen enemy, with enough time to take up sabres and counter charge. We call it the Eugene manoeuvre, sir.'

Koschak's men lifted their charge to the canter.

'Fire!' called Bernasconi.

The troop of sergeants and second lieutenants were engulfed in white smoke as their blank cartridges were fired. Dropping musketoons onto their cross belts and sweeping up their sabres, Bernasconi led his men forward.

Koschak's Milanese troopers fled to the flanks as Rally was called across the field.

'Moench, sound Commanders In,' Jobert said. 'Sir, might I invite you to address our Milanese enemy. They will appreciate your encouragement.'

Rizzoli swept back his thick moustache with a gloved finger.

'I shall. Their *élan* reminds me of Eugene at Vienna.'

De Chabenac chuckled. 'I remember our training escorts around Avignon six years ago. It seems an age.'

Jobert's face was grim. 'Then, we faced a forbidding future with a spirit of confidence. These fellows' morale is shattered. The regiment's reputation is in tatters due to embarrassment and scandal. They have lost comrades to partisans and each other. Weeks away from war they doubt themselves. My aim has been to take small steps encouraging any small success.'

As D'Onofrio and today's troop commanders assembled around Jobert, Fazio trotted down the line of regimental wagons. 'Section Commanders, I want parade states. See to prisoners, wounded and ammunition.' Fazio saluted D'Onofrio. 'Shall I put vedettes out, sir?'

De Chabenac raised an eyebrow of surprise at Jobert.

'Small steps.' Jobert gave a shrug of his head. 'Captain D'Onofrio, all commanders present? Well done, Gentlemen, you ensured security and maintained your soldiers' orientation to priorities. I had the honour of crossing blades with D'Onofrio's regiment in '94 and '95. Their balance of offensive spirit and security made them a formidable and respected foe. I am delighted to see those principles applied today.'

D'Onofrio mumbled his appreciation for the compliment.

'Excuse me, sir,' Bernasconi said, flushed with excitement at his fusillade and resulting canter. 'What was the toughest convoy you ever led?'

Cannon balls hissed just above the waves. Jobert thighs gripped Bleu's saddle as he expected to thud into the gravel as his horse's legs were sheared off. Under the dizzying red light of a suspended flare, musket balls spat from shadows.

Jobert avoided looking at de Chabenac and Moench. Moench had turned his mare and walked away. De Chabenac's twisted face sought something in the high branches.

'Perhaps a story for another time,' Jobert said. 'We are not yet at the convoy's release point. Who knows what lies ahead?'

On a late March day, as Rizzoli and Jobert trotted back to the regiment following Victor's orders, the midday sun took the edge off the crisp northerly pulsing along the Adige Valley.

'General Victor's requirements of the regiment seem reasonable, Jobert,' Rizzoli said.

'The regiment is well prepared, sir,' said Jobert. 'Screening and escorting are the regiment's strengths.'

'I am not sure what to make of General Moreau being replaced by Schérer on the eve of battle. You have served previously under General Schérer?'

'Yes, sir, at Loano in '95 under General Masséna.'

'How did you find him?' Rizzoli asked.

Jobert considered his response. 'General Schérer's plan for the recapture of Savona was sound, sir, and being well served with commanders of the calibre of Masséna, we emerged victorious.'

'And under Schérer, we shall now advance to defeat the Austrians before the Russians can join them. Ah, here is the regiment.'

Off the road, midway across a wide field, nearly six hundred and forty chasseurs sat on parade, sabres drawn, pommels on thighs.

Rizzoli turned and considered Jobert. 'Might I share my initial thoughts on disposing of the regiment during General Victor's coming advance? Bologna and Modena in the left forward screen, Ravenna and Ferrara in the right forward screen, and D'Onofrio's Mantuans and Brescians escorting behind General Victor's forward brigade. I shall hold Milan and Cremona in reserve. Do you foresee any immediate concerns?'

A tremble ran through Jobert's chest. 'Eminently sound, sir. Worthy of Eugene.'

'You have a rapport with D'Onofrio, Jobert. Might I impose on you to keep an eye on him?'

'I am at your service, sir.'

'I am obliged, Jobert. Shall we see if Victor's surprise salute is ready?'

Jobert excused himself from Rizzoli and rode to join Koschak, Moench and Tulloc at the side of the field.

'And?' Koschak asked as Jobert swigged from his flask.

'Orders were simple enough.' Jobert coughed at the water in his throat. 'We are facing fifty thousand kaiserliks on both sides of the Adige. Schérer has thirty-five French and ten thousand Piedmontese, Swiss, Poles and Italians. Schérer wants to attack immediately. We have tomorrow to prepare, and we attack the day after.'

Koschak whistled. 'Your thoughts on Schérer?'

Jobert grimaced. 'I have my doubts. He was lacklustre back in '95 and was propped up by excellent men like Masséna. I have absolute faith in Victor, but I have my doubts about these other generals cast off from the Rhine.'

'Sir,' Moench said, 'here is Victor now.'

Victor's party halted on the road and turned to the silent regiment, with Rizzoli front and centre, the regimental standard flying over his head.

'The Cisalpine Chasseurs à Cheval Regiment, ready!' cried Rizzoli.

Sabres slid onto sword knots as musketoons were taken up from their cross belts. The front rank cocked and shouldered their firearms. The second rank rested their musketoons on their knees.

'Front rank, fire!' Rizzoli called.

Over three hundred blank cartridges exploded.

A barp from Rizzoli's trumpeter.

The second rank moved through the front rank and the wafting smoke as the front rank were loading.

'Front rank ready! Front rank fire!'

Another simultaneous explosion. Another toot caused the original front rank to move through.

Both ranks repeated the process.

'Sabres!' cried Rizzoli, to which the six hundred chasseurs exchanged weapons once more.

Rizzoli rode out to Victor and saluted. 'Would you care to inspect the regiment, sir?'

Jobert grinned at Koschak. 'Seamless.'

Koschak frowned. 'A pretty theatre, sir, but will this be enough to get them through the next few weeks?'

The smile faded from Jobert's face. 'No.'

Two days later, Schérer's Army of Italy, led by Victor's division with the Cisalpine Chasseurs attached, launched the French attack on the Austrian lines.

Waiting in the divisional artillery park, Jobert ran his fingers inside Jaunes girth, checking for tightness and grit.

Three kilometres ahead the guns fired constantly. It was rare to hear muskets except if skirmishers fired as the batteries moved forward. Victor's battleline was drawing further north.

Even the 12th Dragoons, Victor's reserve cavalry waiting behind the depth battalions, had marched forward.

Along the side of the Verona-Legnago road, the Mantua Company stood to horse awaiting the order to move. On the other verge, eight ammunition caissons and their teams warmed in the morning sun.

Jobert leaned against his saddle and peered at the silver boar's head on the side of his pistol. He looked up at the approaching crunch of boots on gravel.

'Sir?' said the artillery sergeant major. The man compressed his lips in agitation. 'We must get these caissons forward. We can wait no longer.'

'I understand, Sergeant Major,' Jobert said with a wink. 'I will put a toe in the arse of the young escort commander.' Jobert turned. 'Captain D'Onofrio! Attend me.'

'Yes sir.' D'Onofrio trotted to Jobert. 'I do not know where these wagons are, sir.'

'A dilemma on your first day of battle,' Jobert said. 'Both convoys are vital, D'Onofrio. May I suggest ...'

D'Onofrio nodded. 'Please, sir.'

'I take Bernasconi's troop to escort the caissons to the gun line,' Jobert said. 'You wait for the water and brandy wagons with your other troop. I will meet you at the casualty clearing post.'

'I would appreciate that, sir.'

'D'Onofrio, parade your company to give your orders. Savour the moment.' D'Onofrio's thick eyebrows creased in confusion. 'This will be the last time you ever see your company all in one place.'

D'Onofrio's lips crimped with worry as he departed.

With orders given, Jobert, Koschak, Moench and Tulloc accompanied Bernasconi's forty sabres and the eight artillery caissons forward to the booming cannons.

Bernasconi's troop halted short of the rear of the gun line.

Each caisson wheeled in beside the emptying caisson and the gun limber. The horse teams faced rearwards, so the gunners had access to the rear of the caissons behind their guns. Civilian drivers raced to transfer remaining ammunition out of the old caissons and into the newly arrived ones. Just in front of the chasseur column, a few caisson drivers unbuckled the harness from a horse dead in the traces.

'Piss off back to your guns!' yelled the sergeant major as soot-grimed artillerymen raced to the fresh caissons seeking water. 'Drink on your own time.'

The crews leapt and swore as they served their six six-pounder cannons and two six-inch howitzers. The mounted battery commander rode along the one hundred and fifty metres of the gun line.

'Fire!'

One by one, down the line, the guns belched iron, smoke and flame. A pall of gun smoke enclosed the fascinated chasseurs.

Cheering, whistling and a short drum paradiddle from a flanking battalion informed the toiling artillerymen of the success of their battery fire.

The smoke lifted. The battery commander peered toward the enemy line. Jobert could see darting green and grey Austrian jäger, but the fusiliers' fire line was a white-grey smudge six hundred metres further down the Verona road.

A puff from the Austrian line.

'Incoming shot!' screamed the blue-coated infantry battalions alongside the battery.

Jobert, Koschak, Moench and Tulloc shortened their reins.

Jobert could not hear the thud of bounce as gunners forward of their muzzles bellowed and pointed their ramrods at the speeding blur.

'Incoming shot!' cried Fazio in the troop behind Bernasconi.

'Sir?' The fear in Bernasconi's voice was palpable.

'Shorten your reins, lad,' Jobert said.

A wheel on one of the centre guns shattered. A piercing clang as the bouncing three-pound ball struck the barrel and ricocheted towards the caissons beside the chasseurs.

The whizzing ball leapt across to cut through the chest of a waiting caisson horse before thumping away towards the depth battalions.

The horse, without front legs, screamed a spray of blood as it was thrown against its mate alongside. The driver threw himself across the horse's neck to stop it from attempting to stand.

Koschak cocked a pistol and sidestepped his horse towards the dying animal.

'Save your ball, sir,' said the sergeant major wielding an axe. With a foot on the horse's throat, the sergeant major chopped the axe into the horse's skull just above the eyes. The horse wheezed, spasmed and lay still. 'Jump lively, boys. Unbuckle this poor bastard.'

Chasseurs in the column leaned out from their saddles and vomited.

Beside Jobert, Bernasconi convulsed.

'Swallow it, Bernasconi!' said Koschak. 'Sit up and drink it down. Do not let your men see you vomit.'

'Welcome to the battlefield, Lieutenant,' Jobert said.

Jobert saw Fazio scowl at the exchange.

'Clear my gun line,' roared the battery captain.

'Move your arses,' the artillery sergeant major yelled at the drivers of the empty caissons.

'Bernasconi,' Jobert said, 'take a platoon and escort the wagons back to the ammunition point. I will take Fazio's platoon and meet D'Onofrio at the casualty clearing post.'

Just as the gun line was identifiable by its noise, the casualty clearing post was found by following the limping and carried infantry wounded. Surrounded by stone sheds and tangled grape vines, a low farmhouse emitted moans and screams.

'Sergeant Fazio.' Jobert evaluated Fazio. Fazio sat steady and awaited Jobert's direction. 'Might I request you leave Corporal Cieno and his section with me. Take the other section to guide Captain D'Onofrio's convoy of water and brandy here. Please.'

Fazio's eyes narrowed with suspicion as he saluted.

As Fazio's ten chasseurs departed, Jobert evaluated how D'Onofrio's convoy would approach, unload and depart the casualty post. A lane ran behind the rear door of the house. It was blocked with a neat line of corpses.

A senior orderly leaning on the gate frame puffed on his pipe and shrugged. 'Sorry, sir, your boys will have to move them. No chance you have any food you can share?' At a shout from within the house, the orderly jerked. 'The surgeon calls.'

When D'Onofrio's convoy arrived, the chasseurs' faces went blank when they were ordered to move the line of dead blocking the lane.

'Some are still alive,' cried a chasseur.

'Do you have any water?' asked an infantry grenadier holding the hand of a dying mate.

Once the lane was cleared, the chasseurs unloaded the wagons of brandy and water and then loaded the wounded, triaged for evacuation.

Inside the back garden by the house's rear door squatted over one hundred Austrian prisoners. Jobert watched D'Onofrio's and Fazio's spellbound expressions as they stared at the huddle of morose men.

Jobert smirked. *Old comrades, perhaps?*

'Water?' some prisoners asked.

'Are you taking them off my hands, sir?' the senior orderly asked Jobert between puffs of his pipe.

Jobert gave the orderly a nod and turned Jaune towards

D'Onofrio. 'Your orders, D'Onofrio?'

D'Onofrio's head and chest twitched with stress. 'Where is Bernasconi, sir?'

'He took a platoon to return the empty caissons. Take the troop you arrived with and escort the prisoners to the divisional cage. I will take Fazio's platoon and return the wounded to the hospital collection—'

An Austrian fusilier burst out of the rear gate and sprinted down the lane.

Jobert squeezed Jaune into a right-lead canter. Jaune surged his great body into the stride. Just beyond the stone barn, Jobert angled his five-hundred-kilogram horse for the prisoner's back and, at forty kilometres per hour, ploughed the escapee underfoot. Jobert sank Jaune to a halt and sidestepped over the writhing man.

'Return to the column, lad,' said Jobert in German, 'or I will spit you like a chicken.'

Once the soldier stood, Jobert grabbed deep into his collar and dragged him back at the trot. He threw the prisoner at the feet of his mates.

'Sergeant,' Jobert said to an Austrian artilleryman, 'keep your men in their ranks.'

'I could, sir, if we had water.'

Jobert's and Fazio's convoy of wounded jolted along the gravel road to the hospital collection post. Bodily fluids leaked through the floorboards into the dust.

'Any water?' asked the wounded, between groans. Should a

water flask be passed across, 'Any food?'

Arriving at the divisional surgeon's tents, the chasseurs recoiled at the stacks of bare hands and arms. A few Austrian prisoners unbuckled gaiters and removed shoes from single, bloodied legs.

'All right, lads, the show is over.' Fazio spat at the scene. 'Unload these poor mongrels. Get moving!'

Once the wounded were unloaded, the chasseurs found the wagon's trays slick with blood and flies.

'Fill buckets from the well and sluice the wagons down,' Jobert said. 'And quickly, Sergeant Fazio. We have to return and keep doing it all again until nightfall.'

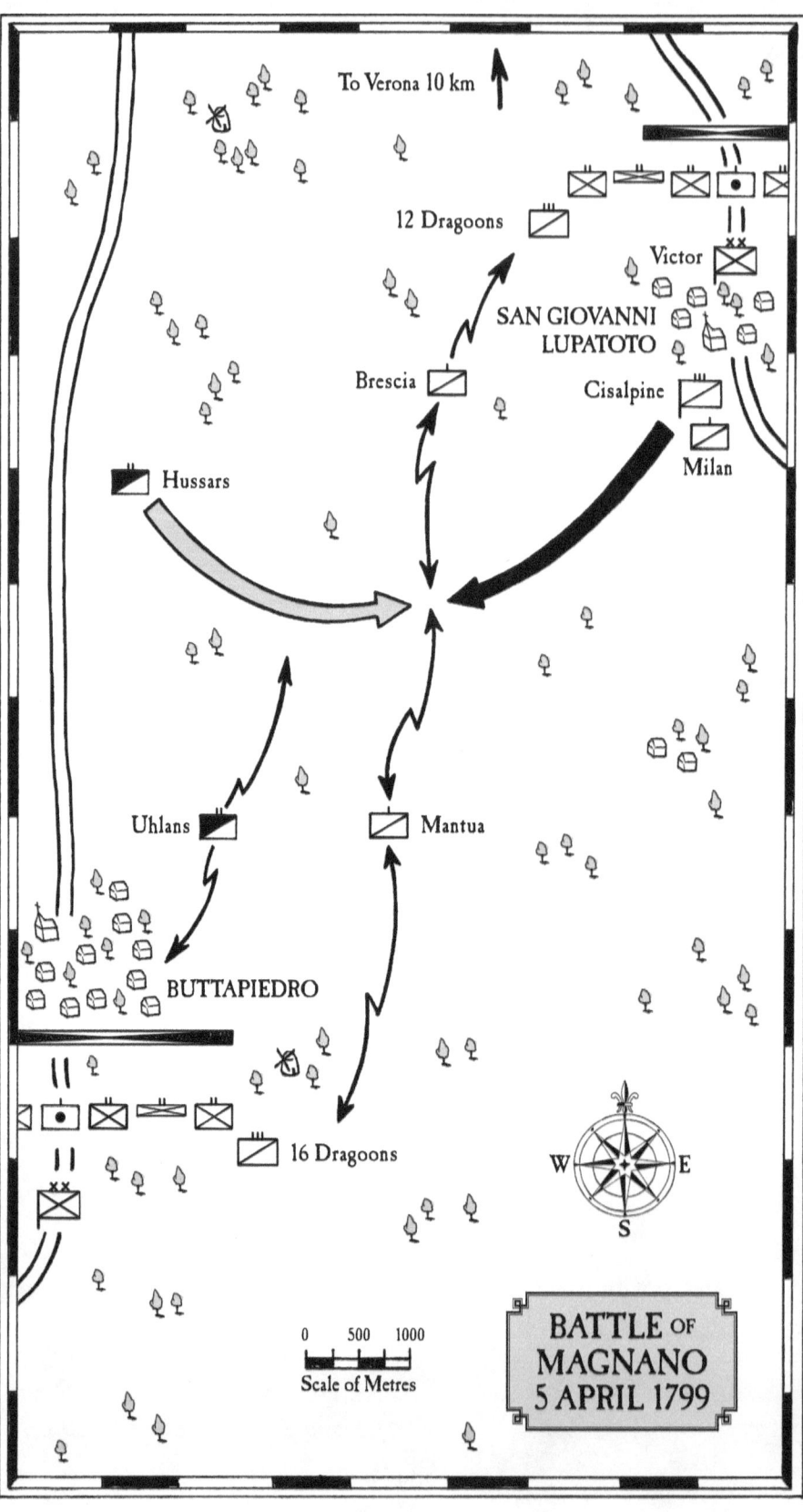

To Verona 10 km

12 Dragoons

Victor

SAN GIOVANNI
LUPATOTO

Brescia

Cisalpine

Milan

Hussars

Uhlans

Mantua

BUTTAPIEDRO

16 Dragoons

W   E

S

0   500   1000

Scale of Metres

BATTLE OF
MAGNANO
5 APRIL 1799

Chapter Eighteen
April 1799, Battle of Magnano, Italy

The lifting of the Adige's early morning fog signalled the slackening of skirmisher fire and the increased rate of artillery fire.

On the fourth morning of the battle, Jobert sat in the middle of a paddock between the two near-parallel roads both converging on Verona. From his position, he could observe the advance of two French infantry divisions, Victor's division on his right towards the Adige and a sister division to his left.

Both divisions advanced north with a similar formation. Straddling the respective roads was an artillery battery. On either side of the road an infantry regiment advanced, with its three battalions in attack column. Towards Jobert, on Victor's western flank, rode three squadron columns of the 12th Dragoons supporting the infantry.

On the eastern flank of the sister division marched the 16th Dragoons.

In the void between the divisions, strung out over two thousand metres, patrolled the four troops of D'Onofrio's squadron of Mantua and Brescia Companies.

Jobert and Koschak rode with Bernasconi's troop on the extreme edge of Victor's division, maintaining contact with the 16th Dragoons.

With a slow gloved hand, Koschak brushed the flies from his face. 'We are going to lose this.'

Jobert considered his friend's brooding stare. After three days of advancing and being repulsed, Schérer's plan for swift victory was unravelling. The Austrian army's full strength was now west of the Adige River. On Schérer's northern flank, seasoned generals such as Moreau and Sérurier had been defeated. The army's mood was lowered further when it was learnt that esteemed General Jourdan had been defeated on the Rhine. Of greater concern to the chasseurs was that Polish battalions, ex-Austrian army who now served France, were given no quarter when they were massacred by Austrian counterattacks.

Koschak jerked a thumb over his shoulder to the ranks of chasseurs. 'It will not take much for these pricks to break.'

Jobert nodded slowly. 'Bernasconi and the younger chasseurs have not coped with being among dead and wounded these past three days.' Last night Bernasconi had confided to Jobert his distress at his brother's and Gianna's fiancé's battlefield deaths.

The sister division's gun fire increased, shifting Jobert's attention west. He extended his telescope at the combat two thousand metres away. 'This other division is having a hard time moving her kaiserliks. The 16th Dragoons are at a standstill. Our line is stretching to keep pace with Victor.'

'If we break Bernasconi's troop in half,' Koschak said, 'I can run the patrol alongside the dragoons.'

'Lieutenant Bernasconi, attend me.' Jobert called. Bernasconi produced his notebook and pencil upon halting. 'You can see our screen line is stretching as Victor advances faster than his neighbour. I want you to report to D'Onofrio that we need to split into platoons to maintain contact along the screen line.'

Bernasconi glanced east to wherever D'Onofrio might be.

'Suggest to D'Onofrio,' Jobert continued, 'that a message is sent to both Victor and the commander of our 12th Dragoons. Our sister division is delayed behind us and our western flank is becoming exposed to counterattack the further we advance.'

Bernasconi's head jerked west to the roiling smoke above the clashing blue and white battlelines. His face crimped in alarm as he pointed his pencil. 'Are they Cossacks, sir?'

Jobert brought up his glass. 'No, lad. Cossacks are Russian, and they have not yet joined the Austrians. The lances you see are uhlans.' Jobert lowered the telescope. 'Also suggest to D'Onofrio that Colonel Rizzoli commit part of his reserve to reinforce our line. Repeat the message.'

Bernasconi repeated the message.

'Are you satisfied, Bernasconi,' Jobert said, 'if Koschak takes Fazio's platoon closer to the 16th Dragoons, and I will patrol with the other platoon in your absence?'

'Yes, thank you, sir.' Bernasconi saluted and departed at the trot.

Koschak lowered his glass. 'You saw sky-blue hussars beyond the uhlans, did you not?'

'Yes, von Maefeld's regiment.' Jobert inspected his pistol holsters. 'Keep Fazio's lads in sight of the 16th Dragoons, and I will drift the others towards our centre. If I sound Figaro, return.'

Over an hour passed and the gap between Jobert's and Koschak's platoons widened. What had started as a two-kilometre gap between the flanking dragoon regiments that morning had widened to six kilometres.

'Why has the fire of the standstill division slackened, sir?' Moench asked. 'And the fire from General Victor increased?'

'Our sister division has run out of puff in the face of a

determined enemy,' Jobert said. 'Now Victor has found kaiserliks standing with the same grit. We will see if the kaiserliks exploit this gaping hole between our divisions.' Jobert raised his telescope. 'Because here comes a hussar patrol. Sound Figaro to recall Koschak.'

Bernasconi and D'Onofrio trotted to join Jobert as Koschak returned with Fazio's platoon.

D'Onofrio saluted. 'General Victor has released us from maintaining contact with the 16th Dragoons. Colonel Rizzoli has brought the Milan Company to support our withdrawal. He requires us to form line on the flanks of the 12th Dragoons.'

'Trot march then, D'Onofrio,' Jobert said, 'or we will be forming on that approaching hussar patrol.'

Bernasconi's troop had no issue maintaining a fast trot the two kilometres to Rizzoli and the Milan Company.

'D'Onofrio,' Jobert asked, 'where is the rest of your Mantua Company?'

D'Onofrio pointed the two thousand metres to a green line of chasseurs. 'They have withdrawn to the 12th Dragoons with the Brescia Company.'

Jobert sucked through his teeth. 'Your troops are far too spread. Next time keep your company together. I am not sure why Milan is facing away, so have Bernasconi's troop face the hussars before you report to Rizzoli.'

Jobert and D'Onofrio saluted Rizzoli seated under the wafting folds of the Cisalpine's *tri-couleur*.

'Why have you formed that troop backwards, D'Onofrio?' Rizzoli asked.

'To cover your flank, sir.' D'Onofrio pointed to the twenty hussars forming battleline four hundred metres from the chasseurs flank. 'A troop of enemy hussars has followed us, sir.'

'Good grief!' Rizzoli said. 'We had best retire to Victor's column. His division has broken. They are in retreat.'

'Sir, our ninety sabres outnumber their twenty,' Jobert said. 'If we just stand firm they will depart. We must protect the 12th Dragoons should the hussars deploy to this flank.'

The hiss of twenty hussar sabres being drawn caused a creak of saddlery as every chasseur twisted in their saddles. A trumpet sounded from the hussars. A collective Italian gasp sounded as the hussars surged into a walk.

In the front rank of Bernasconi's troop, Fazio twisted back to the officers, 'Orders, gentlemen?'

Jobert looked to Rizzoli. Rizzoli was immobile except for the rapid blinking of his eyes.

'Colonel Rizzoli, sir, might Captain D'Onofrio form battleline on Bernasconi's flank to face the hussars?' Rizzoli licked his lips without taking his eyes from the hussars. Jobert drew his sabre. 'Gentlemen, we cannot freeze in battle, or we will remain in that state when they bury us. Cisalpine Chasseurs, sabres! Milan Company, form line to the left at the halt, trot, march! Standard party, take post in the centre, walk, march! Moench, sound Assembly. Koschak and D'Onofrio, on me!'

With a kiss sound, Jobert lifted Bleu into a canter and wheeled among the hastening chasseurs. 'Officers, take post. D'Onofrio, dress the line by the centre.'

The hussar line halted at two hundred metres. A broad-shouldered officer sat forward of the hussar line on a black charger, his hand on his hip, his sabre undrawn.

Von Maefeld!

'Cisalpine,' Jobert spun Bleu to call to the chasseurs, 'stand firm by our standard and they will yield.' Koschak trotted along the back of the line growling instructions.

'Jobert?' came a faint call.

Moench jabbed the mouthpiece of his trumpet towards the hussars. 'Sir, the kaiserlik officer wants you.'

Jobert turned to face front.

'Jobert?' called von Maefeld. 'It is you! Are they Italians?'

The horses threw their heads in unison as fear pulsed though saddles and bits.

'Stand fast, Cisalpine!' bellowed Jobert. 'Moench sound Figaro.'

As the long notes of the call floated across the green fields, Rizzoli reined in alongside Jobert. 'Jobert, I must insist—'

'Shorten your reins, sir, we are less than ten seconds to—'

Von Maefeld drew his sabre. 'Italians! Traitors to the emperor. Massacre them.'

The hussar line erupted into a canter. Their battle-cry was screamed through their bared teeth.

Jobert pumped his blade. 'Cisalpine, advance, trot, march! Moench, sound Advance.'

Unfrozen by the order to trot, many chasseurs peeled away to the flanks and spurred for the distant block of Brescia Company. In a moment Milan Company had dissolved from trotting forward to galloping to the rear.

'Milan, stand fast!' cried D'Onofrio.

Rizzoli's wide eyes bulged from his white face. 'I shall rally Milan.' Rizzoli turned his horse to follow the fleeing troopers.

'On me, Mantua, on me!' called Fazio from the right of the line.

Koschak boxed the chasseurs in on Mantua's left flank. 'Steady in the ranks, lads.'

Seeing that the hussars were splitting into two wings and aiming for the flanks of Bernasconi's troop, Jobert checked Bleu to box in the wheeling standard bearer. 'Duty demands you take post in the centre, Sergeant,' Jobert shouted at the standard bearer.

'You carry it then.' The standard bearer thrust the flag at Jobert before wheeling away.

With hands full of reins and sabre, Jobert dropped the

standard. A quick glance confirmed that the hussars had galloped to the flanks to pursue the routing Milanese. 'Mantua, halt. Moench, sound Halt. Bernasconi, retrieve the standard.'

D'Onofrio cantered in circles. 'Mantua, form on the standard.' D'Onofrio, Fazio and twenty Mantuans around Bernasconi, who held aloft the green, white and red silk.

Jobert and Koschak kept their horses stepping short on a tight rein. 'Where are Tulloc and Jaune?' Jobert asked over his shoulder to Moench.

'Just behind Mantua.'

Within an arc of a dozen hussars fifty metres away, sat von Maefeld. He held up a pistol. It blazed in the sun's rays. 'Jobert, it is time.'

Jobert lifted his matching pistol from its holster. 'Koschak, take Moench and Tulloc and go.'

'What the fuck are you doing?' Koschak asked.

Jobert squeezed Bleu forward away from the standard. 'I have business with von Maefeld, and you know it. Go!'

'Why here? Why now?'

'Because this is all I have,' Jobert screamed, spinning Bleu to face Koschak. Spittle flecked his red face. 'This is the only thing in my life over which I have control. This decision is the only one I am allowed to make.'

'If you stand, I stand.'

Jobert ground his teeth before nodding. 'Moench, take Tulloc and go!'

Moench looked over his shoulder to Tulloc. 'If you stay, we stay.'

'Then make it count, Jobert.' Koschak cocked his musketoon. 'Mantua, ready!'

Jobert swept Bleu in an arc towards von Maefeld as the chasseurs cocked their hammers back.

Von Maefeld swept his loose fur-trimmed pelisse clear of his left shoulder. 'Capture the traitor's standard, boys. The emperor will enjoy wiping his arse on it. Charge!'

Von Maefeld and his dozen hussars launched at the canter.

With blade point extended, Jobert lifted Bleu into a gallop straight at von Maefeld.

Behind him, the chasseurs' musketoons stuttered their fire. With a defiant cry, the hussars crashed into their ranks.

Von Maefeld spun his charger to receive Jobert on his sabre-side.

Jobert's right knee kept Bleu's rush straight. As Bleu's chest collided with the charger's rump, Jobert's blade lifted von Maefeld's. While von Maefeld maintained his balance on a faltering horse, Jobert rolled his wrist under to slice at von Maefeld's open ribs.

Von Maefeld coughed a laugh and spun his horse out of the clinch to parry Jobert's blade.

With a glance at von Maefeld's heels and hips, Jobert could predict von Maefeld's next instructions to his charger. As von Maefeld spun and maintained his guard, so Jobert curved Bleu towards the charger's hindquarters and threatened von Maefeld's kidneys.

The momentum of their spinning duel stepped them into the swirling melee for the standard.

As better horsemen and more confident with their blades, those few hussars who survived the fusillade maintained their furious efforts to secure Bernasconi's standard. The chasseurs emboldened by the fight or terrified of being given no quarter if they submitted, parried and cut.

Jobert and von Maefeld became locked in a struggle side by side, with von Maefeld on Jobert's right. Jobert clubbed down with his high hilt on von Maefeld's head.

Von Maefeld punched his hilt across his reins at Jobert's chest. One blow caught Jobert in the mouth. Jobert spat his shattered dentures clear in a stream of blood.

Jobert swept his trapped right leg under von Maefeld's left and tipped von Maefeld forward off balance. Von Maefeld caught his momentum on his and Jobert's pistol holsters. He scrabbled to grab Jobert's silver-inlaid pistol.

Jobert brought the hilt down hard at the base of von Maefeld's skull. Reeling with pain, von Maefeld gripped Jobert's reins.

'Get off him, Jobert!' Fazio appeared at Jobert's left knee, pushing on Bleu's shoulder. 'Bernasconi is under you, you bastard. You are trampling the standard.'

'Fazio, pass it to me,' cried D'Onofrio. He thrust the torn silks at Jobert. 'Jobert, ride the standard clear.'

'Piss off, idiot. I am busy.' Jobert punched the staff away with his rein hand.

Fazio snatched at the falling flag. 'You bastard, Jobert!'

'Come with me, you prick.' Jobert grabbed von Maefeld's pelisse and pulled. Von Maefeld choked as he was hauled clear of Jobert's reins. With loose reins and a sabre hand full of pelisse, Jobert backed Bleu with his feet.

The pelisse's cord, which connected the outer jacket when draped around the hussar's shoulders, sliced into von Maefeld's throat. Von Maefeld scratched at the straining embroidered cord.

The pelisse cord snapped.

Both Bleu and the charger slumped to a stop.

Jobert held the sky-blue jacket in the air.

Coughing, von Maefeld dropped his sabre to clutch at his throat.

A trumpet called the remaining exhausted hussars clear of the chasseurs.

Von Maefeld glared at Jobert. 'Until next time.'

Jobert stood in his stirrups and thrust his sabre at von Maefeld. 'Stand your ground, you cur. Finish this here and now.

You owe me and my brother a debt of blood.'

Von Maefeld looked at the blood on the palm of his glove. 'My family and I have waited six years for you.' His voice croaked a whisper. 'You will die by my hand at my convenience.'

With a nod, von Maefeld gathered his hussars into a canter and departed to the north.

Jobert gripped his holsters and screamed.

Bleu skittered at the outburst.

Jobert seethed as he spun Bleu towards the remaining chasseurs.

D'Onofrio shot Jobert a look of bitter disappointment before tending to those wounded.

Bernasconi was on his knees hugging the standard to his chest.

Fazio stepped forward, his bleeding arms sending tremors through his extended blade. He spat at Jobert's feet. 'You fucking French turd, Jobert, you did nothing to save the standard.'

'You obtuse shit, Fazio!' Jobert's filthy glove smeared blood across his cheeks. 'Did you not notice I was busy attempting to kill someone?' From the cuts in his mouth, Jobert spat blood back at Fazio. 'What is more, why should I save your pissing standard?'

D'Onofrio and Bernasconi looked up at Jobert in disbelief.

'What has your fucking regiment ever done for me?' Jobert shook with anger. 'Your fucking regiment has only ever given me grief.'

The next morning, Jobert strode through the chaos in the

Mantuan streets to enter the calm of the Bernasconi household. With Signora Bernasconi's evacuation to Milan, the house had been stripped of furniture. Only a few members of the household staff received Jobert and he found Gianna in the drawing room.

'I knew you would come home to me.' Gianna said, as she held Jobert tight. 'Are you hurt?'

Bernasconi strode into the room. 'Ah, Jobert, good. What news from the field?'

Jobert stepped back from Gianna's embrace. 'Schérer's plan has failed, sir. Our losses are great. We are to withdraw.'

'That is a heavy blow,' Bernasconi said. 'And now a limited withdrawal to the Mincio River, no? We cannot fail with an army behind the Mincio anchoring the fortress of Mantua in the south and Lake Garda in the north?'

Jobert dropped his eyes to the bare floorboards. 'I do not understand why, sir, but Schérer has ordered us back to the Adda River to stand in front of Milan.'

'Milan?' Gianna said. 'What of Mantua?'

'Our dear lord protect us!' Bernasconi staggered 'The Austrians will lay siege to Mantua. I must do what I can for the city. Gianna, pack your things and leave with Jobert. Jobert, may I call upon you to take her to her mother in the safety of Milan.'

'I am at your service, sir.' Jobert turned to Gianna. 'What preparations are needed for you to depart?'

Gianna raised a slender finger. 'No, dear André, I am not yet required to obey a husband. I will stay.'

'I do not instruct you, Gianna.' Jobert placed his fingertips together. 'Your bravery is admirable, but no one willingly seeks to endure a siege.'

'No, you must leave,' Bernasconi said. 'I command you, my darling.'

'Your commands have no authority over the commands of my heart.' Gianna took her father's hands in hers. 'My brothers fight, my lovers fight, my father fights. I will fight. I will stay as you will have no one. I will care for you.'

'Then I will stay,' Jobert said. 'There is much here I can do.'

'No!' Bernasconi threw up his hands. 'You both must go! Jobert, you must go. You must protect my wife, my son.' Bernasconi shuffled backwards. 'I will ... I will keep Gianna safe. Now, go.'

Jobert stared at Gianna.

Gianna stepped to Jobert and slipped her hand under his elbow. 'Father, your duties call.'

Bernasconi offered Jobert his hand. 'We will meet again. Keep our Silvio safe.' Bernasconi kissed Gianna on the cheek before he departed.

'Dear Jobert, I will be safe here. I will take refuge in the duomo. Save our Cisalpine dream. Protect my mother. Protect my brother. Once this is over, we will be reunited.'

'Gianna,' Jobert said, taking her hands in his. 'Not the duomo. Take refuge in the basilica. It is furthest from the walls.' Gianna looked confused. 'It is further from artillery fire. Pray by the wall close to the vestibule. Do not huddle in the middle of the nave should the roof collapse.'

Gianna's cheeks drained of colour. 'I trust that I will be protected by our Lord's heavenly grace. I will be here when you return.'

Jobert flexed his fingers around her shoulders as his mind raced. *I would feel less pain had I taken a cut from von Maefeld.*

'Come, there is time,' Gianna said. 'We will find a moment of solace in *Romeo and Juliet's* Act Four.'

Jobert coughed a nervous laugh. 'Will this be the end of their story?'

'You do not remember ... no, there is one more act to play

out still. We will finish it when we are together once more. Sit with me now.'

Jobert began to read his lines, but it became more difficult as Juliet prepared to take the sleeping draught. Gianna read on. At the moment Juliet was discovered dead, Jobert asked Gianna to stop.

'See, Juliet appears dead,' Gianna said, 'but she is not. A means will be found for Romeo to return. There is still hope.'

Jobert sat stunned, his eyes on her fingers on the page. Her lavender and orange scent numbing his reason.

'Take the book.' Gianna pressed the play into his hands. 'A belated gift for your birthday.'

Jobert swallowed to engage his voice. 'I will not read it without you.'

Gianna stroked his cheek. 'We will study the final act on your return.'

Jobert placed the book into an inner pocket of his tailcoat. 'The gift I want, the gift denied, stands before me.'

They stood up together.

Their tears mixed as they kissed.

As Jobert walked from the room, the playbook battered against his heart, its weight dragging his tailcoat through the floor. It took every scrap of his strength to walk away.

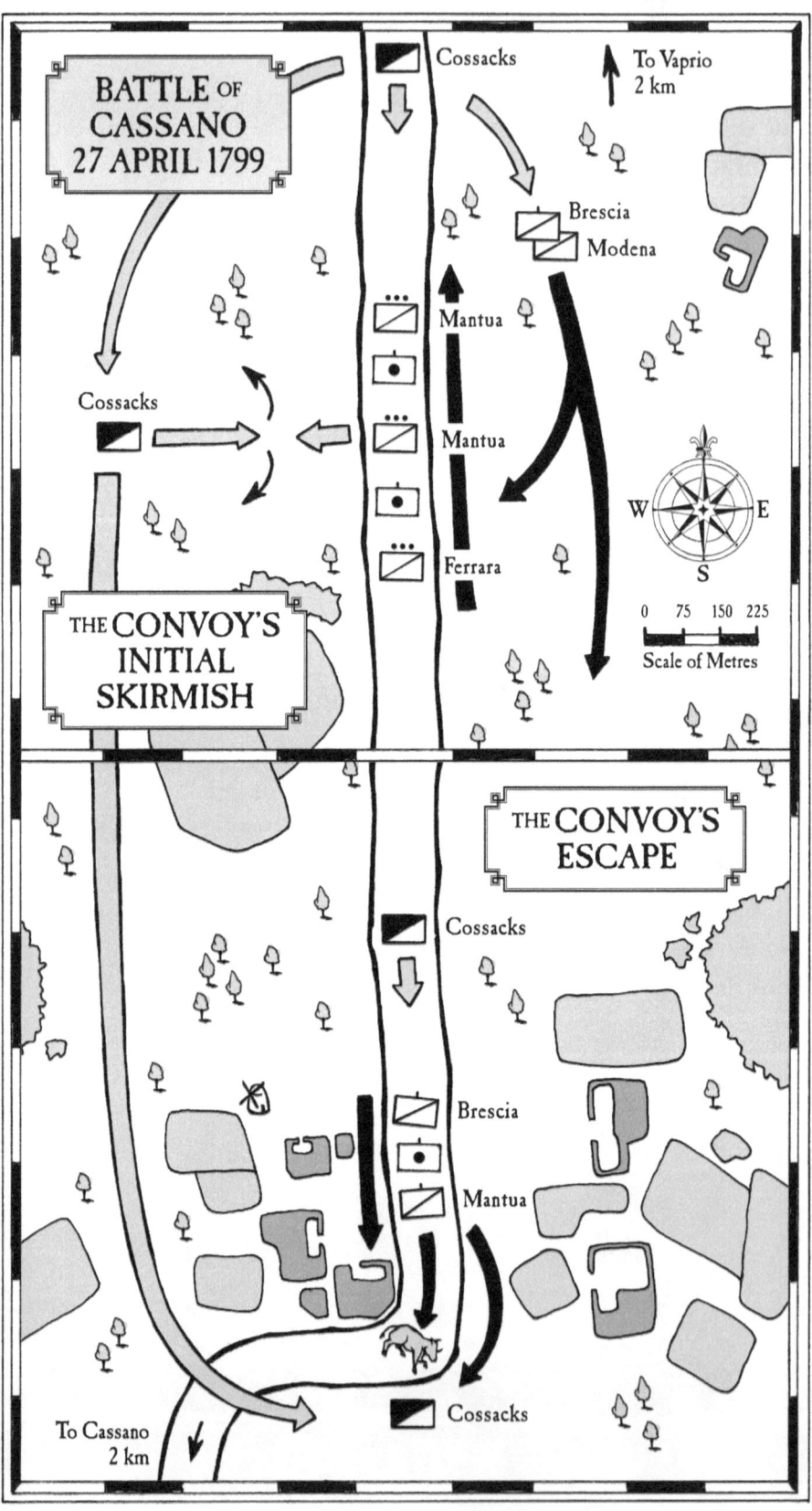

BATTLE OF CASSANO 27 APRIL 1799

Cossacks

To Vaprio 2 km

Brescia

Modena

Cossacks

Mantua

Mantua

Ferrara

THE CONVOY'S INITIAL SKIRMISH

W E

S

0   75   150   225

Scale of Metres

THE CONVOY'S ESCAPE

Cossacks

Brescia

Mantua

Cossacks

To Cassano 2 km

Chapter Nineteen
April 1799, Battle of Cassano, Italy

Three weeks after the defeat at Magnano, a late April moon glowed through the branches along the western bank of the Adda River. Tonight's fire was built on collected willow and produced more smoke than flame. Sited beyond the Mantua Company's horse lines, no singing or banter drifted from the Cisalpine platoon fires. Only the occasional stomp of horses competed with the babble of the river's current.

Jobert rubbed an oily rag over his silver-inlaid pistol. As he rubbed the carved face of the boar, it would change in the firelight. Von Maefeld sneered at him.

I am in an abyss. What have I done to deserve this?

Moench strummed his violin with his thumb as he practiced a tune. The melody from his strings merged with the chirps and clicks of frogs.

'More Figaro? Mozart, right?' Jobert asked.

'No, sir, Bach.' Moench smiled. 'Two violins in D Minor.'

The face on the pistol smiled at him with quivering dimples. The now familiar crush gripped his heart as he thought of their last moments. Gianna's last comments in Mantua were whispered on the river's gurgle. *Juliet appears dead.*

'One month into the war,' Koschak said, pausing the cleaning of his sabre to shake his head at the smoke, 'and we have retreated to the Adda with Milan at our backs.'

Moench stopped strumming. 'Why not stay forward on the Mincio and contribute directly to the defence of Mantua?'

'Who knows what Schérer was thinking?' Koschak poked the willow logs with his sabre. 'Look at the mess he has handed to Moreau. A command of twenty-six thousand men stretched over one hundred kilometres, with an enemy advancing, reinforced by the Russian hordes.'

'Are we too stretched, sir?' Moench asked.

Koschak resumed his rubbing of his steel. 'Our situation is bleak, lad.'

Jobert peered into the darkness for Gianna as the Adda murmured to the reeds. *But she is not.* 'When were we last on the Adda?'

'At Lodi in May '96,' said Koschak.

As Jobert grimaced into the smoke, his fingers savoured the timber of the pistol's butt. 'At the river crossing we found north of Lodi, did we not shoot Wolff's charger?'

A single splash sounded from the gloom as some water creature broke the surface.

'Sir,' Moench asked, 'why has Colonel Rizzoli made these changes to the squadrons?'

Koschak spat at the smoke and wriggled on his blankets to be free of it. 'Speaking of the stupidity of our superiors.'

Jobert lowered the weapon and squinted through the floating haze to Moench. 'Rizzoli is distressed that the government of Cisalpine has been evacuated from Milan. He fears for the loss of Milan. He seeks solutions to a battle fought by Eugene of Savoy here at Cassano over ninety years ago.'

Koschak scoffed. 'Eugene never lost near half his men to desertion.'

'Their desertion is understandable, though,' Jobert said. 'The loss of the chasseurs' homes to the advancing Austrians. Terrified what the Russians will do to their families.'

Koschak slashed the smoke with his blade. 'The boys are shamed at running at their first stand against the enemy. Not chasing partisans in the dark now. The silly bastards came close to losing their standard.'

Moench glanced up from his fiddle. 'And then to have it tramp ...'

For Jobert, the pistol's engraving shifted in turn to the outraged D'Onofrio, Bernasconi and Fazio at Magnano. *Why choose saving their standard over killing Von Maefeld?*

'Rizzoli's idea to reconfigure the squadrons to balance their strengths is a bad idea,' Koschak said. 'The companies have never worked together before.'

'Who is Mantua beside now?' Jobert asked.

'Ferrara.'

Jobert looked up. 'Was there not trouble between the Mantua and Ferrara Companies in Lucca?

'The lads fear the Russians now more than each other. Especially the Cossacks.'

The river rocks mumbled Gianna's words. *A means will be found for him to return.*

'Then we need to capture one.' A harsh grin creased Jobert's cheek. 'Dead or alive. And his horse.'

The willows sighed with the water's flow. *There is still hope. And then she kissed me.*

Jobert slapped his thigh. 'I have chosen to stay with the regiment.'

Koschak swung his blond head towards Jobert.

Jobert straightened. 'It is my best chance to return to Gianna.'

He squinted towards their horses. 'Where is Tulloc?'

'Here, sir.' Tulloc appeared across the fire, holding empty nosebags.

'Tulloc, have Grenzer ready for me to depart for Mantua. I may have to travel into enemy territory. I have a message for Orlande in Milan. Move to Genoa. Our fortunes are too fickle to tuck my cart in behind our column. Tulloc, visit your wife and son.' Jobert held up a stiff finger. 'You have one night, lad. Many others do not have even that. Return tomorrow without fail.'

Koschak leaned back on his blankets, his green eyes piercing the smoke. 'How are you ... we going to get behind the kaiserliks?'

'I do not know. Yet.'

The next day, north of Cassano, the ammunition convoy rumbled along the country lanes beside bramble-choked ditches.

Jobert watched swirling flocks of pigeons disturbed from their grazing by the sound of guns to the north and the smoke on the breeze.

'Russians have broken across the river to the north,' Rizzoli had said this morning. 'Take heart, men, Eugene succeeded here at Cassano in 1705. Victor is dispatching a brigade north to reinforce the line at Vaprio. Two squadrons are required in support. Zenari, take Brescia and Modena to screen the flank. D'Onofrio, with Mantua and Ferrara, escort eight caissons forward. Jobert, might I prevail upon you to assist?'

Jobert remembered D'Onofrio sagging at orders this morning with Jobert's reassignment as D'Onofrio's shadow. Any small gains of rapport with D'Onofrio prior to Jobert's clash with von Maefeld were now ash.

Behind Jobert in the column, Fazio snarled. Jobert turned to the morose chasseurs slumped in their saddles. Fazio made a show of turning his face away.

'Have you fought Cossacks, sir? Bernasconi asked beside him.

'Are you interested in their nationality or their lances?'

A lance ripped into Fergnes' back.

I was not fast enough.

'I admit to being intrigued by the lance, sir.'

Beneath his reins, Jobert's fingers tickled Bleu's hogged mane. 'Then I have fought Croatian uhlans with—'

Shouts came from the escort's advance guard.

The rumble of galloping horses pummelled the ground.

Jobert rocked Bleu into a trot. Koschak and Moench slid out of the column to follow.

Chasseurs cantered south across the meadows beside the convoy. Jobert recognised the routing men from the Brescia and Modena Companies.

Zenari's screen!

'D'Onofrio, call the Brescians to your flank! Mantua, three cheers for Brescia!'

At the ragged cheer from Mantua, the Brescian chasseurs wheeled into the column of their old mates.

The soldiers from Modena yelled 'Cossacks!' and put spurs to ribs.

'Captain D'Onofrio, report,' Jobert said.

'Major Zenari's squadron has broken, sir.' D'Onofrio glanced at the far tree lines. 'They say there are Cossacks flanking us.'

'Sound Assembly. Have these stragglers form on us.'

'Stop that racket!' Zenari yanked on his horse's mouth to

stop beside them. 'You will attract the Cossacks.'

A long low single horn note reached out through the branches.

Jobert snorted. 'Halt your companies, Major Zenari, and take a parade state. Captain D'Onofrio, may I suggest Brescia take post alongside your Mantuans. Remember Lucca. Keep the Ferrara and Modena Companies separate. We have enough difficulties fighting the Russians.'

It was soon established that Brescia paraded with forty sabres and Modena had been reduced to twenty.

'A loss of fifty percent, Zenari!' Jobert said. 'Where are the rest? Did you not sound Rally? Did the Cossacks catch you?'

'The men are cowards.' Zenari stiffened. 'The Cossacks charged us. The companies broke and ran.'

Jobert's nostrils flared. 'There are no bad soldiers, Zenari, only bad officers. Your abysmal attitude to training over the past year has been the architect of their shame.'

'Look!' Fazio shouted. 'Here the bastards come.'

In the shadows of poplars beyond the fields, over a hundred rounded black shapes trotted south. The dappled stripes of lances tipped up and away from their direction of travel as if the slender rods bent with their steady speed.

A horn blurted.

'They are summoning more, D'Onofrio,' Jobert said. 'What are your orders?'

D'Onofrio stepped his horse to Jobert's side. His breathing was shallow, his neck struggled to keep his head up. 'Sir, at this moment ... may I defer to your greater experience?'

Jobert contemplated D'Onofrio.

D'Onofrio nodded. 'Please, sir.'

Jobert's chest swelled with focussed fury. 'Moench, sound Figaro then sound Commanders In.'

Surrounding chasseurs laughed at the trumpeted opening

bars of the opera's overture.

As the officers and the sergeant major commanding the caissons gathered, Corporal Cieno reined in from the advance guard. 'Around one hundred Cossacks on the road ahead, sir.'

Another series of blasted honks confirmed the convoy's dilemma.

'Well done, Corporal,' Jobert said, 'but are they in line or has the road limited them to column?'

'Still squeezed in column, sir.'

'Our orders are to get forward to the guns,' Zenari said. 'We must cut our way through. A good time to blood the men.'

'With French chasseurs, possibly,' Jobert said, 'but not these lads. They are shaken.'

'Then circle the caissons and dismount the troops,' Zenari said, 'That is what Eugene—'

'We have one hundred and seventy sabres to hand,' said Jobert. 'More than enough to handle those raggedy-arsed pricks.'

'I can hear the rate of fire to the north decreasing, sir.' The artillery sergeant major who commanded the caissons shook his head. 'It is breaking my heart. But these Italians are recruits. The mettle is unsteady.'

'But the Cossacks are winning.' Zenari waved his hand towards the dark woods. 'They have forced us to halt. We are of no value to anyone.'

'For once I agree with you, Zenari.' Beyond the circle stood an artillery team of four horses. Jobert recognised the brand on the nearside leader's shoulder. A Chauvel brand. 'Sergeant major, unhitch your teams. The drainage bunds on the roadside will not allow the caissons to be turned.' Jobert raised his palm as the sergeant major opened his mouth. 'There is always more ball and powder. Good gunners and good teams are precious. Captain D'Onofrio, retire the convoy to Victor's defence at Cassano.'

'Sir,' Koschak said, 'the Cossacks on the flank are forming line.'

The lumpy smudges at four hundred metres emerged from the shadows. Their colour shifted to mud brown. Lowered lances no longer pricked their silhouettes but slung muskets poked above their chunky hats. Although no brass or steel glittered on the saddlery or headdress, the long line of lance tips glinted like teeth in the sunlight.

Jobert looked for D'Onofrio, who was forward integrating platoons from Brescia and Modena into the formation. Jobert drew his sabre. 'Bernasconi, fall Mantua out to me. Form line at the ready. Moench, sound Figaro.'

The cossack line rippled into a trot. A bellow of animal delight pulsed across the field. Cavalry four hundred metres apart. Twenty seconds until impact.

Turning off the lane into the paddock's stubble, Mantua Company formed two ranks. Jobert took post front and centre, then backed Bleu into the front rank.

Three hundred metres.

In the centre of the Cossacks swayed a standard, a crucifix from which bunched and braided horsetails swung, surmounted by a brass French dragoon helmet.

But they are still at the trot. The pricks are testing us.

Jobert recalculated their impact at the trot. Ninety seconds. 'Mantua Company,' Jobert cried, holding his fingertips above his head, 'converging fire on the centre.' Two hundred metres. Sixty seconds. 'Second rank, wait for it, wait …' One hundred metres, the Cossacks' eyes were distinct above their beards. 'Fire!'

The explosion rippled along the angled musketoons in the second rank. A few cossack horses stumbled to their knees. A dozen Cossacks reeled in their saddles, their horses dropping to a walk.

The front rank of chasseurs cheered and pressed their weapons into their shoulders.

A whistle shrieked. At fifty metres, the wings of the Cossacks roared with anger and lifted their horses into a canter.

'Front rank, fire!' Bleu cringed as the blast swept past them. 'Sabres! Moench, sound Charge! On me, Mantua, on me!' Steel squealed on brass. Jobert lifted Bleu onto a right-lead canter. Moench's call was drowned by the bawling chasseurs behind him.

With lances raised, the cossack line dissolved by peeling away at the flanks. Like a great flock, the Cossacks wheeled away from the rigid Cisalpine line. Some of the bearded men laughed and jeered. In acts of extraordinary athleticism, dismounted Cossacks swung up behind their mates' galloping horses, or clung between stirrup leathers to be dragged away.

Jobert thrust his sabre into the air. 'Moench, sound Halt.'

The chasseurs moaned with disappointment that their chase had been called off within one hundred metres.

Four or five Cossacks writhed in the mud at the chasseurs' feet. Less than a half-dozen horses with empty saddles sought out green pick between the clods.

'Moench, sound Figaro.' Led by Fazio and Bernasconi, the Cisalpine soldiers let out a cheer.

Jobert spun Bleu to face the company. 'Mantua, form column of fours to the left, at the trot, march! Lieutenant Bernasconi, have Mantua take their place at Captain D'Onofrio's discretion, carry on.'

As loud swearing from Fazio drove the chasseurs to focus on their orders to return to the column, Koschak and D'Onofrio came up beside Jobert and Moench.

Jobert scanned the tree line for the Cossacks. They had gathered and were moving south again.

D'Onofrio's eyes were feverish. 'We did well here, sir.'

Koschak scoffed. 'Come now, sir. Sixty converged rounds at less than one hundred metres at over one hundred enemy, and we have only five birds for our bag. And look,' Koschak leaned from his saddle and spat, 'the pricks are moving to get in behind of us.'

An alien horn wailed a pattern of signals from within the enemy's ranks.

D'Onofrio's thick eyebrows knitted at some internal debate. 'But my men are ecstatic, sir. I have not felt such since—'

'The enemy won, D'Onofrio.' Jobert looked up from his inspection from a nearby Cossack mount. 'Their charge starves our guns. We now have Cossacks to our flanks and rear. See to your convoy.'

'Sir, I can report that, with a little gunner ingenuity, we have turned two caissons and re-hitched their teams.'

'Well saved, D'Onofrio. Our enemy's success is tarnished.'

As D'Onofrio saluted Jobert before departing, their eyes locked. 'And thank you, sir.'

Being turned for home, the column of chasseur horses, with their two caissons and twelve led pairs, stepped out smartly along the lane. Jobert rode as the last man with the Brescia Company's rear guard.

Three hundred metres back in the trees and vines trailed one hundred thick shadows, lance butts resting on right toecaps.

After fifteen minutes of marching beside vine trellises, Moench alerted Jobert to a hubbub behind him. The column shuffled to a stop.

'Colonel Jobert, sir,' Corporal Cieno called, 'Captain D'Onofrio requests you attend the advance guard at your earliest convenience, please.'

With the twist of Jobert's wrist and a press of his knee, Bleu pivoted over his hocks. 'Are you good here?'

Koschak gave Jobert a reassuring nod as Bleu swung into a trot.

Two hundred metres ahead of the halted advance guard, the lane, now lined by stone walls, bent into a right-angled turn around a timber barn. On the outside of the turn, tight against the stone walls, a barricade of barn doors and gates had been erected. On the wall above the barricade, the Cossacks had erected their eerie standard. On the inside corner of the turn lay a dead bull.

Bearded faces and musket barrels peered out of barn windows, over the barricade and from behind the bull.

Jobert looked at Zenari and D'Onofrio for any sense of a plan. Bernasconi was wide-eyed with fear.

D'Onofrio jerked a submissive nod. 'The Mantua Company stands ready at your command, sir.'

Bernasconi exhaled with relief.

Zenari folded his arms with a huff. 'This is infantry work.'

'Major Zenari,' Jobert asked, 'would you be so kind as to command the column while Mantua opens the way? I remind you we still have one hundred Russians behind us.'

Zenari shook his head as he turned his horse back to the column.

Jobert peered at the obstacle ahead. 'D'Onofrio, form your two troops dismounted. You take one troop behind the left-hand wall into the grove and fight, on the outside of the lane, to attack the rear of the barricade. Once you are halfway there, I shall take Bernasconi's troop down the lane and overcome the barricade from within.'

D'Onofrio flinched. 'Sir, your troop will be trapped between the walls in the crossfire from barn and barricade.'

'I know.' Jobert dismounted and handed his reins to Moench. 'They out number us and fire muskets from behind cover.' He tucked all three pistols, his new brace and his silver-engraved, into his waist band. 'That is why we rely on you to secure the rear of the barricade.'

'Gentlemen?' Fazio said behind them.

Jobert looked around to see Fazio roll his head in agitation. 'You have my undivided attention, Sergeant.'

'We could rig up the caissons as rolling grenades,' Fazio said. 'If we push them down the lane and through the grove, they will provide cover as we advance. We could detonate them to unblock the lane.'

'A plan worthy of a fine horse gunner, Sergeant Fazio.' Jobert smiled at the possibilities. 'If fired successfully, it ought to convince the bull to doze elsewhere. Have you, or Prince Eugene of Savoy, ever done this before?'

'No, sir.' Fazio smirked at the reference. 'Well, I have not.'

'Then, Gentlemen,' Jobert turned to D'Onofrio and Bernasconi, 'organise your troops and prepare your contraptions under Sergeant Fazio's strict guidance.'

Soon after, with much shouting, D'Onofrio's bomb-wagon was wheeled through a gate into the plum grove.

Jobert's wagon began to trundle backward toward the barricade. Jobert and a team of six chasseurs pushed the device. They steered it by manipulating the centre shaft to control the front axles. The caisson was loaded with powder bags and case shot, intertwined with quick match. A long length of quick match ran down the shaft. Fazio followed with a sizzling slow match on a linstock. Fifty metres behind, Bernasconi jogged with the remaining twenty men from his troop.

Firing cracked beyond the garden wall. Fruit branches snapped and swooshed. D'Onofrio exhorted his men to keep pushing.

'Now, push, boys, push!' Jobert called. 'Keep her—'

Two dozen Russian muskets exploded from the barn and the barricade. Musket balls pinged off rims and splintered the timberwork.

An explosion roared from beyond the wall. Smoke, stones

and pieces of trees and caisson fell into the lane.

The cossack fire in the laneway paused.

A trumpet sounded Figaro as mounted chasseurs cheered.

'Go, Jobert, go!' Fazio screamed. 'The other has blown too early.'

'Push, lads!' Jobert leaned into the shaft.

Bernasconi's musketoons, now in range, kept a persistent fire at the barn's windows.

A chasseur beside Jobert screamed and collapsed as a ball shattered his knee. 'They are skipping the balls off the lane under the caisson.'

The caisson rammed into the bull.

A whistle squealed. A horn boomed off the walls. From behind the barricade, Cossacks scrambled over the wall. Yelling came from within the barn, and boots sounded on the timber floors within.

'Run clear, lads.' Jobert grabbed at chasseurs and thrust them back up the lane. 'Fazio, fire the quick match.'

From over the wall, fire poured down onto the wagon. A chasseur squatted into the earth with a groan before toppling over. Jobert unclipped his musketoon and fired at the Russian marksmen. He grabbed his two new pistols. A shower of splinters tore at Jobert's exposed face. As he cringed in pain, a glance at the shaft revealed a twist in their plan.

'Fazio! The fuse has been cut.' Jobert wiped the blood oozing across his cheeks.

Waving his smashed and extinguished linstock, Fazio ran to crouch beside Jobert. 'Fucking officers! Give me that.' Fazio pulled the silver pistol from Jobert's waist band. 'It takes a sergeant to do the job properly. When you have finished dabbing at your tears, might you consider covering me when we run like hell.'

Fazio fired the pistol. The pan's flash erupted the quick match.

Fazio dropped the pistol, turned and ran.

Jobert stood and aimed both pistols at the top of the wall. Underneath the horsetail standard, a man with a bulging thick wool cap blew a bone whistle and waved his arms.

Jobert fired.

The match hissed.

He tucked one pistol under his armpit.

The quick match sizzled under the caisson's lid.

Blinded by blood in his eyes, Jobert scrabbled in the gravel for his silver pistol.

Gripping the butt, Jobert sprinted across the lane for a gate beside the barn. He hit it with his shoulder as the blast from the exploding wagon powered him through the air. He cartwheeled into tomato stakes and narrowly missed being impaled.

Jobert gagged to breathe from the stench of cooked shit and baked rock. As he inched into the flattened tomato plants, he groped at his blood-sodden jacket.

Where am I hit?

Bernasconi appeared and was shouting. Jobert could not hear him. His head screeched as if one thousand starlings had taken up residence in his skull. 'The Cossacks have withdrawn, sir. Victory is ours.' Bernasconi pulled Jobert to his feet.

Jobert leaned on Bernasconi as he was led into the lane. 'Where are my wounds?' Jobert shouted to hear himself speak.

'You are fine, sir. You are covered in beef.'

The chasseurs rode past, their faces pale. Their horses shied at the charred remains of the bull's carcass.

Fazio shook the bull's head at his soldiers. 'Ox tongue for our supper.'

Jobert tucked his pistols away before drawing his sabre. With a clean slash, from a shattered hindquarter with only one thigh attached, he cut off the tail. 'And oxtail for your soup. Well deserved, Sergeant Fazio.'

Fazio grinned. 'Thank you, sir.' He stepped closer to Jobert. Contempt burned in his eyes as Fazio tapped Jobert on the chest with the oozing stump of the tail. 'But your sins have not been forgiven.' Fazio spun and squelched through charred innards in search of his horse.

Leading Bleu and Koschak's gelding, and with a face squeezed in consternation, Moench halted his grey mare beside Jobert. 'How are you, sir?'

'Never mind the smudge on your jacket, sir.' Koschak stepped over the rubble of a smouldering breach in the stone wall and held out to Jobert a discarded hat. 'Something for your collection.'

Jobert remembered the piercing whistle and the waving man beneath the standard. 'I just saw this hat.' The hat had a French dragoon's brass helmet encased within a furry cap. Jobert rubbed the foreign wool with his gloved fingers before discovering a ball indented deeply in the brass.

'The prick that lost this will have a headache for a while.' Koschak grinned down the lane. 'But we had better get moving.'

'Not quite yet.' Jobert holstered his pistols and laid his blackened tailcoat across his saddle.

Stepping through the hole in the wall and into the grove, Jobert approached an abandoned Russian horse. The horse sniffed his curled fist. Jobert rubbed its neck.

'Koschak, help me sling one of their dead across this saddle.' Jobert winked at Koschak. 'I have an idea.'

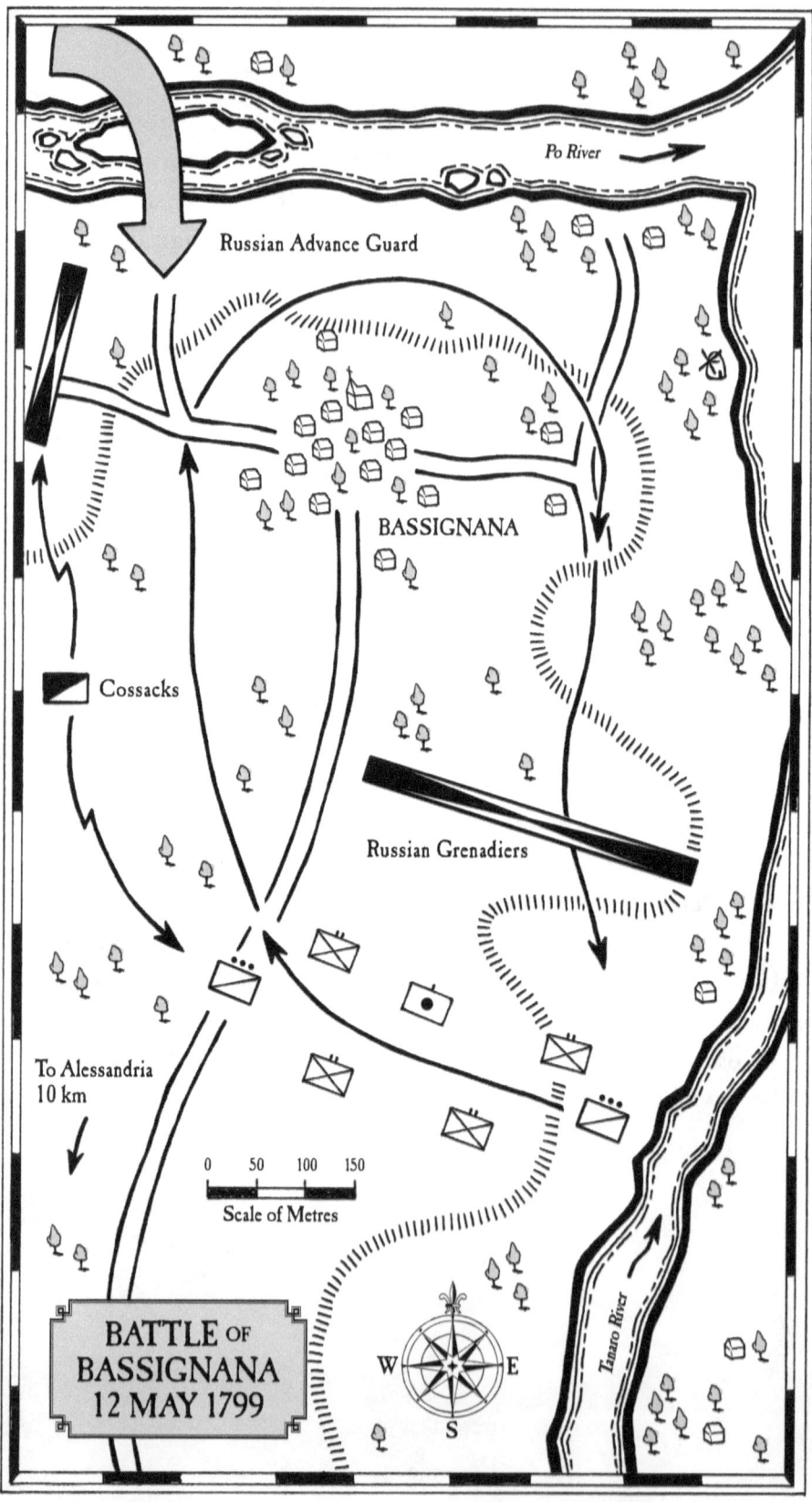

Po River

Russian Advance Guard

BASSIGNANA

Cossacks

Russian Grenadiers

To Alessandria
10 km

0   50   100   150
Scale of Metres

Tanaro River

BATTLE OF
BASSIGNANA
12 MAY 1799

W   E
S

Chapter Twenty
May 1799, Battle of Bassignana, Italy

'Ah, Jobert,' General Victor said, 'I am in need of the company of friends. Join me outside in the sunshine. I have a favourite spot.'

They walked across the aprons and ascended a bastion ramp within the citadel of Alessandria. Beyond the red brick rampart, the Tanaro River frothed over a series of rocky steps between the citadel and the town of Alessandria. On the bastion's banquette, a circle of chairs surrounded a small table upon which glasses, a bottle and a cigar box were set.

Victor poured two glasses of *disaronno*. 'When were we last on the Tanaro? Cigar?'

Jobert clipped and lit the cigar. With the cigar between his fingers and close to his face, he dabbed at the scar beneath his right eye. 'I was up in the Tanaro headwaters in '94, sir, with Masséna when we outflanked Saorgio. The only other time, again with Masséna, when we secured Cherasco in '96.'

Victor passed Jobert a glass. 'All those achievements. All now lost.'

Jobert raised his glass. 'Absent brothers.'

'Absent brothers.' Victor emptied his glass in a swallow. 'Did our fellow get away last night?'

'He did, sir,' Jobert said. Beyond the Cisalpine piquets at two o'clock in the morning, Jobert and Koschak escorted Inoubli to a release point. Before the taciturn enigma slid into the smothering river fog, Jobert passed him an envelope for Gianna. With a shrug, Inoubli pocketed Jobert's hopes and dissolved into the mist.

Jobert savoured the liqueur and considered Victor. 'How are you, sir?'

Victor stretched back on his camp chair. 'For a commander of a demoralised division in a fragmented, defeated army that has lost Lombardy and retreated three hundred kilometres to the border of Piedmont with enemies east, north and west ... I am absolutely fucking wonderful. Thank you for asking, Jobert.' Victor drew deeply on his cigar.

'Then I shall not ask if you have taken in any decent theatre recently.'

'Oh, but I have. Both high drama and great tragedy. Daily! And all performed before me in my headquarters. For example, that uproar by the artillery over your regiment's failure to deliver the ammunition resupply at Cassano. Will that spectacular opera be repeated? Do not hold me in suspense, old friend.'

Jobert blew blue smoke at the grey Tanaro. 'Desertion bleeds the regiment to death. The soldiers are terrified for the families they have left behind. The loss at Magnano, and bypassing the defence of the Mincio, abandoned the regimental communities of Mantua, Brescia, Modena, Bologna, Ferrara and Ravenna. With our defeat at Cassano, the Cisalpine Republic has been abolished and the enemy's rule over Milan and Cremona restored. Our strength of six hundred and fifty sabres before Magnano is now reduced to three hundred and fifty.'

'I appreciate the reasons for the desertion.' Victor topped up Jobert's glass. 'Was it just the lack of training that caused them to break at Cassano? I need to understand the men under my command.'

'The difficulty we all faced at Cassano was that, in light of the desertion, Rizzoli re-balanced his squadron's strengths by undoing established squadrons and coupling depleted companies with more solid ones. Burdened with regional abrasion and lack of trust in their new sister companies, the chasseurs collapsed when faced with their fevered imaginings of Cossacks.'

Victor slumped forward, his elbows on his knees, and sucked on his cigar.

'I quoted Rizzoli an example of Eugene's career.' Jobert smiled. 'The prior structure is now re-established.'

'Pissing Eugene,' Victor said. 'As Saint Thomas of Aquinas said, "Beware the man of one book". How did you find the Cossacks?'

'I examined some equipment I captured at Cassano,' said Jobert. 'Their horses and their kit are of poor quality, but it is all they have and they care for it with their limited means. I sense they are ill at ease in the gardens of Italy, but they are willing to adapt. What is of greater interest is the willingness of Suvorov to release them so far behind enemy lines. Would you ever contemplate such?'

Victor's eyebrows arched. 'To gain the disruption to my enemy that the Cossacks create? Yes, I would. If only I had a body of cavalry I trusted or could afford to give up.'

Jobert ground his cigar butt under his toecap. The Tanaro gurgled Gianna's words. *A means will be found for him to return.*

'What if such a body existed, sir?' Jobert asked. 'Of limited value behind your lines but with intimate knowledge of the ground behind the enemy's lines.'

Victor scowled as he contemplated Jobert.

Jobert nodded Victor a wink. 'Just the sort of guides that can link with the Army of Naples when it marches north.'

'Hmm, interesting,' Victor tipped his head and exhaled his cigar breath. The blue smoke wafted east across the Tanaro and beyond. 'Leave the idea with me.'

The fog crushed the light of the day as if it were still before the dawn. Despite being eight o'clock in the morning, even in a bright May sun, the fog of the mighty Po would hug the river until ten.

Jobert rode away from the column to listen to the shrouded world. The spatter of infantry skirmisher fire was warped by the fog, concealing its direction. Marching in a battery's wheel ruts, the infantry brigade they sought would soon appear to their front.

At Rizzoli's quick orders this morning, Jobert had described the ground to the regimental officers. 'The terrain is dominated by the confluence of three rivers, the Bormida into the Tanaro, then the Tanaro into the Po, and bookended by the fortresses at Alessandria and Valenza.'

The tracks they followed now were along the spine of a small height the slopes of which descended to the Tanaro beside it and the Po somewhere in front.

'Thank you, Jobert,' Rizzoli said. 'As we were at Cassano two weeks ago, General Victor's division faces the Austrians east across the Bormida at Marengo. To our north, the Russians have crossed the Po at Bassignana. May I remind all that this is the site of de Maillebois' success in '45.'

Jobert closed his eyes and gave a small shake of his head.

Rizzoli continued, 'General Victor has ordered a brigade north to block the Russian bridgehead, as does a pincer force from Valenza. Major Zenari, take the Mantua and Brescia squadron. Jobert, if I might impose...'

Jobert resented de Chabenac's gracious smile as he departed the gathering.

Once the chasseurs found the infantry in the mist, the brigade, with its forward battalions in column, was tilted from the summit on the left down to the Tanaro River on its right. With chasseur column halted, Jobert and Zenari soon found the infantry brigade commander among the limbered guns and their plodding gunners.

'Jobert,' the brigadier said, 'thank sweet Mary you are here.'

'I am only an attaché, sir. I do not command.'

'Surely they defer to your advice.'

Jobert nodded towards Zenari. 'May I introduce Major Zenari.'

Zenari drew himself up in the saddle. 'Sir, my chasseur squadron will screen your river flank.'

The general's face soured. 'I have a better idea. If you do not listen to him, then you will listen to me. Then you do what I tell you. Keep these damned Cossacks off my flanks.' He swished a hand at the mist. 'Split your squadron. One company on my river flank seeking any further Russian crossings. The other company seeking to link with the regiments from Valenza. Once deployed, obey Jobert. Do not stand there, man. March! What the hell are your people playing at, Jobert?'

'Excuse us, sir,' Jobert said. 'Come, Zenari. What is your plan?'

Zenari's head wobbled, and his lips pulsed at a raging conversation in his mind. 'Pissing Cossacks. We brushed them off at Cassano.'

Jobert scoffed. 'We did not brush them off, you idiot. You lost half of your command due to the fear of their reputation. No impact! We failed to resupply the battery and gave six full caissons to the enemy. Who will, no doubt, return those balls to us at a heavy price.'

Zenari fidgeted with his reins and rocked in his saddle. 'D'Onofrio, do you have any suggestions?'

'Knowing my squadron, sir, may I suggest you taking Brescia Company and seek the French regiments converging on Bassignana.'

Jobert bent his head as if already knowing the answer. 'Would you accept the services of Lieutenant Koschak?'

'I most certainly will not,' Zenari said.

Zenari's Brescia Company of fifty chasseurs ascended the ridge behind the French line.

Jobert watched the departing soldiers as they rode past. 'D'Onofrio, what are Mantua and Brescia chasseurs wearing on their mirlitons?'

'Sergeant Fazio skinned one of the captured cossack ponies and wrapped a strip of hide around his brim. The rest of the squadron took up the habit. I felt a discreet symbol might bring them together. Do you object, sir?'

Jobert shrugged. 'Not if it binds them.'

The infantry advance was slow. The creases in the ridgeline that ran towards the village of Bassignana, nestled in the confluence of the rivers, created difficulties for the wide infantry formation.

Intense musket fire cracked on the far flank. The flank that was Zenari's responsibility.

An aide from the brigadier's headquarters trotted to find Jobert. 'Cossacks on our left, sir. Our flank battalion has lost contact with your chasseurs beyond the ridge line. The brigadier wishes you to know of his displeasure that he has been forced to bring up a depth battalion to cover his flank.'

Jobert winced. 'I fear, in his eagerness, Zenari has broken contact with our brigade by crossing the ridge line to find the Valenza force.'

D'Onofrio's face showed patient deference to Jobert.

Jobert twisted in the saddle to include Koschak. 'Let us remedy this situation quickly, D'Onofrio. Leave a troop with Koschak and bring Bernasconi's troop.'

'Sir,' D'Onofrio said, 'I would be obliged if Lieutenant Koschak assumes temporary command of the troop in my absence.'

Jobert considered D'Onofrio. 'Ready for your first command as an officer, Koschak?' Koschak grinned. 'Then, your troop until we return. Take post.'

Jobert, D'Onofrio and Bernasconi's troop of thirty sabres rode up the slope away from the river. Jobert scanned the ground as the column trotted behind the three-hundred-metre-long French line. Here and there, in their green coats, lay dead Russian skirmishers and their looted satchels.

'What are you looking for, sir?' Moench asked.

'There are no enemy helmets.'

'Perhaps the infantry picked them up.'

'All of them?' Jobert asked.

As Bernasconi's troop crested the rise beyond the flanking battalion, muted shouts were heard in the fog over the rumble of trotting hooves. Jobert's alarm subsided as the silhouettes were clearly chasseurs. A curtain of cloud parted to reveal a troop from Brescia Company.

'Brescia, stand fast with Mantua,' called Jobert. 'Only half the company? Where are the rest?'

A ramrod straight ex-Austrian sergeant saluted. 'We lost Major Zenari in the fog, sir. I did not know what to do. I returned the column uphill until I found our line.'

'You did well, Sergeant. Take post. Zenari is now lost behind enemy lines. What would you suggest, D'Onofrio?'

D'Onofrio's thick brows furrowed. 'I would split my force to achieve the task. The Brescians will screen the flank. My Mantuans will seek Major Zenari.'

'I agree. Who commands each?' Jobert asked.

'The Brescia troop has no officer. I would confer the honour on Bernasconi.' D'Onofrio fidgeted with his reins. 'But he has little experience. I will stay with Brescia, if you, sir, might take Bernasconi's men to find those missing.'

'I support your initial assessment,' Jobert said. 'Bernasconi, take command of these Brescians. Your first independent command reporting directly to a general.'

'Yes, sir.' Bernasconi saluted briskly.

A horn sounded in the mist. Horses neighed. Foreign shouts.

Bernasconi deflated as he scoured the fog through the trees.

'Bernasconi, remain focussed!' Jobert said. 'Maintain your visual distance with the infantry column. Send a messenger to the flanking battalion commander if the Cossacks come too close.'

D'Onofrio peered into the vale of murk. 'How will we find Major Zenari, sir?'

'Just as you pursued me through Liguria those years ago. We track them. Over twenty shod horses in column of fours. The Cossacks ride unshod.' Jobert tickled Jaune's shorn mane. 'Pass orders to march in silence, D'Onofrio.'

As Jobert followed the shoed hoof prints down the hill, the wall and rooves of Bassignana blurred into view on their right.

The steady tap of infantry drums setting the pace rattled the air, yet their direction from the chasseurs was unclear.

'How do you feel being forced further and further from Mantua?' Jobert asked.

D'Onofrio shifted with discomfort in his seat. 'Someone binds me to Mantua. Her spell is what stops my return to imperial service.'

'What if there was a way to return?'

D'Onofrio's face spun towards Jobert in alarm. 'I cannot believe you would suggest—'

'No! Neither desert nor switch sides.' Jobert held up a palm. 'Listen to this idea. Look at us now, D'Onofrio, we are behind the enemy lines, just as the Cossacks prowl behind ours. This is our land. We could do what they do. Who better? We know the land, the people.'

Jobert met D'Onofrio's suspicious glare. *I know this country. I have lost brothers here.*

Jobert continued, 'I have raised with General Victor the concept of our Italian chasseurs roving behind enemy lines. Do you not want the opportunity to visit your families? Here is our chance to prove the worth of the regiment. Let us show Rizzoli—'

Axles squealed in front. At a treelined road junction, a Russian foot battery turned west onto the Valenza road.

D'Onofrio raised a hand to halt the column. 'Where are they coming from?'

'The river,' Jobert whispered. 'Behind them lies their crossing point. They are reinforcing their bridgehead with guns.'

D'Onofrio bent to examine the ground. 'The print trail leads away to—'

'Shut up! Someone approaches,' Jobert hissed. A rider trotted toward them. 'Stay calm. Fazio, silence in the ranks.'

A Russian officer with a broad bicorne and a dark green jacket saluted. 'Forgive me, gentlemen. Do you speak French?'

Jobert returned the salute. 'Of course.'

'Thank heavens, my German is poor. Are you the Austrian hussars attached to Semernikov's Cossacks?'

Jobert bowed his head. 'At your service, sir.'

The Russian slumped with relief. 'My battalion commander has been directed to support the left of the line, so the brigade can step back across the river. Are you in contact with our sister battalion? How far up are the French dogs?'

At the road junction, more troops marched behind their tapping drummers. The officers wore bicornes. The ranks had tall, tapering mitre caps, not black bicornes.

Grenadiers! A battalion, no … a regiment of Russian grenadiers. No wonder our infantry souvenired their headdress.

'How fortuitous we meet?' Jobert said. 'I have been sent to guide you. Your sister battalion is pressing the French back some five hundred metres. This cursed fog mutes their firefight. The fastest path is behind Bassignana. Have new orders been received to recross the Po again?'

The Russian's face creased with confusion. 'Yes.'

'Then I must make haste to warn Semernikov. We are both unaware. Follow our trail this way.'

'I am obliged. I shall inform my commander.' The aide saluted before departing.

'The fastest path, sir?' D'Onofrio asked. 'Why?'

'A simple delay. It was all I could think of. They have orders to withdraw, not to press south to this side of the Tanaro. We need to inform Victor.'

As Jobert's column followed the horseshoe prints east and then south around the vines and kitchen smoke of Bassignana, the grenadiers' drums increased their rhythm. In the farm lanes close to the junction of both rivers, the column was enclosed in a sunken road crowned by gnarled bushes.

At a curve ahead, muskets cocked and a horse beyond the bend neighed.

'Who goes?' called a French sentry from the mist.

A chasseur's horse in the column responded.

Jobert bent towards Fazio leading the column. 'Horseshoe. What an appropriate password for the day.' Jobert faced front so he would forego the pleasure of Fazio's reaction.

Beyond the curve, horses lined the sunken road. Chasseurs crouched under the crowning shrubs as sentries.

Zenari strode towards them. 'What are you doing here?'

'Where do you think here is, Zenari?' Jobert asked.

Zenari thrust out his chin. 'Somewhere on the Valenza road west of Bassignana.'

'No. You are lost. You are the south-east side of Bassignana.'

'What?' Zenari spun around, his hands reached out as if in the dark. 'D'Onofrio, where do you say we are? We have Russians in front of us. Grenadiers, no less.'

'You have another battalion of grenadiers marching up behind.' The steady drumbeat crept through sodden leaves.

'The Russians have crossed the Po on the wrong side of the Tanaro. They are withdrawing this bridgehead north to join the Austrians. General Victor would welcome your intelligence. We need to move now. D'Onofrio, mount these Brescians.'

'Captain D'Onofrio, sir,' said Fazio, 'there are Cossacks in the mist. They are in skirmish line not column. They are hunting us.'

'A sound evaluation, Sergeant,' Jobert said.

Fazio frowned at the compliment.

Jobert led the column south out of the sunken road. They hugged the willows on the riverbank. The rushing Tanaro engulfed any noise of shod hooves rattling river stones in the mud. Every chasseur scanned the mist for dark lumps with lances.

A sharp fusillade exploded ahead, halting the column. Jobert rode forward to observe dark-jacketed officers on horses behind three ranks of mitre-wearing soldiers. The fog enclosed their gun smoke about them, so the exchange of fire with the French beyond was intermittent.

'There is a grenadier battalion between us and our brigade,' Jobert said.

Zenari rubbed his jowl. 'Why can we not swim the river?'

'D'Onofrio,' Jobert asked, 'have you trained your chasseurs in river crossings?'

D'Onofrio and Fazio exchanged looks of alarm. 'What would you suggest, sir?'

Jobert scowled at Zenari. 'Since we are forced to play a poor hand, I wager with dread. Should we dismount and hold a sunken road, we would deter the Cossacks but swiftly become the target for the following grenadiers. I would place my stake on surprise.' He nodded towards the firefight to their north. 'The Russians are not expecting us. At the canter march, we will aim at the small gap between companies, where the cluster of sergeants are holding spontoons. We will have the chasseurs fire right and left as they pass through. We will slide through them like a hot knife through lard.'

Zenari leaned on his holsters. 'Should their rear rank about face and fire a volley, we are lost.'

'Zenari, if I cover your sword arm will you lead us out.'

Zenari sat up straight. 'I do not require my sword arm covered.'

Jobert bared his teeth. 'Then, at the next grenadier volley, form column of platoon and canter march. Now!'

The grenadiers' line rippled with disciplined platoon fire towards the French line.

'Cisalpine Chasseurs,' Zenari cried, 'column of platoons, canter march!'

Jobert called over his shoulder, 'Moench, sound Charge.'

Through the river weeds, raced the sixty chasseurs, eight ranks of horsemen, seven men abreast.

The Russians spun towards the threat. Junior officers and sergeants in the rear rank came *en garde* with respective swords and spontoons. In lieu of any alternative commands, the grenadier ranks shrank back towards their company comrades.

The gap widened as the leading chasseurs fired their musketoons. The first two ranks flew through with a cheer.

As the third and fourth ranks fired and spurred their horses into the fog beyond, Jobert checked Jaune and fired each of his pistols in turn into the closest command figures standing rear of the ranks.

A tall Russian sergeant charged Jobert with his spontoon.

Jobert fired his last pistol at the running man. The shot went wide.

Holstering his pistol, Jobert trapped his sabre tip with his toe to snatch his grip. As the spontoon's broad blade raced towards his belly, with a roll of his wrist and a bend of the elbow to generate the tip speed needed for a nearside cut, Jobert beat away the spontoon's shaft. The spontoon's head raked down his stirrup leathers and across his booted ankles.

In a digging motion, the grenadier reversed the momentum of his weapon and thrust it upwards at Jobert's throat.

Maintaining Jaune's bend with his heel, Jobert swept his blade up to parry the spontoon high. With another wrist roll, the sabre slashed into the grenadier's left armpit.

My first Russian.

As the grenadier moaned and stepped back, Jobert pivoted Jaune to snatch the shaft of the spontoon.

Gripping his spontoon tight with his right hand, the Russian roared his anger as his left arm fell to his side.

'Sir,' Moench cried, 'We need to go!'

Jobert dropped his sabre onto its sword knot and twisted the sergeant's tall, embroidered mitre cap from his head. With a rock of his hips, Jaune launched into a canter behind the last heels of the fleeing chasseurs.

Ahead a trumpet call sounded Rally. The French line hunkered dark in the mist.

'Moench, sound Figaro,' Jobert called. 'Ride for Koschak, Mantua and home.'

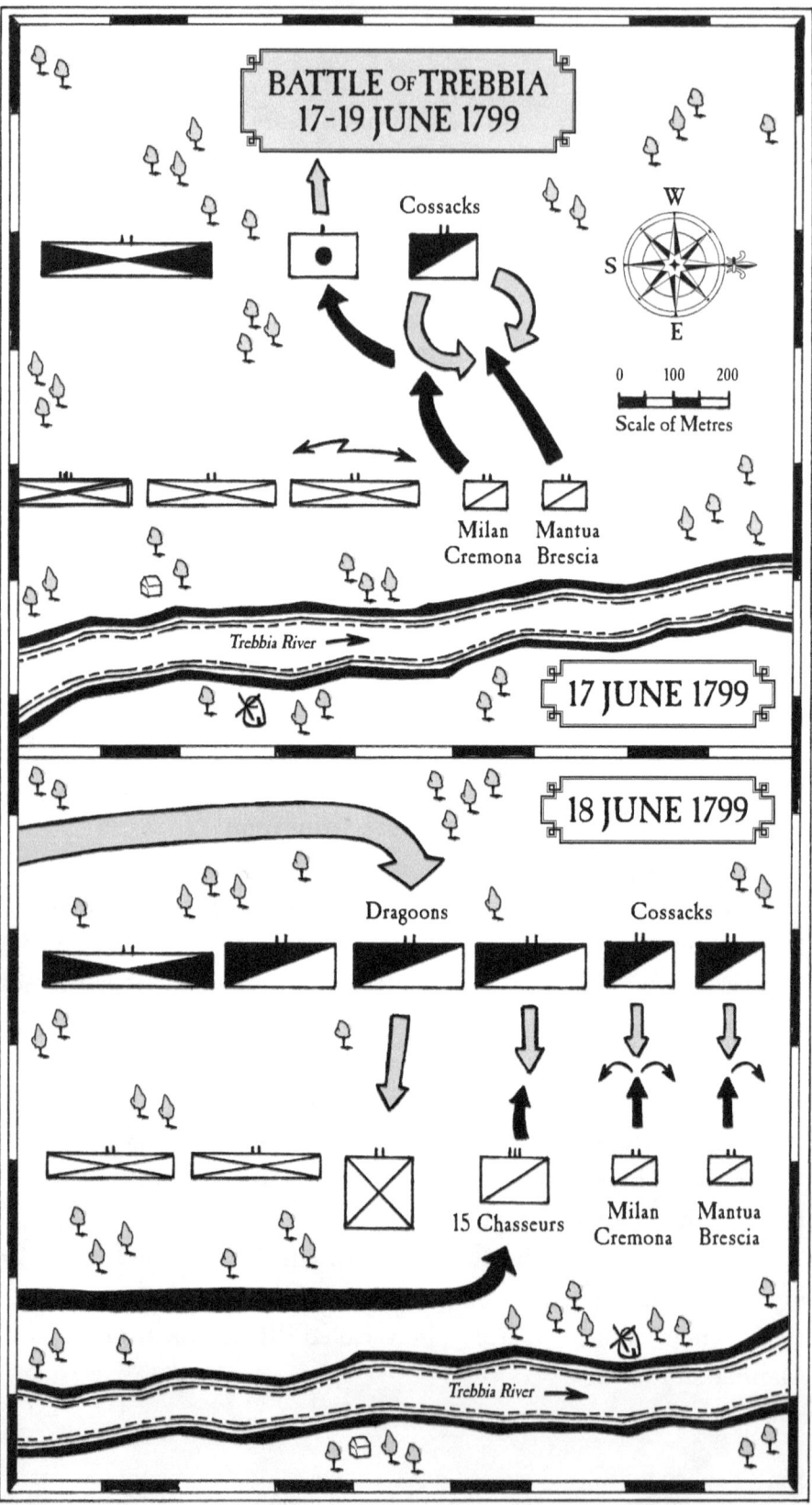

BATTLE OF TREBBIA
17-19 JUNE 1799

Cossacks

W
S · E

0   100   200
Scale of Metres

Milan   Mantua
Cremona Brescia

Trebbia River →

17 JUNE 1799

18 JUNE 1799

Dragoons   Cossacks

15 Chasseurs   Milan   Mantua
               Cremona Brescia

Trebbia River →

Chapter Twenty-One
June 1799, Battle of Trebbia, Italy

With the combined pressure around Alessandria, of the Austrians from the east and the Russians from the north, Moreau chose to withdraw the Army of Italy across the Maritime Alps to the Ligurian coast.

In their farm billet north of Genoa, Jobert added a splash of water to the tot of *vermentino* in his and de Chabenac's cups.

Jobert averted his eyes as Tulloc and Maria shared a small tenderness, their fingertips brushing together as they passed each other in their evening duties. Jobert reached for Gianna's book, kept in his tailcoat pocket.

Returning from the wash tub, de Chabenac accepted his offered cup to hunch in his camp chair. 'Over a month since departing Alessandria.' The last rays of the day's sun etched lines of despondency in his face. 'Did you receive replacement dentures?'

Jobert hooked a finger in his cheek to show his teeth. 'Temporary.' Jobert nudged de Chabenac's boot with his toe. 'Cheer up, old friend. We will not be here long. There is hope.'

De Chabenac shook his head. 'With Turin falling to the Russians, we have lost Piedmont.'

'But not for long,' Jobert said. 'Masséna has taken command in Switzerland and will soon crush the Russians. Moreover, we are saved. Macdonald and the Army of Naples marches north to join us. Admittedly, it has only taken three months for those idiots to realise they would be corked in the bottle.'

De Chabenac winced at the purple sunset over the Ligurian hills. 'With Austrian and British support, the new republic in Naples has reverted to the Neapolitan Kingdom. That infers there is an Austrian, Neapolitan and British force behind our Army of Naples.'

'No, we cannot fail.' Jobert toasted the dusk. 'With a combined strength of fifty thousand concentrated to thrust north into their lines of communication, we have more now than we had with Bonaparte in '96.'

'Our strength on paper does not relieve my despair,' De Chabenac smiled. 'Desertion continues to emaciate the regiment.'

'Have not reinforcements from Bologna to Ravenna answered the call and returned with the Army of Naples?' Jobert gripped de Chabenac's drooping shoulder. 'Have faith in our young men.'

Sixteen-year-old Quandalle approached Orlande's dinner preparations with a freshly plucked and gutted chicken.

I had killed by his age. Jobert's fingers slid for his dagger handle, only to scratch at his bare wrist emerging from his shirtsleeves.

With no protection from his mirliton cap, Jobert's face stung in the June heat. The dust haze from the summer's wheat stubble did little to avert the searing rays. Jobert licked his lips and forced back the temptation of his water flask.

Victor's division was attached to the recently arrived Army of Naples. On the northern end of line, with the Po River on their right, Victor's lead brigade advanced west across the Trebbia, a north-flowing tributary of the Po. D'Onofrio's eighty Mantuans and Brescians held the right of the line. As the French battalions pushed onto the plain beyond the Trebbia, Jobert watched Austrian jäger and Russian Cossacks retire their skirmish lines.

Every now and then Jobert would check over his shoulder to the east.

Mantua and Gianna are only three days hard riding from here.

'Is it an omen, sir? asked Bernasconi. Jobert darted an irritated glance away from the retiring enemy line. 'That on this very Trebbia plain, two thousand years ago Consul Sempronius was defeated by the invading barbarians?'

'No, Bernasconi, it is not an omen. Our victory over Suvorov today will avenge Italy's loss to Hannibal.'

Bernasconi beamed over his shoulder at the chasseurs behind him. 'The men are buoyed by their success over the Cossacks at Cassano and deceiving them at Bassignana.'

Beyond Bernasconi, D'Onofrio grimaced.

Jobert glared at Bernasconi. 'We do not face partisans today, nor are we an escort escaping an ambush. As we were at Magnano, Bernasconi, today we do our duty in the line. Keep your eyes and your mind on your troop.'

Bernasconi's exuberance sobered.

The commander of the flanking battalion, beside which D'Onofrio's chasseurs marched, trotted towards them. 'Jobert, the Austrian line blocks Victor's left, yet we overlap their line here on the right. They have brought up horse artillery.' The chief of battalion waved an arm into the yellow haze. 'Victor sees an opportunity to envelop, but I cannot expose my skirmishers to those Cossacks. My regimental commander requires you to move the Cossacks and cause the kaiserlik guns to flee.'

Jobert looked to Bernasconi. 'Having bested the Cossacks before, are you ready to best them again?'

Bernasconi blanched and swallowed something that had risen in his throat.

'Sir.' D'Onofrio looked behind his chasseur line.

Rizzoli and Zenari arrived with one hundred sabres of the Milan and Cremona Companies. Jobert and D'Onofrio rode to meet them.

'I have been ordered to drive off the Cossacks,' Rizzoli said.

The ominous crack of Austrian six-pounders, five-hundred metres on Jobert's half-left, shattered the cacophony of musket fire, drumbeats and shouting.

'Take heart, sir,' Zenari said. 'Pinned between us here and Moreau's force behind them, we have this army trapped. We will drive them north, sever their lines of communication, secure Milan and restore the Cisalpine Republic.'

Rizzoli gave a wan smile. 'Before we overwhelm Suvorov's entire army, Zenari, might we confine our attention to the swarm of Cossacks before us. Jobert, what has your study of Eugene informed your views of this situation.'

Jobert stiffened. 'This northerly breeze will drive our dust before us and cover our movement. The Prince of Savoy would demand alacrity, sir. Attack or be damned.'

Rizzoli breathed and swallowed with discomfort. 'Then, D'Onofrio, see off the Cossacks with your Mantuans and Brescians. Zenari, with Milan and Cremona, on my order, either support D'Onofrio or charge the gun line.'

'Will you remain here with the standard, sir?' Zenari asked.

'We do not want to provide Jobert another chance to lose it.'

In an effort not to draw his sabre, Jobert clenched his fist to the point of cramping.

As Jobert and D'Onofrio returned to the front of the Mantuans and Brescians, D'Onofrio asked, 'May I ask for your guidance, please, sir?'

Jobert glanced at Bleu and tickled his hogged mane. 'Cock all hammers. Draw sabres. Then straight at their heart, D'Onofrio.' Jobert scanned the line of apprehensive men. 'Sergeant Fazio, we are to shift the Cossacks to shift their horse guns. Sweaty gloves on sweaty reins. Stow the lads' left gloves.' Jobert held up his hand, removed his glove and pushed it deep into his holster.

Jobert stood in his stirrups. The forty-metre-long line seemed so meagre.

'Mantua and Brescia,' Jobert called, 'this is our dust. Our heat. From their frozen wastes, the barbarians wilt before our Italian sun. If we can confound Cossacks in Italian fog, then we can confound Cossacks in Italian dust.'

Bernasconi led the cough of hoarse cheers.

'Koschak, on me,' Jobert called. 'There is no time to train chasseurs to parry lances when they have never parried their own sabres. The trained sabre tip will always have leverage over a trained lance tip. Koschak, you and I can parry them easily enough. If we stay toe-to-toe on Moench, we will break their line.'

Koschak gave a wicked smile. 'I understand.'

Moench jerked in shock. 'Toe-to-toe on me?'

'Moench,' Jobert said, 'stow your trumpet, present your musketoon. The three of us will lead the chasseurs. Keep your heels down. Koschak and I will crush you from both sides. Fire at whatever is ahead of us. Our pistols will be at your knees. Use them. Koschak and I will lift the first lances, then we will be through. Watch our backs. These scruffy pricks ride too loose in their line to have impact, but they will come at all angles in a melee.'

'Mantua and Brescia,' D'Onofrio called, 'squadron battleline, trot, march!'

The chasseurs' line surged.

In response, without hearing any signal, the Cossacks flowed from skirmish line to untidy mass. Despite the wasted condition of their warhorses – *ponies really*, thought Jobert – and the poor seat of their riders – *they ride too high and too short, and far too harsh on their horses' mouths* –, the Cossack formation flowed into a canter.

'At them at the canter, Moench,' Jobert called. 'D'Onofrio, we will break the line. Follow us through.'

The ground blurred as Bleu leapt into a canter. Jobert's left knee and boot toe held Bleu's surging stride neck and neck against Moench's grey.

The cossack line sped towards them.

'Moench, kill their commander.'

The bearded rider rose from his stirrups and flung his lance at the trio.

The lance arced through the air.

'My lance,' called Koschak.

Moench fired.

Koschak caught the plunging lance and guided it wide.

'Give point! Heels down.' Jobert stretched forward out of his saddle.

Lance tips in three strides.

The Cossacks ahead split. Their lance tips remained trained on the thundering chasseurs. The rider on Jobert's left thrust as Jobert passed.

Jobert dropped his blade to sweep the lance to his rear. He heard a sharp clack as Koschak disposed of his lance. Jobert rolled his wrist to bring the sabre back on point.

'Second rank,' yelled Moench.

'Pistols,' yelled Koschak.

Not riding toe-to-toe, the second rank of sabre-wielding Cossacks split apart.

The rider on Jobert's left swung a strong nearside cut down onto Bleu's face. Jobert twisted his wrist to parry the blow past his boot.

'Check, Jobert,' cried Koschak.

Jobert extended his little finger on his sabre hand and shortened his reins. 'Split left, lads. Moench, on me.' Jobert gripped Bleu between his knees. Bleu bounded shorter, changed his canter lead and swept to the left.

Jobert saw the Cossack formation had dissolved. The chasseurs coughed a cheer in the thick dust as they plunged ahead. Jobert saw the seamless canter of the Cossacks wrapping for the chasseurs' flanks.

Jobert checked Bleu and stood in his stirrups to twist backwards. 'Koschak, find D'Onofrio. They have our flanks. Rally clear. Moench, sound Rally!'

Moench fumbled to shorten his reins with a pistol in his hand and grope for his swinging trumpet.

'Drop it, Moench, sound Rally.' Jobert glanced down to see if it was his pistol that was dropped. It was.

'Jobert, parry left,' called Koschak.

Jobert dropped his blade toward his left boot toe. A lance caught the blade with a clang. Jobert pressed his left heel and lifted his sabre high left. The shaft sizzled up his blade and cracked against his hilt. The iron tip slashed past his shoulder as the rider passed on into the fight.

Moench started to sound the long notes of Rally. He stopped to scream, 'Jobert. Parry nearside hind.'

Still cantering on a left-lead arc, Jobert twisted his hips and lifted Bleu's ribs with his left spur. As Bleu bucked in the stride,

Jobert glimpsed a Cossack just beyond Bleu's rump, oriental sabre extended.

The rider reversed his thrust up at Jobert's face.

Jobert leaned back as the thrust sliced passed his chin.

As the Cossack thundered passed, he punched at Jobert with the handle of his whip.

The strike hit Jobert's jaw like a hammer. His mouth filled with blood and wooden shards.

Just forward of Bleu, the Cossack shut his horse down onto its haunches, spun at right angles and disappeared into the dust.

Jobert spat his shattered dentures clear. *Agile pricks.*

Ahead a chasseur's horse kicked out a lance which had penetrated its left hock. The horse's panicked actions were flaying its tendons. The rider attempted to dismount the bucking remount. It was Fazio. He fell heavily in a clatter of sabre and musketoon.

Seeing he was clear, Jobert dropped his sabre, drew his silver-inlaid pistol and charged Bleu into Fazio's rearing horse. Holding Bleu with his knees, Jobert grabbed at the horse's bridle and fired the pistol just above the browband. The horse collapsed beneath Bleu.

Holstering his pistol and shortening his reins, Jobert pivoted Bleu back to Fazio. 'Fazio, up behind.'

Fazio spat. 'I need no help from you.' Fazio hailed a lost chasseur and swung up behind the man's portmanteau.

In a blare of trumpeted Figaro, a pulse of horseflesh surged into the fight.

Zenari, Milan and Cremona!

The Cossacks about them thinned into the dust.

Riding out of the haze, Jobert glimpsed the final cannons in the Austrian battery limbering.

The long notes of Rally seeped through dust-choked shouts, pistol fire and grunting horses.

French infantry roared as they surged forward, sunlight on their bayonets.

Jobert stood in his stirrups and screamed, 'Victory!'

The chasseurs waved their sabres above their heads.

Jobert spat blood. *Soon to be healed with a kiss.*

The second day of the battle was cloudless. Across the plain west of the Trebbia, farms with double-storied barns broke the flat horizon. The air shimmered beyond the enemy line. Small whirls of dust spiralled between poplar-lined tracks.

Suvorov's Russians and Austrians advanced at eleven o'clock. All the divisions of the Army of Naples, including Victor's, locked into their defensive positions. The guns roared to Jobert's south. Battle was joined at two o'clock.

Eight hundred metres across from Jobert, five hundred Cossacks flanked the northern end of the Austrian line. Standing behind Rizzoli and beside de Chabenac in the withering heat, Jobert closed his eyes against the desire to gaze over his shoulder towards Mantua.

'Your thoughts on the day, sir?' de Chabenac asked.

Jobert shrugged. 'Yesterday we threw them west, but we did not overwhelm them. Today they will launch upon us, and we must bleed them to a standstill. Tomorrow, we must strike.'

'Had you heard?' Rizzoli asked over his shoulder. 'As at Magnano, yesterday another battalion of Poles were trapped and massacred. The news has rattled my boys.'

Jobert and de Chabenac exchanged looks of concern.

Over the random cracks of skirmish fire, a deep rumble of

hooves could be heard and felt.

Jobert could see dust being raised behind the enemy line to the south, but the sound was much closer. He stood in his stirrups to look over the Cisalpine battleline. 'We have a regiment of chasseurs forming beside us.'

The commander of the 15th Chasseurs trotted up, introduced himself to Rizzoli and produced his telescope to observe the enemy. 'To the south, the enemy is attacking Victor's left. Our infantry regiments are moving into reserve. Our line is shortening. We have been sent to support the northern flank.'

Jobert pointed beyond the enemy fusiliers and the patient Cossacks. 'There is the source of the dust.'

One thousand, two hundred Austrian dragoons wheeled into battleline beside their fusiliers. The cossack swarm drifted north to accommodate the six hundred metres of large black horses surmounted by white jackets and black bicornes.

Beside the chasseurs, the French battalion beat to square. Their fire line bent to the clatter of jostling fusiliers and the roar of swearing sergeants.

'My four hundred shall take the dragoons,' said the commanding officer of the 15th Chasseurs, 'I will leave the Cossacks for you, Rizzoli.'

Rizzoli blinked. 'Are there not reserves? How close is Moreau behind the enemy?'

The French chasseur colonel gave Rizzoli a look of disdain. 'There is no one else. This affair is ours to resolve. My men are ready to see them off. Are yours?'

Rizzoli squirmed in his saddle. 'The Cossacks are twice our number.'

'But they are barbarians and we men of honour. Support my flank, Rizzoli.' The colonel departed at the trot.

Across the summer stubble, a trumpet call rang. The entire dragoon and Cossack line advanced at the walk.

Rizzoli sat so still the flies settled on his shoulders.

De Chabenac cleared his throat. 'How would you resolve this conundrum, Colonel Jobert?'

Rizzoli stiffened.

Jobert raised his eyebrow to de Chabenac and remained silent.

Rizzoli sagged before twisting in the saddle. 'Your thoughts on our ... predicament, Jobert?'

He has had eighteen months to ask, thought Jobert, and he asks within a minute to impact.

'We do not have to accept the role of Sempronius, sir, and be befuddled by such exotic beasts.'

Rizzoli looked at the Cossacks. 'Oh, Hannibal's elephants, of course. Very good.' De Chabenac's eyes flicked in alarm at the approaching wall of white dragoons. 'I am reminded of Eugene at Mohács—'

The trumpets of the 15th Chasseurs signalled the French chasseurs forward at the trot.

'Perhaps a topic at our leisure over dinner, sir,' Jobert said.

'Very well then, Jobert, what might you suggest?'

'Straight at them, sir,' Jobert said. 'Mirror the 15th Chasseurs and echelon D'Onofrio's squadron right.'

Rizzoli's shoulders sagged, raising a cloud of flies which deserted his jacket for his horse's rump.

Jobert turned in his saddle. 'Moench, escort Tulloc and Bleu to camp. Find food and plenty of water for Koschak's and my return.' Moench started to open his mouth. Jobert raised a rigid finger in warning. 'No discussion. Go.'

Cisalpine trumpets reinforced Rizzoli's orders. Rizzoli led the Milan and Cremona Companies forward at the trot.

At four hundred metres, the dragoons and Cossacks began to trot.

Jobert peeled Jaune over beside D'Onofrio's Mantuans and

Brescians holding their trailing position at the walk. Ahead on their left, the fifty-metre line of Rizzoli's squadron was bracketed by the two-hundred metre bulwark of Cossacks.

D'Onofrio's shook his head at Jobert as he signalled Trot March.

Jobert looked back to Koschak. Beyond Mantua's and Brescia's short ranks, Koschak gave a nod of grim determination.

On their left the 15th Chasseurs sounded Charge. Their left-most squadron raced towards the dragoons.

The dragoons roared at their release into the gallop.

Rizzoli's orders were muted as Milan and Cremona struck out at the canter.

At two hundred metres, the Cossack horns bawled as the bearded ranks lowered their lances and charged.

'May the grace of God deliver us,' D'Onofrio said, before dropping his sabre point forward and calling, 'Charge!'

In an instant, Milan's and Cremona's ranks dissolved. Some chasseurs raced across the front of Mantua and Brescia in rout. Some wheeled their horses about and spurred them for home. De Chabenac and the standard bearer sprinted behind Rizzoli.

At one hundred metres, the Cossacks shrieked wildly as their hardy ponies flattened their necks into the gallop.

'I cannot face them alone, sir,' yelled D'Onofrio, signalling with his sabre. 'Mantua! Brescia! Form column of fours to the right, canter, march.' D'Onofrio's line melted into their own dust.

Cossack horns blew. Cossack commanders thrust their curved blades into the sky. Their ranks howled and shook their lances with disappointment as they jagged down hard on their bits.

Jobert cantered Jaune in an arc to confirm all the chasseurs had fled.

Koschak pushed up beside him. 'Now that was a first for me. Where next?'

'All hope is lost, but I am not quitting the field, Koschak.' Jobert jerked his attention from the stationary Cossacks to the rocks and ruts under Jaune's cantering stride to the melee between dragoons and chasseurs. 'Do you fancy filleting dragoon kidneys?'

Koschak shortened his reins and twirled his sabre.

Under a blistering sun on the third day of the battle, Jobert allowed Bleu to pick his way across the three hundred metres of smooth rocks of the Trebbia's riverbed before ascending through scraggly shrubs along the eastern bank.

After saluting Rizzoli, Jobert removed his mirliton and wiped the running sweat from his burnt face. 'Sir, the Mantua Company are set as guides on the far bank. The infantry are unable to shift the enemy's line. We will be stuck in the riverbed as there is no space to form on the infantry's flank.'

Rizzoli and de Chabenac scanned the far bank. From their location the battle comprised the scattered sound of skirmisher fire, immobile blue fusiliers and the dash of trotting couriers.

'We have news for you, Jobert.' Rizzoli shot a dour glance at de Chabenac. 'At Zurich, Masséna has lost against the Russians. Yesterday, Moreau was defeated behind the enemy and has returned to Genoa. Macdonald has given the general order to withdraw to Genoa. We are to hold this bank as Victor retires his infantry to this side of the Trebbia.'

No chance of Mantua? Retreat to be trapped in Genoa.

Jobert flicked a look of concern to de Chabenac, whose face lowered to inspect his reins. 'If you will excuse me, sir, I will inform Mantua Company to withdraw to the home bank.'

As Jobert returned to Mantua Company, Bleu took the opportunity to guzzle at the streams meandering within the riverbed.

Having passed the order to withdraw to a morose D'Onofrio, Jobert fell in beside Fazio's platoon. 'Sergeant Fazio, how are your horses?'

Fazio clenched his jaw. 'Hungry. Most are lame.'

Jobert held his tongue. *Yesterday's long gallop to flee the field will do that.*

Jobert nodded. 'What and when did your men last eat?'

'Ammunition bread and a grass broth last night.' Fazio wobbled his head at some internal debate. 'Is that Moreau's gunfire I hear behind the enemy?'

'More likely kaiserlik caissons coming forward.'

'How about you, sir?' Fazio's eyes burned with hatred. 'Continuous defeats. Continuous withdrawals. How does it feel this time around?'

Jobert pursed his lips, sank Bleu to a halt and allowed Fazio's chasseurs to march on. He rocked Bleu to a walk beside Bernasconi.

Bernasconi wilted under the heat, his burnt face beginning to blister. 'Is this how it was for the Romans two thousand years ago, sir?'

Jobert shrugged. 'How are your horses, lad?'

Strands of white spittle encrusted Bernasconi's lips as he opened his mouth. 'Many mouths and ribs are galled. All are in poor condition.' He hung his head. 'Most are lame from yesterday.'

'How are your men?'

'I am proud to say none of mine deserted last night.' The younger man gulped to staunch his tears. 'Surely, sir, it cannot get worse than this?'

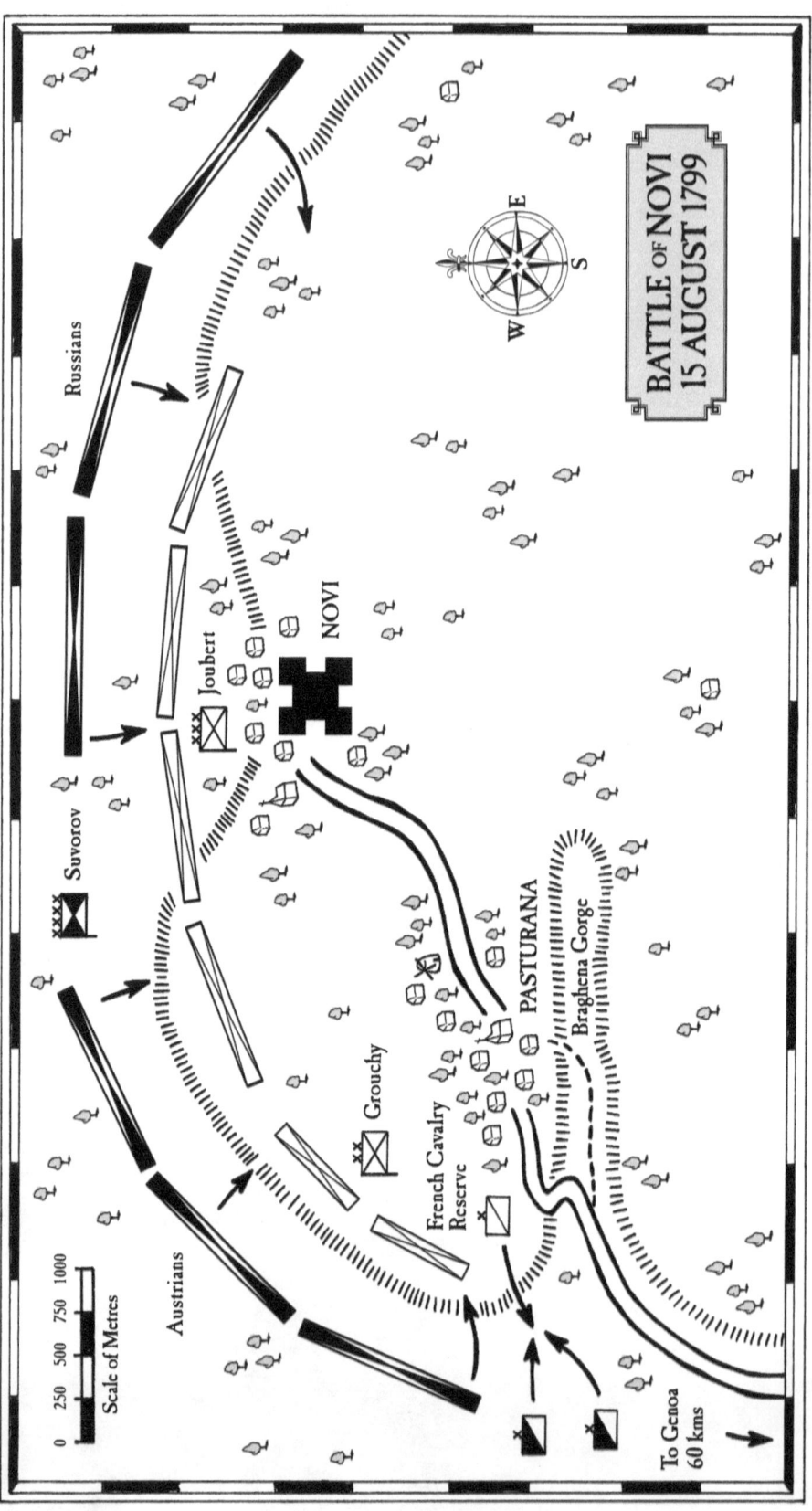

BATTLE of NOVI
15 AUGUST 1799

Russians

Suvorov

Joubert

NOVI

Grouchy

French Cavalry
Reserve

PASTURANA

Braghena Gorge

Austrians

To Genoa
60 kms

Scale of Metres

0   250   500   750   1000

Chapter Twenty-Two
August 1799, Battle of Novi, Italy

Twenty five days after the French defeat on the Trebbia, Jobert sat on a small promontory which bent the Bormida River east to the village of Dego. Below the ridgeline, French columns marched north from Genoa once more.

Except for scratching along Bleu's hogged mane, Jobert sat still as phantoms flitted across the ridge. Five years ago, on this ridge above the Bormida, his 2nd Company of the 24th Chasseurs had chased D'Onofrio's chevau-léger through a nearby olive grove.

A commotion from the column disturbed his memories. The new general's retinue trotted past the labouring battalions. Another general in a whirlwind of useless generals – Berthier, Brune, Joubert, Schérer, Moreau, Macdonald, Moreau, and now Joubert returned.

I remember Joubert at Dego.

Three years ago on this promontory, protecting Masséna's flank, de Chabenac and he had driven back Wolff von Maefeld's hussars. Jobert rubbed his left collarbone as he remembered the next day. Austrian fusiliers snuck through the fog and reoccupied their defence. Jobert screened, then charged, a two-gun redan on the forward slopes opposite.

Heat flushed his face. *What we suffered. The loss of so many.*

Tears stung his eyes.

Bleu threw his head and stomped to disperse the sticky flies. 'Under siege, old friend?' Jobert bent Bleu's neck and wiped his horse's eyes.

A sharp pang erupted in his left temple. Since receiving the news fifteen days ago that the fortress of Mantua had capitulated to the Austrian siege, headaches erupted every time he thought about Gianna.

Where is she? How do I get to her?

He disturbed her book nestled deep in his tailcoat pocket. He pressed the open pages to his throbbing temple, the site where he had fractured his skull at Rivoli.

Ten days ago, in the screen along the heights above Genoa, Jobert escorted the shadow Inoubli onto the secret pathways. 'Did you deliver my letter in Mantua? Any reply?'

'I was not there long enough to receive one.' Inoubli pocketed another of Jobert's letters before blending into the mist.

I will desert. Jobert clenched his fist and his jaw. Bleu flinched at the movement through the saddle. *I will go to her no matter the consequences.*

Five days ago, such opportunity arose for Jobert as he presented himself to his new divisional commander, General Grouchy.

'With Masséna's defeat at Zurich,' Grouchy said, 'the defeat at Trebbia has brought on another coup in Paris. Macdonald has been relieved of command. He and all his generals, including your Victor, have been recalled to Paris to give account of their actions. General Joubert now commands the Army of Italy. You are cousins, I believe?'

'No, sir, we are not related. It is a small amusement of General Joubert's. Our association stretches back many years here in Italy.'

'I see. General Joubert's immediate focus is to strike north from Genoa to Alessandria. While we threaten the Austrians and Russians from the Ligurian coast, Suvorov will not open any offensive into the Alps to support their forces on the Rhine. The bulk of their army lies on the plain between Novi and Marengo. My division is ordered to approach Novi from the south-west. I require a guide. I am told you know the routes along the Bormida Valley.'

Jobert had convinced 'cousin' Joubert to assign D'Onofrio's Mantua and Brescia Companies as guides to Grouchy's division. A mere sixty sabres strong, the force sufficient for Jobert's schemes. Jobert sneered. The paltry squadron was to be commanded by Zenari.

Another stab in the guts from Rizzoli.

In the Bormida Valley this morning, the steady tramp of shoes, human and horse, beat like a dreadful clock.

In the coming chaos, I shall slip away.

He squeezed his copy of *Romeo and Juliet* before he secured it back in his pocket.

Bleu pawed the ground with impatience. His tail flicked at the clouds of buzzing flies on his rump. Jobert lifted his reins and squeezed Bleu to return to the column.

The next morning, dust clung to the sweat on Jobert's face. It lined his nostrils and coated his tongue. He ran his tongue around his mouth, hoping that Tulloc had found water in Novi. His tongue slid over a new set of temporary dentures. Jobert removed them and placed them in his pocket.

North-west of Novi's small, ridgetop citadel, Jobert watched the battle unfold beneath him.

In the hours before dawn that morning, Austrian cavalry probed the Cisalpine piquets protecting Grouchy's infantry.

With first light, the kaiserlik onslaught began. French blue repulsed Austrian white. White surged and blue buckled. White pushed blue backward up the Novi slopes into the terraced vineyards. On the left, or western, flank of the field, cannons and muskets had maintained their unceasing bellow for four hours now. The more the smoke drifted, the locked infantry fire lines blurred to grey. All Jobert knew of the rest of the field was that the Russians pressed Novi's citadel and the French right.

In the last thirty minutes on the Novi plains, phalanxes of Austrian cavalry had formed.

The French cavalry reserve assembled to counterattack.

In the centre sat three regiments of battle-cavalry – grim men in bicornes, blue jackets, buff breeches and tall boots. Beside them in the line, the bronze helmets and green jackets of the 12th Dragoons stood proud. On their flanks sat the remnants of this morning's screen, the 1st Hussars and the 2nd Chasseurs. Each vaunted French regiment bled to a strength of two hundred blades.

On the left of the line, squeezed between the 2nd Chasseurs and the massive chargers of 3rd Cavalry, the sixty Mantuan and Brescian chasseurs formed battleline.

Bernasconi sat beside Jobert in front of the leading rank. His jaw was slack and trembling.

Jobert loosened his shoulders by sweeping his blade forward and back, sword-side and near. Bleu pranced on the spot. 'I remember you telling your parents you wanted to participate in a cavalry charge, Bernasconi. Will an attack by a division of cavalry satisfy your curiosity?'

The wall of white fusiliers began to wrap around Grouchy's left flank.

From the centre of the French cavalry reserve a trumpet called. One regiment of battle-cavalry rumbled into a walk then surged into a trot.

Ahead, Austrian drums urged the forming of squares.

Austrian cavalry lines raised dust as they stepped off.

Beside the Mantuans and Brescians, the 3rd Cavalry advanced with a guttural moan of release. Beyond them, the sky-blue 1st Hussars, Didier's old regiment, marched forward with a cheer.

Two hundred at best.

The 24th Chasseurs had withdrawn from the line when they were skinned to two hundred. Now that strength was considered battle capable.

Zenari, D'Onofrio and Bernasconi sat frozen at the unfolding spectacle.

Jobert urged Bleu to a trot to the end of the line. 'Lieutenant Koschak, review the readiness of the rear rank.'

Jobert then proceeded to walk the noses of the front rank. 'No oilskins cover our colours today, lads.' Ferocity was stamped into Jobert's face. 'We won honour facing dragoons at Trebbia. Today, we shall heap more glory upon the regiment.'

He thrust his sabre above the chasseurs' remounts' ears. The soldiers reached forward and tapped his sabre with theirs.

'Are your chasseurs ready for battle, Corporal Cieno? At Magnano we drove their hussars off our standard. Today, we will drive the bastards into the dirt.'

Moench twitched wide-eyed behind the rear rank.

'Corporal Moench, how many times have we seen this through? Once more, old friend.'

Jobert stopped at the right of the line.

There sat Fazio, streaked with sweat rivulets, teeth bared. Fazio's anger bore into Jobert.

Jobert acknowledged Fazio's battle fever with a nod, before resuming his post between D'Onofrio and Bernasconi.

'The 2nd Chasseurs have received orders to attack their cavalry rallying on their western flank,' D'Onofrio said. 'We are to follow them in.'

Trumpets sounded behind 2nd Chasseurs ranks.

'Our turn, boys,' Koschak called from the rear rank. 'Shorten your fucking reins. Up around their fucking ears.'

Zenari raised then dropped his sabre forward. The Cisalpine line rippled into a walk.

As the slopes' gradient eased, the 2nd Chasseurs, then the Cisalpine Chasseurs, pushed to a trot.

Two hundred metres on Jobert's right, the 12th Dragoons disappeared into the dust.

All of the cavalry reserve committed then.

Trumpets sounding Advance warned figures flitting in the yellow-grey cloud ahead of the one hundred and fifty metre wall of green-jacketed chasseurs. Knots of blue French battle cavalry and strings of white Austrian dragoons spurred their way to the flanks.

A foreign trumpet sounded ahead. A line of sky-blue clad Austrian hussars burst through the cloud at two hundred metres.

Von Maefeld's regiment!

2nd Chasseurs trumpets screamed Charge. French throats roared.

'With them, Zenari.' Jobert tipped Bleu onto a right-lead canter.

Zenari screamed commitment. Trumpets urged action. Throats bellowed fear. Sabres flattened and locked to give point. Over four hundred iron-shod drummers raced to a central crescendo.

In the closing seconds, Jobert sought von Maefeld.

There!

'Our line wraps theirs, D'Onofrio. Sweep left behind them.' Jobert skipped Bleu onto his left-lead. 'On me, Cisalpine, on me!'

As Jobert cantered along the Austrian rear rank, opposing sabres clattered on his left.

Rally sounded.

The Austrian line dropped to a walk before trotting forward again. Fallen green jackets appeared from under the rear hooves of the hussars.

The 2ⁿᵈ Chasseurs have broken!

Jobert twisted in the saddle to look behind him. 'Bernasconi, take our lads home. Now!'

Bernasconi twirled his blade in the air and gathered the band of chasseurs to him.

Jobert dropped his hips. In response, Bleu dropped his hips to halt within two steps. D'Onofrio and Moench converged on Jobert's flanks. Jobert scanned the murk for immediate threat.

Riderless horses stood, either bleeding, ensnared in their reins or grazing. Wounded cavalrymen, in rent uniforms of various hues, stumbled.

'Look, sir,' D'Onofrio said, 'there is the prick who dishonoured us at Magnano.'

The dust parted and, seventy metres away, sat Wolff von Maefeld on a raven-black charger.

Two hussar officers sat either side of him. Jobert marked these wingmen as Black Moustache and Red Plaits.

Von Maefeld swept his sabre up and back to salute Jobert.

Jobert gave a disdainful flick of his jaw. 'Stand fast, D'Onofrio. The big one in the centre and I have unfinished business. Do not follow me in.'

Von Maefeld's rein hand held a pistol aloft. Its silver boar's head winked in the grime-filtered sun.

Jobert drew his own silver-etched pistol. 'The pot is on the table. Deal me in.'

With a flick of von Maefeld's sabre, Black Moustache gave point and his horse leapt into a canter straight at Jobert. Red Plaits came on three strides behind.

Jobert gave point in response and dropped his left heel. Bleu's hindquarters swung to sit flank on to the rushing hussar. The force of the spin sat Bleu into a crouch.

A flicker of doubt crossed Black Moustache's face. The hussar checked his horse. It dropped its gait to a trot.

Too much, idiot.

The hussar sat and urged his horse forward. Without his horse's momentum, he rolled his blade to generate tip speed.

As his opponent's horse propped and his blade dipped, Jobert applied left-calf rhythm to side-step Bleu towards Black Moustache. Jobert drove his sabre into the hussar's upper chest beside the armpit. Six inches into the hussar's body, Jobert's sabre tip jarred against the inside of the man's shoulder blade.

Black Moustache hissed and went limp, his sabre swung by his boots. His horse shied at Bleu's threatening hindquarters.

Red Plaits skipped his horse towards Bleu's head, twirled his sword-side point into a nearside cut down onto Jobert's extended arm.

Jobert twisted his right toe to Bleu's shoulder, lifted the reins to touch the right side of Bleu's neck. Bleu spun on his hocks to the left. Jobert's blade slid free of flesh.

Red Plaits' cut beat down Jobert's extended blade.

As Red Plaits passed behind his pirouette, Jobert halted Bleu's spin beside the wounded Black Moustache. Black Moustache shrugged to test if his shoulder could still yield a blade. A glance showed von Maefeld six canter strides away.

'No, sir! Stay out!' Moench cried behind Jobert.

A clash of blades.

Two sets of canter beats approached behind.

Jobert glanced left.

D'Onofrio! Then Red Plaits is behind my right.

Jobert turned Bleu one step to the right on his haunches and extended his arm to give point. He glanced at von Maefeld, who had checked his charge to receive D'Onofrio.

In Jobert's peripheral vision, Black Moustache covered his face with his arm at D'Onofrio's approach. 'Please, sir, no.'

Anger twitched across Red Plaits' face towards the thundering D'Onofrio.

A thud of blade on flesh. Black Moustache crumpled beside Jobert. D'Onofrio cantered past Bleu's nose towards von Maefeld. Over Jobert's left shoulder, the clang of D'Onofrio's and von Maefeld's blades followed the grunt of effort.

Red Plaits stood in his stirrups at the gallop, his body arced, hilt above his head, tip low for a nearside thrust. He powered his sabre down at Jobert's right thigh.

Jobert's right knee lifted Jaune to pivot left.

My thigh! Bleu's ribs!

Bleu and Jobert's left boot collided with Black Moustache's stationary horse.

Jobert's hilt swept an arc to parry Red Plaits' tip.

The hussar's extended tip sliced into the muscles above Jobert's right knee. Jobert's hilt tapped the hussar's blade tip as it exited. Jobert's guts shuddered as a clammy sensation crawled from his knee.

'*Touché,*' Red Plaits cried as he dashed past.

Forward of Jobert and beyond von Maefeld, D'Onofrio arced back towards the clash.

Red Plaits lengthened his horse's stride toward D'Onofrio. 'Hold fast, sir! My man!'

Von Maefeld checked his horse to let Red Plaits stream past.

Now! Give point!

Jobert dropped his left hip and, with a kiss, lifted Bleu onto a right-lead canter towards the paused von Maefeld.

They sprang at each other. With his hilt covering his face, von Maefeld's eyes were just visible above his wrist.

As Jobert stood in his stirrups for impact, a jelly weakness wobbled his right knee.

Get out!

Jobert sat and slipped Bleu clear to the left. He rolled his blade under and lifted von Maefeld's sizzling steel over his head.

Only nearside cuts off my left leg.

Ahead of him, Red Plaits tugged his racing charger to the left. D'Onofrio sat slumped in the saddle staring at the ground in front of his horse.

'Jobert!' screamed Moench. A clash of steel behind.

'Moench, on me!' Jobert bellowed and skipped Bleu onto his left-lead and aimed Bleu for Red Plaits. Gripping the bounding saddle with his thighs and weight on his left leg, Jobert gave point.

Red Plaits reefed his horse to stop. Frustration flushed his face.

His reins are too long.

Guided by Jobert's left boot, Bleu, with a combined weight of six hundred kilograms, hit the stationary horse's hips at thirty kilometres per hour.

Red Plaits' horse buckled.

Bleu groaned.

Jobert rolled his wrist to bring a nearside cut down under the hussar's collar.

As Bleu staggered backwards and Red Plaits' horse collapsed, Jobert's sabre dragged free of his enemy's chest with a spray of pink mist.

D'Onofrio leaned on his pistol holsters, sabre still in hand.

'Ride for home, D'Onofrio. Now!'

Slumped in his saddle and with a moan at each stride, D'Onofrio trotted towards the Novi heights.

'Jobert!' called Moench.

Moench was on foot. Jobert glanced left and right for Moench's grey. Black Moustache, now toppled from the saddle, anchored his frightened charger. Moench groped his way around the shifting horse, attempting to shield himself from von Maefeld's blows.

'Attend me, von Maefeld. Just me.'

Moench tripped on the outstretched Black Moustache and tumbled in the dust.

Von Maefeld sidestepped his ebony charger towards Moench, sabre arm outstretched.

'Von Maefeld!'

'With pleasure.' Von Maefeld raised his sabre point toward Jobert.

Moench rolled and crawled under Black Moustache's horse's belly to the far side.

Jobert launched Bleu at von Maefeld.

Von Maefeld's charger surged forward on a tight rein.

'Moench, like a Cossack,' Jobert cried.

Confusion creased Moench's face.

Jobert's steel squealed the length of von Maefeld's as they passed. Jobert lifted his opponent's blade. Von Maefeld's sabre sliced through Jobert's mirliton. The cap tugged backwards at speed, the throat strap ripping at Jobert's throat. The strap broke and the hat tumbled free.

Jobert coughed at his burnt throat, dropped his sabre onto its sword knot and extended his hand to Moench. 'Up, Moench.'

Bleu buffeted Moench back onto Black Moustache's mount.

Moench stared beyond Bleu's rump. 'He comes.'

'Get up!' Jobert grabbed Moench's collar.

Moench scrabbled at Jobert's holsters and portmanteau. 'Fly!'

Bleu dropped his head to stretch into the gallop. Von Maefeld's hoofbeats were right behind. Jobert arched his kidneys away from the expected blade tip. 'Pistol!'

Moench released his grip of the portmanteau. Moench's legs dragged beside the struggling Bleu. He fumbled with a pistol butt before firing it just over Bleu's rump.

Von Maefeld's hoof beats ceased.

Moench dropped the pistol, then hopped as he was dragged while reclaiming his purchase behind Jobert's saddle. 'Stop! We are clear!'

Once Bleu sank to stop, Moench hobbled to collect D'Onofrio doubled-over his holsters as his horse grazed. Moench led the blood-stained horse to Jobert.

Jobert checked to see that it was not the silver-inlaid pistol that Moench had discarded. Jobert glanced behind to see how far away one of his new pistols had been dumped.

'As you were with my father at Jemappes, Jobert,' von Maefeld called, sitting still and erect over a hundred metres away. 'You are a coward.'

Jobert's knee pulsed with pain as Moench clambered to mount behind him. 'We need to practice those Cossack vaults, Moench.'

Moench adjusted his seat behind Jobert's portmanteau. 'No, sir, we fucking do not.'

Chapter Twenty-Three
August 1799, Pasturana, Italy

Jobert found the rallied Cisalpine company in a vineyard on the outskirts of Pasturana, five kilometres west of Novi. Their horses were tethered to the branches of the vines, or the stems of the saplings along which the vines groped. All leaves and twigs were stripped from the vines, so the soldiers cringed beside a stone wall for shade.

'Mantua, come care for your captain,' Jobert said. Soldiers rushed to take D'Onofrio from the saddle. 'Cieno, he has taken a cut under the right ribs above the sash.' Jobert shook his head to Cieno's enquiring look. 'Hold his hand and keep his mouth and tongue moist. He cannot swallow. Have Lieutenant Bernasconi attend me.'

Jobert rode to Tulloc with Jaune and Moench's grey.

Tulloc looked at the caked red dust smearing down Jobert's right shin. 'Will you be all right, sir?'

'I am in pain and I am thirsty.'

Moench slid off Bleu's rump. 'Dismount, sir. We need to treat your leg. Tulloc, do you have water?'

Jobert drank from Tulloc's flask. 'Is there a bucket for Bleu?' Bernasconi saluted.

'D'Onofrio will not see another dawn.' Jobert coughed at the influx of water down his throat. 'He has taken a thrust to the liver. You need to secure his personal items. Do you know his family? This girl he admires? What is our parade state?'

Bernasconi dropped his head to nod. 'We are missing nine, sir.'

Jobert groaned as he flopped from his saddle to his left leg. 'Where is Zenari?'

Bernasconi hung his head. 'He has gone for a walk to clear his head, sir.'

'What?' Jobert coughed with incredulity. 'One hundred thousand men from towns across Europe have converged onto this dusty hill to kill each other and Zenari decides to ...' Jobert massaged his thigh above the knee. 'Where is Fazio?'

'He has taken a pair of horses to find a cart for the wounded.'

'Sit down, sir,' Moench said.

Jobert removed his sword belt then bent to lower his weight with his hands. 'Bernasconi, report to General Grouchy's headquarters immediately. Place yourself at the convenience of the Chief of Divisional Artillery. Feed the guns. Keep the lanes open of broken vehicles.'

'And when the road is clogged with dead, sir?' Bernasconi asked.

Koschak took Jobert's weight as he lowered. 'Leave the fallen, Bernasconi. Limber and caisson teams do not stop for bodies under foot.' Jobert gave a nod to Koschak above him. 'I will accompany you.'

Bernasconi looked at Jobert and Koschak with relief. 'Will Lieutenant Koschak command us, sir?'

'No, Bernasconi,' Jobert said, 'you will command your soldiers. No, Moench, do not cut my over-breeches.'

'Then pull them down, sir.'

'What of you, sir?' Bernasconi asked.

Jobert wriggled his bum in the red dirt to drop his pants. The exposed wound throbbed and wept. Dried blood and serum caked a slice ten centimetres long and three centimetres deep.

Koschak shook his head. 'That needs sutures.'

Jobert hissed at the pain. 'That needs brandy.'

'I have vinegar,' Moench said.

'Moench, you will need to sew my—' Jobert swore as Moench sluiced his wound with vinegar.

Moench recoiled. 'Sew it yourself, sir. I will not. Where is Duque when you need him?'

'If you cannot sew it, then splint it,' Koschak said.

Jobert calmed his breathing after the administration of cleansing vinegar. 'I cannot mount in a splint. Bind it.'

'Will you take laudanum?' Koschak asked.

'Not now. Perhaps tonight.' Jobert looked over to D'Onofrio under a blanket spread on vine strings. 'In fact, yes, bring the oil. But, Koschak, you need to get the column moving for Grouchy's headquarters.'

Koschak bent and gripped Jobert's shoulder before turning to depart.

Tulloc lifted Jobert's ankle for Moench to bind his wound.

'My leg is getting stiff. I need to return to the saddle, or I will never mount.'

'Remount in order to do what?' Moench asked.

'Remount and return to duty.'

Koschak, Bernasconi and fifty chasseurs wafted dust across Jobert as they departed the vineyard at the walk.

As Jobert stood and pulled up his over-breeches, Zenari rode into the vineyard.

Zenari's brown eyes were hooded with fatigue. 'General Joubert is dead. The eastern flank against the Russians is collapsing.

Novi is being overrun. The noose is tightening around Pasturana. Any evacuees are being sent to Pasturana as the only road off the plateau to Genoa is through the Braghena Gorge.' Zenari scanned the vineyard of blanket shelters and the lounging wounded. 'What have you done with my men?'

'Your men?' Jobert asked. 'At the time of greatest need you were absent. You failed in your responsibilities, Zenari. You proved yourself irrelevant.'

Zenari shook his head at the reprimand.

Jobert continued, 'Bernasconi and his Mantuans are supporting the feeding of the guns to delay the collapse of the army. You can join the men in their escort duties, or you can go for another stroll.' Jobert pointed to a blanket shelter nearby. 'D'Onofrio has received a mortal wound. Perhaps you can pay your respects before he passes.'

'Do not let me … detain you, sir.' Zenari glanced towards D'Onofrio before he spurred his horse away.

'We need to leave for Genoa, sir,' Moench said.

'D'Onofrio first. Sit him up. Let me cradle him in my arms. A cup of water from the horse buckets, and Moench, fetch the hashish oil from my portmanteau.' Moench looked at Jobert in trepidation. 'Then prepare our horses for departure.'

D'Onofrio's grey face spasmed as he sipped from Jobert's cup.

'Thirsty? Have another sip.' Jobert dribbled the hashish water onto D'Onofrio's black lips and tongue. 'I will find her, my friend. The girl in Mantua.' D'Onofrio's dark eyes implored Jobert. 'I will tell her how important she is.' Jobert continued to tip the soothing mixture. 'She will know the great love that is sped towards her with every heartbeat.' The muscles in D'Onofrio's face relaxed as the hashish oil worked its internal magic. 'She will know she is truly loved.'

How will I find her? The noose is tightening. Crawl or ride. Just go.

'Ride swiftly home, my worthy foe.' Jobert kissed D'Onofrio's dust-encrusted forehead before laying his lolling head in the dirt.

After rolling and crawling to stand, Jobert hobbled to Moench and Tulloc in the midst of their horses. 'I need to leave for Koschak. You both return to Genoa. Koschak and I will catch you on the road.'

'No, sir.' Moench looked to Tulloc. 'Where you go, we go.'

'Moench, Grenzer's panniers are the key.' Jobert gripped Moench's shoulder. 'If we keep Grenzer safe, we survive. We cannot risk him delivering caissons forward. Lads, take Bleu and Grenzer and get moving before the withdrawal becomes a rout and the roads choke.'

Moench looked to Tulloc. Tulloc's face concealed an inner debate.

'Return to Maria, Tulloc.' Jobert smiled. 'But I do need a crutch and a mounting block. Please find me a musket with a sling and tie a bucket on a line to Jaune's bow.'

'You will need a hat, sir,' Moench said. 'If they find you wandering a battlefield with a slung musket and tethered bucket they will think you have stolen an officer's jacket and shoot you.' Moench looked at Tulloc's cap. 'Here, ox-head, give him your mirliton.'

'What will I wear?' Tulloc asked.

'Your bonnet de police, chasseur.'

Jobert inspected the brim of Tulloc's mirliton. 'Phew.' He wrinkled his nose. 'Are there not regulations against the stowage of carcasses within regimental headdress?'

Moench grinned. 'If you lose the bucket, you can use Tulloc's cap as a mounting block.'

Jobert ruffled Bleu's forelock. Bleu pushed his big head into Jobert's thigh to rid himself of flies. Jobert hissed in pain and hopped backwards.

Moench watched him with stern concern. 'What are you doing, sir?'

Jobert shrugged. 'I am good. Just sore.'

'I know you, sir. You are up to something.'

Tulloc handed Jobert a musket with a broken hammer, no flint and no ramrod. Jobert slung the musket across his back, stepped on the up-turned bucket, mounted then drew the bucket up and tied it off.

They rode through the vineyard gate. Moench and Tulloc turned south to Braghena Gorge and Genoa. With one last nod to D'Onofrio, Jobert turned north to Novi.

To Milan and Mantua.

To Gianna.

Hobbling down the lane toward Jobert came Fazio and two bleeding men. Fazio was seething. 'Where is everyone?' Fazio jerked his chin at the vineyard. 'I have wounded. If I take them to a hospital, they die. If I leave them for the enemy, they die. I was abandoned. I will not abandon them.'

Jobert shrugged. 'Then escort them to Genoa.'

'I am trying to do that.' Fazio spat at the ground. 'I took a team to find a suitable wagon. The fucking infantry stole our horses. The remaining horses are the worst of our lame. The pack horse escort carry wounds of their own. If this army routs, they will be torn from their saddles and their horses stolen.'

Jobert rubbed his aching thigh. 'I am busy, Fazio. I have places I need to be. Would you like me to solve your dilemma and give you a direct order?'

'I expect nothing from you, sir. That is all you have ever delivered in the past.'

Jobert rubbed his forehead. 'Prepare your men to move, Sergeant. I am on my way to Zenari and the company at the gun lines. We will collect you on our return.' Jobert shuddered at the lie.

Jobert rummaged in his portmanteau. 'Take this.' He passed Fazio his bottle of hashish oil before rocking Jaune to a walk.

With the Novi-Genoa road crammed with traffic, Jobert guided Jaune through the back lanes and gardens until he sat alone on the eastern side of Pasturana. He drew his telescope and viewed the near horizon. A solid wall of French infantry fired to the north and east, blocking the advancing enemy.

Jobert shifted with pain in his saddle to the west. He considered how to evade the Austrians to the west, then head north to Alessandria.

I will be there by dawn tomorrow if I ride through the night. Jobert turned Jaune to the west.

'Colonel Jobert, sir,' came a call from the flow of foot and wagon traffic entering Pasturana. It was Corporal Cieno. 'Lieutenant Bernasconi is forward at the gun line. I am to return these caissons to Lieutenant Koschak in the artillery park. The kaiserliks are pushing hard. We do not have much time.'

'Well done, Cieno.' Jobert nodded grimly. 'I will guide Fazio's wounded to the artillery park. I will meet you there.'

Once Cieno's caisson escort had moved off, Jobert looked around the small village.

Stay until dark. Where can I wait?

Jobert rode to a small church. Headstones peeked over a low cemetery wall. Beside the church Jobert dismounted with difficulty. It felt as if his wound tore under its bandage. Leaning against his saddle, Jobert pressed the pages of Gianna's *Romeo and Juliet* to his forehead. Once the queasy sensation had subsided, he stowed his telescope and her book into his portmanteau.

Jobert pushed his face into Jaune's neck. 'I trust you to keep it safe, lad.'

'Clear the way for the guns!'

Jobert withdrew back into the buttresses of the church as

the remnants of the Mantua Company escorted a foot battery through the town. Infantry barged against the stone walls as the chasseurs forced the gun teams and their guns through.

Once the artillery had passed, the French infantry streamed through the town, choking any other vehicle movement. Jobert spied a horse team trapped and abandoned. The nearside leader had a Chauvel brand. The image of the patient horse strapped in its harness pierced Jobert's heart.

How can I save you?

'We need everyone in the fire line now, sir.' An infantry officer approached him. Fusiliers crowded the cemetery and took up fire positions behind the cemetery's walls and headstones. 'The Austrians are pressing hard. Leave your horse with my horse, sir.'

'With my wound I cannot reload, sir,' Jobert said, 'but I can fire if you can keep the muskets up to me.'

Jobert checked the western horizon. The height of the late-afternoon sun could not be determined through the smoke and the dust.

Austrians? Russians? Their lines are converging. This is the final stand.

Jobert tethered Jaune to his bucket before tamping and tucking his remaining silver pistol into his waist sash.

Jobert found a tall headstone behind which he could kneel with his right leg extended behind him. The infantry officer allocated some filthy, scared young soldiers to load for him.

Jobert fired aimed shots at the wall of white-jacketed infantry. Under the zip of balls and the crack of ricochets, his loaders hissed encouragement. Jobert fired until each infantryman's cartridge box was empty. 'Fetch more from the wounded, lads.'

'The kaiserliks are losing momentum.' The infantry officer strode between the firers in the cemetery. 'If we can hold them until nightfall, we will see another day.'

From the church, across Pasturana's square to the grain store, the French infantry formed a three-rank fire line. A veritable gale of lead blew out towards the wavering Austrian line.

The infantry officer waved his sword. 'Give a cheer for Grouchy, lads. He will see us through.'

Jobert glanced from his musket's foresight to the pandemonium across the square. Grouchy pushed a reluctant horse and directed the combat with his sword.

Green jackets became more prominent in the Austrian line as Russian musketeers reinforced the assault into the town.

'Fire, boys!' called the prowling infantry officer. 'Those bastards will give no quarter. Stand firm and they will turn.'

With a deep roar, the Russians charged to close with the bayonet. The French line wavered with the impact. The screams and clatter of sword, spontoon and bayonet resounded from the battered stone walls.

'Any more cartridges, lads?' called Jobert as he received a fresh musket. 'Take my ammunition.'

'We have been, sir,' a loader said. 'You are all out.'

'Has Grouchy fallen?' the fusiliers around Jobert yelled to each other. 'No, there, look, Grouchy is captured.'

The French line across the square broke. A savage howl burst from Russian throats.

'Your last musket, sir,' said an infantryman loading for Jobert, 'because I am out of here.'

Jobert fired into the green-jacketed mass. With his injured thigh stiff, he struggled to return to Jaune at the side of the church.

'No!'

Jaune was gone. Jobert ran his fingers along the severed bucket rope.

Her book is gone.

'Colonel Jobert, sir. We need to go.'

Jobert spun in surprise. His wound flared in response. Tulloc caught Jobert's elbow as Jobert staggered.

'Tulloc?' Jobert shook with surprise. 'How did you find me?'

'We found Lieutenant Koschak at the artillery park. Corporal Cieno said you were near the church and were returning to Sergeant Fazio. I was waiting until you stopped firing.'

Jobert hopped on his left leg. 'Where is your horse?'

'I came on foot, sir. I was not sure where you would be.' Tulloc dropped his head. 'I did not want to lose her.'

Jobert gripped Tulloc's upper arm. 'I have lost Jaune.'

Tulloc's face shrivelled in anguish.

'I am so sorry, Tulloc.' Jobert searched the darkening sky.

The Chauvel horse!

'There are horses trapped in their harnesses in the street,' Jobert said. 'Take me there.'

Tulloc looked over Jobert's shoulder. 'The Russians will eat all the horses in the street before we clear the cemetery gate.' Tulloc's face screwed in concentration. 'We could return to our wounded.'

'In the vineyard? Did Fazio not evacuate our wounded?'

Tulloc shook his head. 'No, Fazio is in the morgue.'

'Oh.'

'No, I mean, he is in the morgue with the seriously wounded. He did not come out with Lieutenant Bernasconi.'

The last of the uninjured fusiliers scampered from the cemetery. The Russian drums were deafening.

'Do you know the way? Then take me to him.'

Chapter Twenty-Four

Jobert stumbled on the morgue's uneven stone floor in the dark. Tulloc pushed him to maintain their balance.

'Sergeant Fazio, it is us,' Tulloc called down a pitch-black corridor.

A dim light glowed ahead.

Tulloc assisted Jobert through the morgue's shattered door and into an airless room. Around a stubby candle, sat Fazio and a few wounded chasseurs. Around the sitting, writhed the more seriously wounded chasseurs. Around them, lay the stripped and abandoned dead. The stench of faeces and sour blood draped across Jobert's face.

No horse. No book! All hope is completely exhausted.

Tulloc lowered Jobert to the floor beside Fazio. Jobert grunted to remove the silver pistol from his sash. 'Do you know the enemy has taken the town?' he asked Fazio. 'Prepare for scavengers to seek us. Jar the door open with dead. Scatter the contents of packs as if the place has already been searched. How many musketoons and pistols do we have?'

'Piss off, Jobert.'

Jobert moaned as he turned to face Fazio. 'What is your problem, Fazio?'

In the candlelight, Fazio's filth-streaked face contorted with bitterness. 'My problem? What the fuck are you doing here, Jobert? You do not give me instructions. You are not my commanding officer.'

A brief smirk flashed across Jobert's lips. He slipped the dagger from his cuff. 'Would you like me to be?'

'Piss off. You are not a …a …'

'A what? A nobleman? A gormless idiot? You resent my experience.'

'Bullshit.'

'You resent I am a better sergeant than you. That I have spent my life as a cavalryman.'

Fazio squirmed. 'Bullshit.'

'You think yourself a horse gunner impersonator. You can polish a horse in a stable, you can mount sentries in garrison, but you have no idea how to prepare your men for battle, for patrol, for screen. You are way out of your depth, Fazio.'

'Get fucked, Jobert.' Steel glinted in Fazio's hand.

'But I am right. You are angry we beat you in '97. Now, with the boot on the other foot, you are angry you are with us.'

'Get fucked, or I—'

Jobert lowered his voice. 'I think you have had French cavalry cut up your horse battery. Is that where you were abandoned, Fazio? By whom? Your own cavalry? You actually do want me to command you, Sergeant Fazio. You want me to show you how to be a cavalryman. You want me to lead you out of this morgue.'

Fazio's breathing was ragged. His lips twitched. The steel reflection shuddered.

'How many did you bring with you?' Jobert asked.

The dull reflection on the steel slid from sight. 'Thirteen of us arrived,' Fazio said. 'At least two will stay. Did you bring any water?'

Jobert reached out and squeezed Fazio's arm. 'You know they will search here, Fazio. Make this room look as if the dead have been searched. Once the screams die down outside, we will leave here. Tulloc, assist Sergeant Fazio.'

Once the room was prepared and the few weapons gathered, Fazio took his candle and slumped against the wall opposite.

Tulloc slid down the slimy damp and joined Jobert. 'I hope Jaune will be looked after.'

'Jaune is a clever pony.' Jobert put his arm around Tulloc's broad shoulders. 'Whoever finds him, will value him.' Jobert felt Tulloc shift and wipe his eyes. 'Thank you Tulloc, you saved my life this evening. I am forever in your debt.'

'If anything happens to me, would you ...'

'Nothing will happen to you, my friend.' Jobert drew Tulloc's head onto his shoulder and rested his cheek on Tulloc's grease-matted hair. 'We have fought side by side for six years. Our horses have flourished under your care. Wherever my family has a home, you, Maria and little Andrea have a home.'

'What of your family, sir?'

Jobert breathed deeply. 'Who? Yann and Didier? Michelle and her infant?'

'I mean, when will you marry Signorina Gianna?'

For a moment, the convulsion in Jobert's chest eclipsed the torment in his thigh.

Light flickered across the ceiling. Fazio's candle snuffed out.

'Here they come, brother. Eyes shut.' Jobert wriggled into a pose where he appeared dead but still able to fire at the doorway if required. To staunch the pain that wracked his right leg, Jobert crushed the pistol butt with straining knuckles.

The grunts of those who approached punched along the

corridor towards the door, their stealth betrayed as gravel was crushed under heavy steps. Their torchlight stabbed through the ribs of the door. The swollen tongues of the fallen licked the glow as it slithered over their faces.

The wounded whimpered in the shadows.

'Shut up,' Jobert hissed.

The enemy were just beyond the doorway and aimed muskets, with bayonets fitted, through the opening. Through half-opened lids, Jobert watched a ragged scout creep beyond the broken door. The scavenger pounced on an infantry backpack just beyond Jobert's feet. He upended the backpack before throwing it at the far wall.

Bayonets jerked backwards from their penetration of the doorway. Their boots scurried away.

The corridor choked the retreating light.

'Tulloc!' Jobert shook Tulloc's drowsy form. 'Creep down the corridor as our sentry.'

Tulloc's muscular frame slid into the gloom.

'Fazio?' Jobert struggled to negotiate the criss-cross of corpses on the floor. 'Now is our time. Can we work together to bring these men home?'

Jobert offered his right hand.

Fazio's shadowed head considered the conciliatory hand. He grunted and shook firmly.

'Lads, listen in,' Jobert said. 'Remove your spurs and musketoon cross belts. Carry just your cartridge belts. Fill your cartridge box with cartridges from the dead. Sling your sabres over your shoulders. Dump your mirlitons for infantry bicornes. Our green jackets may fool them that we are a Russian patrol.'

Fazio and Tulloc led Jobert and the wounded chasseurs through the doorway, down the corridor and out into the night. Their anxious hearts drummed any exhaustion from their brains.

Bats and insects hummed and fluttered against the stars. Fires from smouldering houses glowed. Raucous laughter rebounded around stone corners. Random musket fire became a prelude to fierce, but brief, firefights.

'Fazio,' Jobert said, 'there are other French attempting to break out. I expect, just as we did, there will be enemy sentries lying amongst the dead. I suggest we move through Pasturana towards Novi.'

'Deeper behind enemy lines?'

'Who will expect a break out that way? Do you agree? Tulloc knows a footpath at the head of the Braghena Gorge. Our path to freedom.'

'Then lead on, Tulloc,' Fazio said, 'and mind the dead underfoot.'

The shuffling group clung to the shadows as they crept through shattered homes and desecrated gardens.

Tulloc tugged Jobert's sleeve. 'We are at the head of the path down the gorge. Koschak should be at the other end.'

Fazio hissed. 'Silence! Patrol!'

The clank of slung weapons and the rumble of voices sounded close. The echoes off walls confounded any clear direction of their approach.

Jobert patted Tulloc on the shoulder. 'Descend, Tulloc. Find Koschak.'

Now is my moment to depart, to find her.

Jobert counted the other wounded as they passed him. They struggled to descend the earth steps of the path moistened with the evening's dew.

As he reached Jobert, Fazio paused to search for silhouettes of the enemy. 'The patrol is behind us.'

Jobert gripped Fazio's shoulder. 'Fazio, you have not abandoned your men. Take them home. I will follow as last man.'

Jobert waited at the head of the path as the dozen chasseurs hissed in pain as they groped down the slope beneath him. As he had done many times this evening, Jobert ran his fingers over his pistol hammer to confirm it was cocked.

Close by, foreign voices growled. Their patrol clattered to silence.

Jobert pressed back into a prickly vine draping the side of the gorge. He gripped his pistol to his chest. The pressure reminded him of Gianna holding him. He closed his eyes to savour the memory of the press of her body into his.

A clatter below as someone fell. A yelp of pain.

A shout came from the patrol. A musket fired near to Jobert's hidden location.

Chasseurs shouted below to hurry.

The patrol clattered into life and trotted to the head of the stairs.

A few steps beneath Jobert, Fazio cried 'Shit!' as he fell and slid. Fazio panted as he crawled down the stairs.

The patrols' expletives came from the shadows beside Jobert. He could smell their uniforms drenched in gun smoke, garlic and sweat. He shuffled his heels closer to the escarpment face to let them pass.

The first enemy patrolman passed Jobert with musket extended from the hip. He whispered something to the man behind him.

Fazio grumbled as he scrambled just below.

The second man stood right beside Jobert. A third rattled to stop behind him. The second man's bicorne silhouette swung toward the leaf-covered Jobert.

Jobert saw Gianna's smile, Gianna's dimples.

Jobert roared and shoved.

The second man screamed as he toppled into the gorge.

Jobert placed his pistol on the chest of the third man and fired.

As the first man swivelled to present his musket behind him, Jobert grabbed the barrel and pushed it wide.

The infantryman fired.

The barrel seared Jobert's fingers. Jobert cracked his pistol barrel across the man's forehead. The tumbling man dragged his burning musket barrel from Jobert's grasp.

A shot from above. A ball zipped wide. Men yelled on the steps above him.

Jobert stepped down the slope. Fire scorched from his thigh. He spat a mouthful of bile down his chest.

Jobert grabbed Fazio by the collar. 'Hold onto me, you miserable prick.'

A trumpet sounded ahead.

Figaro! Catch up to the others, dump Fazio, then head north.

Balls cracked off the rocks around him.

'Jobert?' yelled Koschak.

'Here! Last man.'

'Lie down. Now. Cisalpine, fire!'

Jobert toppled Fazio and threw himself on top of him. Fazio wheezed at the impact.

A blast of flame roared from the darkness ahead.

'Jobert, it is me.' Koschak groped until he lifted Fazio and shook him. 'Fazio? Why did you save this worthless bastard? You should have left him where he fell.' Koschak lifted Jobert to his feet. 'I knew you would come. We need to start for Genoa.'

Jobert moaned at the sudden movement. 'That will be a long walk. I have lost Jaune.'

'We have Jaune. An officer rode him into the artillery park. Bleu called to him. I removed the gentleman from the saddle. How is the leg?'

Jobert sagged in Koschak's grip. 'Excruciating.'

'I have an axe.'

'Good. Put it through my skull.'

'I was not sure you would come.' Koschak gave Jobert's shoulders a squeeze. 'I thought you might slip us for Mantua.'

Jobert closed his eyes. Gianna was turning away. Jobert breathed the smoke-filled air to catch her scent.

Was it lavender or jasmine?

Chapter Twenty-Five
September 1799, Savona, Italy

Jobert turned at the sound of boots crossing the flagstones on the upper ramparts of Savona's Fort Priamar.

De Chabenac strode towards him. 'Orlande said I would find you here. I have news, sir. Good news! With Masséna's victory over the Russians, Suvorov has failed in Switzerland. The Russians have broken with Austria and are returning home.'

Jobert returned his gaze south along the Mediterranean shoreline. 'Their defeat does not return the Cisalpine Republic from the kaiserliks.'

'Moreover,' de Chabenac continued, 'since Novi, the Russian and British invasion of the Netherlands has been defeated. All within two months of their initial landings. And more welcome tidings. I read in the broadsheets that in July Bonaparte defeated the Turks.'

'Bonaparte, huh! Why waste such talent so far from home? With him, we departed here three and a half years ago and conquered Lombardy.' Jobert wiped sweat from his brow. 'With him here, we could ...'

De Chabenac cocked his head. 'Your fevers persist?'

Jobert dropped his eyes to his right thigh. 'It no longer oozes pus. The sea breeze helps with the fevers.'

De Chabenac stepped to Jobert's side and searched the Mediterranean's grey horizon. 'The Cisalpine Chasseurs have retained my services. The regiment, now reduced to less than three hundred, is to winter beyond Nice and await the new year. Indeed, the new century.' De Chabenac checked Jobert's mournful demeanour. 'Any further possibility of Italian Cossacks?'

'While the kaiserliks have us trapped on the coast there appears little chance of that.'

'I see Orlande and the others packing your trap. Home?'

Jobert smiled. 'Yes. I am looking forward to seeing Duque.'

'Please pass my warmest regards to Duque and my congratulations on his achievements.'

Jobert looked de Chabenac up and down. 'Are you departing as well?'

'I am. Over the winter, I will take the opportunity to visit my mother in Paris. Is there anything I can take to your cousin? While in Paris, is it still your wish I acquire a gimmal ring as an engagement gift?'

The smile vanished from Jobert's face. 'No.'

'Then it is a "no" to this colonelcy in Nice?'

'The commissariat would have only been palatable with Gianna by my side. She is gone now. I need to accept that.'

De Chabenac's eyes tightened as he regarded Jobert. 'Where has she gone? No news from Mantua?'

'No, no letters.' Jobert's lips trembled as he returned his face to the grey Mediterranean. 'Returning to her is impossible. All hope is extinguished.'

De Chabenac's hand reached carefully for Jobert's arm. 'Did you ever read the final act of *Romeo and Juliet*.'

'No.'

'Read it.'

Jobert reached across and patted de Chabenac's hand on his arm. 'Maybe.'

'No, my old friend.' De Chabenac nodded at the toes of his boots. 'Read it.' He released his grip. 'After the farm, where?'

'Perhaps seek out Masséna in Zurich. Rid myself of this cursed Italy.'

'Is this the end?'

Jobert looked towards his friend and frowned. 'The end?'

'Of us in Italy?' asked de Chabenac.

Jobert dropped his view to the waves shoving the rocks at the base of the fort's sea wall.

'It is for me.'

On a chill November day in his grandfather's stone stables, trimming hooves was warm work. To examine the effect of his rasping, Jobert stepped backwards and lowered Bleu's offside hindfoot. The well-shaped hoof on the patchwork of stones somehow invited memories of his grandfather.

They say you have all the time in the world. They are wrong. You do not have a minute to lose.

'André Jobert.' A gruff voice sounded behind Bleu. 'What has the world come to? A lieutenant colonel trimming his own hooves.'

Jobert turned and peered over Bleu's rump. 'Duque!'

Jobert gripped his boyhood friend in a tight, muscular hug.

'You are a welcome sight in these hard times.' They parted, still holding each other by the elbows. 'Five years is too long. Look at you. A sergeant-veterinarian.'

Duque regarded the scar under Jobert's right eye. 'I can suture better now if you want me to redo that.'

'My thigh could have done with you three months ago.' Jobert's eyes ran across Duque's missing right ear. Duque turned his cheek to shield his scar.

'You know the last of those pricks are dead,' Jobert said.

Duque gave a half-smile. 'It will not return my ear or my fingers,' Didier flexed the remaining three fingers in his glove, 'nor Didier's foot. Now there is another one, I hear.'

'A von Maefeld nephew stole one of my pistols.'

'Then what is stopping us hunting this arsehole down.'

'Indeed, what stops us ...'

'How was Italy?' Duque asked.

Jobert shrugged. 'We held a good hand when we won the pot in '96. This year we lost the lot. We lost a lot of good men. All for nothing.'

'Your horses are well?' Duque removed his gloves and ran his fingers down Bleu's hindleg. 'Good old Bleu.'

Jobert watched Duque feel the tendons with his thumb and forefinger of his right hand. The only fingers of his right hand.

Never able to wield a sabre again.

'Who is this?' Duque asked.

'Grenzer.'

Duque opened Grenzer's eye socket. 'How did he lose it?'

'I did it. A sabre flick to unbalance my opponent.'

'You kept his horse?'

'I did,' Jobert said. 'This is Jaune.'

'Hello, Jaune.' Duque looked at Jaune's teeth. 'Where is Rouge?'

In a surge of emotional surprise, tears burnt Jobert' eyes. 'He stands post on the field of honour. Rivoli. Nearly three years ago.'

Duque gripped Jobert's forearm. 'Michelle says you took a beating in that affair.'

'The worst blow was losing Rouge.' Jobert smeared his tears.

Duque pulled him into a hug. 'He was a damn fine horse.'

'He was.' Jobert choked.

'What of the senior colt herd?' Duque asked. 'Convoys still run to Raive in Italy. How is that slippery bastard?'

'Raive has done well. Our convoys are lucrative for him. Do you remember Fergnes?'

'Another loss?'

'Yes, Caldiero,' Jobert said. Duque shrugged at the reference. 'Three years ago.' Ice whistled through Jobert's heart. 'Raive married his widow.'

Duque cocked his head on one side. 'An odd thing to mention. Were you fond of the widow?'

'Ah, no ... you spoke of Raive, my thoughts wandered to convoys and veterans and ...'

Duque shrugged. 'The loads are not placing undue strain on the colts?'

'Yann would never allow it. He keeps a sharp eye on the returning teams.'

'How is Yann with only one arm?'

'You could not kill that old mongrel with a stick,' Jobert said. 'He is disappointed I will not remain here, but I am compelled to return.'

'You stay on the farm? Piss off!' Duque gave a grim half grin. 'Compelled to return? Who is she?'

Jobert shook his head. 'It is nothing.'

'How old?'

'Twenty-four,' Jobert said. 'We met two years ago. She compromised her reputation to secure my release from prison.'

Duque's eyebrows raised. 'I promised to marry her.' Duque huffed in surprise. 'The war is taking me further and further away. I am unable to fulfil my promise to her ... my desire—'

'Michelle shared your letters with me. I saw snippets. This woman's father—'

'Her name is Gianna.' Jobert looked away. 'How is Michelle? Her baby? These de Colbert brothers?'

'Michelle's days are full of Aunt Sophie and little Jacques. Two of the three de Colberts are trapped in Egypt. Be thankful—'

'André?' A voice called from outside the stables. 'Duque?'

'In here, Didier.'

Didier entered on his cane. 'There is news from Paris. I am unsure of its implications. There has been a coup.'

Jobert rolled his eyes. 'Another one?'

'Not just a reshuffle of the Directory, but the overthrow of the Directory. A consulate has been established.'

'Surely, a different word for ineptitude and corruption.'

'Perhaps not,' Didier said. 'Bonaparte has been appointed First Consul.'

'Bonaparte!' Jobert said, exchanging a look of incredulity with Duque. 'Has Bonaparte returned from Egypt? Has he brought his army with him?'

'No,' Didier said, 'he has returned without them, but Bonaparte now heads the government. He intends to retake Lombardy.'

'You ask what implications, brother?' Jobert slapped Didier on the shoulder. 'This changes everything. Bonaparte would accept Italian Cossacks.'

'André, you wanted to re-join Masséna, yes?' Didier asked.

Jobert wobbled his head to consider.

'If so,' Didier said, 'Masséna now commands the Army of Italy and the defence of Genoa.'

Jobert's eyes widened. 'Is that right? Good old Masséna. Then it is fate. Genoa, it is.'

Jobert squeezed Duque's lapel. 'Duque, come with me to Genoa. I will arrange to have you assigned to the Army of Italy. With you by my side we can hunt that bastard von Maefeld.'

Six weeks later, on New Years Day 1800, Jobert stood around the warmth of Masséna's hearth with Raive, Rizzoli and de Chabenac.

'Gentlemen, I have received word from our esteemed First Consul,' said General Masséna, the latest commander of the Army of Italy. '*Monsieur* Bonaparte has informed me of a plan to re-establish the Cisalpine Republic.'

Jobert's face flushed with more than the heat from the flames.

'My part in that plan,' Masséna continued, 'is to make a vigorous defence of Genoa to maintain the attention of our adversaries south of the Po through their defence of the Maritime Alps and the Apennines. Thus, I require information as to the dispositions of the enemy.' Masséna gave Jobert a wink. 'I am informed of a scheme, Jobert, where Cisalpine Cossacks might scout the Austrian's lines of communication. Could you remain at large in Lombardy and Piedmont until Consul Bonaparte arrives with the Army of the Interior?'

Rizzoli stiffened. 'I beg your pardon, sir? What arrangement is being discussed?'

'Am I mistaken?' Masséna shot a look of concern to Raive. 'Has this possibility not been discussed?'

'A proposal had been muted in broad outline, sir,' Raive glanced at Rizzoli, 'of the Cisalpine Chasseurs playing a significant role in the liberation of Lombardy.'

'In broad outline, sir … a strong possibility, sir.' With a handsome smile to Masséna, Rizzoli smoothed his moustache with the back of his finger. 'With general agreement from all parties for its success.'

Masséna gave the fire a firm nod. 'Jobert?'

'I am ready for the task, sir.' Jobert straightened, 'but I am unsure of the Cisalpine Chasseurs.'

Rizzoli raised his eyebrows in alarm.

With a harsh glance at Rizzoli, Masséna rocked back on his heels. 'Yes, I remember the Cisalpine Chasseurs performance in Rome two years ago.'

Hurt flashed in Rizzoli's eyes.

'These last two years,' Jobert said, 'the regiment's mettle has been proven in the heat of battle.' Jobert stared hard at Rizzoli. 'I can vouch for that. My concern lies with their recovery from a severe campaign. Colonel Rizzoli has orders to join the new Italian Legion in Dijon. Men are travelling from Lombardy to enlist. I hesitate to strip veterans from their ranks as they assimilate recruits. Perhaps a company from the 15th Chasseurs would—'

'No, no, no.' Rizzoli upraised palms pushed against the glow of the flames. 'If the reconquest of Cisalpine is underway, then the republic's chasseurs will play an active part. I shall comply with the First Consul's orders to concentrate with the Army of the Interior, but I feel most able to detach the Mantua and Brescia Companies for this vital mission.'

'A squadron?' Masséna's eyes tightened in calculation. 'Of what strength, Rizzoli?'

'Fifty sabres, sir.'

'Do you feel that sufficient, Jobert?'

'Indeed, it is more than sufficient, sir.' Jobert gave Rizzoli a slight nod. 'Colonel Rizzoli, who now commands Mantua Company?'

'Young Bernasconi has been promoted captain. But such a delicate task demands a chief of squadron in attendance, sir.' Rizzoli dropped his eyes to the coals. 'I will assign Major Zenari, sir.'

Jobert's mood soured as if a bucket of piss had been poured on the fire. 'But—'

'There you are, Jobert, your trusty second-in-command.' Masséna glanced at Raive. 'Raive, when can they begin?'

Raive smiled at some private success. 'The gentlemen here gathered need return to Nice, where Jobert shall collect the squadron. Once the snows in the passes melt, Jobert will procced over the Maritime Alps he knows so well.'

'Excellent!' Masséna clapped his hands. 'Then make it so. Gentlemen, until we next meet in Milan.'

With a salute, the chasseur officers departed Masséna's office.

In the anteroom, Rizzoli retrieved a bound volume from de Chabenac. 'Allow me to return your Bourcet.' Rizzoli hesitated at passing over Jobert's manual of mountain warfare.

'I have appreciated the gift you shared, Jobert. Truly.' Rizzoli's sad smile played briefly across his face. 'Thankfully, I paid attention, Jobert, as we now follow Hannibal over the Alps.'

With a nod, Jobert received the book.

'Allow me to say farewell, Jobert,' said Rizzoli. 'I have a long march to Dijon ahead. Zenari and Bernasconi's ... Cossacks will await you in Nice.'

Jobert saluted. 'Until Milan, sir.'

Rizzoli's eyes were tinged with pity. With a slight bow, Rizzoli departed down the corridor.

'Jobert, your purgatory is at an end,' Raive said, giving Jobert's elbow a squeeze. 'I knew your Italians would come through.'

Jobert cocked a sceptical eyebrow. 'Indeed, sir.'

'Now, for the task at hand.' Raive bounced on his toes. 'I imagine you will be travelling quite light into Lombardy. Without Orlande, the cart, Maria and child. Just your packhorse?'

Jobert's face flickered with calculation. 'Yes, sir. I imagine so.'

'I have recently established a house in Nice,' Raive said. 'Would it be to your advantage to have Orlande set camp there whilst you are away?'

'That is very generous, sir.'

'Think nothing of it.' Raive cocked his head to one side. 'Perhaps you might do me a small favour in return?'

Jobert frowned with suspicion. 'Sir?

'Nothing onerous.' Raive wriggled his fingers. 'Since you are travelling that way, would you escort Marguerite, Camille and the children to Nice. I expect Genoa could become ... uncomfortable as the campaign continues. A small convoy of domestic necessities carried by your family's wagons will accompany them.'

Marguerite!

Jobert inclined his head. 'I am at your service, sir.'

'I am obliged, sir,' Raive said. 'Will you ride directly to Mantua?' Raive wiggled an envelope between his fingers. 'Perhaps a letter to spur your mount.'

Juggling the book under his arm, Jobert flipped the envelope to read the sender's address.

Gianna!

The envelope sizzled in his fingers.

'Good luck, Jobert,' Raive said. 'As is the fashion, gentlemen, until Milan.' Raive gave a polite bow and departed the room.

De Chabenac snatched the book from Jobert's grasp. 'Open the damned letter, man.'

Jobert broke the seal and unfolded the note. Jobert's chest shuddered as a hint of lavender and orange ascended from the pages.

The Prefetto's Residence,
Mantua, Lombardy
1ˢᵗ of August 1799

To my darling André,

Your letter, dated early June, has delivered much joy and light during the darkest of days. How are you, my dearest love? I pray this quick note finds you unharmed. How I ache to be with you once more. My heart is flattened as if a vast stone lies upon me. Do you still have our book? Return swiftly, my sweetheart, as we still have the final act ...

Upon your safe arrival, Father is hoping you might approach him with a proposal of which I know he would be delighted to accept. How is Silvio? Send him all our love. Please keep him safe until you arrive ...

This is my first note to be sent since the siege was raised this week. My father and I have passed through that misery as safe and well as can be expected. It saddens me to sign off, but Father is eager to travel to Milan to be united with Mother.

All my love...

'Is the lady well, Jobert?' de Chabenac asked. 'Has your banishment been overturned? Does she encourage you to return?'

'All is well.' A range of emotions played across Jobert's face. The letter trembled in his grasp. 'Should I say all was well, as the letter is dated five months ago. Despite the burden of Raive's convoy, I will ride swiftly to Lombardy.'

De Chabenac considered Jobert. 'Would this be of any value?' He passed Jobert a small black velvet pouch.

Jobert tipped two interlocking bands of a gimmal ring into his palm. The top of the engagement band was encrusted with emeralds. Jobert grinned like a fool.

'Her green eyes.' He gripped de Chabenac in a tight hug.

Upon release, de Chabenac squeezed Jobert's shoulders. 'Ah, it is untrue. He can be happy.' Concern flickered across de Chabenac's face. 'Safe travels, my friend. Until Milan.'

A single candle on a long, silver candlestick lit Jobert's bedroom for the evening. Raive had arranged accommodation for the trip from Genoa to Nice of appropriate comfort for the wife and household of a senior officer. In Savona on their first night on the road, Jobert relaxed in his embroidered chair and rested his gaze upon the ornate panels of the door.

A light knock penetrated the timber.

The polished brass doorknob rotated. Light from the corridor and rich perfume swept towards Jobert.

Marguerite stepped lightly into the room. She wore the shimmering gown she had worn to dinner. She let her shawl slide to the floor.

'Not yet preparing for bed, darling?'

A smile was the only change of movement from within Jobert's seated position. That, and perhaps, a crinkle around his eyes.

Marguerite glided to the bed. Her dark lashes widened as she viewed the room.

'No wine to toast our reunion?' She lifted the waist of her dress to sit on the bed. Her fists wrapped the sheer fabric around her hips. Her buttocks and thighs pressed in soft relief. Marguerite stroked the thick quilted silk bedcover with her white hand.

'What ails you, darling boy? This girl from Mantua? Your desire for her surely needs slaking? What scent does she wear? Come now, it would be fun to pretend? Not even for old times' sake?'

Jobert remained immobile in his corner chair.

'Oh, how disappointing,' she said. 'Very well, play the smitten Romeo.'

Marguerite rolled onto her belly, her chin in her hands. As she waggled her lower legs in the air, the hem of her dress slithered to her knees.

'I was so looking forward to this evening. I always enjoyed your attentions. Raive said an opportunity exists for us all to be together in Nice. Perhaps we might renew our affections then?'

Marguerite rolled onto her back. She arched her smooth neck to watch him. Her breasts strained from her dress. 'Nice will allow you to spend more time with the boys. Have they not grown since you last saw them? You will want to see both children, will you not? Master Fergnes is five and your son, oops ... your godson, is two.'

The tip of Marguerite's tongue darted across her lips. 'Being quite aware of your potency, my darling, I have no doubt your young wife will be constantly pregnant. You will need a dear friend to pass the occasional dreary evening. I am sure we can make arrangements that assure mutual discretion.'

Smiling, Jobert stood and held out his hand to her.

'Marguerite, come to me.'

Marguerite slipped her soft hands around his rigid fingers. She pressed her body towards his.

Jobert's iron grip and locked elbows kept her at bay.

Bruised hope arched across her open lips.

Jobert's brace softened. He rubbed his thumb across the ring upon her finger. The ruby flared in the candlelight. Its nest of diamonds scratched at his skin. Jobert's voice caught in his throat.

'Such future arrangements, dear sister, require me to arrive in Nice with a bride. Such matrimonial bliss is not yet assured.'

Scooping up her shawl, Jobert led Marguerite through his bedchamber door and into the corridor outside.

'Until then, Madame Raive, good night.'

Chapter Twenty-Six
April 1800, Piacenza, Italy

Jobert blew a stream of cigar smoke towards the stars. Beneath him, Bleu threw his head and pawed the earth in impatience. 'Not long now until my birthday fireworks, lad.'

Thirty-five. That cannot be right.

A pair of horses galloped towards him.

Earlier today, an Austrian powder convoy had been ferried south across the Po at Piacenza. It had camped between the Turin Gate and the Trebbia River to the west of the city.

Too good a gift on such an auspicious day.

Koschak and Fazio reined beside Jobert and the long dark column of Cisalpine Chasseurs.

'Not long now,' Koschak said.

A muffled explosion woofed behind the tree line.

Jobert sucked on his cigar. 'Well done, Sergeant Fazio.'

With three months to prepare the squadron before the alpine paths became traversable, Jobert had spoken to Fazio. 'I command this squadron now, Sergeant. Colonel Rizzoli will depend on experienced men, such as yourself, to train the new draft of enlistees in Dijon. If you think that is a better application of your talents, I will support your reassignment.'

Fazio's eyes twitched with internal debate. 'When Mantua Company dwindles to just you and I, I might consider it. Until then ...'

'The men will want to go home. If they do, a wailing mother will confess to the priest who will whisper to the magistrate who will alert the garrison commander.'

Fazio thrust out his jaw. 'I will ensure the men content themselves, as spirits of the night, to watch over their families.'

The other ammunition caissons caught alight in a ripple of greater and greater explosions. The screams of the wagon teams tethered in their lines carried across the ripening fields. The chasseurs' horses shifted with distress.

'Look!' Zenari pointed with glee at a red-hot wheel rim spinning through the air.

Jobert savoured the cigar smoke in his mouth and watched the flames consume the wagons.

Zenari, your debt from Mantua remains outstanding.

On receiving the assignment three months ago, Zenari had whined. 'This squadron of Mantua Company and Brescia Company is nothing more than a troop,'

'It may be only fifty sabres,' Jobert had replied, 'but it is the heart of two fine companies. To give honour to lost brothers I name it the Cisalpine Squadron. Bernasconi will command Mantua and you, Zenari, will command Brescia.'

'Command a platoon. Why bother?'

'Either Brescia, Zenari, or join Sergeant Duque in the pack horse section.'

The whoosh of the explosions' blast waves bent the green seed heads of the spring wheat. Jobert rocked in the saddle as the acrid-tinged shock punched him.

Above Savona a week ago, a regimental raid had distracted

the Austrian screen at the Col di Cadibona. Jobert's sabres waited in the shadows, before their column slithered into the mist to pass behind the enemy's forward piquets. Two days later, Jobert's squadron heard the gunfire as the Austrian assault began on Genoa.

Jobert knew the Bormida Valley well. By night the chasseurs crept their horses until they blended with the Austrian military traffic on the Po's road network.

Throughout the camp of the powder convoy, men bellowed. Loose horses cantered their flapping lead ropes into the gloom. North of the dark horsemen, Piacenza's bells clanged in alarm. Drums rattled to stir the bastions' garrisons. Gun smoke swept across the chattering and pointing chasseurs.

Jobert watched the grey cloud pulse outwards across Trebbia's river flats, the same plains where ten months ago Jobert had faced the Cossacks.

I will be in Mantua in three days. If she is not there, I will be in Milan soon after.

He flicked his cigar butt at the smouldering wreckage of the powder convoy.

'Cisalpines, in column of fours, right turn, walk, march.'

Jobert and Silvio Bernasconi, in the guise of labourers, froze in the shadows as Milan's bells chimed midnight. Once the city's dogs had stopped howling and the pigeon flocks had resettled, Jobert rapped on the gate of Bernasconi's uncle.

A nightwatchman slid open a grille in the gate's panel.

'Fetch your chamberlain to the door,' Jobert said. 'I have a message for your master.'

Within fifteen minutes, the grille slid open again.

'Recognise me, Pietro?' Silvio asked his uncle's chamberlain. 'Is my father within? Take me to him.'

Jobert and Silvio were shown into the drawing room as the family assembled. Illuminated by a single candlelight, the family flocked around Silvio. Urged hushes could not suppress the cries of joy. Dressing gowns swished as arms flapped to either wrap around Silvio or wipe tears.

Jobert, in the room's shadows, had eyes only for Gianna. His unsteady pulse convulsed his throat.

Is she the one for whom I have ached for years?

Once clear of his mother's embrace, Silvio swept a hand to Jobert's shadows. 'I have brought a friend.'

The family froze as they appraised Jobert.

'There are rumours that enemy chasseurs have infiltrated into Lombardy,' Bernasconi said. 'Is that you?' Prefetto Bernasconi face had lined considerably, his hair greyer and sparser since Jobert had departed his company before Mantua's siege twelve months ago.

Jobert bowed. 'I bring news of a French Army led by our General Bonaparte. Stand ready to resume your administration, sir.'

Signora Bernasconi gasped as she fought her tears. 'Your time is over, Jobert. Release my child and return to France.'

'The full weight of French arms marches to Milan, Signora. Captain Bernasconi's squadron is in the vanguard. Soon, your family shall be united and at peace once more.'

Gianna's arms trembled as they folded across her chest. 'You are well, sir?'

Jobert swallowed to clear his throat. 'I am quite well, thank you, Signorina. And you?'

Gianna's jaw clenched as she fought tears. 'I am very well

indeed, now that you are here.'

Her mother grimaced and gripped Silvio's arm even tighter.

'How long can you stay?' Gianna asked.

'Just this night.' Jobert's heart sunk. 'We must depart at dawn.' The family moaned. 'We will be hanged if captured.' Jobert turned to Bernasconi. 'Your household must be sworn to silence. Silvio and I have a commitment we are bound to fulfill. The Austrian assault on Genoa has begun. We must go.'

Gianna took a faltering step towards Jobert, her hands unsure if they should reach for him. 'Where will you go?'

'I march for Turin with fifty Cisalpine Chasseurs. Should I dally so close to their homes they will desert.'

'You both must desire a wash before supper.' Bernasconi clapped his hands and looked to the chamberlain. 'Prepare basins, a tray and beds.'

Soon after, shirtless, Jobert bathed himself over a washbasin when a knock sounded from his door.

Gianna entered in her dressing gown bearing a platter of *salame Cremona*, a wedge of *Gorgonzola* cheese and bread and a jug of *Arneis* white wine. With her entry came a waft of lavender and orange.

Jobert fumbled to pull a clean shirt over his head, regretting the moment any sight of her was obscured.

'I have ached for you.' Before him, Gianna trembled. Her face creased in anxiety. 'Only one letter in a year.'

'Two armies disrupted my correspondence. I sent two.' Jobert had never seen her long hair cascading over her shoulders. 'I have established a household in Nice. You will be safe in Nice. I shall ask your father for your hand as soon as the sun rises.'

'No.'

Ice filled Jobert's chest. 'No?'

She gripped the front of his chest and pushed her face into his throat. 'No, my darling.'

Jobert's chest melted as if a volcano erupted in his belly. His hands shook as he ran his fingertips down her ribs to her waist and the swell of her buttocks.

'I am drowning in desire.' Her eyes closed and her head wobbled as she raised her face. 'Kiss me.'

They devoured each other with mouths and hands.

Our passion rages too far.

Jobert's breath was ragged as he gently eased her backwards.

Gianna scratched at his chest. 'I am torn. I want you so much. I belong to you. The anguish of withholding such gratification is unbearable.' Gianna spun and stepped to the window. 'But darling André, a greater pain terrifies me. A searing pain I have known too many times. I have longed for you these last two years. And for how much of that time have you been absent?'

A bracing clarity purged Jobert's mind. 'A French army marches for Lombardy. Once victorious, I will retire and devote myself to you. I promise. Do you promise to wait for me?'

'I do, of course, I do. But ...' Her look of worry returned. 'Can you cease being a soldier?'

'For you, yes.'

'Then cease your service now. Let us take to Nice this dawn.'

Jobert licked his lips.

'Ah, see you cannot.'

'Beautiful Gianna. I have lost too many dear friends here in Lombardy.' Jobert opened his palms in appeal. 'This last campaign will redeem my devotion to them. Peace has not yet been concluded. Battles are still to be fought.'

Gianna dared her face to smile. 'Once peace is declared, we would fly to Nice together.'

'Yes.'

Gianna's dimples flickered. 'Is that where you will remain. Beside me. You would stay by my side forever?'

Jobert blinks. 'I have been offered a post in the commissariat.

We will create a home in Nice. I may be on the road for short periods.'

Gianna deflated. 'Ah, there you have it.'

Jobert approached her. He slid her hair behind her ear. She watched him study the curls on her throat. He bent to brush her lips with his. 'Like Romeo, my banishment from you has been a torture. I must have you by my side. To be enfolded in your arms. I belong to you.'

Gianna caressed his face. 'Your duty snatches you from me. The demands of the guns are greater than the enticement of my kisses.'

'I have our book.' Jobert groped in his tailcoat's pocket. 'It has never left me.'

Jaune, keep my lapse secret.

'Can we not conclude our study of the play?'

'My memories of our study together sustained me through the four-month nightmare of the siege. Perhaps the final act when you arrive back?' Gianna compressed his hands to close the pages of the play. 'Do you not remember how it ends?'

'No. It was years ago and in Italian.'

Jobert wriggled his hands free and dropped the book on his bed. From a small black pouch, he tipped a ring into his palm. 'I can wait no longer.' The candle-lit emeralds had their reflection sparkle in her eyes.

Jobert dropped to one knee. 'Gianna Bernasconi, will you do me the honour of becoming my wife?'

She sank to her knees, took his head and kissed his forehead. 'I must spite my desire for you.' Her breasts beneath her nightgown rose and fell. 'I will neither marry you nor lie with you, while you serve as a soldier.'

Jobert's mind reeled. 'It is not as simple as that.'

'Then I shall make it simple, my gorgeous man. War has consumed three beautiful young men that I adored, two who had promised themselves to me. I cannot … I cannot endure such pain again.' Gianna began to sob. 'I am so afraid.'

She kissed his lips. Her tears filled his mouth, before she fled his room.

Her salt in his mouth dissolved any final barrier to the release of his own anguish.

'I accept your price, Senor,' Jobert said. 'Will you accept payment in coin?'

Across the grimy table, the tavern keeper's eyes opened at the prospect of hard payment.

Jobert glanced to the other occupied tables. In one corner sat Koschak and an elderly shepherd. Fazio and a whore sat in the other.

'I shall fetch your payment. I will return to collect my loaves.' Jobert exited the tavern through the kitchen.

On the heights east above Turin, the back lane was bathed in a mid-May moon. Having departed Milan in mid-April, the Cisalpine Chasseurs had snuck through Lombardy and around Piedmont. In four weeks, they had established small courier posts from Turin to Genoa through which messages filtered back to the Ligurian coast.

Jobert found the chasseur holding six horses and thrust a bottle into his hands. 'Stash this for your troubles. How goes the night, lad?' Jobert withdrew a small purse of coin from his portmanteau.

A whistle.

Jobert and the chasseur stiffened at the sentry's signal. The horses' ears pricked as they shuffled.

A sentry jogged to them from the end of the lane. 'Hussars, sir. Maybe twenty.'

'Call in the other sentry. Mount. Musketoons ready. I shall fetch Koschak and Fazio from the taproom.'

Jobert entered the tavern through the kitchen to find a woman balling dumplings at a bench. 'Senora, for your husband.' Jobert dropped the purse into an earthenware jar of rice. He parted a hessian curtain a fraction and peered into the taproom. Jobert slid into the shadows beside the door to avoid being silhouetted by glow from the kitchen fire.

Four Austrian hussars entered the front door. Their tall leather shakos scarlet red, their uniforms sky-blue, their embroidered pelisses draped from their left shoulders. They called for the tavern keeper.

Acting the drunken letch, Jobert hoped, Fazio and his local woman ambled out the door toward the tavern yard, with every amorous appearance of completing the night together.

One clear. Now for Koschak.

As more hussars entered the small room, Koschak and the shepherd stood. The shepherd created a minor interference as he attempted to exit the front door as the hussars entered. Their abuse of him distracted their observation of Koschak walking towards Jobert at the kitchen door.

'That shepherd says the French army has crossed the Great Saint Bernhard Pass,' Koschak said. 'He knows secret paths around the fortresses on the Swiss border.' Koschak tipped back the hessian curtain to the kitchen. 'Are you coming?'

Jobert watched a tall, blond hussar officer stride across the room to the tavern fire and open his cape to warm his belly. From his waistband, a familiar silver pistol twinkled at the heat.

Von Maefeld!

'Do you want it?' Koschak asked.

'It is mine. I have earned it.'

Koschak jerked his chin at the other hussars. 'Too many of them now. Do you want to steal it when they sleep?'

Jobert shook his head. 'I want to look him in the eye when I reclaim it.'

'Then capture him and remove him from his escort. Flay him at your leisure.'

Jobert eyes tightened as he calculated.

The hussars entered the room with their portmanteaus.

'Your advantage is draining away,' Koschak said. 'There he is. Call him out. They will stand clear.'

Jobert backed through the kitchen curtain pushing Koschak as he went.

'What can there be to consider?' Koschak asked. Once inside the kitchen, Koschak stood firm with his hands on his hips. 'You created these Italian scouts to see Gianna. She did not accept your proposal. She did not come away with you. What stays your hand? Cut this bastard's ears and fingers off and present them to Duque.' Koschak sneered. 'Or is that pistol no longer important?'

Jobert glanced back into the taproom. 'Bonaparte marches an army over the Alps.' Sufficiently heated, von Maefeld pivoted and appraised the room's patrons and shadows. 'My oath to France trumps my oath to him.'

Just before von Maefeld's inspection reached the kitchen screen, Jobert made a silent promise to the pistol.

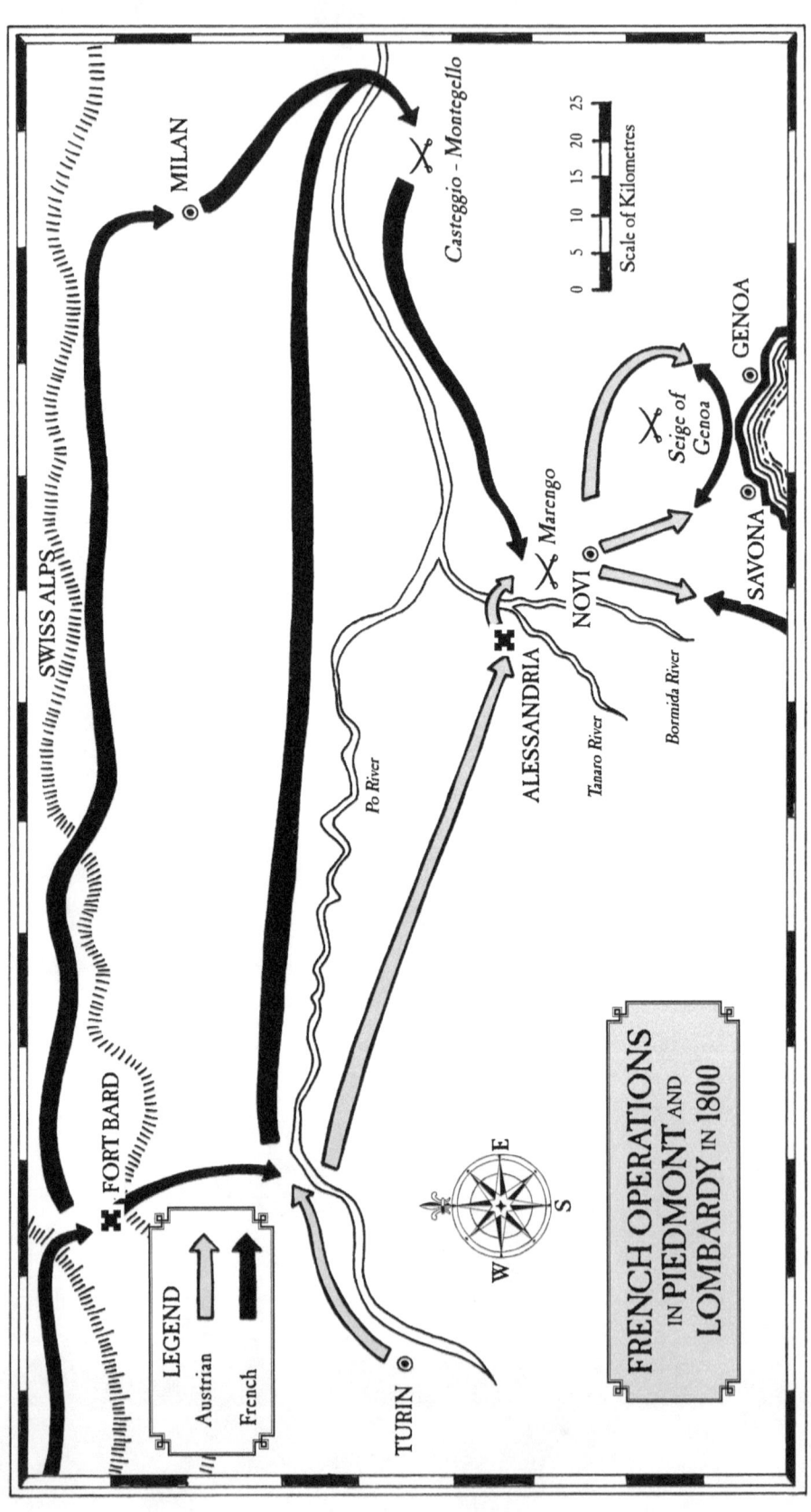

FRENCH OPERATIONS IN PIEDMONT AND LOMBARDY IN 1800

LEGEND
Austrian
French

SWISS ALPS

FORT BARD

MILAN

Casteggio - Monteggello

GENOA

Siege of Genoa

Marengo

NOVI

SAVONA

ALESSANDRIA

Tanaro River

Bormida River

Po River

TURIN

Scale of Kilometres
0 5 10 15 20 25

N
E
S
W

Chapter Twenty-Seven

June 1800,
Battle of Casteggio-Montebello, Italy

For the next week, Jobert and his chasseurs listened to the guns booming in the Swiss valleys to their north. In late May, Jobert entered the headquarters of General Lannes, commanding Bonaparte's advance guard.

'Welcome Jobert.' Lannes returned Jobert's salute by slapping his upper arm. 'Very good to see you.'

'How was Egypt, sir?' Jobert asked.

'Hot. Sandy. How did you get around Fort Bard?'

Jobert smiled at Lannes' impatience. 'There are shepherds' paths, sir.'

'This fortress blocks my advance, and I cannot wait to reduce it. What is the capacity of your paths?'

'Infantry only. Impassable to horses.'

Lannes squinted at Jobert with hope. 'Perhaps three- or four-pounders packed on men's backs?'

Jobert grimaced. 'Possibly.'

Lannes clicked his fingers. 'Then I can resume my advance, even with just my battalions. Thank you, old friend, your time minding Italy for us has been repaid.'

Jobert rolled his jaw to mask his irritation.

Lannes beckoned Jobert to a map-strewn table. 'Jobert, I march an advance guard directly south for Turin. The kaiserliks will be stretched dealing with me to their north, and Masséna and Suchet to their south. All the while, Bonaparte marches the bulk of the army for Milan.' Lannes stopped pointing to look up with a mischievous grin. 'Not only will he cut the Austrian line of communications, but he will also re-establish the Cisalpine Republic. The Austrians will attempt to drive east and break out of encirclement.'

Jobert reached forward and pointed at the town of Romano. 'The enemy currently between you and Turin are a brigade of fusiliers with at least two batteries of six-ponders. Four regiments of cavalry watch the valleys entering the plain. They will reinforce rapidly from Alessandria.'

Lannes squinted and rubbed his chin. 'I shall leave my engineers and gunners to reduce Fort Bard. I shall resume my advance with my infantry with best speed.' Lannes shot Jobert a calculating smile. 'Jobert, stay here and assist my engineers with any support you can provide from behind the enemy. Keep this secret path of yours open. Once the road past Fort Bard is open, escort my artillery to me wherever in Italy I might be.'

Jobert responded with an affirming nod. 'I am at your service, sir.'

Three weeks later, Jobert arrived at Lannes' headquarters on the southern bank of the Po.

'Thanks to Jobert's Italians for escorting the artillery to us,' Lannes said to his assembled commanders. 'We are whole again, and just in time. Good news, Bonaparte has secured Milan. The Cisalpine Republic has been re-established and the Austrian lines of communication are cut.'

The fatigue-worn colonels and majors around the room huffed and grunted with grim delight.

Lannes raised a warning finger to his audience and winced. 'The bad news is Genoa has fallen. Masséna has been unable to hold Genoa for as long as we hoped. The force our enemy had dedicated to the siege now marches north to reinforce those who delay us along the Po. Consul Bonaparte orders me to march west and find the enemy. Jobert, you know the country around Alessandria, east of the Bormida and Tanaro rivers?'

'Around Marengo, yes, sir.'

'Then we race against the clock. My advance guard shall march tomorrow, with Victor's division in the main body being our immediate support.'

Jobert twitched with surprise.

Victor returned?

The next day, Lannes' advance guard and Jobert's Cisalpine Squadron marched west to locate the enemy. At six o'clock that morning, Lannes' vanguard engaged a small Austrian force on the east-west Piacenza-Alessandria road and, after three hours of fighting, pushed them back.

'They now know where we are,' Jobert said to Bernasconi, 'but where are they?'

At eleven o'clock, on the eastern outskirts of Casteggio, Lannes' column was engaged once Austrian infantry fired on the west-marching French column from the lumpy heights south of the road.

Jobert sat at the rear of a group of staff officers clustered around Lannes. Through his telescope, Jobert watched small groups of sky-blue enemy hussars move on the flanks of the kaiserlik fusiliers. He lowered his telescope to check his remaining pistol in its holster. The silver boar's head twinkled in the overhead sun.

'This morning I felt we pursued an Austrian rear guard,' Lannes said. 'I now believe I am facing their advance guard attempting to break out east. Have Victor march forward to reinforce me.'

A smile flickered over Jobert's face as he sensed an opportunity to reconnect with his old commander and friend.

Lannes turned his glass west to Casteggio. 'What force holds the town?'

The commanding officer of the 12th Hussars cleared his throat. 'Your infantry is committed to this distraction to the south, sir. My hussars request the honour of testing the strength of Casteggio.'

Lannes gave a quick smile and nod to the hussar colonel. 'Jobert, perhaps your Cossacks might assist?'

As they trotted to their waiting columns, the colonel said, 'There is little fifty Italian blades can do, Jobert, that five hundred hussars cannot.'

'I agree, sir,' Jobert said. 'With your permission, might I cover your right flank and seek any crossings on the Coppa stream as it flows north of the town?'

'As you, please.'

As Jobert re-joined the chasseurs, hussar trumpets called Skirmishers In and soon after Advance.

Random musket fire sounded in front of Casteggio. Drums beat urgently from within.

Bernasconi stood in his stirrups for a better view. 'Are the hussars charging the town, sir?'

'Koschak, skirmishers out,' Jobert said. 'Bernasconi column of fours, follow the paths north of the town.'

French trumpet calls for Charge were greeted with a roar of yells and a solid volley of muskets. The yelling and trumpets continued until ragged musket fire echoed through the town.

As did many of his chasseurs, Bernasconi craned his neck towards the pandemonium from Casteggio. 'Are the hussars into the town, sir?'

The paths curved until it crossed the Coppa at a wide wooden bridge covered in sheep droppings.

Jobert rode across the bridge and, once clear of the obscuration offered by the stunted elms along the Coppa's banks, extended his glass and observed the town. 'The kaiserliks have cavalry behind Casteggio.'

Foreign trumpets called. A rumble of hooves. A French call to Rally. Cries of effort rebounded from the rock walls. A sizzle of passing blades.

Drums.

Jobert swept his telescope to the right. On an isolated hill, the next village west of Casteggio was Montebello, where a hamlet of stone clung to the outer walls of an ancient castle. 'The 12th Hussars have stirred a hornets' nest. The kaiserliks are marching up reserve infantry from Montebello. Moench, sound Commanders In.'

The firing had ceased in the town. A broken column of brown-clad hussars limped east out of the town.

Bernasconi, Koschak and Fazio formed a tight circle around Jobert. Zenari halted his horse on the outer of the group and angled it away.

'Gentlemen,' Jobert said, 'the enemy hold the town and the routes around it to the south. Here we have an unopposed bridge around Casteggio to the north. The way west to Montebello, and then Alessandria, is open. General Lannes must be informed of this opportunity. In the meantime, the squadron shall form a bridge guard.'

'Do not be ridiculous, Jobert,' Zenari said, 'chasseurs cannot defend a bridge.'

Koschak shook his head at Jobert. Fazio mumbled something to his horse. Bernasconi lowered his face.

Jobert regathered his reins.

Somewhere, sometime, I will have my revenge.

'We cannot defend the bridge, Zenari,' Jobert said, 'but we can deny its use to a small force or delay a larger enemy force from securing it against us. If you find the task daunting, perhaps you might take a walk to clear your head.'

Bernasconi coughed a laugh.

Zenari's hooded eyes rolled towards Jobert, and his droopy moustache curled into another insubordinate comment.

Jobert raised a warning finger. 'Zenari, General Lannes would appreciate our discovery. May I rely on you to deliver him this vital intelligence?'

Zenari snorted and spurred his horse away to the east.

Fazio straightened in the saddle. 'Give us your orders, sir, and we will comply.'

Koschak head swung slowly to regard Fazio with suspicion.

Jobert's eyes tightened as he considered Fazio. 'As we would for a screen, Sergeant, form an inlying piquet for the bridge. Bernasconi, half of Mantua on guard, half at rest. Koschak, half of Brescia form an outlying screen on the Coppa's far bank, the other half rests within the inlying piquet's camp. Sergeant Fazio, may I rely on you to maintain discipline in the camp? No loose girths. Fire one kettle only. Ready to mount on my call.'

Fazio looked Jobert in the eye and saluted. 'Yes, sir.'

On Fazio's departure, Jobert raised an intrigued eyebrow at Koschak. Koschak narrowed his eyes and shook his head.

Once Duque passed him a wooden mug of bouillon, Jobert toured the squadrons deployment. 'Is your bridge guard at their posts, Bernasconi?'

'They are set, sir.' Bernasconi shifted in his saddle to look around him as Jobert gathered his reins to depart. 'May I say, sir, that ... I am very glad you will become my brother-in-law, and not ... von Poschinger.'

Jobert jerked with alarm. 'Who?'

'Ah, sir ... did you not ...' Bernasconi's face flickered with unpleasant realisation. 'After Gianna's fiancé passed, we saw a great deal of his brother.'

'The Austrian who lost an arm at Rivoli?'

'Yes, sir.' Bernasconi swallowed hard. 'He and Gianna became close before he returned to Salzburg.' Bernasconi dropped his face. 'They still correspond.'

Jobert's heart exploded in flame. 'Thank you for the sentiment, Bernasconi. Before we become brothers, might we see to our duties and our chasseurs.'

Bernasconi saluted and departed swiftly.

Jobert crushed her book in his grip through his jacket.

Two hours later, General Victor, his commanders and staff approached Jobert's bridge.

Jobert saluted. 'Welcome back to Italy, sir.'

Victor returned the compliment. 'It seems the infernal country will not release us from its grip, Jobert.'

'How was your sojourn in Paris?'

Victor grinned. 'Collective knuckles rapped for our supposed failings, but all that is behind us now. Our dear friend, and First Consul, Bonaparte has graciously reinstalled me. Do you still have your Italian Cossacks?'

'I do, sir.' Jobert swept his arm at the guard on the bridge, the reserves smoking and oiling weapons as horses grazed, and the skirmish line in the green wheatfields on the far bank.

Victor walked his charger onto the bridge. 'And this opportunity exists to continue our advance west, yet Lannes has not secured it. Why not?'

'His advance guard is fully committed to the Austrian threat to the south.'

A prolonged rattle of drums drifted across the spring crops. Out in the screen, Figaro was called. Chasseurs scrambled to scoff soup and mount.

Jobert looked at Victor. 'The enemy marches for us, sir.'

Within the hour, three blue-jacketed fusilier battalions surged over the bridge to confront an Austrian fire line. The firefight between the blue and white lines roared for an hour.

As the gun smoke and cartridge papers swirled across the June sky, Bernasconi and Zenari held the chasseurs in line in support on the infantry's northern flank. Jobert and Koschak held their posts well forward in the screen line and watched the Austrian line waver and step backwards.

'They are breaking.' Koschak said. 'Do you see him?'

'I do.' Jobert watched a hussar aide canter clear of the Austrian fire line. A solid man in sky-blue on a jet-black charger could only be von Maefeld.

With a roar of rage and a thrashing of drums, the French surged forward with the bayonet. The white-jacketed fusilier broke and ran.

'I want a prisoner,' Jobert said.

Interest glinted in Koschak's eye.

Jobert smirked. 'Why not ask our new friend for help? Sergeant Fazio, attend me.'

Fazio saluted as he drew up beside.

'Sergeant Fazio, I require a junior officer from that breaking kaiserlik battalion as a prisoner. Could you assist me?'

'With pleasure, sir.'

'And a stray horse, if you can.'

Fazio saluted, spun his remount around and shouted, 'Cieno, fall your section out. On me. Trot, march.'

Within half an hour, square-nosed chasseur horses breathed hard as they trotted to re-join the chasseur line. Moench welcomed the troopers back with Figaro. Leading the grinning parade, Fazio dragged a young infantry lieutenant by the collar to dump him at Jobert's feet.

The Austrian gasped for breath. 'Sir, I must protest.'

Jobert pushed Jaune forward.

The man wriggled back from Jaune's hooves.

'See that hussar aide behind the jäger screen towards Montebello,' Jobert said, 'the one in sky-blue? Do you know him?'

The infantryman wobbled with confusion. 'Ah ... yes, sir. General Ott's aide de camp.'

'Mount that horse and take this note to him.' Jobert passed a folded page from his notebook.

The Austrian scowled as he took Jobert's note and departed across the field at the canter.

'I have demanded von Maefeld attend me at the end of the line.' Jobert's nostrils flared. Jaune's ears flickered at the tension through the saddle.

At five o'clock, one of Victor's infantry regiments supported by the Cisalpine Chasseurs, advanced towards Montebello. In the open fields surrounding the village, Austrian fusiliers and grenzers raced to form a screen line within a thicket-choked stream meandering between large squares of vines.

'Colonel Jobert, sir.' Bernasconi pointed. 'Is that the fellow who attempted to take our standard at Magnano?'

Far out to the end of the line of opposing skirmishers sat von Maefeld.

The chasseurs growled with contempt.

Fazio spat. 'Colonel Jobert, sir, permission to catch the bastard. I will mount his head on a pike like a Cossack standard.'

Jobert halted the Cisalpine Squadron in line. 'No, Sergeant. He is mine.'

Jobert glared into Koschak's red-rimmed eyes sunk deep into his filthy, unshaven face and lowered his voice to a growl. 'I have horse and sabre but no honour. With the former I will claim the latter or be released from my Italian purgatory.'

Koschak leaned across and lifted Jobert's silver pistol. 'Only one?' Koschak cocked one of his pistols and passed it to Jobert. 'You may need this.'

At the walk on a short rein, Jobert and Jaune approached von Maefeld. Jobert glanced at the chasseur line three hundred metres across the green crops. He searched around von Maefeld for a trap. Pairs of grenzers over two hundred metres from Jobert retired back towards Montebello.

Von Maefeld lounged on his horse, his sabre hand on his hip. He dangled his silver pistol from his little finger. 'You are the architect of our family's misery, Jobert. No one retires today.'

Jobert lifted his pistol from its holster.

'Who was the other one?' von Maefeld asked. 'North of Trento. September of '96.' Jobert stiffened. *Didier.* 'Was he something to you? He crawled on the ground rather than stand and face me. I would imagine he perished from his wound, if not his shame.'

Jobert snorted and shook his head. 'You may prefer schoolyard taunts, boy.' Jobert slid his sabre into the air in a fluid movement. 'But how do you respond to steel?'

Von Maefeld's shako shuddered as he flicked his face to one side.

A trumpet call sounded To Mess.

Jobert jerked with recognition at the old 24th Chasseur call. Jobert looked over his left shoulder towards Casteggio. Koschak was galloping towards him waving.

No, thought Jobert, *he is waving me away*.

Jobert felt the impact of the balls, just as he heard two muskets fire slightly apart over his right shoulder. One round hit the corner folds of Jaune's saddle blankets, just above his offside shoulder. Jaune groaned in shock and struggled to stand. The other round cut Jaune's chest, slicing through the breastplate straps.

Heart shots! Jobert slipped his feet clear of his stirrups.

Koschak was close enough to yell. 'Ambush! Jäger snipers! Ride clear!'

Over one hundred metres away, two jäger rose from a fold in the ground, perhaps a field boundary ditch hidden by the green stems.

Rifles!

They fired.

One round punctured the pistol holder and shattered the woodwork of Koschak's pistol. The hammer blow carried through the holster to punch Jaune's wither. Jaune screeched with distress and staggered further.

The other round flew wide.

It hit Koschak's horse in the chest. At the canter, the horse crumpled onto its knees and head. Koschak pitched forward over the horse's ears and ploughed into the field. The horse coughed blood and thrashed to stand. Koschak remained face down and struggled to push his chest out of the ploughed ruts.

'Forward!' von Maefeld bellowed to the jäger in the ditch. 'He must die! Do not let him flee!'

The jäger emerged from the fold in the ground. Their approach was slowed due to the cumbersome process of reloading their rifles.

Jobert dismounted with his sabre trailing off his sword knot. His fingers found a swelling over Jaune's ribs under the multiple folds of Jobert's blankets and paillasse beneath his saddle. Blood streamed down the long slice across Jaune's chest.

He will live.

With a glance at the focussed jäger, Jobert dragged a wheezing Jaune towards Koschak. 'Can you stand?'

'My chest! I cannot fucking breathe.' Koschak strove to get his hands underneath himself to roll to one side.

A trumpet sounded Figaro.

Jobert led a trembling Jaune to stand beside Koschak. 'Climb Jaune's leg. Stand so I can put you in the saddle.'

Jobert took Koschak's pistol from the crumpled offside holster. The jäger shot had struck and buckled the hammer. Jobert drew his silver pistol, placed the muzzle against the temple of Koschak's horse.

'Thank you for your service,' he whispered and squeezed the trigger.

Jobert looked to the jäger. They tucked their ramrods into the rifles' sleeves and slipped their mallets into their cartridge boxes.

'Winded or broken ribs? What is your injury?' Jobert reached to unclip Koschak's musketoon.

'Broken ribs—' Koschak hissed in pain as Jobert manipulated the musketoon clipped to Koschak's cross belts. Jobert released the cross belt. The musketoon's muzzle was clogged with soil.

With an eye on the creeping jäger, Jobert loaded his silver pistol, the only firearm he had available.

The jäger prowled closer in the green wheat, rifles pressed hard into their shoulders.

Jobert walked beyond Jaune's rump, away from Koschak.

Jaune turned to follow. Jobert raised a finger. The bay horse dipped his face and nipped at the surrounding seed heads.

As Jobert stepped wider into the field, the jäger barrels followed him.

Why does von Maefeld not take me dismounted?

Von Maefeld shouted at the jäger pair but looked towards Casteggio.

A thunder of hooves behind Jobert sounded louder than the blood pounding in his ears.

Turning sideways to be ready for any flash from the jägers' pans, a quick glance revealed the chasseurs, led by Bernasconi, charging towards him. Appearing more as a Cossack swarm than a line formation, they swept around Jobert and Koschak to form a barrier to the jäger.

Moench swung out of his saddle to assist the groaning Koschak. Duque, leading Bleu, trotted towards Jobert. With a whinny of delight, Jaune limped to follow Bleu.

Jobert held out his raised palm. 'No, Duque, stand clear.'

Duque sat immobile staring at von Maefeld. 'It is him.' Duque's voice wavered with emotion. 'He looks like all of those bastards. Why are they all obsessed with these pistols?'

'Duque!' Jobert shouted. 'Drop Bleu's rein. Lead Jaune clear.'

The grey-clad jäger knelt and cocked their weapons, their wide-brimmed hats swivelled as they sought the distance to the cover of the ditch. Von Maefeld attempted to urge them forward by swinging his sabre.

Bernasconi's chasseurs dressed their two ranks.

'Converging fire on the bastards, sir!' Fazio cried to Bernasconi.

Bernasconi touched his fingertips above his head. 'Converging fire on the jäger. Present!'

The chasseurs shouldered their musketoon at forty-five degrees.

Von Maefeld spun his horse into a gallop for Montebello. The jäger fled for the blackberries in the draining ditch.

'Fire!'

Both jäger fell in an ellipse of flattened wheat stalks.

'Shall I secure their rifles?' Fazio called.

Jobert watched von Maefeld cantering towards Montebello.

This is no longer about pistols. Where and how?

Jobert aimed the silver pistol at the retreating silhouette and fired.

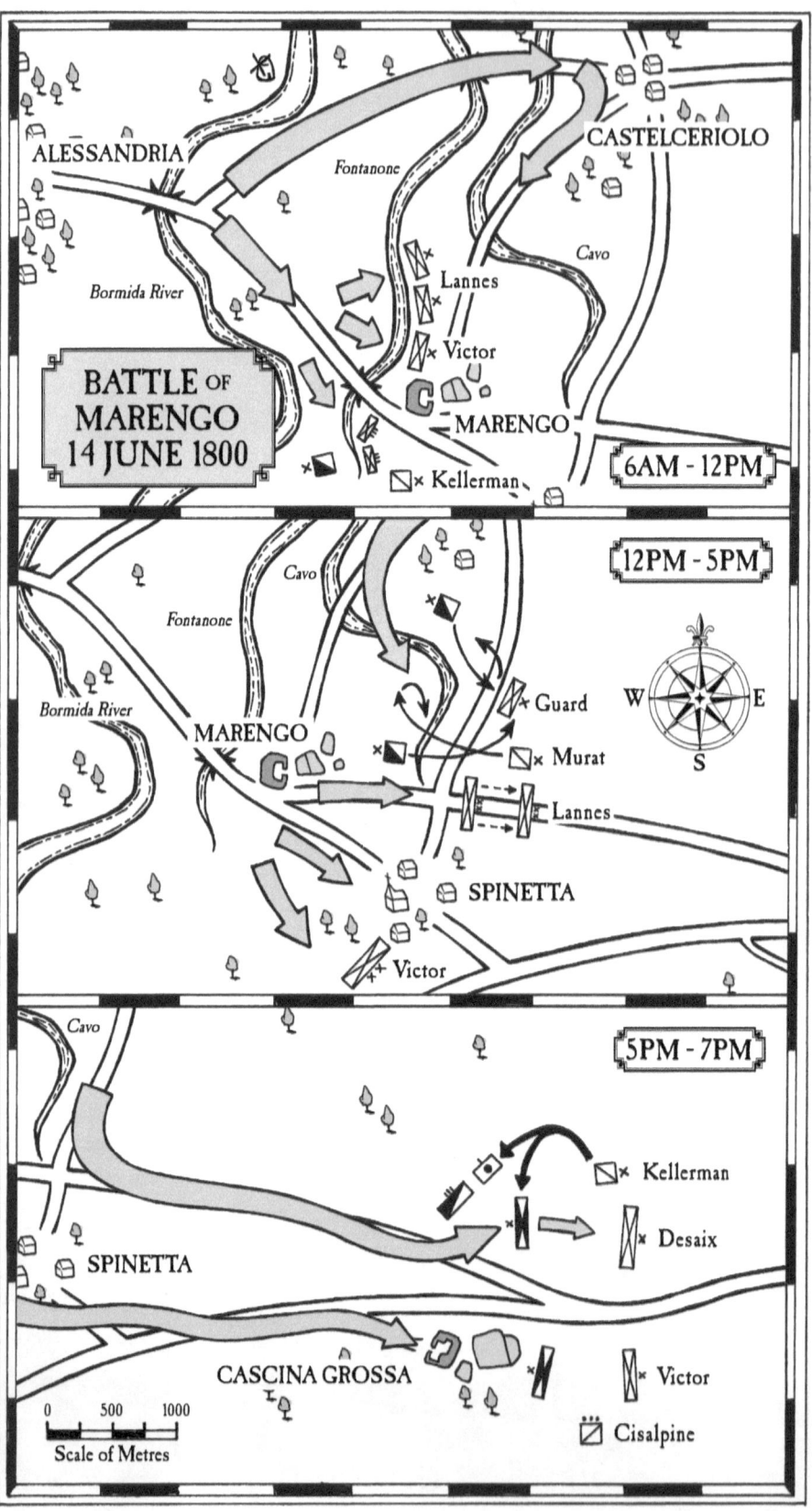

BATTLE OF
MARENGO
14 JUNE 1800

ALESSANDRIA
Fontanone
CASTELCERIOLO
Cavo
Bormida River
Lannes
Victor
C
MARENGO
Kellerman
6AM – 12PM

12PM – 5PM
Cavo
Fontanone
Bormida River
MARENGO
C
Guard
Murat
Lannes
SPINETTA
Victor
W N E S

5PM – 7PM
Cavo
Kellerman
Desaix
SPINETTA
Victor
CASCINA GROSSA
Cisalpine

0   500   1000
Scale of Metres

Chapter Twenty-Eight
June 1800, Battle of Marengo, Italy

Musket shots crackled from the hedgerows two hundred metres away. French light infantry skirmishers prowled along the base of hedges and stone walls as enemy jäger sought the limits of the French force.

Jobert raised his face to the west.

Here they come.

The westerly breeze that brought the whiff of gun smoke cleared the wisps of Bormida fog to a clear morning lit with mauve. In the four days since the battle of Casteggio-Montebello, Jobert's Cisalpines had guided Victor's division the fifty kilometres to the banks of the Bormida River. This morning, in the French outposts just west of Marengo, Jobert stood four kilometres from the citadel of Alessandria.

The marching was done.

Now for the fighting.

Victor's division occupied a battleline anchored to the large farm of Marengo and sighted behind the bramble-clogged Fontanone stream. Jobert smiled at the absurdity of the reverse positions of the day. Over a year ago, Victor's division faced east to protect Alessandria from Austria, while the Cisalpine Chasseurs reacted to the Russian river crossing at Bassignana. Today, Victor faced west on the same ground.

With the sun well up by nine o'clock, the rippling of drums announced the approach of the enemy's line infantry. Within the hour, the enemy's forward batteries opened the cannonade on the outlying farms.

Jobert saluted as he entered Victor's headquarters in Marengo's milking barn.

'Ah, Virginian, just the man,' said General Berthier, who had come forward from Bonaparte's main headquarters somewhere in the rear. 'Jobert, a message for Lannes.'

Jobert reached for his notebook.

The general continued, 'It is Victor's and my understanding the enemy are breaking out of Alessandria. This is not a feint. Victor will hold Marengo. Lannes is to secure Victor's right, or northern, flank along the Fontanone. I will depart to inform Consul Bonaparte of the developments.'

Jobert reread the message, saluted and departed the headquarters. 'Moench, sound Commander's In.'

Within a grove of cherry trees behind Victor's headquarters, the Cisalpine Chasseurs shared a breakfast of ammunition bread and a cup of rabbit broth. The officers and non-commissioned officers gathered around Jobert as chasseurs scoffed their soup and tightened girths.

'Gentlemen,' Jobert said, 'the enemy mean to break us to re-establish their control over Lombardy.' The officers shuffled. 'What part shall we play in denying the enemy their victory? I have longstanding relationships with the generals on the field, and I know the ground, so I predict I will be used as an aide to convey key messages. Today, you will escort me as I deliver those messages, and fill gaps in threatening situations as they arise. Questions?'

'How ridiculous, Jobert,' Zenari said. 'Is there not a better application of our abilities than to play nursemaid to a general's courier?'

Bernasconi and Fazio rolled their eyes and shook their heads. Koschak's shoulders rolled as he bristled.

Jobert levelled a malevolent stare at Zenari. 'The Cisalpines can have no greater honour this day than provide vital, timely information to our commanders. Gentlemen, we march to Lannes headquarters. Mount, column of fours, trot, march.'

As they strode to their horses, Koschak stepped beside Jobert. 'Kill him during the combat today. If you will not, I will.'

'No, old friend.' Jobert slapped Koschak on the shoulder. 'I want to inflict a punishment on that prick, where he knows he suffers due to his arrogance. How are your ribs?'

'Duque has strapped them so I can ride faster than a walk. I cannot wield a blade.'

Jobert smiled. 'Good, then your skills in scrounging food will come to the fore.'

Two hours later, the Cisalpine Chasseurs guided Lannes division forward to the rear of Marengo. Victor's hotly contested defence spread one thousand metres north and south of the red-brick farm and its dominating tower. Despite the persistent westerly breeze clearing the gun smoke and twirling spent cartridge papers in the haze, humidity seeped from the long grass and crops.

'I see where I shall place my line beside Victor's,' Lannes said. He swept the flat horizon with his telescope. 'Jobert, what are those white spires to the north.'

'The village of Castelceriolo at one thousand, five hundred metres, sir,' Jobert said. 'Once the road from Alessandria crosses the Bormida it splits. The southern arm runs through Marengo. The northern arm runs through Castelceriolo.'

'So, a possible threat to my right flank.' Lannes shook his head. 'Jobert, take a company of light infantry and secure Castelceriolo. Warn me of any enemy movement on my right.'

'I am at your service, sir.'

Jobert and the chasseurs escorted a company of fifty muskets to Castelceriolo. The light infantrymen established sentries around the perimeter of the village, while the chasseurs maintained a piquet on the road towards Alessandria.

'Excuse me, sir,' Fazio said once Jobert had returned from inspecting the vedettes. 'We have acquired a little food.' Fazio passed a loaf and a dozen carrots to Moench before departing.

'Who was that?' Koschak frowned. 'He looks like someone I know, but it cannot be him.'

Jobert took his chunk of loaf and two carrots from Moench. 'Perhaps—'

Bernasconi trotted into the village square. 'Sir, enemy dragoons and jäger approaching the village.'

Jobert rode to the outskirts of Castelceriolo and drew out his telescope. The dragoons spread in two wings either side of a long line of skirmishing grey coats. 'I estimate over two hundred dragoons and over two hundred jäger. Look, a long column of whitecoats behind them. We will return to Lannes and warn him. Moench, sound Skirmishers In.'

Having departed Lannes headquarters ninety minutes before, Jobert reported back to Lannes. 'You have an advance guard north of you, sir. Behind them marches a division of infantry.'

'Let us assume an infantry corps of three divisions has appeared on my flank. Leave them with me, Jobert. Press on and inform Victor of the threat.'

At Marengo farm, Jobert reported to Victor.

Victor clicked his watch closed. 'One o'clock.' Victor dropped his head over a map and traced the Fontanone north of Marengo to Castelceriolo. He then traced his finger south-east to the village of Spinetta. 'My lads have repulsed two divisional attacks. We need ammunition, Jobert. Have your Italian Cossacks raid any idle teamster hanging back in Spinetta and bring my ammunition forward. As you move to Spinetta, inform Kellerman and his heavy cavalry to anticipate enemy cavalry movement to our south.'

Outside among the chasseurs, Fazio stepped forward to Jobert. 'Permission to speak, sir.'

Jobert returned Fazio's salute. 'What is on your mind, Sergeant?'

'If the infantry need ammunition, sir, could we not halve the ammunition we are carrying. Possibly, take our ammunition mule to the nearest battalion.'

'I concur. Make it so. Thank you, Sergeant.'

Zenari scoffed. 'What a ridiculous waste.'

Jobert swung up into Bleu's saddle. 'Zenari and Koschak, take Brescia and scour Spinetta for ammunition. Locate a camp for our packhorses. Bernasconi, bring Mantua. We shall find the cavalry reserve.'

Jobert's chasseurs trotted south to seek Kellerman's cavalry brigade. He halted the chasseur column behind a formidable line of French battle cavalry over three hundred metres long. Despite the three cavalry regiments' depleted strength, the two ranks of blue jacketed, black-bicorne-wearing heavy cavalry exuded strength. Their straight cavalry swords rested on their thighs. Their thick-boned horses tossed their heads.

Jobert approached Brigadier Kellerman's mounted head-quarters, pulsing with action as riders came and went to a core of central officers.

Kellerman waved to Jobert's salute. 'Jobert, my piquets have reported kaiserlik dragoons sweeping around Victor's southern flank. I am sending in our dragoons to disorder them.'

French trumpets screamed. A two hundred metres–long line

of green-backed dragoons trotted forward, their black manes flying from their brass helmets.

'My message from General Victor, sir,' Jobert said, 'supports what is already underway. Victor observed a body of enemy cavalry move across his front towards his left. He requested your support in securing his flank.'

Kellerman watched the green French dragoons swirling around the white Austrian dragoons. 'We have them where we want them. Clear the dragoons. Sound Rally.' The combined trumpets of the three regiments screamed the order. Green jackets peeled out of the fray. Kellerman raised his sabre. 'Join us, Jobert? A good education for a chasseur.'

'If I was not attending Victor and Lannes, sir, then—'

'Then stand clear, chasseur.' Kellerman dropped his sabre and over six hundred battle-cavalry stepped off. Watching from behind, the blue jackets and powerful rumps thundered into the disordered white-jacketed dragoons.

'Where next, sir?' Bernasconi asked. 'Return to General Victor?'

Jobert looked north to the Marengo farm, engulfed in a cloud of gun smoke which pulsed with cannon blasts. 'I am of a mind to visit Lannes before we return to Victor.'

Leaving Mantua with Bernasconi and Bleu with Tulloc, Jobert and Moench dismounted and followed the gunners of a battery of foot artillery manhandling their guns forward. Jobert found Lannes in the middle of a regimental fire line. Beyond the fire line, jäger traded shots with the French skirmisher line. Moench cringed at the hiss of ball and cannister flew above the bicornes and bayonet tips of the infantry. Apart from those balls which thudded into the bodies packed in tight ranks.

'We are being encircled by the Austrians to the north, and we are being assaulted frontally.' Lannes stood with his hands on his hips as a regiment, over one thousand muskets strong, waited for the Austrian assault. 'Look at these bastards crossing the Fontanone, Jobert.'

Across the narrow rivulet, Austrian soldiers, stripped to their shirtsleeves, lugged great ten-foot beams forward to the edge of the Fontanone. Another column of men, stripped to their drawers and shoes, raced forward and, without bearing any timber beams, leapt into the Fontanone. Up to their chests in the water, they gripped the shoulders of the men in front of them and bowed their heads. A column of grey jacketed jäger raced across their backs to establish a skirmish line on the French bank.

'Here comes a column of fusiliers across their human bridge.' Lannes waved to the regimental commander. 'Fire, colonel, fire!' Over the musketry blast, Lannes shook Jobert's lapels and shouted, 'Jobert, inform Victor that Marengo is lost, but not the day. Tell Victor I am encircled and cannot hold here. I must withdraw to better defensive line north of Spinetta.' Lannes slapped Jobert's shoulder. 'See you in Spinetta, Jobert.'

Within half an hour, Jobert entered Victor's headquarters in Marengo. Infantry and cavalry couriers raced in and out of the barn. The few scribes did not look up from their reports as they snatched the next piece of paper thrust at them.

Victor entered the room with two aides and an escort of four fusiliers. 'Water!' Victor cried. 'Ah, Jobert, what news.'

'General Lannes reports he is encircled from the north. The enemy have broken our line between Lannes' division and your northern regiments. Lannes is withdrawing to a defensive line north of Spinetta.'

Victor gulped a cup of water from a bucket he shared with the fusilier escort. 'An assault of grenadiers and dragoons is forming across the Fontanone from us. I too am evacuating Marengo for Spinetta.' Victor gripped Jobert's sleeve. 'I need every barrel and every sabre, Jobert. Do what you can to cover the withdrawal of the infantry. It is a long kilometre from here to Spinetta for exhausted infantry running before dragoons.'

The muffled thunder of drums was backed with the calls of trumpets.

'Here they come.' Victor turned on his heel to depart with his escort.

Jobert walked from the barn into the farm's courtyard.

What can I do?

Fusiliers fired from holes in the walls. Wounded were helped into a casualty post in a stable.

Jobert ran into the stable and found the battalion surgeon drenched with blood. 'Surgeon, I have fifty horsemen who can assist in the evacuation of the wounded. How many do you have?'

'Near four hundred,' said the exhausted man. 'Do you have carts?'

Jobert returned to the lane behind the farm. The chasseurs of Mantua had been rejoined by the men of Brescia. They clustered in small groups to lean on their horses and listen to snippets of news. The soldiers jerked and nudged as Jobert strode down the line.

'Commanders in,' Jobert called.

Koschak, Bernasconi and Fazio trotted to gather around Jobert. Zenari walked to stand behind the group.

Jobert breathed deeply and assumed a mask of confidence. 'Koschak, have we established a packhorse camp in Spinetta?'

'Yes, sir. Duque commands the post.'

'Listen in, men.' Jobert looked each in the eye and emphasised his points with a firm chopping action of his palm. 'The enemy are breaking through our first line of defence. Lannes and Victor are withdrawing their divisions to Spinetta. The Cisalpine Squadron will assist with the transfer of wounded to Spinetta.'

Zenari snorted. 'What a waste of time. Why can we not charge like Kellerman?'

Bernasconi and Fazio rolled their eyes and shook their heads.

'Just shut up, you stupid bastard,' Koschak said. 'You have served a year in combat, and you still fail to realise where you are.'

'Zenari,' Jobert said, 'we are in the middle of a battle. A place where you have no value. You are relieved of command of the Brescia Company. You have my permission to depart on whatever task you feel suits your superior talents.'

Zenari's mouth opened and closed beneath his moustache, but he remained standing behind the group.

Jobert swept his hand and closed his fist to regain the group's focus. 'Pairs of chasseurs will evacuate the wounded in the following manner. Two wounded unable to walk up in the saddle. If needed, a chasseur on behind to stabilise the fusilier. One badly wounded supported between the horses. Two lesser wounded hanging onto the shabraques on the horses' shoulders. We have twenty-five pairs of chasseurs. We could evacuate over one hundred and twenty casualties per trip.'

Jobert looked to each commander. Koschak, Bernasconi and Fazio nodded to assure Jobert they understood.

'Koschak,' Jobert continued, 'attend the surgeon and triage the wounded. Fazio, bring forward pairs of chasseurs and their remounts to be loaded. Bernasconi, lead the first wounded back to Sergeant Duque in Spinetta and establish a casualty post there. Questions?'

'Yes, sir.' Fazio raised his hand. 'I am concerned that the commander of the Cisalpine Squadron is incorrectly dressed.'

Jobert scowled at his blackened tailcoat and over-breeches. 'In what regard, Sergeant?'

'Your headdress, sir.' Fazio held out a loop of green leather.

Jobert took the gnarled and furry coil supposedly cut from a Cossack horse.

'Does Prince Eugene of Savoy have one?' Jobert asked.

'No, he does not, sir.' Fazio's thick moustache curled as he spoke form the side of his mouth. 'He is not fucking good enough for the Cisalpine Chasseurs.'

Jobert slipped the noose down onto his mirliton's brim and replaced his hat. 'Have I got it right now, Sergeant.'

Fazio gave a grim smile and saluted. 'You have, sir.'

Behind Fazio, Zenari's jaw clenched as he stared at the leather strip looped on Jobert's cap.

Jobert returned Fazio's salute. 'Excuse me, Sergeant, duty calls. Moench, with me.'

Jobert ran back into Marengo's courtyard. 'Moench, I need to understand how long we have before we need to leave.'

A wall on the western side of the courtyard exploded with bricks. A small black dot bounced on the hard packed surface to disappear into, and implode, a wall beyond.

Moench rolled his eyes. 'Could I assist your evaluation, sir, by saying we need to leave right now.'

Jobert raced into the brick building where the cannonball had entered the courtyard.

Infantrymen coated in white dust, scrabbled to pull the dead and wounded from the rubble. 'They have bought up their four-pounders.' The fusiliers began to return fire beyond the wall. 'Our muskets cannot reach them.'

Jobert looked through the breach in the wall. 'Moench, fetch Tulloc with his rifle. Stay with the horses.'

Tulloc soon knelt beside Jobert in the brick shards.

Jobert pointed at the pair of Austrian four-pounders two hundred metres away on the far side of the Fontanone stream. 'I will load. Give me your ramrod and mallet. Drop the firers and the ventsmen.'

Tulloc aimed and fired.

A cheer sprang from the fusiliers around them.

Jobert worked to reload the rifle, biting open the cartridge and tapping the ball down the rifled barrel with the weapon's small mallet. 'She is double charged.'

Tulloc aimed and fired again.

The cheers along the loopholes changed to calls of urgency.

A sharp boom sounded from the Austrian guns.

'Ball inbound!'

The room pulsed with mortar dust as bricks rattled across the timber uprights.

Jobert was struck in the right side of his face with a brick. Pain gripped his head and shoulders. On his hands and knees, he spat out his bloodied dentures. His ribs were buffeted by fusiliers around him dragging away wounded and attempting to fire through the breach.

Jobert saw Tulloc being dragged clear by the bluecoats. Tulloc was dusted white, and his pulped chest oozed brown mud. Jobert rolled Tulloc on his side.

Tulloc choked on his own blood.

As Jobert leaned forward to listen, rough hands pulled him upwards.

'We need to go,' Moench said. 'Now!'

Moench dragged Tulloc by the arms out of the building and into the courtyard.

Jobert, clinging to Moench's cross belts, saw Tulloc's eyes widen with fear. 'Stop, stop.'

Moench released Tulloc to flop on the ground.

Jobert gathered Tulloc in his arms and tilted his head to allow the blood in his throat to drain. 'Tulloc, I am with you. Maria and Andrea will always have a safe home with my family. Your parents will meet your son. Your boy will grow into a fine horseman.'

Tulloc head shuddered, in either understanding or fear or both. He coughed at his bubbles. His eyes blurred with tears.

He gripped Jobert's lapels.

Moench squeezed one of Tulloc's hands and mumbled the final sacraments through his tears.

Tulloc heaved. His eyes opened wide before they rolled upwards. His hands fell from Jobert's tailcoat.

Chapter Twenty-Nine

Tulloc lay between Jobert and Moench, his face whitened with mortar dust and speckled with blood.

With his fingertips, Jobert probed the side of his face where he was struck by the brick.

Moench spasmed and panted with shock. 'We enlisted together.' Moench squinted at Jobert's injuries. 'We need to go, sir. Will Tulloc be all right here? We will come back for him, yes?'

Moench supported Jobert out of the Marengo farmyard. The French surgeon, lounging against a stable post, gave Jobert a nod. 'Change of ownership expected anytime soon. Travel well.'

Koschak, waiting in the lane with the horses, twisted in the saddle and stretched his arms against the pressure on his ribs.

'Have they taken the wounded to Spinetta?' Jobert asked.

Koschak regarded Jobert's coating of mortar dust, his ripped jacket and his bleeding ear with suspicion. 'As many as they could. Where is Tulloc?'

Jobert and Moench replied with pained looks.

Koschak's face curled into an ugly grimace. 'Fuck!'

In Spinetta, Jobert found the chasseurs behind a wayside shrine in a devastated vegetable garden surrounded by apple trees stripped bare of fruit and leaves. Over the road, a tavern and its stables were overflowing with wounded.

'Dismount, Jobert.' Duque took a bottle of brandy from his portmanteau. 'Where is young Tulloc?'

Jobert's lips crimped with sadness, and he shook his head.

Duque slumped. 'When Tulloc was to be kicked out for being a poor rider, I was the one who suggested he become an apprentice farrier.' Duque blinked at his tears. 'Come, Jobert, let me dress that wound.'

Duque dabbed Jobert's swelling with brandy then, when Jobert had stopped swearing, bound his right temple and ear with a boiled bandage.

Zenari stood over Jobert. 'Jobert, your injuries render you *hors de combat.*'

'Not at all,' Jobert said. 'Once this wound is bound, I am reporting to Victor's headquarters.'

'You may do as you please, but I am taking command in your absence.'

Jobert looked up. 'If you do, Zenari, then you will be hanged for mutiny.'

Zenari scoffed. 'Temporary command, Jobert, until you are fit to return to duty.'

'Why are you doing this, Zenari?'

Zenari spoke through gritted teeth. 'I am tired of being wasted with escorting wounded and wet nursing a general's aide. These are not actions of great honour. If we are to save the republic,' he pumped his fists, 'we need to be in the thick of the fight.'

'I have never doubted your courage, Zenari, but your judgement is appalling.' Jobert stood, placed on his mirliton and rolled his neck against the pressure of the bandages. 'I am reporting to Victor, where I shall receive further orders. Upon my return I expect the command granted to me by General Masséna, the commander of the Army of Italy, to be here on parade ready for tasking.'

Bernasconi stepped forward to Jobert, his eyes wide with concern. 'Sir, what should I ...'

'Whatever happens,' Jobert gripped Bernasconi's arm, 'stay with your soldiers.'

Jobert checked his watch before entering the mayoral residence in Spinetta. Three o'clock. Around the dining room table, Victor, Lannes and other officers bent over scattered charts.

Victor brightened as Jobert entered the room. 'Jobert would know. Jobert, what terrain lies north of here towards Castelceriolo?'

Not only did Lannes look up at Jobert, but Bonaparte, the First Consul of France, turned and appraised the filthy and bandaged chasseur officer. Bonaparte's slim face twitched in a smile of recognition.

Jobert saluted. 'Gentlemen, the terrain is flat. Wheat fields and vineyards. The only feature of tactical significance is a drainage ditch, the Cavo, which runs from Spinetta to Castelceriolo parallel to the Fontanone stream.'

Bonaparte's grey eyes narrowed. 'An obstacle to what degree?'

'At fifty metres out, it would enhance an infantry fire line, sir.'

'Are you still with the Italian chasseurs, Jobert?'

Jobert flinched. *He remembers my assignment from three years ago.*

'Yes, sir,' Jobert said, 'I have fifty Italian sabres at my command.'

'Good.' Bonaparte turned to the table and scribbled a note. 'Might I impose upon you to guide the three battalions of the Guard to the right of Lannes' line?' He passed the note to Jobert. 'This is the authorisation they need to march. They wait two kilometres down the Alessandria road.'

'I am at your service, sir.' Jobert pocketed the note and saluted. 'Would you excuse me?'

Jobert emerged from the headquarters and returned to Koschak, Duque and Moench. The chasseurs had gone. 'Zenari has taken them?'

'Pack horse section and all,' Koschak said.

The four chasseurs departed Spinetta and found the tall bearskin helmets of the Consular Guard battalions along the road east of the town. Jobert presented the regimental commander Bonaparte's note.

'Lead on, Jobert.'

Jobert and his companions guided the Guards to a gravel road parallel to the Cavo. 'Sir, Castelceriolo is to your immediate north. Spinetta lies to your south, with Lannes north of the village, Victor to the south.' Jobert pointed to the west towards the Austrian fire. 'You have an enemy force advancing across the Fontanone and another marching south from Castelceriolo.'

'This will do nicely,' said the Guard's regimental commander. 'Thank you, Jobert. Leave it to us.'

'With your permission, sir,' Jobert said, 'I shall inform the next commander along of your presence.'

As the Guard battalions and their four guns set as a west-facing line on the road behind the Cavo ditch, Jobert and his three shadows trotted south to reconnect with the regiment on the right of Lannes' battleline.

Foreign trumpets sounded over the thunder of hooves. The line infantry regiment which Jobert approached beat to square.

Jobert looked in alarm at the exposed Guards. The Guards did not form square. They received the charging Austrians with rhythmic half-company volleys.

The enemy dragoon retired with many empty saddles.

'Now that was impressive,' Koschak said. 'Why form square when you can outstare them?'

As the defeated dragoons cantered away to reform, French trumpets called the Advance and then Charge. Jobert spun in the saddle. A thunder of hooves crushed the grain crops behind the four observers. Rank upon rank of green-jacketed French dragoons cantered past.

'Who is that?' Duque pointed at the commander leading the counterattack.

'It is Murat, no?' Jobert said. 'Another returnee from Egypt.'

Over the pounding of dragoon hooves a clear trumpet sounded.

'Figaro!' Moench said.

'And look who seeks honour with the dragoons,' Koschak said.

On the left of the dragoon line, led by Zenari, the Cisalpine Squadron cantered, yelled and waved their sabres in the air. They disappeared from view in the gap between Jobert at the extremity of Lannes' line and the left flank of the Guard.

'Into the thick of the fight,' Jobert said. 'To save the republic.'

Although their view was obscured by the Guards' line, they heard the belch of artillery.

'Canister,' Koschak said.

An extended crackle of volley fire sounded, then another, and then again.

Jobert winced.

Trumpets sounded Rally.

Small groups of dragoons trotted back around the Guard line. Many riders lolled in the saddles propped up by their mates.

'Can you see any chasseurs?' Moench asked.

Jobert searched the groups with his glass. 'Will that letting of Italian blood satisfy Zenari's vanity?'

When the four guns in the Guard's fire line exploded as one, the four chasseurs jerked. The Guard's fire line then rippled with exact bursts of half-company fire. The time between volleys, punctuated by steady cannon fire, and the initiation of the firing cracked like clockwork.

Koschak growled. 'You would go a long way to see anything that precise on a parade ground.'

At one hundred metres across the Cavo, the Austrian guns responded to the Guard. Smoke pulsed down the line.

Jobert shook his head. 'But the kaiserliks have more—'

An infantry aide reined in and saluted. 'From my colonel, sir, a message for the commander of the Consular Guard. The Austrians have brought up dragoons and a battery of horse artillery.' The captain pointed to the dragoons across the Cavo. 'The Cavo is insufficient to hold the dragoons back. If we form square, the horse gunners will massacre us. General Lannes is having us withdraw to the vineyards.'

The aide departed and soon after Lannes' infantry stepped back towards the safety of the vineyards.

The fire from the Austrian infantry subsided and their drums thrashed a new order.

'They have lowered their bayonets.' Koschak pointed to the Austrian infantry in front of the Guard. 'The kaiserliks are going to charge over the Cavo. I want to watch this.'

Foreign trumpets sounded. Across the Cavo, reformed

Austrian dragoons surged into a walk.

'Good grief, look!' Jobert pointed to the flank of the Guard. 'A five hundred metre gap has opened between the Guard and Lannes. I need to warn them. Koschak, stay with Duque. Moench, with me.'

Jobert lifted Bleu to a canter toward the centre of the Guard line.

'Sir,' Moench cried, 'the kaiserliks are following us.'

Jobert glanced over his shoulder. A wall of white-jacketed dragoons, sabres glinting, trotted one hundred metres behind the Guard's line. 'Moench, sound Charge over and over to warn the Guard.'

As the Guards' volleys ripped into the oncoming enemy fusiliers, guardsmen on the left of the line began to notice Jobert's shouts and waving. The warning was to no avail. The massed squadrons of pounding black horses, flanked by green-jacketed light cavalry, smashed into the rear of the Guard's line. The length of blue jackets and bearskin helmets shuddered at the impact.

Guardsmen on the right of their line broke formation and ran clear.

'Follow me.' Jobert waved his sabre to the fleeing guardsmen. 'To the woods.'

The guardsmen yelled to each other. One guardsman ran past with a *tri-couleur*. 'To the woods.'

The dragoons and the attendant light cavalry surrounded most of the Guard.

'What can we do, sir?' Moench asked. 'Can we not go in and pull them clear on our stirrups?'

Although small pockets of guardsmen presented their bayonets at the circling white and green horsemen, many guardsmen threw down their muskets and surrendered.

'I think not, Moench.' Jobert grimaced at the loss of such fine infantry. 'If we could evade dragoon swords, our green jackets will be confused for those of the kaiserlik light cavalry. The guardsmen would just as likely shoot us than believe we were there to whisk them to safety. I need to report this calamity to Victor. Moench, find Koschak and Duque and meet me at Victor's headquarters in Spinetta.'

Jobert kept a sharp eye as Bleu trotted towards Spinetta. Victor's defensive line was under intense bombardment. Balls bounced deep into the town, cracking walls into stone splinters and snapping branches from orchards.

At five o'clock, Jobert entered Victor's Spinetta headquarters. 'Sir, the Guard have been destroyed. The right flank has gone.'

Victor leaned on his map table with both hands. 'After eight hours in battle, I have lost two-thirds of my division. As the enemy rebuilds their strength for their next assault, we are to withdraw two kilometres further down the road. Lannes is to hold north of the road, and I am to defend Cascina Grossa. Kellerman's cavalry will screen us.' Victor ran his hands through his grime-matted hair. 'The day ... the French Republic hinges on Desaix's division arriving from the south.'

Jobert emerged from the headquarters. Koschak, Duque and Moench chewed carrots beside the tavern's casualty post. 'The army continues to withdraw,' Jobert said as he tightened Bleu's girth. 'Prepare to mount and march.'

'Have you received a task?' Koschak asked.

'No.'

'Head for Nice.' Koschak grinned. 'Or Mantua?'

Jobert rubbed the stubble on his chin. 'Why not? There is nothing for us here.'

Moench flinched with alarm. 'We cannot leave Tulloc.'

Koschak raised an appeasing palm. 'We will collect him, either—'

Duque grinned over Grenzer's panniers. 'Well, look who

returns weeping honour from every cut.'

The rolling clack of horseshoes on cobblestones announced the arrival of the chasseurs led by Zenari and Bernasconi.

'Fuck them.' Jobert mounted Bleu. 'They are no longer my problem.'

Zenari halted the column and approached Jobert. 'Excuse me, sir.'

Jobert twitched with suspicion. *What did he just call me?*

'What further disgrace do you intend to inflict, Zenari?' Jobert asked.

Zenari raised his downcast face with effort. Zenari saluted Jobert. 'The Cisalpine Squadron is on parade and ready for your tasking, sir.'

Jobert scanned Zenari's pale face for any hint of malevolence. Zenari was mounted on a horse with dragoon saddlery. His over-breeches were crusted with dirt. His thumb hooked into his waistcoat cradled the arm on which dried blood framed a slice in his sleeve.

Jobert slid his gaze along the chasseurs' line. 'Thirty men in the saddle. You have destroyed two-fifths of your command, Zenari. Was the honour worth the gamble of other men's lives?'

Zenari's brown eyes wandered over Jobert's face and chest. 'I do not ... know what to do.'

Jobert shook his head. 'You have never known what to do.'

Zenari lowered his face. 'I ... seek your guidance, sir.'

'Now?' Jobert scoffed. 'After two and a half years? When all that is dear to us is being swept away? You beg me to save those who revile me?'

Zenari glanced at the strip of horse hide on Jobert's mirliton. 'You are not reviled, sir.'

'This is all too late, Zenari.' Jobert shrugged. 'The single requirement of cavalry right now is to cover the withdrawal of the infantry. A fundamental task these soldiers have never been trained to do. Your determined arrogance, Zenari, has rendered them utterly useless at the time of greatest need.'

Zenari's hand flopped. 'We can form a screen line, sir.'

Jobert ground his dentures into his gum. 'Piquets are not needed. Skirmishers are needed. They cannot skirmish.'

'We can charge, sir.'

Jobert punched his holsters and yelled, 'These men cannot charge, Zenari! They have not been trained to charge. They broke at Magnano. The Cossacks tested them and peeled off at Cassano. They charged the rear of the grenadiers at Bassignana to breakout. They charged Cossacks at Trebbia twice. The first time the Cossacks surrounded them. The second time they broke. They were forced to flee the field at Novi when the French chasseurs beside them broke.' Jobert's fists trembled as he gripped the shabraque over his holsters. 'As you are in temporary command, Zenari, march your survivors to the rear. Do not let me detain you.'

'Would you resume command, sir? Please.' Zenari shrank into his saddle. 'We need you to lead us in battle.'

Jobert seethed as he looked at Koschak, Duque and Moench and then along the chasseur column.

All eyes were upon him.

Chapter Thirty

Jobert gritted his teeth as he regarded the wilted Zenari. Jobert closed his eyes, took a deep breath and shook his head. 'Moench, sound Figaro, then sound Commanders In.'

All along the column, the notes of Figaro blew spirit into sunken chests.

Zenari pressed his horse to halt front and centre of Jobert. Bernasconi and Fazio grinned as they gathered their reins and urged their horses on either side of Zenari.

'Victor's division is withdrawing east.' Jobert looked down the road towards the large farm. 'Vineyards dominate the road to Cascina Grossa. We cannot skirmish mounted in vineyards, but we can dismount and use the vines to our advantage. Moench, order the chasseurs to stand to horse.'

Moench spun towards the column.

'Koschak, command the horse holders and pack horses.' Jobert jerked a thumb at the casualty clearing post. 'Load as many wounded onto the horses as you can. Head down the road to the next casualty post.' Jobert shrugged. 'We will find you after dark.'

Koschak nodded with a grunt.

'Zenari, Bernasconi and Fazio, create three teams of around eight chasseurs each, then halve them. Have the braver men as your marksmen. Have the other half who are feeling the strain of the day load for them. Sling your musketoons on your saddles as you load wounded onto your horses. Take the infantry's muskets and as many cartridge boxes as you can from the casualty post. Questions? No? Move.'

Zenari, Bernasconi and Fazio spun to attend to their preparations.

'Shall I take our horses?' asked Moench.

'No,' Jobert said. 'You are with me. Duque, keep our horses with Koschak.'

When Koschak's horse group departed with the wounded, Jobert's dismounted chasseurs joined the throng of columns of silent, exhausted infantry, walking wounded and stragglers moving east towards Cascina Grossa. Most of the guns were manhandled by the gunners as any available horses drew the caissons draped with wounded.

In the first vineyard south-east of Spinetta, Jobert set out the three sections within fifty metres of each other. Between the trees lining the roads, other infantry skirmishers set their pairs. They stared with curiosity at the chasseurs taking up firing positions among the trellises.

The flow of stragglers dwindled to an empty road.

Jobert lowered his telescope. 'Stand to! Bernasconi, select individual skirmishers as targets, fire two volleys and then retire, at a walk. Move through the vines until you are fifty metres beyond the last group. Here they come.'

Austrian skirmishers crept beside the walls at the edge of Spinetta, their jackets a dark grey from the grime of battle.

'Bernasconi, follow my example.' Jobert stepped forward, sabre drawn. 'Lads, ready.' The four soldiers in Bernasconi's section designated to fire shouldered their muskets. 'Kaiserlik in green gateway.' The soldiers swung their barrels and grunted their acknowledgement. 'Fire!'

Four muskets sparked and cracked. Gun smoke filled the air beneath the vines.

'Swap. Reload. Ready.' Jobert peered through the lifting haze. Two Austrian fusiliers lifted the sprawling skirmisher who was the team's earlier target. 'Two kaiserliks in green gateway. Fire!'

Four muskets fired. The French infantry skirmishers shouted a cheer.

'Swap. Reload. Retire. Bernasconi, carry on.'

One or two balls zipped through the branches causing a few twigs to fall. Bernasconi and his men scurried back through the vines.

Jobert and Moench stepped back through the string and saplings the vines were strung on to Zenari's and Fazio's teams and repeated the process.

At the end of the vineyard, the chasseurs pressed through the boundary brambles and entered a field of wheat. In the centre of a field, a dozen battle-cavalrymen watched for any Austrians exiting the vineyards.

Directing the chasseur teams to the next roadside vineyards, Jobert kept to the road and waved to the cavalry patrol with his sabre.

Between Jobert's chasseurs, the French skirmishers and the cavalry patrols, the Austrian skirmish line and teams of their light cavalry crept forward. Behind them the steady beat of drums urged the enemy columns forward.

After half an hour of firing and falling back, Jobert heard, not far to the north, the sharp cracks of battery fire followed by an intense fusillade. Like their horses in the crops, the ripple of fire caused the cavalrymen's heads, both French and Austrian, to swivel in the direction of a rising cloud of gun smoke. The musketry peaked before French drums beat Quick March.

A cavalry corporal surged through the long wheat to Jobert. 'Sir, my captain sends his compliments. Desaix's division has arrived on the field and has set battle line to the north. The cavalry screen is rallying as a reserve to the north. You are on your own. Will you inform the infantry?'

The soldier saluted and departed at the canter.

The most senior infantryman Jobert could find to pass the news was a ragged sergeant major.

'The cavalry screen has been withdrawn, Sergeant Major,' he said. 'We had better push our lads for the shelter of Cascina Grossa. My chasseurs will cover your company.'

With a series of whistles from the sergeant major, around forty infantry emerged from beneath shrubs and out of fields to shuffle down the road towards the high-walled farm.

Jobert's marksmen increased their rate of fire as the emboldened Austrians, mounted and dismounted, pushed along the roadside.

Jobert's chasseurs entered the silent ransacked farm to find the infantry scoffing water from a well-bucket with their blackened hands.

The sergeant major limped towards Jobert. 'My regiment, or what is left of it, is forming a fire line on General Victor four hundred metres down the road. The kaiserliks will soon have the farm. I am taking post to the front of the line.'

Six o'clock. Jobert snapped his watch closed and looked across the fields at the activity along the French fire line. 'The Austrians will form their own line east of this farm. I will form my lads in the vineyards to the south. We will keep an eye on their flank.'

Austrian light cavalry began to encircle the farm. The chasseurs, bounding south in their teams, raced through the fields to the vineyards.

Drumming reverberated off the walls as the Austrian infantry marched into the farm. As Jobert's teams settled into fire positions along the vineyard's boundary, the Austrian infantry emerged from the farm's eastern gate and formed a fire line against the French blocking the road.

To the north, artillery fire intensified.

'Theirs or ours, sir?' Fazio asked.

'I do not know.' Jobert scanned the horizon for clues. Only treetops silhouetted the yellow wheat fields. 'Either way, it sounds like someone's final stand.'

The horizon emitted sharp bursts of musketry. 'Regimental volleys. Someone is receiving a flogging.' Trumpets sounded. Jobert listened to the calls between the volleys. 'They are French calls.' A roar of voices then drumming.

'Look, sir.' Fazio pointed to a white-jacketed aide galloping up to the Austrian line.

A crescendo of drums sounded in the Austrian line. Skirmishers and cavalry patrols forward of the line jerked to attention and searched the fields.

The French battalions across the field started to cheer.

The Austrian infantry formed column and marched back into the farm and then up the road to Spinetta. The light cavalry trotted to the west of the farm in response to trumpets. The remaining skirmishers crept backwards.

'That surge in fighting to the north,' Jobert said, 'perhaps we have won the latest hand. The kaiserliks are retiring. Let us see them on their way. Moench, sound Assembly. Form two ranks clear of the vines.'

The chasseurs raced at the trumpet's urging and took their place in the ranks.

'Cisalpine Squadron, converging fire, ready,' Jobert yelled.

Austrian skirmishers called and pointed at the unexpected

formation on their flanks. Some aimed and fired at the short green line.

As enemy balls zipped close, Jobert called 'This is for Magnano. Fire!'

As the blast pulsed past his head, Jobert thought, *For Rome.*

The chasseur's second rank stepped through and presented their muskets.

'And this for Cassano. Fire!'

For the dungeons of Mantua.

His facial wound pulsed through his bandages.

'For Bassignana. Fire!'

For Turin.

The Austrian skirmishers had ceased firing and were retreating for the farm.

'For Trebbia. Fire!'

For Lucca.

'For Novi. Fire!'

For Tulloc.

'Sabres!' cried Zenari. 'Charge!'

The chasseurs dropped their muskets in the grass, drew their sabres and ran cheering at the retiring Austrians.

Jobert shook his head at the foolish glee. 'Moench, sound Rally. Someone will get shot.'

'Colonel Jobert, sir,' said Fazio behind him.

Jobert looked back to see Fazio squatting beside Bernasconi. Fazio's face was solemn.

White-faced, Bernasconi sat on the ground, his legs askew and looked up at Jobert in confusion. Blood pumped from his abdomen into his clenched fingers then flowed down his thighs.

Jobert slumped and found his steps towards Bernasconi unbearably difficult.

Jobert knelt beside Bernasconi and took his hand. 'Silvio, Sergeant Duque will put this right. I will take you home to your parents. You will be up and about in time to be my groomsman at my wedding.' Jobert squeezed Bernasconi's hand. 'All will be well, dear brother.'

Bernasconi smiled through his panting. 'Is the day ours, sir?' Bernasconi's voice rasped against his blue lips.

'The day is ours, Captain Bernasconi.' Jobert lips quivered into a smile. 'The Cisalpine Chasseurs hold the field with honour.'

'With glory, sir.' With a wheeze, Bernasconi folded backwards to stare at the sky.

'Fuck, sir.' Fazio spat into the stalks around him. 'He was a good one.'

Jobert bowed his head. 'Reform the men on parade, Sergeant Fazio.'

Fazio gave a curt nod and shuffled away through the long grass.

Hoofbeats alerted Jobert to Koschak, Duque and the horse holders trotting across the field towards him.

'There has been a counterattack to our north,' Koschak said. 'The kaiserliks are routing. Victor has ordered us to pursue.'

'The day is ours.' Jobert blinked. 'Moench, sound Assembly.'

As the chasseurs mounted under Fazio's direction, Jobert, Koschak, Duque and Moench wrapped Bernasconi in Jaune's canvas horse rug and slung him across Jaune's saddle.

'We have run from the kaiserliks for over a year,' Jobert called to the chasseurs once formed in their ranks. 'Who is tired of running? Let us give it to these kaiserlik bastards. Moench, sound Figaro.'

The chasseurs screeched hoarsely over Moench's long notes.

Jobert turned to Koschak, Duque and Moench. 'Let us find Tulloc and take him home.'

The chasseurs followed the Austrian skirmishers who tailed their rambling columns up the road to Spinetta.

Upon reaching Marengo, twilight descended across the battlefield. The chasseurs had set camp between Spinetta and Marengo, when Jobert rejoined them from Victor's headquarters.

'Tulloc?' Jobert asked Koschak.

Koschak grunted in the affirmative.

Fazio stood up from the central campfire. 'A place by the fire, sir.'

'No,' Jobert said, 'I am to deliver a report from Victor to Bonaparte's headquarters. I am riding east. I will not be riding back.'

Jobert looked at Zenari. Zenari stood. 'Major Zenari, Victor has signed an order for the Cisalpine Squadron to return to the regiment in Milan. In the morning, march the squadron to Milan.'

'Yes, sir.' Zenari saluted then pursed his lips. 'Thank you, sir.'

Jobert considered Zenari's steady gaze, before ending the exchange with a nod.

'Duque and Moench,' Jobert said, 'take Tulloc and Grenzer to Nice. Collect Orlande, Maria and Quandalle and return to the farm. Koschak and I will take Bernasconi home then meet you there.'

Jobert and Koschak, with Bernasconi slung across Jaune, rode east into the clear, dark evening. Torches of work parties seeking wounded flickered in the fields. The swirl of tiny bats flitted across the stars.

They found Bonaparte's headquarters sited within the mayor's house of a village further back along the road to Milan. Jobert dismounted, unbuckled his sword belt and opened the front of his trousers. He tucked in his shirt, refastened his sword belt and flapped at the front of his ripped tailcoat. 'How do I look?'

Koschak snorted. 'Like shit.'

Jobert moved past Bonaparte's Consular Guards into the

anteroom. A hussar aide indicated General Berthier's office where Jobert could submit his report.

Berthier's door opened and out strode First Consul Bonaparte.

Jobert braced to attention and saluted.

'Ah, Virginian!' Bonaparte slapped Jobert's arm with his gloves. 'Your Italians did well. I am grateful.' Bonaparte gave a quick bob of his head before he swept out to his waiting escort.

Jobert remained rigid.

There it is. After two-and-a-half years. His eyes glazed. *My reward.*

Chapter Thirty-One
June 1800, Mantua, Italy

The shroud of morning fog pressed Mantua's causeways deeper into the mud of the dead calm lakes that surrounded the city. Slimy with mist, the footfalls of each person and beast that entered the maw of the black gates was muffled. The early morning traffic crossed themselves and made a wide berth around Jobert, Koschak and the wrapped corpse slung over Bleu's saddle.

Four dawns since the battle of Marengo, Jobert knocked on the gate of the Bernasconi residence.

'Fetch your master,' Jobert said as Bernasconi's chamberlain appeared in the gate's grille.

Jobert led Bleu and Silvio through the opened gates. The faces of the gathered staff shifted from trepidation at news from the battlefield to alarm at Jobert's bedraggled filth. On sighting the slung corpse, the scream of a maid shattered the silence of the courtyard.

The men and women of Bernasconi's kitchens and stables fell to their knees and wailed.

Prefetto Bernasconi rushed from the entrance hall, his hands groping the air to contain the sound of collective distress. 'What ... what ...'

Jobert met Bernasconi's searching fear then bowed his head. 'My condolences on your ...'

Blind with tears, Bernasconi groped down Jobert's arm and Bleu's neck to pat at the aura around the wrapped body.

Jobert's face jerked up as a shriek burst from an upstairs window.

Signora Bernasconi gripped the windowsill. Her piercing anguish echoed off the stone walls across the lane. Hands pulled her back into the room.

Jobert and Koschak unlashed Silvio's cords and lowered his body. 'Clear a table in the house,' Jobert said to the shaking chamberlain.

Bernasconi, not willing to touch the canvas horse rug which swaddled his son, wafted his hands at the bundle.

Jobert and Koschak carried Silvio inside and laid him on a bench within the kitchen. Jobert unwrapped the flap of canvas to reveal Silvio's head and shoulders. The pungent odour of decay caused the gathered household to gag. Jobert and Koschak had bathed Silvio this morning at the lakes edge, but his face was a plump purple from being up ended across a saddle for four days. Jobert stepped back to allow the family to grieve their loss and to watch for Gianna's entrance.

The sobbing of those downstairs staff was drowned in moans of sorrow as Signora Bernasconi and a number of attendant women arrived at the base of the kitchen steps.

Signora collapsed, her voice croaking with misery, her hands clawing at invisible demons. Her maids, Jobert assumed, reeled to support her weight and their own despair. Gianna was not among those who lifted their matron towards the man on the table.

Bernasconi hands spasmed as they touched the lapels of Silvio's tailcoat. Then his fists curled into balls clutching the filth-matted fabric as he plunged his face onto Silvio's chest.

'No, no, no ...' Bernasconi's voice choked on his ingested tears.

Signora's eyes bulged as she beheld Silvio's mottled face and she gasped for breath unable to scream. Her hands cupping his cheeks, Signora dropped her head to vomit. Her projected stream of misery splashed Silvio's hair and epaulettes.

Bernasconi twitched his bleary vision at the sorrowful crowd around the table. 'Fetch a priest. Unwrap him. Fetch warm water to bathe him. Prepare his bed. Go! Now! Quickly!'

The chamberlain nominated maids and footmen to ascend the kitchen stairs to prepare Silvio's arrival home. Jobert watched the kitchen steps for Gianna's entry. One or two maids and footmen had crept into the room only to recoil at the central spectacle.

The chamberlain re-entered the kitchen and jerked a solemn nod to Bernasconi.

Bernasconi stroked Silvio's chest and neck as he asked the room, 'Help me lift him. Carefully.' Stable hands and footmen stepped forward. Jobert reached to carry Silvio's feet. Bernasconi glanced at Jobert, and with a look of disgust, flicked his fingers to dismiss Jobert.

Jobert laid his fingertips on Bernasconi's sleeve. 'Where is Gianna?'

Bernasconi recoiled at Jobert's touch.

The men shuffled to lift Silvio from the table.

'Take your hands off my baby,' Signora screeched, her throat husky with torment. 'Never again will I let anyone take—' Her grasping fingers tore at the shroud wrapping his lower body. She swooned when she spied the black crust around his abdomen's mortal wound. She stumbled backwards in horror.

Jobert buckled to his knees as he caught her.

Signora writhed and scratched at Jobert. 'Do not ... not you ... release me ... you vile ...' Her voice was hoarse, her energy spent.

Bernasconi convulsed with rage. 'Unhand my wife.' Bernasconi waved to hesitant maids to assist their matron.

The women wrapped around the distraught Signora Bernasconi, helping her to stand and ascend the stairs behind the men bearing Silvio's corpse.

'You have delivered my son, Jobert.' Bernasconi flung the blood-stained horse rug out through the courtyard door. 'You can go.' Bernasconi turned on his heel for the stairs.

Jobert struggled to his feet. 'Where is Gianna?'

Bernasconi's shoulders sagged. 'She has gone.'

Jobert lurched as if punched. He gripped the edge of the table. His fingers scrabbled for the book in his pocket. 'Gone where?'

'Von Poschinger returned,' said Bernasconi. 'She went with him.'

'Von Poschinger?' Jobert sought the answers in the smears of Silvio's body fluids on the tabletop. His fingers crushed the pages of the book to recall the name. 'The brother who lost an arm at Rivoli?'

Bernasconi mounted the stairs.

'Went with him?' Jobert gulped at the insufficient air in the room. 'How?'

'She married him and went as his wife.' Bernasconi turned a grey, exhausted face to Jobert. 'She said with him she knew his days of war were done.'

Bernasconi leaned against the wall as he clumped up the stairs and disappeared from Jobert's view.

Jobert slumped over the table. He felt he had been slammed in the sternum with a musket butt. Air could not enter his lungs. His mouth dribbled as he could not close his jaws.

His body trembled with fever. Hunched, he took tremulous, halting steps, like a monstrous marionette. His splayed fingers sought the edges of the door. He panted as he searched the courtyard for understanding.

Koschak dropped the reins of their horses and ran to Jobert, hands ready to catch his fall.

Jobert shrank from Koschak's approach and flapped his hands to avoid his support.

Koschak rocked back and cocked his head to catch any sign from Jobert's drooping face. 'What?'

'She has gone.' Jobert's heart withered into his guts. He continued to stumble towards the courtyard gates.

Bleu's great nose thrust into Jobert's ribs.

Jobert moaned as his knees buckled. He collapsed against the gatepost. His elbow caught an iron hinge as he collapsed. The sharp pain scalded his arm.

I can feel pain. Good.

On his hands and knees, Jobert crawled out of the gate and across the street. His hands pushed into scattered balls of horse manure. His knees dragged against the cobblestones. His nostrils filled with the stale urine at the base of the walls.

Passers-by in the lane paused around him and then, with some unseen sign from Koschak, hurried past.

Jobert slumped against the far wall.

He looked through the Bernasconi gate at a house he did not recognise.

He brought the book from his pocket. Its pages were besmirched with grime. He looked at his hands. He wondered to whom they belonged.

Had they ever touched her? He wiped his hands on his thighs.

As his fingers flicked the pages, a hint of lavender and orange rose, like the fog, dissipated in the morning sunshine.

Jobert blinked. Act Five. He read the final pages.

Chief of Squadron de Chabenac's long legs stretched beyond the shade of the cloisters surrounding Milan's Piazza Duomo. His battered, but polished, riding boots extended from patched, *chasseur*-green over-breeches. De Chabenac poured Cortese white wine from an earthenware jug into both their glasses. 'You do not care for the salami?'

Jobert dropped his eyes to the platter of cheese, meat and fruit, and shook his head.

A week after returning Silvio to his family, this morning Jobert attempted to make sense of his thoughts by observing the birds flocking over the morning markets in the piazza. Doves, crows and finches soared and swirled over the bustling human trade.

'Attend the theatre with me.' De Chabenac prodded a playbill pinned beneath the platter.

Jobert shuddered when he saw a playbill for *Romeo and Juliet*.

'No, not that one?' De Chabenac screwed the paper into a ball and tossed it into the street. 'Perhaps, this one. Surely, a welcome distraction before you depart?'

Jobert glimpsed the woodcut print for *The Marriage of Figaro*.

De Chabenac raised his eyebrows as he looked at Jobert. 'Exultant in our hard-won victory over Austria, why ever would we not—'

'No!' Jobert raised a firm hand. 'One last decent night's sleep before Koschak and I return home.'

'Will you call upon Rizzoli while you are here? Zenari and

the Mantuans returned the day before yesterday.'

'I am here in Milan to see you, old friend.'

De Chabenac popped a combination of pear and salami into his mouth. 'Home for summer then? No intent of slipping into Austria and seeking—'

'No.'

'I was going to suggest von Maefeld, not—'

'No!'

De Chabenac straightened the front of his threadbare tail-coat. He picked up the wine jug and shuffled in his chair to seek a waiter.

Jobert leaned over to rest his elbows on his knees. 'I need to go to the farm. Duque and Moench took Tulloc home to Avignon. They were to collect Orlande and Quandalle in Nice. Koschak and I will follow them to the farm.'

'What of Maria and the child? The boy must be three years old.'

'Maria will be offered a place in our house in the Auvergne.'

'Will Quandalle replace Tulloc as your groom?'

'Yes.' Jobert glanced at de Chabenac. 'He is seventeen. Koschak will have him enlist with the 24th Chasseurs as they pass through Avignon.'

De Chabenac brightened. 'Oh, the 24th Chasseurs. I wonder where they are now?'

Jobert snorted. 'Gone. All gone.'

De Chabenac turned his sunburnt face towards Jobert. 'Will you call on Marguerite as you pass through Nice?'

'No.'

'Not even the young Fergnes? The boy will be five and Raive's child must be two by now. I remember how much Fergnes' son enjoyed your visits. He is the spitting image—'

'No.'

De Chabenac took a deep breath and resumed his lounging

posture, legs extended. 'Then what next? Come to Paris for Christmas with Michelle and Valmai. How long has it been since you were in Paris? Return refreshed.'

Jobert blinked in calculation.

Paris? Jobert winced. *After Jemappes. After the von Maefeld brothers. Eight years.*

A waiter topped up their glasses from a fresh jug.

'Will you return to the Army of Italy on Masséna's staff?' de Chabenac asked. 'Or join Bonaparte's new Army of England?'

Jobert shook his head slowly as his eyes followed the darting birds.

With a serene smile, de Chabenac bowed his head. 'Where are you, my friend?'

'Crushed under a mountain.' Tears burnt Jobert's eyes. 'I have the senses of a ghost.'

A bell tolled from within the cathedral's spires. The cloud of birds swept up the face of the edifice.

Jobert stood and pulled his tailcoat tight around him. 'I must away.'

De Chabenac glanced at Milan's towering medieval spires. 'Communion or confession?'

Jobert raised his gaze to the swirling birds. 'Worse.'

Jobert's adventures, in 1801, continue in
If God Wills It.

If you enjoyed Jobert's adventure, it would be
deeply appreciated if you would provide a review
in your favourite online bookstore.

Visit **www.jobert.site**
to discover more about the Jobert series.

Author's Note

A powerful sensation once writhed in my chest. I released that feeling by writing.

I chose a historical European setting. I scoured maps, old and new. I enlarged online images for details. For five years, I explored these locations in my imagination. Four stories have emerged since.

For thirty years I wanted to travel to Europe. The opportunity finally arose. For three weeks, in October 2022, I walked around southern France and northern Italy for the first time.

For three weeks, I chased Jobert. The experience was extraordinary. May I share how it felt?

For five years I had been connected to this landscape. I was excited when I greeted, for the first time, terrain features I knew well. I tracked Jobert through narrow cobble-stoned lanes, across steep slopes of pine and beside green rivers, some still wild, some now tamed. Although many forests and fields through which Jobert rode are now asphalt and concrete, I gripped with certainty ancient stone that he had brushed against.

What I felt as I chased Jobert was a sense of loss. I might never return. An epilogue. The end of my part in these stories. If someone had been beside me, I might have shared this sadness with them. Since writing is solitary, only my baguette watched my pen scratch its notes. Village bells punctuated my phrases. With a Provencale beer, I toasted the settling dust of Jobert's horses' hoofprints.

Jobert's trail, his second and third adventures, led to Italy. I crossed the frontier in pursuit. Jobert's advance march has now been denied by apartment blocks, his flanking manoeuvres thwarted by supermarkets. These moments of fading recognition gripped my chest. Whilst ensnared in the crawl of Ligurian traffic, I glanced sideways to get a sense of Jobert's presence. A squawk from a scooter shoved me forward.

One evening I planned – my research for this fourth story – to arrive where Jobert had not been. It is a place that I had not imagined. A place that was not yet special. Would I design a reception for him? A trap?

I travelled to a tilled field on the banks of the river Po. For ten thousand years, families had hunted and farmed this mud. For two and a half thousand years, soldiers had slept on it. Bled into it.

On my arrival Jobert was already there. I was surprised I had not got ahead of him.

Jobert was in earnest conversation with his support characters. Combat was imminent; a plan was needed. Although I merited an appraising glance from the narrator standing just behind Jobert's shoulder, no one else noticed my presence. I listened to their conversation. I nudged the narrator to indicate salient terrain features that might assist the plan. I scribbled down what they said, all the while standing on the dirt where the action would take place.

Their story slid from the mud under my boots into the ink on my page.

Rob McLaren
Veresdale, Queensland
June 2023

Bibliography

Arnold, J.R., *Marengo and Hohenlinden – Napoleon's Rise to Power,* London, 2015

Berkovich, I., *Motivation in War – The Experience of Common Soldiers in Old-regime Europe,* Cambridge, 2017

Bourgeot, V., *Les Tresors de l'Emperi,* Paris, 2009

Bucquoy, E., *Les Uniformes Du Premier Empire, La Cavalerie Légère,* Paris, 1980

Bukhari, E., *Napoleon's Cavalry,* London, 1979

Calvert, M., Young, P., *A Dictionary of Battles, 1715-1815,* New York, 1979

Chandler, D.G., *Napoleon's Marshals,* London, 1987

Chandler, D.G., *The Campaigns of Napoleon,* New York, 1966

Chartrand, R., *Napoleon's Guns 1792-1815,* Oxford, 2003

Dodge, T.A., *Warfare in the Age of Napoleon, Vol. 2,* 2011

Duffy, C., *Eagles over the Alps,* Grand Rapids, 1999

Duffy, C., *Fire and Stone – The Science of Fortress Warfare 1660-1860,* London, 1975

Devereux, F.L., *The Cavalry Manual of Horse Management,* Cranbury, NJ, 1979

Elting, J.R., *Swords Around A Throne,* London, 1988

Erkmann, E., Chatrian, A., *The History of a Conscript of 1813,* London, 1946

Fremont-Barnes, G., *The French Revolutionary Wars,* London, 2001

Haythornthwaite, P., *Austrian Specialist Troops of the Napoleonic Wars,* London, 1990

Haythornthwaite, P., *Napoleonic Light Cavalry Tactics,* London, 2013

Haythornthwaite, P., *Uniforms of the French Revolutionary Wars 1789-1802,* Poole, 1981

Hollins, D., *Marengo 1800 – Napoleon's Day of Fate,* London, 2009

Letrun, L., Mongin, J., *Chasseurs à Cheval, 1779-1815, Vol. 1-3,* Paris, 2013

Maughan, S.E., *Napoleon's Line Cavalry – Recreated in Colour Photographs,* London, 1997

Muir, R., *Tactics and the Experience of Battle in the Age of Napoleon,* Bury St Edmunds, 1998

Napier, C.J., *Lights and Shades of Military Life; The Memoirs of Captain Elzear Blaze,* London, 1850

Petard-Rigo, M., *La Cavalerie Légère du Premier Empire,* 1993

Shakespeare, W., *Romeo and Juliet,* New York, 2009

Smith, D., *Napoleon's Regiments, Battle Histories of the Regiments of the French Army, 1792-1815,* London, 2000

Tranié, J., Carmigniaini, J.C., *Napoléon Bonaparte 1ère campagne d'Italie, Paris,* 1990

Walter, J., *The Diary of a Napoleonic Foot Soldier,* London, 1991

Weston-Phipps, R., *Armies of the First French Republic and the Rise of the Marshals, Vol. 4-5,* London

Wise, T., *Artillery Equipments of the Napoleonic Wars,* London, 1979

I also acknowledge the insights and detail provided by the Wikipedia, Google Maps and YouTube websites.

Chronology of Events

The following chronology lists the historical events that are referred to within the story.

1797

7 Jan– 2 Feb	France controls Lombardy following victory over Austria at the Battle of Rivoli and the Austrian capitulation of the fortress of Mantua.
22-24 Feb	French expedition to Wales fails.
18 Apr	Napoleon forces the Peace of Leoben on Austria.
27 Jul	Cisalpine Republic, based on Milan, established.
4 Sep	France declared bankruptcy causes a coup d'état.
17 Oct	Treaty of Campo Formio confirms peace between France and Austria.

1798

28 Jan	France invades Switzerland.
15 Feb	French troops occupy and pillage Rome. Roman Republic established. Pope Pius VI taken prisoner and exiled in France.
12 Apr	Helvetic Republic (Switzerland) established.
11 May	An internal coup realigns the French Directory.
19 May	Bonaparte and the Army of the Orient sail for Egypt.
1 Aug	British naval victory over the French fleet at the Battle of the Nile.
10 Sep	Piedmontese Republic, based on Turin, established.
19 Oct	General Brune fails in a coup attempt in Milan.

29 Nov	Kingdom of Naples occupies Rome. French troops counterattack, resecuring Rome and occupying Naples.
6 Dec	Joubert occupies Turin. King Charles Emmanuel IV abdicates.
22 Dec	French troops occupy the port of Livorno and pillage the city of Lucca.

1799

12 Jan	Parthenopean Republic, based on Naples, established.
12 Feb	Bonaparte invades Syria.
25 Mar	Jourdan's invasion of the Rhine defeated.
5 Apr	Schérer defeated at the Battle of Magnano and relinquishes command to Moreau.
27 Apr	Moreau defeated at the Battle of Cassano.
7 May	Austrian troops besiege Mantua.
12 May	Moreau withdraws to Genoa following victory over Russians at the Battle of Bassignana.
25 May	Austrian and Russian forces secure Turin.
7 Jun	Masséna defeated at the First Battle of Zurich.
18 Jun	An internal coup realigns the French Directory.
20 Jun	Macdonald defeated at the Battle of Trebbia.
30 Jul	Mantua capitulates to Austrian troops.
15 Aug	Joubert defeated, and killed, at the Battle of Novi.
31 Aug	Combined British and Russian expedition to the Netherlands.

15 Sep	Suvorov enters Switzerland.
25 Sep	Masséna defeats Austrian and Russian forces at the Second Battle of Zurich.
6 Oct	France defeats British and Russian forces at the Battle of Castricum.
28 Oct	Suvorov withdraws Russian troops from Switzerland and marches to Russia.
9 Nov	Bonaparte stages a coup, overthrows the Directory and ends the French Revolution. A Consulate is established, and Bonaparte becomes the First Consul.

1800

6 Apr	Austria launches attacks against Genoa.
14 May	Bonaparte's Army of the Interior advances across the Alps.
21 May	Fort Bard blocks Lannes' advance guard.
2 Jun	Bonaparte secures Milan.
4 Jun	Masséna's defence of Genoa capitulates to Austrian forces.
9 Jun	Lannes' advance guard is victorious at the Battle of Casteggio-Montebello
14 Jun	Bonaparte is victorious over Austria at the Battle of Marengo.

Ready Reference –
Military Organisations

A very quick and simple overview of military organisations:

Squad/File/Patrol – Cavalry soldiers were grouped together in threes or fours to patrol, cook and sleep together as well as ride together in larger formations.

Section – Twelve men, when at full-strength, or three squads/files, commanded by a corporal.

Platoon – Two sections, twenty-four men at full-strength, commanded by a sergeant.

Troop – Two platoons, fifty men at full strength, commanded by a second lieutenant.

Company – Two troops, one hundred men at full strength, commanded by a captain.

Squadron – Two companies, commanded by the senior captain of the two companies.

Regiment – Three or more squadrons, commanded by a colonel. The regimental commander had two chiefs of squadron who could assist him by commanding one to three squadrons on independent tasks.

Brigade – Two or more regiments of infantry or cavalry, with supporting artillery, engineers and logistic support, commanded by a brigadier (a rank of general).

Division – Two or more brigades, with associated support, commanded by a major general.

Corps – Two or more divisions, capable of significant independent operations, commanded by a lieutenant general.

Army, or Army Wing – Two or more corps, commanded by a general.

Ready Reference – Measurement Conversion

A very approximate conversion of metric measurements:

One inch is approximately two and a half centimetres.

One metre is approximately one yard, or three feet.

One thousand metres, or one kilometre, is approximately two-thirds of a mile (five-eighths).

One mile is approximately one and a half kilometres.

One kilogram is approximately two pounds.

One litre, or one kilogram of water, is approximately two pints.

Dramatis Personae

This story is a work of fiction within a historical setting. In the list of characters below, those with their names underlined actually <u>existed</u>, otherwise the character is a creation of the author's.

<u>Bonaparte</u> Commander of the Army of Italy. Future Napoleon I, Emperor of France.

<u>Berthier,</u> **<u>Brune,</u>** **<u>Joubert,</u>** **<u>Masséna,</u>** **<u>Moreau,</u>** **<u>Murat,</u>** **<u>Schérer and</u>** **<u>Sérurier</u>** Berthier, Brune, Joubert, Masséna, Moreau and Schérer were general officers commanding France's Army of Italy at various times during the period. Murat was a senior aide of Bonaparte's. Sérurier was a commander within the Army of Italy. All, except Moreau, became Marshals of France under Emperor Napoleon.

Raive Colonel, a staff officer on the headquarters of the Army of Italy.

André Jobert Lieutenant colonel, a staff officer on the headquarters of the Army of Italy, attached to the Cisalpine Chasseurs à Cheval.

Koschak Lieutenant, Jobert's aide de camp.

Moench Corporal, Jobert's trumpeter.

Orlande Jobert's valet and cook.

Tulloc and Quandalle Jobert's grooms.

De Chabenac Major, a staff officer on the headquarters of the Army of Italy.

Rizzoli   The Commanding Officer of the Cisalpine Chasseurs à Cheval.

Zenari   A chief of squadron of the Cisalpine Chasseurs à Cheval, and Rizzoli's nephew.

Bernasconi   Bernasconi (senior) is a minister in the government of the Cisalpine Republic. Bernasconi has a daughter, Gianna, and a son, Silvio, a lieutenant in the Cisalpine Chasseurs à Cheval.

Fazio   A sergeant in the Cisalpine Chasseurs à Cheval.

Fergnes, Marguerite and Camille   Fergnes, a close friend of Jobert's, died at the Battle of Caldiero, October 1796. Marguerite is Fergnes' widow. Camille is Marguerite's cousin and companion.

Didier Jobert-Chauvel   Jobert's brother.

Yann Chauvel   Jobert's uncle. Ex-sergeant veterinarian. Manages the family farm in the high country of the Auvergne.

Michelle Chauvel   Jobert's cousin, daughter of Yann. Seamstress. Lives in Paris with her great aunt Sophie, Madame de Chabenac and Valmai de Chabenac, mother and sister of Captain de Chabenac.

Inoubli   A pair of identical twins revealed to be Austrian spies, now turned to work for the French Republic.

The Jobert Series

Brothers of the Capucine (1793)
Duty on a Lesser Front (1794-1795)
Yet Another General (1796-1797)
Neither Up Nor Down (1798-1800)

Coming soon

If God Wills It (1801)

www.ingramcontent.com/pod-product-compliance
Lightning Source LLC
Chambersburg PA
CBHW020508020726
47493CB00001B/241